"You can do this, Lucinda. You have nothing to fear from a man on the dance floor. The vast majority of us don't even bite."

"Don't they?"

"You are trying to joke your way out of this. Although I heartily approve of the tactic, I shall not allow you to do it."

He launched into his favorite waltz. After a brief hesitation, Lucinda joined in.

"*Enjoy* the music, Lucinda. Feel it, in your bones." He reached again for her hand, feeling a burst of pleasure as it slipped easily into his.

They were moving now, tracing a small circle in the center of the room. She kept her eyes fixed on his. Her lips parted slightly, her front teeth briefly tugging at her bottom lip in an artless gesture that was undeniably appealing.

Lucinda appeared completely transported by the dance. Her mouth opened to a smile and a small sigh escaped her. And that's when a thought crossed his mind that was more dangerous than any yet: *Lucinda is beautiful.* Not just pleasant, or passingly pretty. From her soul to her soft brown hair, inside and out, she was the most beautiful woman he had ever known...

Praise for
The *Love's* Grace Trilogy

A Lady Most Lovely

"A touching, tender romance...Delamere reaches out to readers yearning for a lovely story that is sensitive yet passionate. The power of love, second chances, and even the joy of the holiday season combine to create the perfect atmosphere for this charmer."
—*RT Book Reviews*

"Intense...the undercurrent of attraction between Margaret and Tom is a powerful force that keeps the story moving." —*Publishers Weekly* (starred review)

"A wonderfully sweet, faith-inspired romance that I truly enjoyed. I found immense satisfaction in the ending and couldn't keep myself from smiling."
—RomanticHistoricalReviews.com

"Though this was book two in the series, it was a good standalone romance that tickled your interest and kept you turning the pages...the romance was sweet and ended delightfully...a good book and a fun romp through history."
—CleanRomanceReviews.com

An Heiress at Heart

"Engrossing and heartbreaking...*An Heiress at Heart* is poignant, profound, and lovely."
—*USA Today*'s Happy Ever After blog

Also By Jennifer Delamere

The Love's Grace Series
An Heiress at Heart
A Lady Most Lovely

A *Bride* for the Season

Jennifer Delamere

FOREVER

NEW YORK   BOSTON

Copyright © 2014 by Jennifer Harrington
Excerpt from *An Heiress at Heart* Copyright © 2012 by Jennifer Harrington
Excerpt from *A Lady Most Lovely* Copyright © 2013 by Jennifer Harrington
All rights reserved. In accordance with the U.S. Copyright Act of 1976, the scanning, uploading, and electronic sharing of any part of this book without the permission of the publisher constitute unlawful piracy and theft of the author's intellectual property. If you would like to use material from the book (other than for review purposes), prior written permission must be obtained by contacting the publisher at permissions@hbgusa.com. Thank you for your support of the author's rights.

Forever
Hachette Book Group
1290 Avenue of the Americas
New York, NY 10104

www.HachetteBookGroup.com

Printed in the United States of America

First Edition: November 2014
10 9 8 7 6 5 4 3 2 1

OPM

Forever is an imprint of Grand Central Publishing.
The Forever name and logo are trademarks of Hachette Book Group, Inc.

The Hachette Speakers Bureau provides a wide range of authors for speaking events. To find out more, go to www.hachettespeakersbureau.com or call (866) 376-6591.

The publisher is not responsible for websites (or their content) that are not owned by the publisher.

For my dad

Acknowledgments

Being a writer is not nearly as solitary a profession as it is made out to be. I'm thankful for all the help and support I have received along the way.

First, I would like to thank *you,* my reader! It has been a joy to share my stories with you. Meeting you (in person or online) and hearing you've enjoyed my books has been heartwarming and delightful.

Many thanks to David Parker-Ross for answering my questions on obscure points of English history and customs, helping me keep my terminology accurate, and giving me the fantastic idea for locating James and Lucinda's photographic adventure on the rooftop of Westminster Palace.

Thanks to Ann Collette for a wonderfully entertaining crash course on opera in general and *La Traviata* in particular. Your enthusiasm is contagious!

Abundant thanks to my fantastic and ever-supportive agent, Jessica Alvarez.

Many thanks to my editor, Lauren Plude, for loving

my books from the beginning and for helping me improve as an author.

Thanks to Elaine Klonicki and Karen Anders for reading my drafts and giving me invaluable feedback.

As always, my love and thanks to my husband, Jim; my family; and the Raleigh area fellowship for your continual support and cheerleading, and for always giving me that extra boost I need when the deadline looms.

Finally, and most especially, I am thankful to God. Psalm 68 says, "Blessed be the Lord, who daily loadeth us with benefits." I see this truth every day.

Author's Note

As an avid reader of history, it's no wonder that I would set my historical romances against the background of real places and events. *An Heiress at Heart* has several scenes set at the Great Exhibition of 1851. *A Lady Most Lovely* includes the Duke of Wellington's funeral and also a cameo appearance by a police detective of the time named Inspector Field.

When writing *A Bride for the Season*, I took a slightly different approach. It would be more accurate to say this book was *inspired* by the people and culture of the time. For example, Lucinda Cardington's school to help "fallen women" was based on a similar project developed by wealthy heiress and philanthropist Angela Burdett-Coutts and the author Charles Dickens. Like Lucinda, Miss Coutts objected to the subject matter of the opera *La Traviata* from both moral and social standpoints, believing that it glorified prostitution and was overly harsh in its judgment of women. Miss Coutts always insisted her box at the opera house be kept empty whenever *La Traviata* was performed. (One minor liberty I took with the historical record was setting the London premiere of *La Traviata* in the summer of 1853; in fact the real date was in May 1856.)

Daniel Hibbitt's statements regarding cholera and the need for better sewage systems in London are an accurate reflection of what was known at the time. Although design and planning efforts were under way by 1853, the project did not become a reality until the 1860s, when the problem had grown so bad it could no longer be ignored.

Everything about photography in this book is as accurate as I could make it. In 1853, photography had been around for only about a decade. The wet plate method used by James Simpson was the newest advancement in the technology at that time. James's custom-built wagon for carrying his photographic supplies was inspired by Roger Fenton, who designed just such a wagon and took it to the Crimea in 1855, where he became one of the very first war photographers.

James Simpson's favorite sport is rackets (also spelled racquets), a game played with a ball and a strung racket in an enclosed court. The game had initially gained popularity in Fleet Prison and taverns, but by the 1850s it was moving to indoor courts and had become a gentleman's game as well. In 1853 (the year *A Bride for the Season* takes place) the Prince's Club opened with two rackets courts and two tennis courts. According to the *Encyclopaedia Britannica*, "The building of old Prince's Club in London in 1853 is regarded as marking the beginning of a new era in which rackets became the game of the clubs, military services, and universities." In this, as with photography, James was on the cutting edge!

I love weaving these historical tidbits into my stories, and I hope you've enjoyed this taste of life in mid-Victorian England as well.

He hath made every thing beautiful in his time...

ECCLESIASTES 3:11

Chapter 1

July 1853

James Simpson sent a smile and a wink across the ballroom to Miss Emily Cardington and was pleased, as
he always was, to see her reaction.

Emily blushed prettily and leaned in to whisper something to her friend. She had been watching the dancing
with a little cluster of debutantes who were almost as
charming as she was. There was a lot to be said for ladies
whose primary aim was to look pretty, please the gentlemen, and have a good time while they were about it.
James had adored the company of such women for years,
and he had yet to tire of it. Plenty had fished for a marriage proposal, too, but their hints had been easy enough
to dance around.

Emily detached herself from the females giggling
behind their fans and began to thread her way through
the crowd. She paused to smile and return greetings from
those she passed, so that her movement in his direction

would not be noticeable to a casual onlooker. What a delight she was. She was beautiful and vivacious, but she also knew how to be discreet when necessary. Tonight, under the eagle eyes of her elder sister and her parents, who disapproved of James on the somewhat plausible grounds that he was an untrustworthy rogue, was just such a time.

James remained by the open French doors, leaning casually against the wall as he watched Emily's approach. From this vantage point he had a good view of the ballroom. It was crowded tonight. A mild evening after scorching-hot weather had lured many people out tonight. No doubt it would have been heavily attended anyway—invitations to Lord and Lady Trefethen's balls were always highly sought after.

James's gaze traveled across the glittering scene, taking in the dancers, the wallflowers, the matrons chatting by the punch table, and one young couple who were quietly slipping behind a large potted palm for a private tête-à-tête. He loved these large affairs. There must be two hundred people in the room, yet it was not simply one block of people. Groups large and small collected, broke up, and then re-formed, each taking a different dynamic from the people who were in it. For James it was a continual feast. He always craved something new, and tonight was no exception.

As he finished his survey of the ballroom, James was happy to see that Lord Cardington, Emily's father, was nowhere in sight. No doubt he'd retreated to the large library to enjoy a cigar and brandy with the other old men who had no penchant for dancing. Lady Cardington was hard to miss, though. Her corpulent frame was perched precariously on one of the chairs near a food table, and she was deep in conversation with the tall and shrill Mrs. Paddington. Clearly Lady Cardington was not concerning herself at the moment with the whereabouts of her younger daughter.

Oddly enough, the only person he could not account for was Emily's sister. Lucinda tended to stick to the edges of a crowded ballroom, and James usually had no trouble locating her. She was not among the dancers, but that was no surprise. Lucinda rarely danced, which was good news for the men whose toes she invariably trod on. But neither was she to be seen with the other spinsters-in-training who were whispering together along the far wall. Perhaps she had joined her father and the other ancients in the library. Lucinda was always more comfortable conversing with gloomy old men about science and politics than in partaking of any real fun.

Emily had made it halfway across the room by now, and she sent James a quick, apologetic smile as she was intercepted by Lady Trefethen's nephew, a tall, lanky fellow who had spent much of the season trying to win Emily's favor. Poor fellow never stood a chance. Emily was this season's bon-bon, and she could have her pick of the men. Naturally, she had made James her favorite. She was his favorite too, for the moment. He enjoyed these innocent flirtations with debutantes, although he found greater satisfaction in very different dalliances with far less innocent ladies—and far from well-lit ballrooms.

He knew it would not take long for Emily to politely separate herself from Lady Trefethen's nephew, and then it would be a matter of mere moments before she reached James. So he stepped out the French doors and walked

toward the balcony railing in order to wait for her, and
to gauge whether his favorite seat in the arbor—the
one perfect for admiring the moonlight with a willing
companion—was available. What he saw instead as he
looked out over the garden surprised him. A lady was
walking along one of the well-manicured paths. Her face
was shrouded by shadows, but she moved with a furtive
air, as though she'd been doing something naughty and
was afraid of being caught. James leaned on the railing,
admiring her slender figure as she approached the house,
trying to figure out who she was. It wasn't until she'd
reached the steps leading up to the balcony that James
realized with great astonishment that the woman was
Lucinda Cardington.

On a night like this, the garden was the perfect place
for a few stolen kisses—exactly what James had planned
for himself and Emily. James tried to picture Lucinda in
a lover's embrace, but gave it up instantly. It was impossible even to imagine, and in any case she was clearly
alone. Why then, was she here? What could possibly lead
her away from the ball and into the lonely shadows? Suddenly, James had an irresistible urge to know.

He noticed she kept her hands behind her, as if she
was hiding something. When she reached the top of the
steps, she pulled up short when she saw James. Even in
the flickering light of the torches he could see a furious blush begin to spread across her cheeks. When she
turned beet-red like that it was impossible to miss.

"What are you doing here?" she demanded, as though
James were the one being caught doing something
untoward, and not her.

He looked at her askance. "It is I who should be asking that question. Why are you sneaking about in the dark?"

She drew herself up. "I am not *sneaking about*. I merely went for a walk. It's terribly hot inside and I needed some fresh air."

"You went out to the garden alone?" James did not bother to hide his disbelief.

"Of course," she replied defensively. "What did you think?"

"A moonlit summer night is much more enjoyable with company." He was amused to see her eyes widen and her blush spread down her neck—which, he suddenly noticed, was not slender in a gangly way but was pleasingly delicate. "Come, now," he chided. "I know you're hiding something."

He took a wide sidestep in an attempt to see what was behind her. She moved too, trying to keep her back hidden, but James was too quick for her. She was holding a book, which he deftly plucked out of her hands.

"Mr. Simpson!" Lucinda cried out, affronted.

James tilted the spine toward the light in order to see the title. "*Elemental Photographic Methods*," he read aloud. "Did you tiptoe out to the garden to read this?" He was torn between confusion at her actions and admiration at the book's subject matter. Photography had become a passion for him.

She snatched the book back. Her hands were icy cold as they brushed his, sending a small wave of shock through him. She hugged it close, sending a cautious glance around to be sure no one was watching. As though it were illegal to be found at a dance with a book in one's hands. In her case, it probably was. Given the way Lady Cardington was pushing to get her elder daughter married, she'd be livid if she knew Lucinda was reading in a hidden corner instead of luring some gentleman into the velvet noose. "You can't have been able to read very well," he observed. "That quarter moon isn't providing much light."

She was still blushing, which, against the backdrop of her defiant look, made an arresting picture. "There is a small lamp near the rear of the garden, by the back gate. I came out here because I did not want my father to see me. He does not believe photography is a suitable pastime for a young lady."

"Really? Why ever not?" He took a step closer to her as he spoke, closing the distance between them to mere inches. Something about her crisp starchiness always amused him, and he enjoyed seeing her squirm.

"The dangerous chemicals, the darkroom..." Her voice trailed off.

"Ah yes, the darkroom," he said, bemused. "I can see why he'd object to that. Heaven forbid you find yourself alone, in the dark, with a *man*."

She tried to take a step back, but James had her effectively pinned against the railing. Instinctively he took a quiet inhaling breath, for he was always curious to discover the scents used by the ladies he encountered. Lucinda seemed to favor almond and lilac—an agreeable combination. "So am I to understand that Miss Lucinda Cardington is not above breaking a rule now and then?" He was enjoying the idea of this prim young lady as a covert rebel.

She straightened under his scrutiny and even lifted her chin. "I'm fascinated with photography. I know you understand its appeal. We've—we've discussed this before."

"Ah yes, so we have." James could now dimly remember a conversation they'd had on this topic some months ago. Somehow he'd forgotten about it.

She was still blushing. Two bright red splotches seemed to have taken up permanent residence on the apple of her cheeks. "I hate being forced to do these things behind my father's back, but he simply won't listen to reason. When I saw this book in Lord Trefethen's library, I thought I'd just borrow it for a few minutes to see if it's worth buying."

"Buying?" James thought ladies never spent money on anything other than clothes or jewelry. Lucinda was becoming more intriguing by the minute. "Do you mean to say you've bought other books—despite your father's ban on them?"

"I've got a good hiding place for them at home." She said this with an air of triumph, but this quickly dissolved into anxiety. "Please don't tell him!"

He held up a hand in an appeasing gesture. "Rest assured, I am the world's best keeper of secrets. When I want to be." This was perfect, he thought. Lucinda would be in his debt, and he could get her to keep quiet if he were to take a harmless foray into the garden tonight with Emily. But suddenly he wanted to gain more than her grudging acquiescence. He wanted her entirely on his side. She'd hitherto been immune to his charms, but perhaps he'd at last found a way to breach her wall of staid seriousness. He leaned toward her and said with a confidential air, "This book is not nearly as good as Alderson's *New Photographic Methods and Applications*."

He had been right in his guess, for she brightened immediately. "I have that book!"

"Well, then, you have no need of this one. The instructions for the wet plate process are faulty, and some crucial steps are not well enough described. However, I don't understand why you need either book. Without the materials to actually take photographs, what's the point?"

"I have every intention of buying my own equipment very soon, and building a darkroom too, when I have a home of my own."

"Is that so?" Now his interested was really piqued. "Does this mean you've found someone who will allow you to indulge in this hobby after you are married?"

She scooted away, putting a yard or so distance between them. "Marriage is not the only way to obtain a home. There is money in a trust that I shall receive on my twenty-sixth birthday. Then I shall set up housekeeping on my own."

"On your own!" Was this woman really planning to go against one of society's most stringent dictates? Perhaps there was more to her than met the eye. James found himself grinning in approval. "How delightfully scandalous."

She clutched the book closer and gave him a cold look. "I'll have a companion—Miss Parsons, my former governess. It will all be quite respectable."

"Oh, I see." Apparently this woman's rebellious streak only went so far. James found it hard to believe he was spending this lovely night chatting with a woman who was planning her spinsterhood with such zeal. She was so unlike her sister, whose aims lay in an entirely different direction. "Perhaps when Emily is married, you might live with her?"

Lucinda made a sound that was suspiciously close to

a snort. "I have no desire to subject myself to that. She's bound to mismanage her home, and I shudder to think what living there will be like. I pity the man who marries her. Oh!" The red blotches on her face began to stand out again. "I shouldn't have said that. I'd hate for you to get the wrong idea about her."

James did not like the implication behind her words. He enjoyed flirting with Emily and indulging in the occasional stolen kiss, but that was the limit of his interest. "Why should it matter to me?"

"It's just that—I mean, well..."

James sighed. Lucinda's habit of stammering when embarrassed could be trying at times. At last she gave up and stared at James, unable to speak and clearly mortified about it.

"See here, Miss Cardington. There is nothing serious between Emily and me—"

"James! There you are!" Emily's high little voice pierced the night air as she slipped through the door. "Why did you duck out here? You had to have known I was coming for you—" She cut herself off when she saw her sister. The playful smile that had been lighting her features sank into a pout. "Lucinda! I never thought I'd find *you* on the terrace. Shouldn't you be inside, haranguing some Member of Parliament about a public works project or something?" Her eye lit upon the book in Lucinda's hand. "Don't tell me you've been reading! Papa will have a fit if he catches you!"

"As a matter of fact, this belongs to Mr. Simpson." Lucinda thrust the book at James with such force that it winded him as it hit his chest. "He was simply showing it to me."

"Really?" Emily's eyes narrowed as she studied James. "I didn't see you with that earlier."

James playfully tweaked her chin. "I desperately needed something to occupy my mind. I was pining away, waiting for you."

As a rule, Emily always fell hard for James's compliments. It didn't work this time, however. She turned her distrusting gaze back to her sister. "You still haven't answered my question. Why are you out here?"

"I've a perfect right to be here," Lucinda huffed. "I needed some air, that's all. You know the closeness of crowded ballrooms makes me lightheaded." She took Emily's arm and tugged her several feet away from James. "If I've prevented you from stealing into the garden with Mr. Simpson, I am glad for it," she said in a harsh whisper. "You know what Papa told you about such acts of impropriety."

"And *you* know what Papa told you about this photography nonsense," Emily retorted. "It would appear we both have something to answer for. Besides, *you're* the one who has just been caught in the shadows without a chaperone, not me."

The two sisters stared heatedly at each other. It was actually rather comical to watch them. James saw something flash across Emily's face that could only—absurd as it was—be described as jealousy. Why Emily should fear her spinster-like sister he could not imagine. He knew he ought to say something to defuse the tension, but he was too absorbed in watching them to try.

In the end, someone else interrupted the sibling feud. "Here he is," a jolly voice rang out. Bob Chapman and his fiancée spilled out onto the balcony, followed by two other couples. "We've been looking all over for you," Chapman said. "We need you to complete the set for this next dance." He slapped James on the back and winked at Emily. "Come on, then, you two. The music's about to start!"

James could see Emily's emotions warring between anger at having her clandestine meeting prevented and relief at leaving her disagreeable sister behind. It didn't take long for the latter sentiment to prevail. She pushed away from Lucinda and took hold of James's hand. "Yes, let's dance!"

James could see he wasn't going to get any private time with Emily after all. "It seems I am outnumbered," he said with a showy sigh of resignation. "Very well, I shall accept my fate. But only if Emily and I are allowed to start out as top couple. If we leave it to Hopkins, the set will fall hopelessly out of order before we're ten steps in."

Hopkins, a contentedly buffoonish sort, laughed heartily at this jab. "Too true, my good fellow."

For his part, James was glad to see the pert smile return to Emily's face. She had always been tagged as the "pretty one," but James observed that neither sister was very fetching when they were wearing angry frowns. Especially not Emily. She was like a perfect little china doll, and unless her smile was painted on just so, the whole effect was ruined. "Let's go!" she urged, tugging at James's hand.

No one spared a word, or even a glance, at Lucinda. Nor had she encouraged them to do so. She had taken several steps back and was now half-obscured by shadows. It appeared she was retreating to her usual spot away from the limelight. Or perhaps she feared repercussions for being caught reading at the ball. This he could not allow. Having now plenty of witnesses handy, James extended the book to Lucinda. "Miss Cardington, I have been reading this, but now that I have been called upon to dance I'm worried that it might get misplaced. Would you be so good as to return it to Lord Trefethen's library for me?"

A look of gratitude passed across Lucinda's face, and a hint of a smile. Both were quickly gone, however, to be replaced by the stoic expression she normally wore. "I shall be happy to return this for you, Mr. Simpson."

As she grasped the book, James tugged at it in order to pull her close enough to whisper in her ear, "I like it when you stand up for yourself. You should do it more often."

Her brown eyes opened wide and her mouth fell open to a tiny, delicate *O*. She closed it, swallowed, and said nothing.

James could feel Lucinda's gaze on his back as he led Emily into the ballroom. He'd been unaccountably disarmed by tonight's encounter. He wondered whether she would try to read more of the book before returning it. For the briefest of moments, he half-wished he could accompany her and point out another excellent photography book he'd seen in Lord Trefethen's library. But as he and Emily took their places on the dance floor, James decided to dismiss it from his mind. He was bound to see Lucinda at some future event, and he would be sure to tell her about it then.

Chapter 2

"Come along, Emily," Lady Cardington admonished. "We shall catch cold if we stand here dawdling."

"Mama's right," added Lucinda, giving her sister a nudge. She wanted nothing more than to get home. They were in the front hall of the Trefethens' home and had gathered their cloaks in preparation for leaving. But Emily kept fiddling with her ties, and Lucinda knew she was deliberately stalling. She was looking for James. By the time Lucinda had quietly returned Lord Trefethen's book to the library and made her way back to the ballroom, she saw that James and Emily were no longer dancing together. James had, in fact, been waltzing with Miss Shaw, and Emily was none too happy about it. Lucinda never could make sense of the silly rivalry between those two for James's affections. He'd then proceeded to spend the next hour or more dancing with a dozen different ladies. At the moment he was nowhere to be seen, and Lucinda did not even wish to guess at what he might be doing. Or with whom.

"I don't know why we should be in such a hurry," Emily said petulantly. "It's barely midnight."

Lord Cardington came back inside. "The coach is here, my girls. Let's go, or you will all turn into pumpkins."

Emily rolled her eyes. "It's the *coach*, not the people, who turn into pumpkins, Papa."

But her words were unheeded, as Lord and Lady Cardington were already halfway to the carriage. Lucinda took hold of Emily's arm. "Come on. You've thrown yourself at Mr. Simpson enough for one evening."

"At least I make the effort to find a beau," Emily sniffed. "I don't hide in the library with fat old men."

"You're right," Lucinda snapped, tugging her sister down the steps. "I don't go chasing after gentlemen. I prefer to keep my self-respect instead."

"What a cross creature you are," Emily returned. "I think it's because you know no one will have you."

Lucinda did not reply. She was too inured to her sister's biting comments by now. Instead, she gave Emily a final shove to get her into the carriage.

Once inside, Emily took the seat by the window facing the Trefethens' residence—still hoping, Lucinda did not doubt, for another glimpse of James Simpson. If so, she was immediately rewarded because James came bounding out the door and down the steps. Emily gave a little cry of delight and suddenly, without intending to, Lucinda found herself watching him, too. It was hard to resist, for he had a jaunty, carefree air that easily drew attention. He was tall and lean, but well proportioned, always moving with a light step and athletic grace.

Someone called his name, and he strolled over to a hackney that was parked in front of them. "Don't forget,

Simpson," said the man who had called out to him from the carriage. "The Gypsy Cave, in an hour."

"I'll be there," James called cheerfully. "Order me a bottle of their best, cheapest wine, and be sure to tell Mirela to save me a place at her table."

"Oooh," Emily whispered excitedly to Lucinda. "Did you hear that? He's going to the Gypsy Cave."

In fact, Lucinda barely heard James's words. She was captivated by his blue eyes, which sparkled in the torchlight, just as they had done earlier when he'd found her outside. She'd always known James was a handsome man. So did Emily and every other woman in London who kept dangling after him. But Lucinda had never been carried away by such shallow things as outward appearance. Therefore she'd been baffled by her response to him tonight, the way his laughing eyes and teasing smile had so completely riveted her. Equally disturbing had been her inability to stop thinking about him for the rest of the evening. She'd concluded with some embarrassment that having a man's full attention—however briefly—had been unexpectedly gratifying. *"I like it when you stand up for yourself,"* he had said. What did that mean, exactly? Lucinda gave herself a mental shake. He could not have been serious. He never was. It had been a joke and nothing more.

Emily poked her in the ribs.

"What?" Lucinda asked distractedly, too caught up in her own thoughts to use the more polite *I beg your pardon*. She tore her gaze away from James.

"He's meeting Mr. Chapman at the Gypsy Cave! That's the café in Cremorne Gardens where the gypsy ladies dance." Emily was still whispering so she wouldn't be overheard, although there was little danger of that. Their mother was half deaf, and both their parents had already begun dozing off. Emily's eyes danced with excitement. "I wish I were going."

"How could you even think such a thing? You know how disreputable Cremorne Gardens is after dark."

"Indeed I do!" Emily replied with relish.

Lord, give me strength, Lucinda thought.

As the carriage pulled away, Emily craned her neck in order to watch James for as long as she could. For her part, Lucinda was determined not to be caught gawking. Yet somehow as they passed James her eyes met his. He smiled and tipped his hat, sending an odd jolt of pleasure through her. She pulled her gaze away and concentrated on retying her cloak. She would not waste a moment in idle dreams about any man—least of all a rogue like James Simpson. She would leave that sort of nonsense to her sister.

*

Lucinda sat on the window seat and gazed out at the street, watching as the moon slipped among the clouds, sending dappled light along the neighboring buildings. She had been anxious to come home, eager to escape both the physical and emotional discomfort she always experienced in an overcrowded ballroom. Yet now that she was finally alone she still felt strangely out of sorts. Lonely, almost. She recalled the way Emily had danced and laughed so effortlessly with the gentlemen at the ball, holding them entranced in a way Lucinda could never hope to do. Lucinda usually considered herself better off to be the "intelligent" sister rather than the "pretty" one. Surely that was the more useful, more lasting trait. But every now and then she was taken with the tiniest twinge of envy, thinking how wonderful it would be if she could be so at ease in social situations. Lucinda had tried her best, but at some point during her debutante year she'd realized such a thing would always be beyond her abilities.

Sleep, too, was out of her reach tonight. Lucinda went to her bed and pulled out a small box tucked underneath it. She lifted the lid and pulled out a book from the small stack inside the box. It was the photography manual that James had said was the best. She opened it and began to read.

After several minutes she finally admitted to herself that she was hearing every word in her head as though James Simpson were reading it aloud. What a foolish fancy! She closed the book with a snap and returned it to the box. As she pushed the box back into place, she concentrated again on the future satisfaction of one day having her own home and not being forced to such secretive measures.

With a sigh, she rose and reached for the bell to call for Susannah, her maid. But before she could do so, she heard the door to Emily's room open and close. It was probably Emily's maid. Lucinda decided to ask her to call for Susannah instead. She opened her door and poked her head into the hallway, but the girl was already at the far end of the corridor and slipping through the door that led down to the servants' hall. The dim light of Lucinda's candle must have been playing tricks on her eyes, for she thought she caught a glimpse of Emily's bright pink gown before the door closed. It had to be the maid, though. Perhaps she had taken Emily's gown to mend or to clean.

She pulled the bell for her own maid and, while she waited, went to the window once again. The moon was still high, brighter now that the clouds had blown away, adding its light to the street lamps below. Lucinda blinked in surprise as she saw a figure coming out from the side of the house. She was wearing a hooded cloak and hurrying down the street toward a hackney cab waiting on the corner. When the woman reached the cab, she lifted her face to speak to the driver, and Lucinda's heart seized with fear. It was Emily.

It took Lucinda no time at all to conclude where her wayward sister was going. The thoughtless girl was probably heading to Cremorne Gardens, putting her honor and reputation in jeopardy in the process. She had to be stopped.

There was a light tap on the door and the maid entered. "Ready for bed, miss?"

Lucinda rushed over to her. "Susannah, something terrible has happened, and I need your help."

The maid's eyes grew wide but she said without hesitation, "Certainly, miss."

Susannah had only been in the Cardingtons' employ for a few weeks, and her loyalty and discretion had yet to be tested. No doubt it would be tonight. Lucinda had no choice but to rely on her. "I need you to find me a cab."

Her mouth fell open. "At this hour? Surely you're not going out alone?"

"I need you to go with me, if you would be so kind. We must go quietly, and my parents must not know!" Seeing the maid still frozen in shock, she added, "I'll explain everything on the way. For now, I'll tell you that we must find Emily and bring her home before irreparable damage is done." She reached for her reticule. Thank

God she had not yet undressed, or it would have taken an additional quarter of an hour to get out of the house.

"Miss Emily has gone out?" Susannah said. "No wonder I saw Joan comin' in from outside, like she'd been running an errand. When I asked where she'd been, she rudely told me to mind my own business."

"She'd probably gone to fetch a hackney. Now we'll need to do the same. Hurry!"

Lucinda and Susannah took the servants' stairs to the kitchen, and Lucinda waited while Susannah made sure there were no other servants about. They had to get out of the house without being seen. All was quiet in the Cardington household. They went out the servants' door on the lower level, then up the outside steps that led to the street. As they hurried toward the corner where cabs were known to wait, Lucinda prayed that one would be there. Fortunately, there was.

"Where to, my ladies?" the driver asked with a cheeky grin. When Lucinda said, "Cremorne Gardens, please," his smile broadened. Lucinda would have loved to slap the leer off his face, but given how things appeared, the man's assumptions were not altogether unjustified.

While the carriage made its way briskly along the nearly empty streets, Lucinda kept twisting her hands in her lap over and over again. She could only hope she was able to find Emily before her reputation was ruined.

"Don't worry, miss," Susannah said. "We'll find her, surely."

As they approached the entrance to Cremorne Gardens, the traffic once again grew thicker. The hackney came to a stop at the elaborate wrought-iron gates that served as the entrance. "Wait here," Lucinda instructed her maid.

"But you can't go by yourself—it's not safe!" Susannah protested.

"I'll be fine," Lucinda assured her, although her rapidly beating heart apparently disagreed. "I need you to stay with the carriage and be sure he doesn't leave."

Lucinda paid the driver to wait, thanking heaven she'd been saving the money her father had given her, instead of spending it all on luxuries the way Emily did. How Emily had found money for cab fare, Lucinda couldn't even begin to guess.

Music and laughter filled the air. The park was thronged with men and women in search of wilder pleasures. None of the ladies here would have been in the Trefethens' ballroom this evening. But plenty of the gentlemen had been. After their polite turn in society, they were now seeking very different company.

Lucinda had been to Cremorne Gardens during the daytime, when it was a pleasant place for enjoying music and tea. One afternoon she had even watched people going up in a hot air balloon. But at night the park held a very different allure. She'd heard all kinds of lurid tales about the fate of innocent ladies who ventured here after dark. She would have to be on her guard.

As she strode through the gates, she was instantly met by two gentlemen holding papers that looked like handbills of some kind. One of the men thrust a paper into her hand. "We're here to spread information about the Caring House for Wayward Ladies," he informed her.

Lucinda looked at the paper. It described the school where she volunteered many hours a week, helping poor women learn skills that would help them find better work.

"I beg you to consider this," the man said earnestly.

Lucinda straightened, affronted. "I am well aware of the Caring House. I am one of its patrons."

"Patron?" the man repeated, flummoxed. Clearly he had not expected to find a proper lady wandering the park at night unescorted.

Lucinda did not have the time or willingness to explain. "I've come to find one of the women," she said briskly. "Did either of you perchance see a blonde lady in a bright pink gown, who would have arrived here by hackney cab not too long ago?"

"Indeed we did," the other man answered. "She gave us a bit of a rude sendoff when we approached her."

"Which way did she go? Was she alone?"

"She was alone. I believe she went that way." He pointed toward a path. The one Lucinda knew led to the Gypsy Cave. The lamps lighting the path were broadly spaced, affording plenty of shadows for the couples walking along it to conveniently step aside and talk—or whatever else they were doing—without being observed. Lucinda wondered what else might lie along that path. She envisioned men lurking in the shadows to lure or even abduct unsuspecting women. Disquiet rose up within her, as she feared not so much for herself as for her sister. Emily would have little defense against a sweet-talking man, and none at all against a more serious threat. What Lucinda could possibly do in the latter case, she had no idea.

Sending a short prayer heavenward and taking a deep breath to quell her trepidation, Lucinda set off resolutely down the path.

Chapter 3

W here can Mirela have gotten herself off to?" James said, pouring himself more wine. The crowded tent was abundantly filled with gypsy ladies, but his favorite was nowhere in sight. His friends Chapman and Hopkins were content to sit here and drink themselves into a happy stupor, but James needed a more interesting distraction.

"I saw her leave a few minutes ago with another man," said Hopkins, taking the carafe and clumsily refilling his own glass. James had lost track of just how much the man had imbibed this evening. "Sorry, my lad, but she appears to be occupied."

"You idiot," Chapman rejoined. "That was her brother she left with, I'm sure of it."

"Her brother?" Hopkins made a sloshy sort of tsking sound. "Those gypsies are a strange lot."

James ignored the banter of his friends. Normally he'd be right in the middle of it himself, but tonight he felt unaccountably agitated. Most likely it was the aftereffects of the ball he'd just attended. From the moment she'd found him on the terrace with her sister, Emily seemed determined to monopolize his attention. Even worse, her conversation kept veering toward the one subject he keenly wished to avoid. In the beginning he had enjoyed their stolen kisses in anterooms or behind garden shrubs. Her virginal enthusiasm was charming, and her blind adoration provided no small boost to his ego. But like all good things, the simple fun of it was coming to an end. Now she had plainly set her sights on a more permanent connection, and James had to tread carefully. Not that it would be all that difficult to keep from getting engaged to her. Emily's determined pursuit would ultimately be thwarted by her father's disapproval.

He threw a glance at the tent opening, anticipating Mirela's return. She was a clever girl, as well as luscious. She never asked for anything but a good time and an extra piece of gold or two. She could always take his mind off his troubles. If only all women could be that way, the world would certainly be a more congenial place.

"There she is," Hopkins said.

James craned his neck. "Where?"

"Just outside the tent, waving to you."

Sure enough, in the dim shadows beyond the lights of the tent, James could see Mirela's bright blue and pink silk shawl. At the moment it was draped over her head and the lower portion of her face, as though she wished to remain unrecognized. That was unusual for her. Was she hiding from someone? She reached out an arm and beckoned to him.

"Looks like she wants a private interview," Hopkins said. "I recommend the arbor just beyond the large oak at the curve in the path."

"Thanks," said James, rising from his chair. "I'll keep that in mind."

He worked his way through the crowded tent, but was surprised to find that by the time he stepped outside, Mirela was no longer there. In the dim flicker of the sparsely lighted path, he caught a glimpse of her disappearing behind the large oak tree Hopkins had mentioned. So a private meeting *was* what she wanted. James smiled to himself and strode after her. Now that he thought about it, it seemed an excellent idea.

When he reached the shady arbor by the oak, he saw her sitting on a marble bench with her back to him. The bench obscured her lower half, while her upper half was still covered by the shawl. "Mirela, is something wrong?" he asked, concern reluctantly overtaking him. He wasn't in the mood to listen to anyone else's problems just now. He'd come to Cremorne Gardens to lose himself in light-hearted revels. However, he was fond of Mirela, and if she needed his help, he would give it.

She turned her head slightly. "Please join me," she whispered, tracing a welcoming hand along the unoccupied half of the marble bench.

James sat down. Their feet were on opposite sides of the bench, and she had once again turned demurely away, but she leaned into him, enticing him to take hold of her. The moment he did so, he knew this was not the woman he sought. Her shoulders were too narrow and delicate to belong to the more voluptuous Mirela. James took hold of the shawl and pulled it away from her face and hair, only to find himself staring into the shining eyes of a lady far too young and innocent to be hazarding Cremorne at this hour.

"Oh, no, no, no, no," he stammered in disbelief. "You

cannot be here. It isn't proper—" She cut him off with a kiss, which, pleasant as it was, also stunned him into silence. He disentangled himself and stood up, taking several steps away from the bench. "Emily, do you have any idea what you've done?"

"Indeed I do—I fooled you!" she said proudly. "You thought I was a sultry gypsy lass!" She rose and walked toward him, swaying her hips suggestively.

Too suggestively. James took her by the arms in an effort to still the unladylike movements, but quickly let go when she took this as a cue to melt against him. "Emily, you are very naughty to come to Cremorne by yourself. Don't you know how dangerous it is here for an unprotected lady?"

"I can take care of myself." She ran a hand along his cheek. "Besides, I'm not alone. I'm with you."

"That is exactly what concerns me." He took hold of her hand. "Don't you care at all for your reputation?"

She leaned closer, and the clean scent of vanilla drifted toward his nostrils. It was an aroma that always spoke to James of purity and innocence. But now Emily was risking both. "Why are you here, Emily?" he asked, his voice rough with frustration.

Her blue eyes widened. "Why, to be with you, my love. You'll keep me safe. And besides—" She began to thread her fingers through his hair. "What's the worst that could happen?"

Her hands were sending dangerously pleasant sensations along his scalp. James swallowed, feeling sweat break out on his forehead. "The *worst* is that you will be ruined, and forever ostracized from polite society."

"Not if you marry me. Wouldn't that be a lark?"

Married? The mere word set off a spark of panic. "Emily, listen to me—"

"Then we could spend all the time together we want. Including nighttime…" She pressed her body against his, the motion itself an invitation to kiss her, a siren call to disaster.

He was trying hard to resist, but her allure was rapidly pulling him in. A gentle breeze brought the soft scents of flowers and greenery, and the moon's silvery light illuminated her enticing lips. He had badly underestimated this lady, James realized, his chagrin deepening. He'd thought her a silly girl who played innocently with fire, but her knowledge of the game was far greater than he could ever have imagined.

He cleared his throat, grabbing for sanity. "Marriage is more than a mere lark, Emily. You can do far better than me for a husband, as I'm sure your parents have pointed out to you. I am neither wealthy nor respectable."

Emily scrunched her nose in distaste. "My parents are insufferable bores. What do they know of love?" Her fingers slid down to the nape of his neck, drawing him close to her once more. "We can make each other very, very happy…"

James took hold of her hands, clasping them firmly in front of him. He wasn't ready for marriage, and despite what she might think, neither was she. "Emily, listen to reason. This…flirtation…can never lead to anything. Your parents will not have me, and really, for your sake, it is best."

"You don't mean that." Once again she kissed him, clinging to him with single-minded determination. The only way to stop her would be to push her away rudely, and James didn't want to be callous with her. So he remained stock still, his mind frantically searching for an argument that could sway her. But his thoughts were brought to a complete halt when Emily gently tucked his hair behind his ear, kissing the tender skin below it in a way that was simple and yet alarmingly sensual. And heaven help him, he had been the one who taught her that.

She nibbled his earlobe. "I know you return my affections, James. Now I want proof. If you don't take me in your arms and kiss me right this minute, I will scream bloody murder." Her voice was still soft, sultry, but the words chilled him. "It will be easy to blame the scandal on you. So you see, I intend to have you one way or the other."

She pulled back a few inches, and he saw her inhale, preparing to scream. She really meant it! Instantly he covered her mouth with his, if only to keep her from ruining them both. She clung to him, returning his kiss with unwarranted passion.

It served him right, James thought, as resignation began to filter through every part of his being. Everyone considered him a danger to sweet young ladies, when in fact the opposite was true. Any of the delicious debutantes who'd come under his tutelage could take what he taught them and use it to their advantage. A few had done so, but they'd used their newfound arts to capture bigger game. Now, James realized with alarm, Emily had just shown herself to be his most apt pupil, and *he* was the prey.

He had only two choices, and they were not choices at all. He must either appease Emily and get her quietly home or allow her to ruin her reputation by causing a scene. He would have to take the former route if he wanted any chance at all—however slim—of avoiding the marriage trap. Well, no one could put on as good a show as he could, he told himself wryly. And it wasn't the

first time he'd had to sneak a girl home. He disengaged
his mouth from hers just enough to murmur, "You're a sly
one, aren't you, my dear? You've caught me out at last."

*

Lucinda kept her eyes on the path, but her ears were attuned
to everything around her. She worried lest any of the men
who had been lounging near the entrance should decide to
follow her. She grew more nervous every time she passed
one of the lamp-bearing statues. Each one threw a circle of
light onto a small section of the path, illuminating Lucinda's face as she hurried past. Even though she was wearing
a hooded cloak, she feared someone might recognize her.

Several couples walked past, but they were too
absorbed in one another to spare a glance at Lucinda.
About twenty yards ahead, a woman whose gown was
cut so low that her breasts were nearly falling out laughed
as she pulled along a well-dressed young man who could
not have been more than twenty. "I'll bet I can teach you
a few things you never learnt at Oxford," she said, running a hand suggestively over her ample curves. The man
was willing to be led, and he followed her with shy eager-
ness. "I daresay you can," he rasped, ogling her exposed
flesh as the two of them stepped into the shadows.

At the thought of something similar happening to her
sister, Lucinda walked even faster. When she passed the
place where the man and woman had disappeared, she
averted her eyes and did her best to ignore the laughter
and rustling sounds that came from behind the bushes.

To her relief, loud music and the raucous noise of a
crowd soon drowned out any other noises. The Gypsy
Cave was brightly lit and bustling with activity. Men and

women danced energetically to music from a sprightly fiddle or else drank gaily and tried to make themselves heard over the music. The place was packed, and more people spilled out into the moonlight, carrying bottles and glasses and laughing uproariously.

Lucinda slowed her pace as she approached, wondering how she could possibly locate her sister among all those people. Then she realized it would probably be easy. Emily loved nothing more than to dance; she would most likely be in the center of the dance floor. Hesitantly, Lucinda worked her way to one of several openings in the tent. To her dismay, two men blocked her path. Their clothes were clean enough, but not fine. Tradesmen, Lucinda guessed.

They, in turn, thoroughly looked her up and down, no doubt drawing their own conclusions about her. Lucinda wished she had changed into one of the plain day gowns she usually wore when visiting the Caring House. She drew her cloak more tightly around her shoulders.

One of the men lifted his battered hat. "Good evening, miss," he said, affecting a gentlemanly air that was at odds with his attire. "Fancy a good romp?" The second man said nothing, but gave her a salacious grin.

Lucinda's throat tightened. "I'm looking for someone," she choked out, reminding herself that she had worked among the lower classes for several years, and surely there could be nothing to fear. Of course, she had never been among them alone and at night, when they were at leisure to indulge in drink.

The man who had doffed his cap drew nearer. "Well, if you're lookin' for someone, I'm available!"

He smelled of beer and sweat and tobacco. Lucinda took a step back. "What I mean is that I'm trying to find—" She paused, at a loss. Perhaps it would be better to find James first. If he came here often, these men might know him. "I'm searching for a man named James Simpson. Do you know him?"

"Simpson?" The man scratched his head. "What's he look like?"

"Tall, with curly brown hair and blue eyes. Tonight he was wearing—" A memory of James, laughing, handsome, and irrepressible, filled her mind once more. "A dark blue coat with a matching cravat and waistcoat."

The second man stepped forward. "A toff, then?" He turned to his friend. "You know who she means, Joe. He's the one what always nabs Mirela, then makes her think she's too good for us."

"Ah," said Joe, nodding. "Mirela's chap. As a matter of fact, he just left."

"Was he…" Lucinda's mouth went dry. "Was he alone?"

"I'm pretty sure he was."

"Oh." This was bad news. Where could Emily be?

The second man looked surprised at Lucinda's crestfallen expression. He gave her another wink. "Ain't that a good thing?"

"I'm not seeking an assignation," Lucinda said tartly. "I need to speak to him."

"Well if I was you, I'd check that arbor just beyond the oak tree." He pointed down another path, which was, like the others, conveniently shrouded in darkness. It was also lined with dozens of oaks.

She looked at the area uncertainly. "How far down the path?"

Joe replaced his cap and grabbed a torch from its stand near the tent. "I'll be happy to light the way for you."

Lucinda took another step back, trying not to show her alarm. "That won't be necessary."

But the second man stepped up too, leaving Lucinda sandwiched between the pair of them. "We insist. It's dangerous for a lady to be alone around these parts after dark."

His leer reappeared, and Lucinda felt far from safe. But she couldn't think of any way to get rid of them. So long as the one called Joe was carrying a bright torch, she told herself they weren't likely to try anything untoward. And if she could just get to James, he would surely help her find Emily. With a nod, she said, "Thank you for your help, gentleman."

Both of them stood a little taller at being thus addressed. It was nearly comical, and Lucinda's trepidation lightened. Joe said, "Pardon me, miss, but you look familiar, though I'm sure I ain't never seen you here before."

"I go to Spitalfields sometimes. Perhaps you've seen me there?"

"You? At Spitalfields?" the other man said in disbelief. "Why would a lady like you set foot there?"

"I do charitable work at the Caring House. Teaching the girls to read and write."

"Blimey!" said Joe. "You don't say! My cousin Kate lives there." He added hastily, "She fell in with a bad lot for a while after her mum died, but she's a good girl at heart."

"You needn't feel embarrassed on her account. She's a lovely girl, eager to start fresh and make something of her life. You should be proud."

Joe beamed, and Lucinda's tension eased even more. She had a sense this man would prevent the leering one from attempting anything improper. How often her mother had fretted over Lucinda's forays to the poor and

dangerous parts of London, worried she might be set
upon by unscrupulous men. She would certainly be surprised to know it was precisely because of those trips that
Lucinda was just a little bit safer tonight.

Some of Lucinda's apprehension returned, however,
as she noticed a third man about twenty yards to her
left who was staring at her with undisguised curiosity.
He was better dressed than these two, and seemed to be
coolly observing the festivities rather than participating
in them. Now as Lucinda and the two men began walking down the path, she became uncomfortably aware that
he had broken away from the crowd and was following
them. "Do you know that man?" she asked her escorts,
indicating him with a brief tilt of her head.

Joe frowned. "Don't know who he is, but he seems to
be around a lot. Keeps to himself, though. Sometimes I
see him scribbling things in a little notebook."

His friend guffawed. "Imagine coming here and doin'
nothin' but writing!"

Lucinda decided to press forward, hoping the curious
man wouldn't follow them. When they reached a bend
in the path, Joe put out a hand to stop her. "It's just over
there," he said, pointing. "But I do believe there are two
people there after all." He looked at her quizzically. "Are
you sure you want to go on? You might not want to interrupt a private, ah, *conversation*, if you know what I mean."

"You are mistaken; I want very much to interrupt it."
She stepped forward, beyond the glare of the torch, so
that she could see better into the darkness. When her eyes
adjusted, she saw two people in a passionate embrace.
The bright pink of Emily's gown was unmistakable, and
although the man's back was facing Lucinda, she had no

trouble discerning who it was. Now she had to find a way to intervene without causing a commotion that would bring attention to themselves.

She returned to the men. "I can't thank you enough, gentlemen," she said, placing herself beyond them so that they would have to turn their backs on Emily and James in order to look at her. "However, I must ask you . . . if you would be so good . . . that is—"

Joe nudged his fellow. "Come on then, Henry. She don't want us to be no part of this."

"But that bloke's occupied," Henry objected. He gave Lucinda a wink. "If you stay with us, I guarantee you'll 'ave our undivided attention."

"Please." Lucinda took two coins from her reticule. "Here's for your trouble."

The men gasped as she placed a half crown in each of their hands. "Anytime at all," Joe said, tipping his hat to her. "Send my love to Kate, won't you, miss?"

"I will."

Joe gave his reluctant friend another shove, and they strolled away. Lucinda took a moment to calm herself before returning to the darkened nook where she had seen Emily and James. It was only later, after it was too late, that she realized she had forgotten about the third man.

James and Emily were still kissing, unaware they were being watched. Emily's arms were clasped tightly around James's neck, and she was pressing her body shamelessly against his, from her chest all the way down to her—Lucinda's own chest tightened. Such contact had to be arousing unpardonable feelings in both of them. And James's hands—dear Lord! They were moving down Emily's waist . . . and beyond. Emily let out a throaty murmur of delight. Lucinda could only hope the pair of them had not indulged in such behaviors before, and that she was not too late to preserve her sister's very last piece of honor.

James's hands were now massaging Emily's bottom.

Lucinda knew she ought to be rushing in and forcibly separating them. Yet her own heart was pounding so hard against her chest she could barely breathe, and her legs seemed to be suddenly made of rubber. She reached out to steady herself against a tree, closing her eyes tight to block out the sight of her sister in such a compromising position.

While she stood there, unable to move or speak, the two of them finally came up for air. James pulled away slightly, although this brought a soft moan of protest from Emily. "My dearest," James said softly. "We really ought to leave. Anyone might come by, and—" James stopped himself as he caught sight of Lucinda.

When their eyes met, his face registered a multitude of emotions in quick succession: surprise, worry, something that looked strangely like relief, and then, remarkably, shame. This gave Lucinda the strength she needed. Pushing herself off the tree, she said, "Yes indeed, anyone might come by and see your wanton actions." In her effort to force out the words, they ended nearly in a shriek.

Emily turned sharply. "Lucinda! What are you doing—trying to ruin everything?"

Lucinda took a step forward, happy to discover her legs remained under her. No doubt they were bolstered by the rage coursing through her. "I should ask the same thing of you! How could you be such a reckless fool?" She turned on James. "And shame on you sir, for luring her to this place!"

"Miss Cardington, I beg you will keep your voice

down," James said, lifting his hands in a placating gesture. "It's not what you think. We were kissing, nothing more. I was just telling Emily we ought to leave."

"And where were you planning to take her? To some private room where you could finish ruining her?"

His eyebrows lifted. Lucinda's anger increased when she realized he actually looked amused. "As a matter of fact, I was trying to get her home before anyone realized she was gone." He finished dryly, "Apparently I didn't succeed."

"Do you really expect me to believe that? Or perhaps you were merely planning to complete the nefarious deed while in the carriage on the way home?"

He *was* smiling now, curse the man. "*Nefarious deed?* What an imagination you have, Miss Cardington. Have you been reading gothic romances in addition to photography books?"

His utter lack of chagrin, plus his infuriating look of amusement, only fed her anger. "I...saw...your... hands," she ground out. Her face felt like it was on fire, but she was not going to back down. How dare he treat this crisis so nonchalantly?

"Lucinda, you are a nosy and pestilent old busybody," Emily said crossly, still clinging to James's arm. "What difference does it make where we were going? We are betrothed, so we are as good as married."

"Betrothed!" Lucinda repeated, horrified at her sister's criminal naïveté. "He'll never marry you."

"And what would you know about it?" Emily shot back. "I am old enough to make my own decisions and I don't need your interference. Go home."

"I'll be going home, all right, but I'll be taking you

with me. Don't you realize that men like him are not to be trusted? The way he was touching you—"

"You had no right to spy on me!" Emily broke in, looking truly affronted, as though she were not the one who was at fault.

Lucinda ignored her accusing stare. "There is no way you could convince me you would have returned home with your virtue intact."

"That is exactly what would have happened," James asserted, speaking with a cold authority that was so unlike his usual affable nature that Lucinda looked at him, startled. The amusement she had seen earlier was gone. Now he looked irritated and even troubled. "I would have taken her home and advised her against repeating such imprudent actions, and no one would have been the wiser. Now, I am not so sure."

"What are you saying?" Lucinda asked, confused.

James took Lucinda's arm and turned her to face the path once more. She was about to protest this brusque treatment when she saw a man leaning against a tree, watching the scene with interest and jotting down something in a small notebook. It was the gentleman she'd spotted earlier.

"Who the devil are you?" Lucinda said. Her agitation at finding Emily and James in that indecent embrace had so shaken her poise that the rude words flew out of her mouth before she could stop them. Instantly she felt James start in shock at her unladylike swearing. Where in the world had she gotten that? Too much time spent at Spitalfields, her father would say, if he ever got wind of it. Which, to judge by the exultant look on Emily's face, he probably would.

The man grinned and tipped his hat. "Mr. Harris, of the *Times*, at your service."

Chapter 4

"We are ruined, I tell you! Ruined! Oh, what shall we do? Oh!"

Lady Cardington's cries echoed down the long hallway. The butler's measured pace never changed as he led James toward the closed parlor door, which did little to muffle the ungodly sounds. No doubt he was used to such histrionics from the lady of the house. James could barely resist the urge to plug his fingers in his ears. Lady Cardington was hard to take at the best of times, and this was definitely *not* the best of times.

"Will you be quiet!" a deep male voice bellowed. It had to belong to Lord Cardington, although James had never before heard him raise his voice. James had heretofore thought of him as a docile, soft-spoken man, always in the shadow of his booming wife. "Sit down right this minute!" Lord Cardington yelled. "You will give yourself apoplexy."

"It would serve both of them right if I did!" came the ridiculous response. "After all I've done to keep our immaculate standing in society, they have tossed it away in the blink of an eye!"

The butler reached for the door handle, but James put out a hand to stop him. "A moment, if you please," he whispered. "I need to fortify myself against the onslaught."

In truth, James wanted to eavesdrop on more of this conversation. The butler must have sensed this, for he threw a worried glance down the hall—probably to assure himself there were no other servants nearby who might observe them. Seeing no one, he gave James a grudging nod of acquiescence.

"Foolish, wanton girls!" Lady Cardington was shrieking. "They will be the death of me."

"Don't blame both of them," Lord Cardington corrected. "Lucinda was only there because she was trying to avert this disaster."

"And you believe her story?" Lady Cardington said it more as an accusation than a question.

"Lucinda would never lie. It's not in her nature."

This declaration brought a loud huff from his wife. "You would say that. You have always preferred Lucinda, thinking she can do no wrong. But if she had gotten herself married two years ago when she *ought* to have done, none of this would have happened."

"What sort of twisted logic is that?" Lord Cardington demanded.

James found himself scratching his head over that one, too.

"If Lucinda had done what I had told her to do—" Lady Cardington spoke the words slowly and with deliberate emphasis, the way one would explain a mathematics

problem to a child. "If she'd followed my orders and forced
Lord Somerville to keep his promise to marry her—"

"There was no promise!" Lord Cardington roared.
"How many times do I have to point that out to you?"

There was a long pause, during which James imagined the two of them staring each other down. Or perhaps
Lord Cardington had forcibly taken hold of his wife in
an attempt to quiet her. Or...such a woman could drive
a man to any number of rash acts. James sincerely hoped
Lord Cardington wasn't standing within reach of the fireplace poker. He leaned closer to the door, holding up a
hand once more in response to the butler's affronted glare,
in a silent plea to remain where they were. James wanted
to hear Lady Cardington's wild denial of this obvious fact.

The lady did not disappoint. "With as much time as
the two of them spent together—at times so far out of
earshot as to be nearly *unchaperoned*—there was a vir-
tual promise, if not in actual fact."

That was stretching things, to be sure, and James could
well imagine Lord Cardington's exasperated reaction.

"And remember the way he leaned in to turn the
music for her when she played the piano at Lady Thornborough's dinner party?" Lady Cardington continued.
"Everybody noticed it. You mark my words: Lucinda
could easily have pressed her case, and Lord Somerville
would have done the right thing. He is honorable enough,
I'm sure."

"Even if I were to accept this wild premise," Lord
Cardington said, in a voice of barely concealed irritation,
"how does it follow that her marriage would have prevented last night's catastrophe?"

"Why, because Emily would already be engaged!

Your obstinate insistence that Lucinda get married first—and her equally obstinate refusal to oblige—is the root of all this trouble. I don't know how she continues to be your favorite daughter."

"Lucinda will come around in time," Lord Cardington insisted. "Besides, Emily is too young to get married. Can you imagine her trying to keep house? The place would be in utter chaos. It would be only a matter of time before everything fell down around their ears."

"But she must get married now! It is the only way to salvage her reputation!" Lady Cardington's screech was probably peeling the paint off the ceiling.

"Perhaps. But you know how I feel about that James Simpson. He is a good-for-nothing lazy scoundrel."

James couldn't help wincing at this, although he had to admit it was a fair assessment. He threw a glance at the butler, but the man was standing ramrod straight, nothing in his face betraying that he was listening to this conversation with as much interest as James was. James supposed he could add *encourages servants to eavesdrop* to his ever-growing list of offenses.

"I'm aware that Emily has been mooning over Simpson for months," Lord Cardington went on. "But I refuse to have him as a son-in-law. Look at his disreputable actions so far. Lucinda claims he was not at fault, that he never encouraged Emily to join him at Cremorne—"

"And Lucinda *never* lies," Lady Cardington reminded him, her voice laden with sarcasm.

"She is perhaps too inclined to believe the stories others tell her," Lord Cardington allowed. "I, however, remain unconvinced. There is nothing about Simpson's manner of life that indicates he would make a proper husband for Emily. He would more likely run through all her money and then abandon her."

This was too harsh. James was used to being seen in a bad light, and for the most part he deserved it. But mistreat his wife? *No.* That was one thing he would never do. It was a conviction and a determination that ran through him more deeply than anyone would ever know. Once he was married, he would carry out every one of his marital obligations, including that of being a faithful husband. Ironically, he had been avoiding marriage for precisely that reason.

However, James could tell from the Cardingtons' reaction that the time had come to stop putting off the inevitable. Although this whole debacle had not been his fault, he would make it right. Never had his affairs been blown so badly out of proportion, for he'd always been careful in his dealings with innocent ingénues. Most had been content to flirt with him in ballrooms and at other public events. But for once, this particular ingénue had followed him right into scandalous territory and taken him off guard. She was the last person he'd expected to do it, and that was precisely why he knew it was time to get out of the game. Clearly he was losing his edge. So, marriage with Emily it would be. It really might not be so bad. By finding her way to Cremorne and cornering him there, she'd displayed an impressive resourcefulness. But then, he had also been heartily surprised by the actions of her sister. Perhaps life among the Cardingtons would be more interesting than he had anticipated.

James turned to the butler and gave him a nod. Without missing a beat, the butler smoothly opened the door and announced him. The scene before James was just as he imagined it. Lord and Lady Cardington were standing by the fireplace, staring one another down. Both turned as soon as James entered.

"You!" Lady Cardington advanced on him as though she fully intended to inflict bodily harm.

James deftly took hold of her hand—primarily to ensure she didn't strike him with it. He dredged up what he hoped was his most charming smile. "May I say how well you are looking today, Lady Cardington." He gallantly kissed her hand.

These actions took her by surprise, as they were meant to do. James had long since learned this was the most efficient way to handle irate mothers. In fact, he'd come to think of himself as a master at taming the angry beast.

Unfortunately, Lady Cardington could not be won over so easily. She wrenched her hand from his grasp. "Don't try to be coy with me, Mr. Simpson," she retorted, her lips pursing and her tremendous jowls wagging. "You were caught in a compromising situation with my daughter, and—"

"And I am here to make amends," he interrupted smoothly. "I will do everything I can to remove the taint of scandal from your daughter and from this family."

Lady Cardington gaped at him. She had clearly been intending a fight—perhaps expecting James to insist he was innocent in the whole affair. But if the Cardingtons had not accepted Lucinda's explanation of what had happened, they would be even less likely to believe him. There was no point in trying that road.

Nor was there anything to be gained by delay. He tipped his head to the scowling Lord Cardington. "Thank you for receiving me, sir."

"I got your note," Lord Cardington said gruffly. "I have

allowed you in my home today because Lady Cardington insists upon it. Normally, I do not bow to her whims."

"I have no doubt you lead your family most admirably," James replied. It would probably have stroked the man's ego if James had said "rule" rather than "lead," but he was trying to gain the good graces of both Lady Cardington and her supposed lord and master. It was a fine line to walk.

"State your business, then, Mr. Simpson."

James had expected the man to at least offer him a chair, but he remained standing, as though to show by his posture that he had no intention of giving way on his decision.

"I deeply regret the circumstances that led to last night's . . . ah . . . indiscretions."

"Indiscretions!" Lady Cardington burst out. She thumped him in the chest in a most unladylike manner. "You rogue! You villain! You have made our family a laughingstock and ruined my daughter's reputation—" She began flapping her arms, and James had to work hard to protect his face without accidentally striking her back.

"That's enough, Esther," Lord Cardington said, pulling her away from James. It was an amusing sight to see a short, portly fellow manhandling his taller and stouter wife, who at the moment seemed to be nothing but a windmill of flailing arms. No doubt the poor man had had years of practice.

"You will pay for this!" Lady Cardington gasped at James.

No doubt I will, James thought. He could not truly believe he was fighting so hard for Emily's hand, when at this time yesterday he had considered her little more than an amusing addition to the season's festivities. It was too ironic, even for him. *Do it, man,* he told himself sternly.

Time to walk off the plank. Once more he addressed himself to Lord Cardington. "The truth is, sir, I wish to marry your daughter."

This declaration brought Lady Cardington to a complete standstill. Somehow she managed to gape and glare at him at the same time. Clearly she had not expected James to be so amenable to making things right. Even now, he could not say why he was convinced that marriage to Emily was the best and only course.

Now that he was plunged into the icy water, it was uncomfortable to be sure, but not so deadly as he had feared. At least it had shut the old woman up. "For weeks I have desired to speak to you, and to ask you for the privilege of Emily's hand in marriage. I was merely waiting until I could find a way to convince you of my good intentions and the sincerity of my affections."

It was pure blather, but it seemed to work on Lady Cardington. Immediately she switched from angry to ecstatic. So the woman could be steered after all. As long as she got what she wanted. "Oh, my dear boy!" she exclaimed, clapping her hands together in excitement. "Why didn't you approach us sooner! I'm sure you might have convinced us. We must begin the wedding preparations immediately—"

Once more Lord Cardington restrained her. "Not so fast, if you please."

"But my dear, we must get them married as soon as possible! It's the only way—"

"Yes, yes, so you have been telling me, nonstop and without ceasing, *all morning.*"

Lady Cardington stared at him blankly. Something in his tone must have taken her by surprise. It certainly did James.

They were both downright flabbergasted when Lord Cardington began pushing his wife toward the door. "Esther, go and have the servants prepare tea. And be sure to have them bring up those muffins I like so much."

"But I can ring for those things," she pointed out, trying unsuccessfully to dig her heels into the elegant Persian carpet. "Why must I go?"

"I want you to do it *personally*," he insisted, giving her one last shove to get her dislodged and out the door. "And don't come back for at least a half hour." He shut the door firmly behind her, even as she sputtered in protest, then made the door fast by turning the lock.

"Lord Andrew Cardington!" she cried out, loudly enough to be heard through the closed door. "If you do not get our daughter wed by the end of the season, I shall never forgive you! I shall make your life miserable, see if I don't!"

"As if you don't already," Lord Cardington muttered under his breath, and James had to stifle a laugh. "Go away!" Cardington shouted at his wife through the door. "Mr. Simpson and I will discuss this man-to-man, without your interference."

"But—"

"No buts! You may rest easy about Emily's marriage. I fully intend to see *both* our daughters wed within the year, and Mr. Simpson is going to help me do it."

James blinked. He had no idea what Cardington meant by that statement, but he suspected it wasn't good.

Accepting defeat, and apparently somewhat mollified, Lady Cardington said no more. She was still miffed, however, to judge by the house-shaking thumps as she stalked an angry retreat down the hallway.

At last the room settled into an uneasy silence. Thinking

over Cardington's last remark to his wife, James said, "With all due respect, sir, I do not think I can marry *both* of your daughters—the laws of England being what they are."

This ridiculous remark brought a grunt of amusement from Cardington. "That's a fate I would not wish on any man, even if it were legal." He pointed toward two chairs at the far end of the room. "Let us sit down. My wife has worn me out." He led the way, pausing at a sideboard, which held a brandy decanter. James took a seat while Cardington filled two glasses. Although it was too early in the day for brandy, James had no objection. He could use its bracing effects.

Cardington handed a glass to James, and then settled into his chair with a groan. This turned into a sigh of contentment as he relaxed his large frame into the cushions. He took a long sip of the brandy and once more fixed his stare on James. "Tell me, Simpson, why exactly do you want to marry my daughter?"

James took a drink from his own glass before answering. "Well, sir, as I was saying earlier, I have grown quite fond of her." Even in these circumstances, James refused to stretch the truth so far as to talk about *love*.

"I see." Cardington did not appear in the least bit convinced. "Do you suppose she returns your affections?"

"Oh, I'm positive of it, sir. Emily has the delightfully innocent belief that I am the most wonderful man in the world—which is the main thing a man requires in a wife."

Cardington grunted again, but this time there was no amusement in it. With a glance at the door that Lady Cardington had just exited—or rather, been shoved through—he added morosely, "That will change, I assure you." He finished his brandy and set the glass down with a thump on the small table between the two chairs. "Let's get down to the truth, shall we? I doubt we'd be discussing marriage at all, but for the events of last night."

Yes, there was no pulling the wool over Cardington's eyes, James thought.

"Tell me exactly what happened," Cardington directed. "If you want to be my son-in-law, I demand complete candor. Did you convince my daughter to go out to Cremorne Gardens, knowing what it would do to her reputation? Or did she really go there on her own and somehow manage to track you down?"

James was growing uncomfortable under this inflexible questioning. It was a side of the man he had never seen before. Cardington was typically a genial sort of fellow, but evidently he became very different if you threatened his family. Or his personal property. No doubt he considered his daughters to be in both of those categories.

"Mind you," Cardington went on, "I'm inclined to believe the latter is true, knowing what an impetuous girl she is, except I'd never believe she'd have enough intelligence to figure out how to do it."

"I'm afraid Miss Emily is more clever than any of us gave her credit for." Too late James realized the chagrin in his voice was all too clear. "I mean that in a good way," he amended lamely.

"No, no, don't apologize. I believe you hit the nail right on the head." He slapped the arm of his chair for emphasis. "I would have preferred to think the worse of you, rather than to believe my daughter initiated such stupidity. And you can understand that, given your reputation, it's an easy assumption to make."

"Yes, sir, I do," James said humbly. For perhaps the first time in his life, James felt a genuine twinge of regret at the way he'd been living. His own family had been after him for years to change, beginning with his formidable great-aunt. It struck him again that now everyone would consider him the guilty party when in fact it was the first time he'd been innocent. "You asked me for the truth, and I will give it to you. I had no idea Miss Emily was going to come out to Cremorne Gardens last night. But she did. She also managed to bribe a gypsy lass named Mirela who was, I'll confess, a particular friend of mine—"

He paused, wondering if this was too much information to share with a prospective father-in-law. But Cardington's expression showed only cool cooperation. He'd asked James for the bald truth, and evidently he was gratified to be getting it. "Go on," Cardington said. "She bribed a gypsy to do what, exactly?"

James sighed. There was no point in being evasive. This man wanted the truth about his daughter, and he would get it. "Emily borrowed Mirela's scarf, and from a distance she fooled me into thinking she was Mirela. She led me to one of those little grottos that are designed for—" But here he stopped again. Surely Cardington was a man of the world and knew exactly what those grottos were designed for.

He did. He gave another short nod. "And then?"

"As soon as I discovered it was Emily, I was immediately concerned for her reputation. Believe me, sir, my first thought was how to return Emily to her home without anyone being the wiser."

His primary reason for keeping Emily's reputation safe was to keep himself out of the marriage noose, but there was no reason to spell that out to Cardington. In any case, he had a feeling the man knew that already.

"And then Lucinda arrived and caused a fuss," Cardington supplied, finishing the story for James. "And this whole affair was, unhappily, observed by the gossip columnist for the *Times*."

"Yes, sir."

"Well, the story makes sense, much as I hate to admit it. Do you swear to me this is all true?"

"Yes, sir."

Cardington sat back in his chair and sighed, rubbing his hands on his face. "And now we have a mess to clean up."

"I should like to add that, although I have been honest with you, I will never tell this version of events to anyone else. I am happy to allow everyone to put the blame on me."

Cardington stopped rubbing his eyes long enough to throw a glance at James that showed a glint of amusement. "That's very gentlemanly of you, I'm sure."

"With your permission, I will go to the registrar's office as soon as I leave here and see about procuring a marriage license."

Cardington held up a hand. "There's no need for haste." Once more his eyes bored into James. "Is there?"

"What? Oh—no, sir! I assure you her, ah . . ." He gulped. This was not a conversation he wanted to have with *any* young lady's father. There was a limit to how candidly one could speak. "Her, ah, maidenly virtue, is intact."

"Good." The single clipped word showed a hint of relief. "Then there is another matter to address first."

James braced himself. He assumed Cardington would

want to discuss his concerns about James's suitability as a husband, and he was prepared to answer for that. He would also have to find a way to bring up the subject of the dowry, which he'd heard was thirty thousand pounds, and which he desperately needed in order to take on a wife and all the attendant responsibilities of keeping her in style.

"The problem, you see, is that there is more at stake here than Emily's reputation," Cardington said. "My greater concern is that Lucinda has also been implicated in this scandal."

This was a direction James was not expecting. "Yes I know, but she was only trying to save her sister. Surely you don't think anyone would accuse her of being at Cremorne for illicit reasons?"

Cardington picked up a newspaper lying on a table by the chair and gave the offending document a slap. "It's in here! Of course she stands accused of such a thing!"

"But this is bound to blow over—especially after Emily and I are married."

"Now we are at the crux of the issue," Cardington replied, tossing the paper aside. "Lucinda is my elder. Unlike her sister, she has a sensible head on her shoulders. I am aware she is not regarded as a great beauty, but nevertheless she will make someone a fine wife."

"I don't doubt it," James said.

"It is therefore unacceptable that Emily should be married before Lucinda is. I simply will not have it."

James had known for months that Cardington wanted to have his elder daughter married first; it was a big reason why Emily had been so attractive. Her unavailability had made her safe to flirt with. Or so he had thought. On the other hand, Cardington's intractability on this point might give James a reprieve. "You mean, you do not wish me to marry Emily?"

"On the contrary. You must marry her." He wagged a finger at James. "Furthermore, I'll see to it that you do."

"What about Lucinda, then?" James asked, confused. "Does she have a marriage prospect?" James considered himself pretty well attuned to these things, and he had not seen Lucinda with anyone he would label a suitor. In fact, no one seemed even remotely interested in her. Nor had she appeared to be looking for a beau—quite the opposite, in fact. She had crept away from a sumptuous ball filled with single men in order to be alone with a book. Although her interest in photography was laudable, only a woman intent on being a spinster would waste a perfectly good moonlit garden for it.

"I am sorry to say Lucinda has no suitors at the moment," Cardington said, confirming James's suspicion. "After last night, she is even less likely to get one. That's where you come in." He leaned over and poked James in the chest. "You are going to find her a husband."

"Me?" James said, recoiling in disbelief.

"You know everyone in London. Your powers of persuasion are legendary. In three days' time I expect you to give me a short list of candidates. Once I have approved them, you will get to work securing one of them for her."

Cardington spoke as though this were as easy as choosing cloth for a new coat. James shook his head doubtfully. Although he often enjoyed playing matchmaker, this situation was entirely different. He could think of nothing more daunting than to find a mate for a woman who had no wish to be married and whom no one desired to marry. "Excuse me, sir, but I don't understand why this task should fall upon me. I have already made it clear to you that, despite my *not* having caused the current scandal, I am willing to put it to rights. Why then should I be responsible to find a husband for Lucinda?"

"I'll give you one very good reason," Cardington said, tapping the tips of his fingers together with a self-satisfied smile. "Emily's dowry hinges upon it."

A chill ran down James's spine. "Her…dowry?"

"Let's not fool ourselves, Mr. Simpson. I know the real reason you are so willing to marry Emily. She has an excellent dowry. Therefore, I'm letting you know right now that this is how you are going to get it. I want my Lucinda married first. When she is married to a man who has my approval, then we can get serious about discussing the marriage settlement." A malicious glint came to the old man's eye. "Did I mention that her dowry is fifty thousand pounds?"

"Fifty?" James repeated, suddenly realizing his mouth was dry. The rumor mill, which was usually accurate in these matters, had held that the amount was thirty. Had the gossips been incorrect, or was Cardington slyly raising the sum? Either way, this whole business was beginning to take on the characteristics of a wager. Cardington was betting him fifty thousand pounds that he could find a husband for Lucinda. But could he? Win or lose, he was still bound to Emily. If she came without a dowry, James's financial status would be grim indeed.

James swallowed. "Did I hear you correctly? *Fifty* thousand pounds?"

"The same goes for Lucinda," Cardington affirmed. "However, I want you to keep the exact amount confidential. I don't want some cad marrying her just for her money."

That seemed a direct jab at James, and he shifted uncomfortably in his chair.

"Well, Simpson, are you up to the job?" Cardington demanded. "Will you help me procure a husband for Lucinda?"

James tossed back the last of the brandy, savoring its effects, using the action to gain a few moments to reflect. There was no way he could refuse. But could he really get Lucinda married? She'd always been eclipsed by her sister, the lovely and spritely chit who had come into society before her eighteenth year and taken it by storm. Emily had an endless string of admirers. Lucinda had been her opposite in every way; she was quiet and withdrawn and spurned the very idea of marriage.

Come on, man, he chided himself. *No matter what she says, in her heart of hearts surely Lucinda wants to get married. Every woman does.* Knowing what he did about women, James considered the idea that Lucinda was only pretending indifference to men because they had not shown any interest in her. It could simply be her defense against wounded pride.

Without speaking, Cardington rose and poured James another glass of brandy. He seemed content to wait while James thought over the situation. No doubt he'd learned a lot about patience when dealing with his unruly family.

Lucinda wanted to get married. From now on, James was going to hold fast to that belief, come what may. And if she *mistakenly* thought she did not, James would find a way to persuade her otherwise.

The bigger problem was likely to be finding a man he could persuade to marry her. Doing so without trumpeting the huge dowry would make it more challenging, no doubt, but James could not really fault Cardington for this stipulation. The man was genuinely concerned about his daughter and didn't want her married off simply to the highest bidder. The situation was not impossible, however. After all, Lucinda had many good points. She had an engaging personality, once you could get her talking. She played piano well and had a pleasant singing voice. James personally thought her love of photography was a strong point in her favor; perhaps another man would think so, too. James thought he could begin by making a list of eligible bachelors who had this same interest. It would be something to draw them together from the start, would it not?

He sighed. Most men, shallow as they were, would have a hard time seeing past Lucinda's awkwardness. And then there was her appearance, which many had spoken of as plain. But was it? As James sat there, recalling her gleaming chestnut hair and her eyes that often looked brown but were actually hazel, he suddenly realized she could at times be rather pleasing to look upon. And until he had seen her in the garden last night, he had not really noticed her fantastic figure . . .

He pulled himself up with a start. *Where had that thought come from?*

He downed the second glass of brandy in one go and slapped it down on the table. Standing up, he reached out to shake Cardington's hand. "Sir, may I say it is a pleasure to be welcomed into your family. I assure you I will ably perform my duties as a husband to Emily. And I guarantee," he added, with more confidence than he felt, "that we will find a suitable husband for Lucinda."

Chapter 5

Lucinda sensed something was amiss the moment she stepped into the front hall. An eerie calm pervaded the place. This was rare even on a good day, as her mother or Emily were usually up in arms about one trivial thing or another. But today, after the disaster of last night, the stillness was disquieting rather than peaceful.

There was a hired carriage standing out front, and Lucinda guessed this meant James Simpson was still here. Had he convinced her parents that the whole affair would soon be forgotten? Or had he offered marriage to Emily, and they had accepted?

Perhaps, she thought with a wild jolt of her heart, her father had shot him dead and her parents were at this very moment gloating over his corpse as it lay sprawled and bleeding on the carpet. Given the rage she'd seen this morning on her father's usually composed face, she could easily believe it. But the idea was preposterous. If James were dead, the maid would not be standing placidly in the hallway, waiting to take her bonnet and shawl. Perhaps Lucinda ought to read fewer gothic novels after all.

Mr. Jennings, the butler, approached and said, "If you please, Miss Cardington, your parents have instructed me that your presence is requested in the drawing room as soon as you return."

"Is everything all right?" she asked anxiously.

Jennings did not answer directly, but merely said, "They are all taking tea with Mr. Simpson."

"Is Emily there, too?" Like Lucinda, her sister had been instructed to stay away from the house while the interview with James was taking place. Lucinda had gone to work at her charity school, and Emily had been sent off shopping, with a maid and two footmen to keep a close eye on her. Lucinda was not surprised that Emily had returned home as soon as possible; she'd be desperate to know the outcome of the meeting. Lucinda had to admit she was curious too. Would Papa really allow an engagement? If so, perhaps her parents would stop nagging her about getting married. There was comfort in that thought. She hurried down the hall and into the drawing room.

She found Emily and James seated next to each other on the sofa, sitting just far enough apart to qualify as proper. Emily was sipping tea with unnatural tranquility; Lucinda had never known her sister to be able to control her fidgeting. She smiled at Lucinda with the complacency of a cat who has just swallowed a canary.

James stood up immediately, as did her father, whose expression Lucinda would have described as closer to resignation than contentment. But at least the signs of anger were gone—a complete turnaround from this morning. James gave her a bow and a polite greeting that was entirely devoid of his usual playfulness.

Lucinda could only stand and stare. The whole atmosphere of the room was weirdly off-kilter. Had everyone gone mad?

Her father took her hand and drew her into the room. "We've been waiting for you, my dear." He led her to a chair with an assiduous attention that was completely unlike him. She stared at her father in mute inquiry.

"Sit down, Lucinda," Lady Cardington commanded imperiously. "We've important family business to discuss." She set down her teacup and began to dust sandwich crumbs from her fingers with a napkin.

Here, at least, was something that had not changed. Lucinda seated herself and accepted the teacup proffered by Emily. She took a cautious sip; Emily always put too much sugar in her tea. But today it was exactly as Lucinda liked it. She threw a wary look at her sister. "Are you well, Emily?"

"Oh, perfectly!" Emily answered, her eyes shining. "We've been making such wonderful plans, and—"

"—And your *father* is going to tell you about it," her mother broke in, peering significantly over her pince-nez at Emily.

"Yes, Mama," Emily replied demurely.

Too demurely. Emily never failed to bristle whenever their mother interrupted or corrected her. Now Lucinda was sure something was very wrong indeed. As all eyes in the room settled on her, she had a sudden mind picture of a gazelle being separated from the herd for a kill. It would be better to have this out as soon as possible. "So are Emily and Mr. Simpson to be married, then?"

"We are!" Emily clasped James's hand and gazed at him like a schoolgirl whose head is filled with romantic fantasies about love. James did not appear quite so ecstatic, but he returned Emily's smile with a warmth that Lucinda deemed sincere.

"Well, I'm glad that's settled," Lucinda said truthfully. She dared not ask why her father had abandoned his foolish insistence that Lucinda get married first. "My felicitations to you both. When is the happy day to be?"

"A week after yours," her father said.

"I—I beg your pardon?" The teacup slipped from Lucinda's hand, cracking as it landed sideways on the saucer. "But Papa, you know I don't have any—" She paused. James had settled his beaming smile on her, which was more than a little unnerving. "That is, there is no one—" Again, she could not finish the sentence. Everyone here knew full well she had no beau, nor was she likely to get one. Not that she was in the market. She'd made up her mind on that score. Nevertheless, it was embarrassing to say these things out loud. And there was the fact that James kept *looking* at her.

At last Emily began fidgeting, in the way she always had when she wanted to get a word in. Not surprisingly, the plan was not being told quickly enough to suit her. "You will have a suitor by the end of the week," she blurted out. "James has promised to find you one. We are going to get you married off, and then—"

"Hush, child!" Lady Cardington scolded. "Or I shall make you leave the room."

"Listen to your dear Mama," James soothed, patting Emily's hand. "We don't want to overwhelm your sister with these details all at once." He gave Lucinda a smile that was almost apologetic—rather like a doctor who has just informed a patient she has only a few days to live.

Lucinda stood up. "Papa, what's this all about?"

He put his hands in his waistcoat, striking a pose that was meant to look authoritative. "Lucinda, I'm going to tell you how it stands. I have decided on a course of action that is for your own good."

Lucinda took hold of the wingback chair for strength. "Go on."

"Last night's affair at Cremorne Gardens has damaged your reputation as well as Emily's. There is no denying it."

"I don't care," she said defiantly. "Let them talk. Emily and James are to be married, and that will be the end of it. I don't care what people say about me; I have no wish to be married anyway."

"No wish to be married!" Lady Cardington repeated shrilly, as though it were the most preposterous thing she'd ever heard.

"I will not have any daughter of mine left on the shelf," Lord Cardington said stoutly. "You are the elder, and you must be married before Emily. After last night, Emily must announce her engagement soon. That doesn't leave us much time. I have tasked Mr. Simpson with compiling a list of candidates."

"Mr. Simpson!" she repeated in horror. "Why should *he* be responsible to find me a husband?"

"Because our whole future depends upon it!" Emily said fervently. "Papa will not release my dowry money until you are married. So you see, you must do it!"

Lucinda looked at her father aghast. "Would you really use money as a means to force me into marriage, Papa?"

"Now, now, no one is forcing you," Lord Cardington insisted. "We will find a man who is acceptable to you." He wiped a hand briefly across his brow. "Surely there must be such a man out there *somewhere*."

Lucinda had never had any illusions about her feminine charm—or lack thereof. But even so, this idea that someone else must find her a husband—and the implication that it would be such a horrific chore—was too insulting. Lucinda lifted her chin and crossed her arms. "I won't do it."

"What?" Lady Cardington's jaw dropped in surprise.

Lucinda knew she was shocking them with her mutiny, but she didn't care. "I've spent my whole life trying to be your dutiful daughter. Ever since my presentation at court I've spent season after season at balls and dinners, not to mention countless weeks at house parties in the country. I've been ignored, mocked, and overlooked, and I've had my own wishes belittled for long enough. I won't go along with it anymore." She turned to face James Simpson full on. "And I'll thank you *not* to go husband-hunting for me. I shall never get married."

"You can't possibly mean that!" Emily moaned.

"How do you intend to repair your reputation?" Lady Cardington demanded.

"Surely my modest lifestyle and my charitable works speak for themselves. I care nothing for the opinions of those who believe words in a newspaper rather than clear evidence."

"But Lucinda!" Emily wheedled. "You can't tell me you truly wish to remain a lonely old maid?"

A lonely old maid. That was what everyone thought of her. Even now they were all looking at her with misplaced pity. She had to find a way to show them she was content. "The Scriptures tell us to seek first the kingdom of God and His righteousness. My faith is what gives my life meaning, and my volunteer work fills my days. I shall be happy to stay on this course for the rest of my life."

"For heaven's sake!" Emily cried in frustration. "Can't you for once think of anyone but yourself?"

Lucinda let out a contemptuous laugh. "You're a fine one to judge, little sister. When have you ever thought of anyone else? If you had even once come down to the school, you would have seen for yourself what positive changes we are bringing about in the lives of the poor and downtrodden. But you could not be bothered. You were too busy with your silly schemes. Your self-centered, foolish actions have gotten you into this mess, and now you must get yourself out."

She marched to the door and flung it open. She paused, feeling all eyes upon her back, and realized she had one more thing to add. She turned slowly and sized them all up. No one spoke, but Lucinda knew it was just the shock of her actions that had temporarily shut them up. Any second now the chaos would resume. She threw a triumphant glance at James. "Mr. Simpson, have I stood up for myself today?"

James presumably had the most to lose from these events, since he was at risk of being tied to a penniless wife. And yet Lucinda was surprised to see he was the only person in the room who did not appear angry. Rather, a kind of wonder lit his face. His eyebrows were raised, and somehow she got the impression his estimation of her had risen as well.

But this foolish notion passed, as did the moment of

silence. Both Emily and Lady Cardington began shrieking at the same time, begging Lord Cardington to do
something.

"This is not the end of the discussion, Lucinda!" Lord
Cardington bellowed.

"With all due respect, sir, I beg to differ." She turned
and stalked out. Her face still burned white hot, and her
heart was pounding so hard she thought it would burst.
But she'd done it. For once in her life she had stood up to
her family. Was this what triumph felt like? If so, why did
it feel more like guilt than elation?

"Come back here, young lady!" Her father's words
followed her into the hallway.

Lucinda did not stop. She had to get away, go some-
place where she could be alone and sort this out. "Dear
Lord, what have I done?" she murmured as she hurried
up the stairs to her room. No doubt she would have plenty
of time to mull over what these events signified. For now,
though, she had to believe she had done the right thing.
She had put her foot down, and her father was bound
to relent. He wouldn't really allow Emily to be married
without a dowry, would he? Lucinda would have to speak
to him again, try to get him to see reason. But she would
do it without her mother or sister present, and certainly
without James Simpson.

For some reason he worried her more than the rest of
them put together.

*

"Foolish, uncaring, ungrateful girl!" Lady Cardington
fumed, struggling to get her large frame out of the chair.

Lord Cardington set a hand on her shoulder to

restrain her, even as James took hold of Emily's arm to prevent her from racing after her sister. He had no doubt both these ladies would happily drag the girl back into this room and tie her down if necessary in order to force her to submit. And while the prospect was an interesting one, it was surely not the wisest way to go.

It seemed Lord Cardington was of the same mind. "Let her go," he said, wearily but firmly.

"But—but—" Lady Cardington sputtered like a faulty steam engine.

"You can't just let her go like that, Papa!" Emily cried. "You must make her come back here right this instant!" There were tears streaming down her face now. Combined with the heat of her anger, they turned her face a blotchy red. It was a look James had never seen on Emily before, and he found it most unflattering.

She tried to pull away, but he kept his grip. A sample of things to come, he thought grimly. No doubt Emily was going to be a handful to govern, and he might as well start training for it now. "Your father is right. We must all remain calm." He reached up to brush away the tears from her cheeks—not because he had any particular desire to do so, but because he suspected it would help settle her down.

Sure enough, her big blue eyes looked into his and her mouth softened into a tremulous smile. "But what shall we do?" she implored.

"We will allow her to think it over," Lord Cardington said. "She needs time to adjust to the idea, that's all. She's a sensible creature, and I have no doubt her desire to do the best by her family will ultimately prevail."

"If that's your plan, you'll be waiting a long time,"

Lady Cardington pronounced. "She has always been a willful girl, intent on getting her own way."

Willful? Lucinda? This was a new thought for James. He'd always thought Lucinda to be somewhat docile, but after what he had just witnessed, he had to admit he might have been wrong. The words she had flung back at him about standing up for herself were still ringing in his ears.

"At times Lucinda has fallen short of our expectations, I'll grant you that," Lord Cardington said. "But that's no sin—"

"Don't you go making excuses for her!" Lady Cardington broke in. This time she made it out of her chair and began to advance on her husband. "Lucinda could easily have met our expectations. All she had to do was take that hard-headed tenacity she wastes on charities and use it to secure Lord Somerville like I told her to."

"Oh, not that again!" Lord Cardington shouted, throwing his hands up in annoyance. "Will you leave off! What's done is done."

James cleared his throat. "Pardon me, but I feel compelled to point out that Lord Somerville and his wife— my cousin Lizzie—will soon be part of your family, since Miss Emily and I are to be married."

"Married," Emily repeated dreamily. She let out a sigh and clung unpleasantly to his arm.

"You are correct," Lord Cardington said to James. He pointed a finger at his wife. "So you must stop your invective against that situation once and for all."

"Humph," Lady Cardington replied, giving him an indignant stare. But it appeared her husband's words were finally sinking in.

"In my opinion, Lucinda is the last person at fault here," Lord Cardington went on. "We ought to put the blame where it belongs."

Emily gripped James's arm tighter, as though expecting to be reprimanded. She had achieved her aim of being betrothed to James, but she knew her father was far from happy about it. James was also prepared for an onslaught, but to his surprise Lord Cardington pointed both of his thumbs at himself. "The blame must be placed squarely upon my shoulders."

Emily said uncertainly, "*You*, Papa?"

"That's right," Cardington replied brusquely. "I have been too lax in my discipline. I have allowed her to indulge in pastimes that are not healthy for a young woman. I allowed her to spend too much time reading books and discussing politics. I agreed to her becoming involved with that school, but she has spent far too much time with base and uncultured people as a result." He rubbed his hands together. "It is time to rein her in. And just like a horse that has been given too much of its head, it must be done firmly, but gently."

"Now you are talking sense," Lady Cardington said.

James found himself cringing at this assessment. He couldn't help but think it was far wide of the mark. Lucinda's insistence that she'd spent the past few years faithfully following her parents' dictates rang true to him, and he'd hate to think of her few freedoms being heartlessly curtailed because of something her sister had done. But what better explanation or advice could he give? He had only a scrap of wisdom he'd gleaned from wallflowers in general, but it was as good a place as any to start. "Sir, if I might interject."

"Yes?"

"Perhaps the problem is that Lucinda does not feel she has the ability to attract a husband."

Lord Cardington's eyebrows raised. "Why? What's wrong with her?"

"Nothing," James hastened to assure him. "Lucinda has lovely qualities, to be sure. But since her previous efforts have not yielded much success, perhaps she has not . . . er . . . learned to make the most of her assets."

Unfortunately, Lord Cardington took this as proof of his previous statement. He nodded vigorously. "That is precisely what I mean. She's wasting her time on the wrong things." He pointed at Emily, who was still clinging to James's arm. "Therefore, you must help her."

"With what?" Emily squeaked.

"With all those . . . *womanly* things." He waved a hand in a general indication of Emily's gown and hair. "Drag her to your modiste and order up some new gowns. Get a proper ladies' maid to fix her hair."

"But I've tried that before!" Emily whined. "She always rebuffs my suggestions. And in any case, how can I help her now if she won't even talk to me?"

"Give her a day or so to calm down," James suggested. "In the meantime, I will try to come up with a few additional ideas."

"See that you do," Lord Cardington ordered. He strode over to James. "As my future son-in-law, I'm counting on you. You know what is at stake."

James tried to swallow a knot that had lodged itself in his throat. He thought of the years stretching ahead with Emily as his wife. She was pleasant enough, but if she came to him without a dowry, he would be placed in a precarious position. Living in town, in the manner to which he was accustomed, was expensive. His father had left him no inheritance to speak of, and for years James had been dependent on his mother's side of the family. His great-aunt, Lady Thornborough, had taken him into her home and treated him as a son. But even her resources were limited. Without an influx of cash, the estate in Kent that would be his after her death could easily fall into decline or even ruin. For years James had shirked his responsibilities, emulating his father's carelessness, telling himself that one day he'd get serious about taking the proper road. Now he worried he might have waited too long. There was a very real danger he'd turn out to be the complete failure his father had been.

Know what was at stake? Indeed he did.

Chapter 6

"You're late, James."

Lady Thornborough scowled at James from her bed, where she was supposedly laid low by a bad cold. But she was sitting up and alert, her back supported by a mountain of pillows. So far as James could tell, his great-aunt was looking as imperious as ever.

He crossed to the bed and placed a quick kiss on her cheek, careful to avoid the cup of tea in her hands. "My sincere apologies, Auntie. Something came up to detain me."

His aunt frowned. "Something is always detaining you, James. I wish you would learn how *not* to be 'detained'—it's most aggravating."

James dropped into a chair and surveyed her—what he could see of her, at any rate. She was swaddled in woolen shawls and had blankets drawn up to her chest, even though a bright fire was keeping the room uncomfortably warm. "I'm sorry, Auntie, have I kept you from something? You were planning on going out, perhaps?"

She set the teacup on the bedside table, where it

landed with a clatter. "Always jesting, aren't you? No concern for the fact that I waited half an hour to take my tea, because you said you would be joining me."

James had long since learned to allow his great-aunt's reproving remarks to glance off him. "Is there any more tea?" he inquired, looking hopefully glance toward the teapot.

"It's cold," she answered uncompromisingly.

"What a pity. I could use a cup just now." He gave here a rueful grin, which he hoped she would accept as a sign of contrition. "I truly am sorry I'm late. I promise I have a reason which even you will find valid. But first I must ask, how are you doing?"

He asked the question sincerely, for underneath her still formidable presence he sensed a growing frailty, and this worried him. James had come to live with his great-aunt when he was just fourteen years old, right after his mother had died. She was in many ways his anchor, although he had never told her so outright. Her "colds" were becoming more frequent, and James could not bear to think of her leaving this earth—not yet, when he still had so much need of her help and guidance.

Hearing the genuine concern in James's question, Lady Thornborough's expression softened. "I'm getting old, James." She pulled her shawls closer around her with a tiny sigh. "Some days the ache in my bones simply will not leave me."

"Don't say that, Auntie." He leaned in and took one of her cool hands, chafing it to warm it. "We'll have you back on your feet in no time. Have you had some of Cook's miracle-working broth?"

"Yes, yes," she said impatiently. "All the servants do

their best to coddle me. I don't need that from you, as well." She drew her hand back. "On second thought, you are not trying so very hard to coddle me, seeing as how you kept me waiting for my tea."

This reproach actually set James's mind at ease a little. So long as she was railing at him, James knew she still had plenty of life left in her. "On any other day I would deserve such chastisement. But not today. I have just come from a very important meeting. One that will affect us both."

"Oh? Let's hear it, then."

James found himself under the intense scrutiny of her steely gray eyes. This was nothing new, however. Even when he was a reckless and disrespectful youth who was afraid of very little, he always felt some trepidation whenever his great-aunt looked at him that way. Over the years he'd learned how to cajole her into a better mood—most times. He wondered how she would react to the news he was bringing today. "Auntie, I shall tell you straight out: I am going to be married."

"Married?" She was so surprised that it came out as a gasp. "To whom?"

"Miss Emily Cardington."

She looked at him incredulously. "That foolish little slip of a girl? Nonsense." Her eyes narrowed. "Oh, I see. You're jesting. I should have known."

"Unfortunately, I must assure you I am in earnest."

"But James, how can you be serious?" she protested. "I know that girl has been following after you at every opportunity—anyone with eyes in their head could see that. But surely you can't think she'd make a suitable wife. She's such a flighty one, and totally lacking in common sense. How could she possibly manage her duties as mistress of an estate like Rosewood?"

His aunt was voicing the worries James had as well. Problem was, now he was in the unenviable position of having to defend the match. "Emily may be a trifle immature in some areas, but she's still young. She will learn. For now, you are the proper mistress of Rosewood, and as far as I'm concerned you will remain so, even after I am married."

"Why her, then? And why now?" Again she pierced him with a look. "Have you gotten her into trouble?" There was no mistaking what she meant.

"There was trouble, Auntie, but not the kind you are thinking of. I promise you I would never compromise an innocent young lady in that way."

Her only response to this declaration was a small *humph*, which James ignored. "I don't blame you for jumping to that conclusion. You must have read about last night's incident at Cremorne Gardens."

"I've left off reading the gossip columns, precisely because too often *you* are their subject," she replied archly. "My bones are already giving out on me; I don't need heart failure as well. Don't tell me you took Miss Cardington to Cremorne!"

James held up a hand. "Certainly not. She was there, but I had nothing to do with it. Unfortunately, I now have rather a lot to do with the result."

Lady Thornborough crossed her arms and regarded him coolly. "Perhaps you had better start at the beginning."

So James related the whole story, from the time he had been told the gypsy girl wanted to see him in the arbor through to Lucinda's arrival and their subsequent discovery by the reporter from the *Times*. "I did my best to persuade the man not to print the article. He seemed sympathetic to my plight, acting as though he believed my explanation of what had happened—especially after I threatened him. Thinking I had gained his silence, I took the ladies home and got them inside safely and quietly. But that reporter was a sly devil. As soon as he was free of me, he must have gone straight to the newspaper and made his report. When Lord and Lady Cardington read it, they were beside themselves with rage."

"They have every right to be," Lady Thornborough said. "Both their daughters' reputations have been ruined in one night. So I suppose that's where you were this afternoon—at Lord Cardington's home?"

"Yes."

"I'm surprised you came out of that meeting alive."

"Lady Cardington wanted to murder me, that's for sure," James agreed. "But then they would have lost their best hope for salvaging the situation. I don't think they are thrilled to have me for a son-in-law, but we all agree it's the only honorable thing to do under the circumstances."

"I suppose you are right," Lady Thornborough said grudgingly. "Well, when's it to be, then? Soon, I suppose."

"No, not until next spring. Lord Cardington is adamant that we not get married right away, just to prove to the gossip-mongers that his daughter's virtue is still intact. In the meantime, I was hoping you could take Emily under your wing and give her the benefit of your wisdom. I'm certain that many a responsible lady started out as a foolish girl. Surely you were young once, Auntie?"

She gave another *humph* and shook her head. "I was never so empty-headed as that one. Why could you not marry Lucinda?"

This question took James completely off guard. "Marry Lucinda?" It was a novel idea, albeit an absurd one. "I couldn't possibly do that, and in any case the announcement of my engagement to Emily has already been sent to the *Times*. It would be like changing horses in midstream, don't you think?"

Lady Thornborough bristled. "Women are not cattle," she remarked sourly.

James sighed and rubbed a hand on the back of his neck. Usually he enjoyed sparring with his great-aunt, but this topic was beginning to cut too close to the bone. "All right then, let me put it this way. Emily has her heart set on me. Why else do you think she went through all that trouble to follow me to Cremorne Gardens? If I didn't marry her, she would be devastated."

"I suppose that's true," Lady Thornborough admitted, although the reluctance in her voice was unmistakable.

"As for her sister—well, Lucinda has no interest in me." He sighed. "Nor in anyone else for that matter."

His aunt raised one gray eyebrow. "Are you disappointed that she does not find you irresistible, as do all the other ladies?"

"You will say my ego deserves a good bruising," James replied with a dry laugh. "And you would be right. But no, that's not the reason why the situation rankles me."

"No? What is it, then?"

Now it was time to discuss the hard facts. "You know there has always been another important reason why I must get married. A wife who brings a good dowry with her will provide a vital boost to Rosewood."

"Yes, I know," Lady Thornborough said with a note of regret. "It is a shame to have to think of marriage in that light, but in our circumstances we must. At least in that regard you've chosen the right woman. I've heard her dowry is thirty thousand pounds. That is true, isn't it?"

"It *was* thirty thousand," James said. "Now, it's fifty."

"Fifty!"

The old woman's eyes lit up, but James knew her elation stemmed from relief, not avarice. She loved Rosewood fervently—certainly more than James ever had. Occasionally he felt bad about that, but he'd always told himself he would grow to love it in time. "There is one thing, though," he added. "The dowry hinges on me finding a husband for Lucinda. Otherwise, the settlement will be only a fraction of that amount."

Lady Thornborough's smile evaporated. "*You* must find her a husband? And how does Lord Cardington propose you do that?"

"I'm to compile a list of candidates, then approach each man individually and try to generate his interest in her. Lucinda also has a sizeable dowry. Money can smooth over a lot of other things." He felt a cad for stating it that way, and even more so when he saw his aunt's pained reaction. But there was no getting around the fact that it was true.

"But you said Lucinda is not inclined to get married," she pressed. "How do you intend to change her mind?"

"She *says* she has no interest in getting married," James corrected. "But I can't believe it. I think it is merely a way of hiding her disappointment that no one is interested in her. And in any case, as Lord Cardington pointed out to me, my powers of persuasion are legendary."

His aunt looked unconvinced. "A short while ago you acknowledged that your boundless charms had no effect on her. I think you will find this to be a greater challenge than you are willing to acknowledge."

James opened his hands wide and shrugged. "If you have any ideas, Auntie, I'll be glad to hear them."

She considered this for a moment, her brows knitting together. It was an important question, as they were both well aware. This would impact not only their lives but future generations of their family as well. For years he had blissfully ignored her admonitions that she "would not be around forever" and he would have to take personal responsibility for his future. Now he could no longer deny that in this, as in so many other things, she was right.

"I can think of two avenues," she said at last.

"That's two more than I have thought of."

"James, use your head for once," Lady Thornborough chided, effectively quelling his morose thoughts. His aunt never looked more invincible than when she was scolding him. "First, remember that Lucinda has become close friends with Margaret."

"Yes, that's true," James agreed. Last season, Margaret Vaughn had captured the heart of Tom Poole, who was the half brother of James's cousin Lizzie. They'd had plenty of obstacles to overcome—including facing down the man who had purposefully ruined Lizzie's good reputation. But now Tom and Margaret were married and ecstatically happy. James snapped his fingers. "I think I see what you're after. We could get Margaret to extol the joys of married life—persuade her how wonderful it can be."

"Precisely."

"And the second thing?"

"Perhaps there is a way to put your powers of persuasion to work. It's all in the approach, right? What about your mutual interest in photography? I believe you and Lucinda have been engaged in lively conversation on this topic more than once."

"Yes, we have!" James found himself unable to repress a smile. The memory of Lucinda on the Trefethens' moonlit terrace defiantly clutching a book was one he would not soon forget.

"Cultivate that mutual interest. It can be an open door to get to know her better. Find out what she likes—and dislikes. Lucinda is not like so many other ladies who care only about money or social standing. I believe she is holding out for a man who is her intellectual equal, someone who shares her passions. Find her someone like that, and she'll be married before you know it."

James leaped out of his chair, took the woman by the shoulders, and planted a big kiss on her wrinkled cheek. "Auntie, you are a genius!"

"I'm glad to hear you acknowledge it. After all those years when you were certain you were far more clever than I."

James gave her a chastened look. "Even with your gruff exterior, I never doubted that you had my best interests at heart."

There was, for the tiniest fraction of an instant, a gleam in his aunt's eye that James could have sworn was a tear. But she gave a little cough and gathered her shawls around her, her voice becoming businesslike once more. "No one is more concerned than I am that your future—and the future of Rosewood—should be made financially secure. However, we are dealing with more than dowries or what a father wants for his daughter. We are dealing with a human heart. It is abundantly evident to me that

Miss Lucinda Cardington does not approach the idea of marriage as frivolously as her sister."

Or me, James thought. His aunt may not have said it aloud, but James had no doubt she was thinking it. And she was right. James *had* been approaching the idea of marriage frivolously, at least in his actions. He had not wished to drill down to the core of his feelings and admit that marriage scared him. At least with a wife like Emily he could maintain both control and distance. She would never press him to uncover the long-buried hurt and the fear of what a marriage could become when two people loved each other too much.

Truth be told, that was the real reason he would never marry a woman like Lucinda. She was the sincere, earnest type, the kind who would expect things of him—things he was not sure he'd have the ability to give, even if he wanted to.

"Lucinda is a person in her own right," Lady Thornborough said. "She is not a mere path to the things you and Emily want." She ran a hand across his cheek in a brief, tender motion. His aunt's slender hand felt dry and rough. The skin, covered with age spots, was drawn taught across delicate bones. It struck James that they looked more gnarled than he had remembered. "Promise me you'll do your best for Lucinda. Always treat her with respect."

All too often he had fallen short of her expectations for him, but now he was going to put those days far behind. He nodded solemnly. "Yes, Auntie. I will."

*

James sat at one of the desks in his club's massive library. This was his favorite room, expansive and filled with comfortable chairs and acres of books lining the walls. The comforting scents of leather, cigars, and brandy always hung in the air. It was the perfect place to retreat and regroup, and tonight he certainly needed to do some serious regrouping.

He looked down at the sheet of paper in front of him. At the top he had written "Prospects for Lucinda." The rest of the page was blank. *A fine start,* he thought wryly. He stared at the paper, gathering his thoughts, mentally reviewing all the men of his acquaintance.

"Aren't you coming, Simpson?"

James looked up to see Chapman standing in the doorway, looking at James expectantly. Beyond him, several other men were donning their hats and gloves in preparation for going out.

James sighed. "Not tonight, my boys. I've something else to attend to."

He had to complete this list. And in any case, there would be no more nighttime trips to Cremorne Gardens for him. As of tomorrow, all the world would know he was an engaged man.

After subjecting James to some good-natured teasing about how London's best roué was losing his touch, the men departed. They chatted energetically while working their way down the hall, their voices gradually fading as they went out the massive front doors of the club.

When they were gone, the cavernous library fairly echoed with quiet. Only occasionally was there a sound— a rustling from across the room as the only other man there, Daniel Hibbitt, turned the pages of the newspaper he was reading. True to his usual manner, Hibbitt had paid no attention to the men who had just gone, nor did he act at all aware that James was still in the room. He was the club's anomaly: a quiet man who seemed to enjoy having the bustle of people around him but took no part in it himself. He was known as the club's "hermit"—albeit a hermit who happened to live among other people.

From behind the newspaper Hibbitt's hand reached out for the brandy glass on the table next to his chair. James saw the glass disappear behind the paper, then reappear as Hibbitt set it down again. This was not the way James would have preferred to spend the evening. He'd been engaged for less than a day, and already he missed the parties and raucous laughter his friends would be enjoying. It was as though the silence around him magnified the weight of his new responsibilities. This task of finding a husband for Lucinda pressed on him most heavily of all. With a quiet sigh, James set pen to paper and began to write.

A few minutes later he looked down at a short list of twelve names. They were all men who were well known to James; all had incomes and social status that made them worthy to marry the daughter of an English peer. "Look at that," he said softly. "A round dozen. Surely there must be one man among them who could be persuaded to marry Lucinda."

Across the room, the paper rustled again as Hibbitt turned another page, reminding James he was not alone. Instantly he regretted having spoken aloud. There was a need for discretion, after all. It would not do to have everyone know he was desperate to get Lucinda married and actively scheming for it. But he need not have worried; Hibbitt was clearly absorbed in the news of the day and paying no heed to James's mutterings.

What did worry James was his great-aunt's admonition, which was annoyingly lodged in his thoughts: *"A man who is her intellectual equal, someone who shares her passions."*

Who would be such a match for Lucinda? What type of man would want a wife who was intelligent, if somewhat awkward, who cared more for science than fashion, who was pitifully shy in a group but so obstinate once she'd set her mind on something? James feared it was a mixture of traits not many men would find appealing.

He looked back at his list and reviewed the names. Reluctantly he took his pen and scratched out four of them. During his years of matchmaking for mere amusement he'd often been successful at pairing those who were polar opposites, and yet he also knew when two people would simply never be suitable for each other. The four names he'd just scratched certainly fell into that category.

In truth, he could not think of anyone who seemed exactly right for Lucinda. Perhaps she also felt that way, and this was why she was so convinced she would never marry. If he was honest with himself, James had been convinced of it, too. But at least the remaining names on his list showed some potential.

The man at the top of his list, George Wilson, was someone James had recently met at the London Photographic Society. Wilson was a tall, thin man, the smartest in his graduating class at Cambridge. His talent in chemistry and math had made him a natural for the pursuit of photography. James found him a tad egotistical and self-absorbed, but perhaps those traits would prevent the man from feeling threatened by a woman as intelligent as Lucinda.

The second man on the list, Myron Stonewell, was a music lover whom James frequently spotted at the opera. Like Lucinda, he was an accomplished piano player. James could make sure they met during an interval at the next opera, and then bring up their shared interests to get the conversation going. Once he'd been introduced to the Cardingtons, they might invite him to their home for a dinner party where he could hear Lucinda play.

James stood up. Knowing he had at least two solid prospects made him feel more confident. This might not be so difficult after all. It would still require a measure of finesse and persuasion, but at least he would have a starting point, a bridge to get the two lovebirds together.

Lovebirds.

James snorted. There was no denying that this entire situation was, at its heart, a farce of amazing proportions. But somehow he would succeed at his task. He picked up his glass of brandy. "Hibbitt!" he shouted.

Hibbitt's newspaper jerked in surprise. Slowly it lowered, and the club's hermit peered at James, with only his bespectacled eyes visible. They must be about the same age, James realized, although Hibbitt's rapidly receding hairline made him look older.

"What is it?" Hibbitt said in his usual sour manner.

The man positively radiated gloom, but James refused to let it dampen his spirits. He lifted his glass as if in toast. "To marriage!"

Hibbitt had thick, bushy eyebrows—as though all the hair that had abandoned the top of his head had jumped down to his brows to compensate for it. He now raised them inquiringly at James. "Whose marriage—yours?"

"I'm only telling you because I know you can keep a secret."

Hibbitt shook his head and raised his paper again. From behind it, James heard a surly, "Better you than me, my friend."

Chapter 7

"We are going to the...mill-i-ner's shop to..."

Lucinda listened patiently as her student laboriously read each word in the sentence. "Go on, Kate," she encouraged, when the girl paused before a word she didn't recognize. It was slow going for some of these older girls whose learning was so slight as to be virtually nonexistent. Kate was learning quickly, though. She'd come to the school just a few short months ago, and yet she had already acquired nearly all the skills she would need to work at a milliner's shop. "Sound out the word," Lucinda instructed. "What is the first letter?"

"*P*," Kate answered. When Lucinda nodded, Kate looked at the word again. "*P-U-R*...Pur-chase!"

"Correct!" Lucinda said happily. "Now read the whole sentence to me."

Kate began again from the beginning, reading with confidence this time. "We are going to the milliner's shop to purchase two bonnets. The bonnets cost two pounds each—" This time she stopped reading for a different reason. "Two pounds! It's a shop for rich ladies, to be sure!" Her quip brought guffaws from the seven other girls who were also seated at this large table where they took their reading lessons together.

"Imagine spendin' half a year's wages on a bonnet!" This came from Fannie, the eldest of the ladies.

"I guarantee you, you'll be earning more than four pounds a year when you leave here," Lucinda said. "And it will be work you can be proud of."

The girls beamed as they tried to imagine what they might do with such riches.

"But you've got to work hard to earn that money," Lucinda reminded them. "Back to work, everyone."

"Hard work it may be," she heard Fannie say to her neighbor, "but it's a darn sight better than making a living on your back!"

Several of the girls laughed. There was once a time when such talk would have made Lucinda blush with embarrassment, but she was used to it now. The banter among her pupils was good-hearted, and they truly wished to put their unsavory pasts behind them. With few exceptions, they were serious about bettering their lives. Those who had come here seeking only a handout were soon revealed by their own actions. There was another place where those who were in desperate need of food or shelter could find it temporarily, but Lucinda's school was for those willing and able to work.

"The sleep of a laboring man is sweet, whether he have little or much," Lucinda told them, quoting one of her favorite verses from Proverbs. "There is nothing like a clean Christian conscience from living as the Lord would have us to do."

"And is *your* conscience clean, Miss Cardington?"

This question, which had the tenor of an accusation, came unexpectedly from a male voice behind her.

Lucinda turned to see a man standing in the doorway, his arms crossed and his expression as harsh as his words. It was Bill Nelson, a rough man, a drunkard and a roustabout. Kate had once been his "particular gal," and he hadn't taken kindly to her efforts to reform.

"I asked you never to come back here, Bill," Lucinda said, speaking in a frosty tone to cover a spasm of fear. Normally her footman, Peter, was here to provide a measure of protection, but Lucinda had just sent him out on an errand. She wondered if Bill had seen him go and taken this moment to approach the school.

It wasn't even noon, but Bill was blind drunk, that much was plain. Unfortunately, he was even more dangerous drunk than sober. He swaggered into the room and launched himself toward Kate. She stood up rapidly, the simple wooden chair tumbling to the floor as she backed away from him. "Go away, Bill. You got no business here."

"Business!" he shot out. "You are my business! You belong with me, and the sooner you come to your senses, the better." He pointed an accusing finger at Lucinda. "And you, with your high-and-mighty airs, telling these girls about *Christian* living. Is that why you spend your evenings carousing at Cremorne Gardens?"

Lucinda winced. She had known the news might reach the ears of her girls eventually, but she hadn't expected Bill to be the messenger. The morning had been going so well; for a few hours she'd been able to forget the nasty scene that had taken place at her home the day before. Now here it was, raising its ugly head, thanks to a man who spent plenty of nights at Cremorne himself. Thank God she had not run into him when she'd gone chasing after Emily.

Bill made a lunge for Kate's arm. "Come on, then, luv. Enough's enough. Come on home now, and I'll forgive ya."

His movements were sloppy and Lucinda could smell the alcohol on him. "Don't touch her!" She spoke with such authority that Bill paused to stare at her in surprise. During her months of volunteering at this school, Lucinda had been discovering a thing or two about how to handle the rougher folks. One thing she had learned was that a certain amount of bluster was required. "Leave now, or I'll make sure the police arrest you for assault and trespass."

"Will ya, now?" he answered with a lopsided grin. "Have you told these here *young ladies*,"—he said this last bit with mock gentility—"that you was in the gossip column of the *Times*? That you and your sister was caught carousing at Cremorne Gardens at night without—oh, what's that fancy word for it—*chaperones*?"

There was a collective gasp from all the students. All except Kate. "I don't believe it," she declared. "You always was a liar and a scoundrel, Bill. Now you want to spread lies about a good woman."

"It ain't a lie!" Bill pulled a folded newspaper from his pocket and thrust it at her. "Read it for yourself, seein' as how you're such a champion at letters now."

Kate dropped the newspaper onto the table without looking at it. "You heard what Miss Cardington said, Bill. Get out. *Now*."

Bill's face darkened and twisted into an ugly sneer.

"Why you ungrateful—" He raised a hand to strike her. Without hesitation, Lucinda rushed toward him with both her hands balled into fists. She stepped between them, deflecting his hands and then pushing on his chest, forcing him back toward the door. He was so taken by surprise at being manhandled by a woman that it seemed he forgot to resist. The alcohol, too, had weakened him. With one final shove Lucinda propelled him outside—and right into the arms of another man who was just about to enter.

"Ho there!" James Simpson exclaimed as Bill stumbled backward into him, nearly sending them both to the ground. "What's going on?"

Bill took a wild swing at him, but James deftly avoided it, thrusting Bill into the street, where he tripped over his own feet and fell on his hands and knees. James watched him intently, poised to fight if Bill challenged him. "It appears you are not welcome here. I believe you should take your leave."

By this time a dozen or more people had gathered. Altercations were common in this neighborhood, as were spectators to spur them on. Lucinda was beginning to think that watching fights was their primary form of entertainment.

Bill was clearly the loser this time, and in his drunken embarrassment he did not appreciate the attention of the onlookers. With a malevolent glance at Lucinda, he clambered to his feet. "You got them weak-minded women fooled, but not me!" he shouted. "You pretend to be all Christian goodness by day, when you ain't nothin' but a strumpet at night." Pointing at James he added, "All you rich folks ain't nothin' but hypocrites. I knows you for what you are."

Lucinda stood looking at him, unable to speak or even move. What had she been thinking? He might easily have done serious harm to her or the women. But she hadn't been thinking at all. She'd been so caught up in her desire to protect her students that she had acted on instinct, giving no thought to the possible consequences.

"Off with you now," James commanded. His fists were clenched, and he was staring down the man with a fierceness that Lucinda had never seen in him before.

Muttering a stream of invectives and curses, Bill turned away. It was only after he had gone some ways down the street and turned a corner out of sight that Lucinda was able to breathe again. "Dear Lord," she murmured.

James took her gently by the elbow. "Are you all right? He didn't hurt you, did he?"

She shook her head, fighting to hold back tears. How dare a man such as Bill Nelson impugn her reputation before the very women whose lives she was working so hard to improve?

"Easy now," James said. "You're shaking."

His touch was gentle and warm. It was meant to be reassuring, but it only made her heart pound more wildly. She must still be in shock from her tussle with Bill. "What...why are you...?" she stammered, dazed by his unexpected appearance on top of everything else that had happened. She caught a scent of sandalwood and fresh linen; for some reason it only made her more unsteady.

Tiny laugh lines crinkled around his cornflower blue eyes as he let out a chuckle. "You are full of surprises, aren't you, Miss Cardington? I must say I'm impressed at the way you tossed that man into the street."

"Ain't that the truth!" chimed in a round, feisty lady

who was standing nearby. She grinned, showing several gaps in her teeth. "I never woulda thought she 'ad it in her."

The dubious compliment nonetheless made Lucinda proud. *I stood up to that bully!* she realized, thrilled by the taste of victory.

James nudged her toward the door. "Why don't we go inside? I'm dying to see your school, and I daresay it's calmer in there. Not to mention less crowded." He indicated the dozen or so people still gawking at them and murmuring to one another. "Go on, then," he said to the crowd. "Nothing more to see here."

All of her students were clustered at the door, staring at Lucinda with a mixture of shock and awe. "I'm so sorry, Miss Cardington," Kate said, wringing her hands. "He could have hurt you. He's been known to break a woman's arm and not think twice about it." She did not need to add that *she* was the woman in question. Every woman here knew it. "It's me what brought him here, and if anything bad had happened—"

"But nothing did happen," Lucinda reassured her. "The Lord protected us." She took hold of Kate's hands. "Do you remember those verses I taught you? How we are more than conquerors through him who loves us, and that he always gives us the victory?" She spoke the words with relish, realizing this was the real reason why she had not hesitated to face down Bill Nelson. God had given her the strength. "So don't fret yourself, Kate. You have every right to be here, and Bill has *no* right. That is how it stands."

Kate nodded, but said nothing. Her eyes, shining with gratitude, said it all.

The girls retreated from the doorway so Lucinda and

James could enter. Naturally their attention was riveted on James. It wasn't every day that such a well-to-do gentleman appeared in this neighborhood, let alone at this school.

Fannie crossed her arms and looked him up and down with approval. "I suppose the good Lord sent us protection in the form of this 'ere gentleman?"

James removed his hat and calmly readjusted his coat, which had been knocked askew. "Good afternoon, ladies," he said, giving the students a formal bow as though he were greeting duchesses at a royal ball. "In fact, I did nothing. Your benefactress is supremely capable."

His compliment sounded genuine. But then, James was a master at flattery. It was yet another reason why the ladies adored him—including these poor lasses who probably had never received a polite bow from a gentleman in their entire lives.

Now that the excitement of her encounter with Bill was wearing off, Lucinda began to grow wary about James's presence at her school. She was still furious that James was complicit in her father's ridiculous scheme to find her a husband. Had her father sent him here for some underhanded purpose? The possibility was both logical and highly probable. With this thought, the warmth she had been feeling earlier toward James began to cool rapidly. But she had to set a good example for her students, so she said with studied politeness, "Ladies, this is Mr. James Simpson."

He bowed again, and they all curtseyed, giggling a little at the idea of acting so genteel.

"And might I learn your names as well?" James asked.

This was quickly accomplished, though not without a

round of giggling and more staring as they took in everything about him, from his carefully groomed hair to his polished boots. No doubt they were finding him very handsome. Everyone always did.

"So this is your fine school," James said, looking around the room, taking in its two plain wooden tables and the few books and simple writing materials scattered on them. "It's most impressive."

"What's impressive is what's going on in these girls' heads," Lucinda replied tartly. "They are learning to read and write, and they are gaining competency in mathematics. When they leave here they will be able to find work in any number of honest occupations. So you see what a huge difference we are making in their lives. If for any reason this school should be disbanded—"

"Whoa!" James said. "You're not on trial here. I think it's splendid what you are doing."

"Really?" She looked at him suspiciously. It was always hard to tell what James was truly thinking. "My father doesn't think so," she said pointedly.

James did not reply. Strolling over to Caroline, who was the youngest of the girls, he said, "Will you show me what's going on in your pretty head?"

Her eyes grew round. "I beg your pardon, sir?"

He winked. "I mean, what have you been reading?" His eye caught the newspaper lying on the table. "Is that what you've been using for a text? I cannot think that reading about the world's bad news would be helpful, but if you say so . . ."

His voice trailed off as he noticed the sudden somberness that fell over the room. The women turned questioning eyes on Lucinda.

She squared her shoulders. "Mr. Simpson, I'm afraid you missed the most exciting portion of our encounter with Bill Nelson. He was the one who brought that paper here."

With a lift of his eyebrows, James picked up the paper and scrutinized it. "I see," he said. "This is yesterday's paper. And it is open to the gossip column." He gave Lucinda a sympathetic glance.

"Is it true, Miss Cardington?" asked Mary, a girl who had only been at the school a few days.

"Not that any of us have a right to judge you," Fannie quickly butted in. "Our pasts certainly ain't spotless. But it is a mistake, ain't it?"

"It is," Lucinda said with a sigh. "And it isn't."

Fannie gaped at her. "You mean, you were there?"

Lucinda could see clearly in her students' eyes just how much she had disappointed them.

"Ladies, this is a *gossip* column," James said. "What it lacks in solid facts, it makes up for in salacious conjecture. Allow me to tell you exactly what happened." With these words he secured their rapt attention. "Miss Cardington was at Cremorne Gardens because she was trying to keep another lady from falling into vice. She had learned that the girl was about to take an unwise and irretrievable step, and she went there to stop her before it was too late."

By this time Fannie had picked up the paper and began reading it. "What about her sister, Emily?" Fannie asked. "Why was she there? It says here—"

"That is where the paper goes off course," James interrupted quickly. "Emily went along to help rescue the young lady in question. She did not want her sister to go alone."

Fannie was still reading the article with great interest. She looked up. "It says you were there, too, and that you and Miss Emily Cardington were discovered in each other's arms."

Every lady's eyes fastened on James with renewed curiosity. And admiration. And—desire? *Good heavens,* Lucinda thought. *Did every woman want to envision themselves in James's embrace?* She became aware of heat rising to her face as she recalled the sight of James and Emily in a passionate kiss. How would James talk his way out of this?

"Well, she was . . . that is, I was with her, for you see, we are engaged."

"You're engaged to *Emily* Cardington?" Kate asked. For some reason she appeared crestfallen at the idea. In fact, all the women did. Lucinda wondered, had they assumed James was here today because he was *her* beau? She brought cool palms to her cheeks in a vain effort to quench the fire there.

"Yes, I am Miss Emily's fiancé," James said with a nod. "The two ladies therefore enlisted my help. They certainly could not go to Cremorne Gardens at night without a man to protect them."

"Oh, certainly not!" Fannie said with facetious prudery. Always an independent and fearless woman, she would not hesitate to go to Cremorne Gardens alone. But she did not challenge James further on this. Instead, she set the paper down and said, "What about the other lady—the one you all went there to rescue? The paper makes no mention of her."

She was a sharp girl, that Fannie, Lucinda thought ruefully. She was not a great one for book learning, but she had a quick mind. Lucinda had always been impressed by how observant she was. At the moment, however, this quality of her eldest pupil only added to Lucinda's distress.

James remained unruffled. "The woman was, shall we say, from the humbler strata of society," he returned smoothly. "I have noticed that such persons are often shockingly under-represented in the press. It's as though newspapermen find them not worth mentioning."

"Don't we know it," chimed in Tessa, the most hardened one of the bunch.

Lucinda stood dumbfounded at the ease with which James had altered the story. He was doing it to protect her and Emily, she knew. Even so, Lucinda could not have told a lie if her very life depended on it. She reflected that James must have a lot of experience talking himself out of tight situations. He exuded an air of simple honesty that made it impossible to disbelieve him.

"Our mission was unsuccessful, I'm sorry to say." James punctuated these words with a regretful shake of his head. "We had hoped to get that unfortunate young lady to this school, but she is not yet ready to give up her wicked ways."

"It is hard," Fannie acknowledged. One of the other girls poked her in the ribs. "Well it is!" she protested. "I confess I do miss a spot of gin sometimes."

"Don't we all," James said.

*

James was pleased to see the ladies' reaction to his story. His sole aim had been to help Lucinda, and he'd succeeded. They were all looking at their benefactress with renewed admiration. Lucinda's expression, however, was something akin to shock. No doubt by telling lies he had lowered himself in her estimation. Well, at least he could say his description of her actions had been completely true. She had gone to Cremorne with only the best intentions, and she was an innocent party in this scandal. She did not deserve to have her reputation tarnished.

"You drink gin, sir?" This came from Fannie, the fulsome redhead with a keen eye and a broad smile. "Surely only fine wine and brandy is good enough for you."

James could see Lucinda about to object to the tack this conversation was taking, so he said, "The key is moderation. Any strong drink can be overdone, and such misuse should be avoided." He felt like a hypocrite for saying this, for he himself had overdone—and enjoyed it—far too often.

"I don't believe we should be even discussing alcohol," Lucinda said briskly. "There is no place for it in a godly, Christian life."

Was she really as severe as that? James thought back to several large dinner parties they'd both been at, and how she'd taken only one or two tiny sips—probably out of politeness. Nor had he observed her near the punch tables at balls, although he'd always ascribed that to a desire to avoid her mother, who usually stationed herself there for the duration of an evening.

How did one function without the ease and relaxation alcohol provides? James could not imagine it. Not that he'd ever been an excessive drinker. He'd never been so blind drunk he couldn't remember what he'd done or where he'd been. That was very bad for one's health, not to mention keeping one's personal affairs in order.

And yet, as Fannie had correctly discerned, James did enjoy his fine wine and brandy. He almost felt sorry for Lucinda, that she was missing out on such a pleasurable aspect of life. Certainly her little sister had no qualms about it.

Lucinda shooed her students away from James and toward the two tables. "All right, everyone, it's time to get back to work. Fannie and Kate, you will each take three others and make sure everyone completes today's task. There will be no time for it tomorrow, because Mrs. Claridge will be coming to give you a housekeeping lesson."

She spoke with firm authority, and although several had a hard time tearing their eyes from James, they all obeyed Lucinda's order without protest. There was no question she ran this school with admirable ability. Was this really the same woman who stood in a corner during dances and spilled her tea whenever men were around? How had this aspect of her personality remained hidden whenever she was outside the walls of this school? James could only shake his head in amazement.

It was only after the women were once more absorbed in their work that he remembered Lucinda's statement about Mrs. Claridge. "Did you say Geoffrey and Lizzie's housekeeper will be coming here?" he asked, as Lucinda returned to his side.

"Yes. These girls have grown up in the slums and have no concept of how proper households are run. Since the Somervilles have elected to remain in Kent this summer, Mrs. Claridge's duties at their London home are not strenuous. She can easily take time to come here."

This mention of the Somervilles' remaining in Kent gave James pause. Lizzie had been away from London since last winter. She insisted it was because the country air was better for her and little seven-month-old Eddie. There was some truth to this, but James knew the greater reason was that she was hiding away from embarrassment. A scandal had erupted late last fall when someone familiar with Lizzie's past had publicly revealed that she'd once run away to the Continent and lived scandalously with a man for several months. This terrible misstep occurred years before she even met Geoffrey, and she'd been living an irreproachable life for well over seven years. Yet now that her past sins had come to light, everyone in London considered her a woman of unclean reputation. This angered James to no end, for such judgments were patently cruel and unfair. "I wish Lizzie *had* come to London," he said fervently. "I told her she ought to attend every ball, dinner, and opera and face down every matron who dares to sneer at her. Lizzie is better than all of them put together."

"I agree with you in principle," Lucinda said. "Although now that I have been the subject of slander myself, I understand how hard it can be to face people afterward."

"But you were wrongfully accused," James protested.

"So was Lizzie, as far as I'm concerned. Her sins are in the past, and no one has a right to judge her in any case."

"Very true," James said, warmed by Lucinda's kind words. "However, I noticed you had no trouble facing down that man—Bill Nelson, did you say his name was?"

"That's different. He was threatening my school. Threatening my girls."

Once more James saw her chin lift and her eyes flash with pride. And once more he was tempted to wonder where this woman had been hiding this strength of hers. Wasn't there some Bible verse about not hiding one's light under a bushel? James decided then and there that he was going to do whatever it took to get this woman to come out of her shell. He wanted the rest of the world to see Lucinda Cardington as he was beginning to see her. Besides, it could well be the key to finding her a husband, for surely any man in his right mind would be bound to fall for such a strong, capable woman. "Miss Cardington, will you allow me to escort you home today?"

She hesitated for a few moments before finally nodding her assent. "Yes, I think that would be a good idea. I've a few questions to ask you."

There was something ominous in the way she said it, but James covered his apprehension with a smile. "You are free to ask me anything you like."

It took another quarter hour for Lucinda to conclude her business for the day, including leaving instructions for her footman when he returned. Then she and James left the school, walking briskly along a damp, narrow lane edged with derelict-looking houses and overrun with dirty children and stray dogs. Although James had enjoyed seeing the school, he was now equally glad to be leaving it. He could not think her parents had any idea just how bad the area was, or they'd never allow her to come here.

Fortunately, it was not long before they reached a broader street lined with shops and taverns. It was astounding, really, how there were still parts of London where an area of abject squalor could be mere blocks away from a respectable neighborhood. It was one of the great contradictions of this city.

"So why did you paint our visit to Cremorne in a positive, almost heroic, light?" Lucinda asked, bringing his mind back from its wanderings.

"Well in your case, it *was* heroic. You were trying to prevent a scandal. In the end you were not successful, but I do not lay any blame at your feet for that."

"That's noble of you," Lucinda said drily. "And yet you also excused Emily's actions by lying about her reasons for being there."

"Would you really have me tell the truth? Do you want to now savage your sister's reputation, after you tried so hard to protect it?"

She frowned, and her eyebrows drew together in a way that James had seen before and did not care for. It always made her look severe and uninviting. He much preferred to look at her when her face was flushed and full of livelier emotions, as it had been when he'd arrived at the school.

"It's just that I hate and abhor lying," she said.

"Have you *never* told a lie?" he challenged, thinking of the night he found her with a contraband book.

Her face contorted in guilt. "Not willingly," she murmured.

"Aha!" James said. "That's an important distinction, isn't it? Sometimes—such as when we wish to protect those we care for deeply—we might be compelled to, shall we say, *recast* reality in a different light. But really, there's no harm done. In today's case, you have been restored to your rightful place of honor before those women. If Emily's stock has also risen, then why not look upon it as a side benefit—the way a plant benefits from the sunshine."

The tiniest glint of amusement lit her eye. "You are comparing me to sunshine?"

"An absolute ray of sunshine," he insisted. "And never more so than when you were tossing that drunken fellow out on his ear and giving him full well what he deserved."

The words rolled easily off his tongue. But if James had plenty of experience giving compliments, he could see plainly that Lucinda had very little experience receiving them. A blush began to rise above the high collar of her gown. It was charming, really. Her sister was a practiced flirt who could blush prettily at will, using it as a ploy to flatter the gentlemen, but James was certain that Lucinda's blushes were unfeigned and deeply felt.

She smiled briefly, but then seemed to think the better of it and tightened her lips to their usual, more serious expression. "Please don't tell my father about that incident."

"Why not? I should think he would be proud!"

"Proud? Heavens, no—he would be livid! He has told me repeatedly that I must never allow the footman out of my presence, that he is there for my protection. He worries too much about the character of the neighborhood."

"It's the *characters* in the neighborhood who are the greater problem, I should think." This pleasantry brought out another brief flash of her fine, white teeth, and James realized that teasing smiles from the straight-laced Miss Cardington could be a hugely rewarding endeavor. In fact, it could be fascinating to encourage Lucinda's better features to blossom. Why had he never realized that peeling a wallflower away from the wall might be fun?

"There are some characters in that quarter, to be sure," Lucinda acknowledged. "But honestly, I never believed myself to be in any real danger. And in any case, I am certain Fannie and the others would have ganged up on him if necessary. They are a tough lot, those ladies."

"I can see that. So it would appear that at this school they are teaching you a few things as well. Good thing, too. One never knows when proficiency at pushing around drunken men will come in handy. Are you sure you don't want to share this triumph with your family?"

"No!" She looked at him earnestly. "Please don't tell them, I beg you."

James looked into her intriguing hazel eyes. Just now the sun was highlighting the green in them. She was always unpretentious and honest, wearing her heart on her sleeve. As she appealed to him for this favor, James knew he had her right where he wanted her. He was in a perfect position to carry out his plan. Even so, he felt almost guilty as he said with a great show of reluctance, "Very well, your secret is safe with me."

She let out a breath. "Thank you."

"But now I must ask *you* a favor."

"Me?" Immediately her look turned wary. "What kind of favor? Did my father send you to try to talk me into giving up the school—or worse, throw myself on the marriage market?"

This lady was too quick by half. He should have known he'd not be able to lead her along as easily as her little sister. The so-called Simpson charm was going to have to work a lot harder with her. He laid a hand to his heart and gave her his most hurt expression. "I cannot believe you would think such a thing! Did you never think that perhaps I came here today simply because I wish to become better acquainted with my future sister-in-law?"

"Really?" She gave him a puzzled expression. "Why?"

James found himself laughing with genuine delight. "You undervalue yourself," he remonstrated. "Do you not think of yourself as a person worth getting to know?"

She straightened. "I know you won't believe this, but what I think rarely mirrors what the rest of the world thinks."

How had James never noticed this sly edge to her wit? Probably because he'd spent so little time talking with her. "You're right, I don't believe you. I want to learn all about you. I was curious to see this project of yours—which, I must add, has impressed me a great deal." Actually, he was more impressed that Lucinda would work here day after day in these truly appalling conditions. "So tell me, what's next for those ladies?"

"The goal is to get each of them settled in a good position. There is a milliner's shop not too far from here. They sell to modest families, nothing fancy, and the owner is willing to take Kate and Caroline as soon as they can be taught to read and do math, as well as some of the niceties of how to interact with customers." Her face was alight now. "Just think, James—they have been saved from a life of poverty and prostitution."

"Yes, I suppose even working twelve hours a day in a shop for a mere pittance would be better than that," James observed.

"Twelve hours of *honest* labor," Lucinda pointed out quickly. "They can live their lives without shame."

"You can't change the whole world, you know," James said.

"I'm not trying to," she insisted. "Only the small piece of it that I can reach."

"And must you really remain single in order to carry out this calling?"

"So we are back to that, are we?"

He held up a hand in defense. "I merely asked an honest question. Is it really so hard to believe that a husband would not share this desire with you—or at least, allow you to pursue it?"

Her mouth twisted in an expression of disbelief. "You really have no concept of what married life is like, do you?"

In point of fact, James was painfully aware that he did not. His own parents had certainly provided no example. A brief flash of his miserable childhood rose up before him: a mother, spiraling into depression, who died when James was only fourteen years old; a father who had always been distant, and never more so than after his mother died; James being shipped off to his great-aunt Thornborough's home to live whenever he wasn't away at school. Growing up, he'd had exactly no family life to speak of. Not that he was prepared to admit any of this. Instead, he allowed irritation at this void in his life to wash over him, and he said sarcastically, "Perhaps you would care to enlighten me as to how *you* know so much about marriage?"

She came to a dead stop, turning to face him. Her face was flushed with exertion as well as emotion. "I've had twenty-five years to observe firsthand how it's done. My mother appears to run the household, and my father is happy to maintain that illusion. But the truth is, he rules with an iron hand, and his word is final. Mama is kept within her own little sphere, having only the right sort of people as friends. She's never ventured beyond the limits my father has set for her."

"She seems content enough," James countered.

"Which is why Papa married her! Suppose she wanted to explore new ideas or try to improve society in some way that he does not consider acceptable. What then?" She waved a defiant hand for emphasis. "I'll tell you what then: he would say *no*, and that would be that. The man is unmovable as a bank vault."

The rage and frustration in her words was unmistakable, perhaps even justified. But there was something wrong with her argument, something James could not put his finger on. He'd have to think on it, decide how to attack this fear of hers. For the moment, he found himself distracted by her reflection in the shop window. She had her back to it, and in the glass James could see a ribbon from her bonnet fluttering down toward her trim waist. It was an appealing sight, and he would happily have kept on enjoying it, but she was still glaring at him, challenging him to refute her words.

"Look," he said in a conciliatory tone, "I do not wish to argue the point with you." This was true. In point of fact, James hated arguments or unpleasantness of any kind. He'd spent a lifetime avoiding them whenever possible. He took hold of her arm and turned her so that they were once more walking down the street. "How about if we talk about something else for now."

She sent him a sidelong glance. "What did you have in mind?"

"Did you know I'm turning one of the rooms at my great-aunt's town house into a darkroom? I would have preferred to use one of the rooms at the club, but they were annoyingly close-minded on the subject."

He felt her relax a little as curiosity deflated her anger. "Doesn't Lady Thornborough object?"

"She did at first, but she eventually gave in. I think she believes it will bring me round to the house more often—which, I concede, it probably will. Of course, she also thinks that with all those chemicals I will blow up the place. She does have a flair for the dramatic."

"That is, I assume, a common family trait."

"Touché, my dear," James replied happily. He snapped his fingers. "I nearly forgot. That favor I mentioned—tomorrow I'll be taking a few photographs in Hyde Park, and I wondered if you would join me."

Once more, Lucinda pulled up short. "Me?"

"And Emily, too. Although it's probable you will be of greater assistance."

She frowned. "Emily is not on speaking terms with me just now."

"Whether she speaks to you or not, she will want to come along. She'll take exception if you and I spend too much time together without her."

"I'm sure she has nothing to worry about on that score." Lucinda's gaze flitted away as the dry edge crept back into her voice.

"Indeed she has plenty to worry about," James contradicted, kissing her hand with a flourish. "She'll be insanely jealous, and rightly so."

He was pleased to see a slip of a smile, even though she clearly didn't believe a word of it.

"We'll have a marvelous time!" James assured her. "I've got a special wagon fitted up with everything we need. I was hoping to take perhaps a half dozen photographs."

"A wagon? I daresay you'll need it for all the equipment. May I really assist you?"

"Indeed you can. I thought you might begin by putting

the first coat on the plates. That part does not require you to be muffled underneath the dark bag."

"It sounds wonderful, but what about Emily? What will she do?"

James shrugged. "I expect she'll be happy just to enjoy a day in the park."

Now that they were away from the tricky subject of marriage and talking once more about photography, it was amazing how easily the conversation flowed. Before he knew it they had arrived at her home.

"Will you come in?" Lucinda offered. "I'm sure Emily will want to see you."

He shook his head. "I'm afraid I must leave you here. I'm overdue for another appointment."

She turned to go up the steps, then paused, turning back to say, "I'm glad you came to the school today."

James felt a burst of triumph. She was warming to him. He tipped his hat. "Until tomorrow, then."

Once more she gave him that bright smile, the one he had seen so little of before today. It was unaccountably arresting. "I shall look forward to it," she said.

Chapter 8

How much longer?" Emily's complaint echoed across the grass to the back of the wagon, where James and Lucinda were preparing the photographic plates.

The cargo area of the wagon was entirely enclosed and fitted with special shelves to hold two dozen bottles of chemicals, several washing trays, a portable table, and various other items, plus the camera and its tripod. Geoffrey had even lent him one of his older and more docile horses to pull it. The horse stood patiently while James and Lucinda had unloaded the needed items, set up the work table, and began the process of preparing the photographic plate.

James stuck his head around the corner of the wagon. Lady Cardington and Emily were seated a short distance away in an open carriage. They both looked out of sorts. "It's so dull just sitting here," Emily moaned. "And we're fainting away from the heat."

"Why don't you take a drive around the park?" James suggested. "That will give you something to do, and the breeze will cool you down."

"But I don't want to go without you!" Emily whined.

James fought to conceal his exasperation. "How about coming over here to watch us prepare these plates? Then Lady Cardington can go for a drive and get some air."

"And leave the three of you here by yourselves?" Lady Cardington objected. "That would be most imprudent."

"It's not as though we were alone," James pointed out. Indeed, no less than four pairs of gentlemen and ladies were standing nearby, watching the proceedings with interest. Carriages slowed as they passed, their occupants staring with fascination at the large wooden camera on a tripod that James had set up on the green. Everyone in Hyde Park today was curious to see wet plate photography in action— *except* his fiancée and future mother-in-law.

"Well, it's clear you are not alone," Lady Cardington huffed. "In fact you are making a spectacle of yourselves."

Her voice had reached an ear-splitting pitch that could be heard all the way to Buckingham Palace. While James normally enjoyed being the center of attention, he preferred to have people drawn to him by admiration rather than by pity. He really had to find a way to curb Lady Cardington's audible negativity. Turning to Lucinda, he said quietly, "Take this, will you?" He handed her the plate he had been carefully coating with the collodion substance. "Just keep tipping the sides as I showed you until it's evenly covered."

James had no qualms about entrusting this task to her. Already today he'd seen that her time skulking away to read photography manuals had been well spent. She understood the chemistry involved and was deft at handling the materials. For a woman whose awkwardness had many times caused her to spill her tea or drop a punch glass, she had shown herself surprisingly coordinated when it came to handling these delicate flat planes of glass which would capture the photographic image. Perhaps one day soon he'd let her try the next step, which involved dipping the plate into silver nitrate and then placing it into a special light-proof frame to be mounted on the camera. But he could not allow her to do that here, for it had to be done beneath the dark tent, a heavy cloth propped up like a tent over the work table. Her mother would surely deem it too indecorous for a lady to be half shrouded, with only her lower half showing. Especially with all these people watching.

Lucinda accepted the plate eagerly, smiling with pride and pleasure. James enjoyed the way she looked at this moment—confident and relaxed, her eyes sparkling with excitement. This was the woman he wanted others to see. This was exactly why they were here today. James decided it was full well time to remind her family members of this fact.

He strode over to the carriage and offered up a hand to Emily, who was still pouting furiously. "Won't you come down, love?" he asked solicitously.

She frowned at his outstretched hand. "You care about photography more than me," she said sullenly.

"I must agree," Lady Cardington put in, with predictable unpleasantness. "You've been messing about for an hour, ignoring your own fiancée. What will everyone think?"

Seeing they were not going to cooperate, James set one foot on the small iron step attached to the carriage and lifted himself up so that he was eye to eye with both of them. Keeping his tone hushed and confidential, he leaned in and said, "Allow me to state again for you the reason we are here. The goal is to win Lucinda over to our plans."

Lady Cardington narrowed her gaze. "What exactly does indulging her silly interest in photography have to do with finding her a husband?" Indicating the onlookers who were staring at the photography wagon she added, "I don't see a single eligible bachelor."

James briefly pinched the bridge of his nose and tried again. "If Lucinda sees we take a genuine interest in the things she is interested in, she will be more kindly disposed toward us, don't you think?"

"Well, I…" Lady Cardington's eyebrows drew together as she tried to follow James's logic.

Emily understood though, and she did not like it. "So today is all about Lucinda," she said, sounding affronted at the very idea.

"No, indeed. Today is entirely about us." He took Emily's hand. "Nothing is more important to me than your happiness."

"Really?" She brightened.

James gave her the most earnestly loving look he could muster. "We may find the present circumstances trying, but let us get your sister happily married and then you and I will be free to spend the rest of our lives together. Trust me, there's nothing I want more."

He was laying it on pretty thick. Yet he knew Emily well enough to be sure this was the way to gain her cooperation. All he had to do was infuse an element of romance into it, and she would be hooked. He kissed her hand and she gave a little sigh, gazing at him with a dreamy expression. Good. This was right where he needed her. Giving her hand a gentle squeeze, he said,

"When it comes to affairs of the heart, an iron hand just won't work. Let's win her over with kindness, shall we?"

There must have been a shred of romance lurking somewhere deep inside Lady Cardington, too, for she gave a wheezy sort of sigh. "If you think it's the best plan, we'll agree to it for now. But we had better see some progress soon. There's no time to waste."

"I'm well aware of that, believe me. But let us at least take this afternoon to liven up Lucinda's spirits, and then—"

"—and then tonight we can broach the subject of marriage once again!" Lady Cardington interjected, finishing the sentence much differently than he'd intended to.

James sighed. "Right." This was probably as far as he was going to get with these two today.

Lucinda came around from the back of the wagon, holding the special light-proof frame that was used to transport the sensitized glass plate to the camera. "It's ready!" she said triumphantly. "We can take the photograph!"

James looked at her with astonishment. "You don't mean to say you've already applied the silver nitrate!"

Her face fell a little. "Do you mind terribly? The plate was ready for the next step, so I thought I'd give it a try."

"But that means you—" He stopped himself, taking note of her disheveled appearance. Her bonnet was askew and one of her hairpins was loose.

"I used the dark tent." She pushed a stray lock of hair from her face, which was, as usual, flushed bright red. However, this time her blush seemed more from exhilaration than embarrassment. "I'm certain I dipped the plate into the correct bath. You showed me which was which before covering the table with the dark tent."

Lucinda's smile—wider and sunnier than he had

ever seen it—left James speechless. His plan to loosen her up was certainly succeeding. Beyond his wildest imagination.

"Lucinda, what have you been doing?" Lady Cardington said shrilly. "And what is that dripping on your clothes?"

"Oh!" Lucinda thrust the wooden frame away from her body. "That's the light-sensitive solution. But it's supposed to drip a little, isn't it, Mr. Simpson?"

"Indeed it is," James answered with a grin. What a woman! James was so impressed by her initiative that he wanted to take her by the shoulders and plant a great big kiss on her cheek. But that action would no doubt be misinterpreted by everybody here—especially Emily. So he settled for a hearty "Well done."

Lucinda's blush turned a shade deeper, and she wiped a bit of perspiration from her forehead with the back of her hand. "You'd better hurry and take the photograph. The heat will dry the chemicals quickly."

"Right you are." He turned back to Emily. "Hurry down, love. We must take the photograph while the plate is still wet." Seeing Emily hesitate, he added, "I want to have you in the picture and preserve your beauty for all posterity."

Her frown softened into a self-satisfied smile. "You do?"

"Naturally! I want the world to see and admire my beautiful bride-to-be."

Lucinda gave a barely audible snort of derision. James, too, was laughing at himself for using such flowery language, but it worked like a charm on Emily. She allowed him to help her down from the carriage. He led her to the spot he had prepared, about ten feet in front of the camera. Behind her, the graceful stone bridge arched over the narrow, curved lake known as the Serpentine, providing a serene and picturesque backdrop. "Now, just stand right there," he instructed. "I have to get the camera ready."

Emily obliged and stayed where James had placed her. She reached up to double-check her bonnet and hair. "How do I look, Mama?" she called over to Lady Cardington.

"Beautiful, as always," her mother cooed. She turned a less approving eye on Lucinda. "But you..." she tsked. "That frock is ruined."

James hastened to take the plate from Lucinda. "Pay her no attention," he whispered. "As a matter of fact, I think you look exceptionally well at this moment."

She looked at him uncertainly. "I never know when you are indulging in insincere flattery."

"Nor should you. That's part of my charm." He gave her a wink.

He had in fact been sincere. But he would not tell her that. Not just yet. He was surprised to find his hand was unsteady as he slid the plate into the camera. He blamed it on the solution, which was still dripping through the frame. "Now, my dear," he said to Emily, "you'll find this much easier than those daguerreotypes we took last year. You won't have to hold the pose for nearly as long."

"Thank heaven for that," Emily said.

Lucinda hurried back to the wagon and returned with a dry towel, which she handed to James. "Here," she said. "To wipe your hands."

"Why thank you. You are a regular photographer's apprentice," he joked, but he could see she was pleased at the compliment.

"Now then..." James set himself to the task of getting Emily posed just right. He had recently seen some wonderful work by two Scottish photographers, and he wanted to emulate a few of their more successful arrangements. "You know, I think this will work better in profile." He turned her to one side, arranging her shoulders. "Now, just lift your chin a little...perfect! Now don't move!"

"Are you sure...?"

"Yes, yes! Don't move!" James ran back to the camera. Emily stood frozen in place, staring into the distance. With the Serpentine and the bridge behind her, it would be an outstanding photograph. "I'm going to start the exposure!" he called out. "Hold that pose for just one minute more!"

With one more glance at the sun to estimate his exposure time, he removed the lens cap and counted the seconds. "And...done!" he announced, replacing the lens cap. "Emily, I'm so proud of you!"

She squealed and raced over to him. "Do you think my beauty has been captured for all posterity?"

Behind him he heard Lucinda murmur, "What there is of it." He had to suppress a smile.

"What happens now?" Emily asked excitedly. "When can I see it?" She looked expectantly as James removed the light-proof frame from the camera, as though she thought he would magically pull out a finished photograph.

"Patience, my love. This special frame holds only the glass negative. There are still a few more steps to complete. At the moment, I've got to get this image fixed." He nodded toward the wagon. "Come along."

*

Lucinda felt a pang of anxiety as they returned to the work table, with Emily trailing behind. What if she had not applied the silver nitrate correctly? The picture would be ruined. If that happened, James might forgive her, but her sister never would.

"What's that?" Emily asked, as they approached the large black bag draped over the table.

"That's the portable darkroom," James said. "I've got to go back under there for a few minutes to get this plate fixed."

She looked at it with large eyes. "You're going under there?"

"I won't be long." With that, he draped the dark bag over himself. Soon, only his legs were visible. The bag moved and rustled as James worked. This brought a few titters of amusement from Emily. "Is this what you were doing back here? No wonder James placed the carriage so Mama couldn't see this." She turned to Lucinda, seeming to take note of her appearance for the first time. Lucinda reached up to straighten her bonnet, but it was too late. "Don't tell me you were under there!" Emily said. "With only your bottom half showing? How scandalous!"

"Shhh. And you are not to tell Mama," Lucinda warned her. "What she doesn't know won't hurt her."

"But—" Emily began. She stopped abruptly when James's foot reached out and nudged her. It was, in fact, nearly a kick. Lucinda expected Emily to protest, but instead her manner changed and she gave Lucinda a stiff smile. "As you wish, dear sister."

These were such unusual words coming from Emily that Lucinda was tempted to pinch herself to be sure she was awake. But this was no dream. Her hands were still sticky from the collodion solution, and Lady Cardington was calling out to them again. "Emily! Lucinda! What's going on over there?"

Lucinda walked out from behind the wagon and went over to the carriage. "James—Mr. Simpson—is fixing the plate. Then I believe he intends to take a few more."

Lady Cardington fanned herself. "But it's so hot!"

"Why don't you take a turn around the park? I assure you we won't do anything to cause alarm." Even as she said this, she thought of James's legs and backside sticking out from under that dark tent. She realized that she, too, had made just such a spectacle. How many people had been watching her? She ought to be cringing from embarrassment, and yet surprisingly she found herself completely unperturbed. *Let them talk,* she thought. *It matters not to me.* Indeed, there was something very freeing about being both scandalous and on the shelf. Soon she would set up her own home and be able to live her life exactly as she wished. It was a hope she clung to, especially on days like this when her dreams were tantalizingly before her, yet still just out of reach.

*

In the end, Lucinda's worries about the plate she had prepared were unfounded. James had pronounced it a spectacular success. After he had finished the chemical baths and a final wash, they laid it out to dry. He held the plate up to the sun, and as they studied the image it was easy to tell that the print would turn out very well indeed.

Because the process was so time-consuming, they'd only been able to take two more photographs before Lady Cardington declared resolutely that it was time to leave. But those few hours had been more than enough for Lucinda. Now back home and alone in her bedchamber, she sat at the vanity table, still thinking over the afternoon's events. She ought to be preparing for dinner, but instead she placed one elbow on the table, her chin in her hand, and savored the feeling of being pleasantly exhausted. How wonderful it had been to gain some real experience with photography! As she idly toyed with her brush and comb on the table, she considered that perhaps having James as a brother-in-law would not be such a bad thing after all. Perhaps they would go on lots of photographic excursions. It was an exhilarating thought, and not even the prospect of Emily's whining (as she would undoubtedly tag along) could quench it.

Best of all, no one had said a single word to her all day on the subject of marriage. Were they really going to allow the matter to rest? Had James actually succeeded in dissuading her father from husband-hunting for her? Lucinda sighed and stared at herself unhappily in the mirror. No, she knew her parents too well to believe they would give up so easily. Not even a charmer like James could get her father to change his mind once it was made up. There were bound to be more altercations on this subject. She began to grow uneasy, recalling how her mother and sister had been unusually yielding to her requests today. In fact, the entire afternoon seemed—as much as was possible with her sister around—to be entirely centered on Lucinda. Were they up to something?

Lucinda straightened and shook her head to clear it. It would do no good to dwell on the matter. Emily was always unpredictable, and in any case her actions today could be seen as attempts to make herself more agreeable to her future husband. Even so, it was clear she had not one ounce of curiosity about photography, other than concern over how she would appear in the picture. What a shame that Emily did not share an interest in this fascinating pastime. And yet, how many husbands and wives actually enjoyed the same things? Not too many, to judge by most of the couples she had known. Certainly her mother and father seemed to have nothing in common. Was that really the norm?

An image came to Lucinda's mind of her friend Margaret Poole, who had been married for nearly a year now to James's cousin Tom. Margaret and Tom shared an almost fanatical love of horses. They were both excellent riders, and Margaret's letters were always filled with detailed accounts of rides they had taken and the new horses they were acquiring for their stables. They were so happy that Lucinda's heart fairly ached with joy every time she was around them. Surely that was the ideal marriage—one based on mutual respect, shared passions, and a similar outlook on life. Lucinda had no interest in getting married unless she could find exactly that kind of harmonious match. Since that was about as probable as a month of full moons, she would content herself with remaining a spinster.

Once Emily and James were married, Margaret and Tom would become part of Lucinda's extended family— they'd be cousins, as it were. This made Lucinda very happy, although she could tell that her mother and father were still getting used to the idea. Like everyone else in London, they had not known what to make of Tom Poole, a newly rich man of humble origins. But even they had begun to perceive that Tom was truly a gentleman now, and not just because of the shipload of gold he had brought with him from Australia. He was showing himself to be a conscientious landowner. There had been many reports of how the vast estate Margaret had inherited was now thriving under his oversight. Slowly, grudgingly, society was beginning to accept him.

This happy state of affairs meant that her parents would not object if Lucinda spent time with the Pooles at their home in Lincolnshire. Margaret had made it clear that Lucinda was welcome to come anytime and stay as long as she wished. Lucinda was counting the days until she could go, for the Pooles' home was one place where Lucinda was sure she would feel entirely at ease.

Yes, she would focus on the many things she had to be thankful for, Lucinda thought, as she arose and went to her washbasin to clean up and prepare for dinner. Ever since that colossal row in which Lucinda had refused to be a marriage pawn, dinners at the Cardington home had been tense. But after things had gone so well this afternoon, Lucinda had hopes that tonight the atmosphere would not be so brittle. Perhaps James really could be a peacemaker.

Still pondering these things, she washed her face and hands. She was just about to begin undressing so that she could change into a dinner gown when she felt a weight in her skirt pocket. Even as she pulled out the object, she remembered what it was. It was the small notebook James had been using to record his observations about the light conditions and the exposure times he had used for each photograph. She would have to return it to James as soon as possible. No doubt he would need it soon, for he referred to this information often to keep improving his judgments of exposure times needed in various kinds of light.

It occurred to her that perhaps James was still at the house. She had seen him and her father heading for the library as the ladies had gone upstairs. A quick glance out the window confirmed that he had not yet left. That odd little wagon was still standing at the curb.

Lucinda turned toward her bedchamber door. She would just go down quickly and return the notebook to James before he left. No doubt he and her father were still in the library discussing business, or the upcoming marriage, or whatever it was that men talked about among themselves.

She left her room quietly, and as she entered the hallway she was glad to see Emily's door was shut. She paused and listened at the door for a moment. There was a soft murmur of voices as Emily's maid helped her to dress for the evening. Her mother, too, would be in her own room, resting up before dinner.

Lucinda went quietly down the stairs. When she reached the library door she knocked lightly. Her father's voice came easily through the door. "Come in!"

She entered and found the two men seated in the leather chairs by the fireplace. James was swirling a glass of brandy, and her father was perusing a piece of paper.

"Lucinda!" her father said in surprise. He hastily set aside the paper. "I thought you'd be changing for dinner."

"I'm sorry to interrupt, but I found this and wanted to return it to Mr. Simpson before he left." She walked over to James and held out the notebook.

"Thank you," James said, accepting it with his usual smile. "I would certainly have missed that tomorrow, as I'm going out again."

Lucinda threw a curious glance at the paper her father had set down on the small table. Ordinarily she would not be so bad-mannered as to read her father's personal correspondence. But she was still uneasy about his possible plans for her, and something in his look as he had quickly set the paper aside had caught her attention. She allowed her gaze to slide sideways and surreptitiously read what was on it. Even from several feet away she could see it was a list. At the top was underlined "Prospects for Lucinda." Beneath it were ten or so names.

Lucinda dropped all pretense and snatched up the list. "What is this? Are you still trying to get me married off?" She turned an accusing look at James. "You told me Papa had given up on this scheme."

At least James had the decency to look abashed, as though he were not used to lying every day. "I did not say that, actually. Well, not in so many words."

Now Lucinda had proof of the real reason why they had all been so unnaturally nice to her today. Rage—and frustration that they would think her so simple-minded—blossomed within her. They were selfish and duplicitous, all three of them. "Our little adventure in Hyde Park—it was just to humor me, wasn't it? You think if you pander to me, I'll do whatever you say."

"I'd like to think we all had a good time today," James said in a placating tone. "You did enjoy yourself, didn't you?"

"That's all that matters to you, isn't it?" Lucinda crossed her arms over her chest in order to keep her clenched fists from doing any damage to his irritating smile. "Either you must be having a good time, or else you must be manipulating other people. I suppose if you manage to do both of those things at the same time you consider it a stellar day! Have you no scruples whatsoever?"

She expected a flippant reply, the kind so typical to James. To her surprise he winced, and when he opened his mouth to speak, nothing came out. For a moment Lucinda wondered if she had actually struck a nerve.

Seeing her attention thus diverted, her father pried the paper out of her hand. "I most certainly have not 'given up on this scheme,' as you put it. This"—he slapped the document for emphasis—"is a list of eligible bachelors who might still consider marrying you, *if* they are approached the right way."

"What do you have in mind?" she said with disgust. "Will you parade me before them like some cow at Smithfield Market?"

"I am your father!" he bellowed. "You will not speak to me in such a manner, and you will do as I say. You will not leave your sister in the lurch. You will get married next spring, and so will she."

This string of uncompromising commands, shouted loudly enough to shake the house, set Lucinda's heart racing. She was trembling, too, but not from fear. It was her own anger, matching that of her father's. "I am of age, Papa. I will not be forced into a marriage I don't want."

"It's really not like that at all," James interjected.

"You stay out of it," Lucinda shot back, but she did not turn her eyes away from her father. She was so filled with revulsion that she couldn't even bear to look at James. Today she had begun to open up to him. She had even been idiotic enough to believe he'd been showing a genuine interest in her. To think, she'd even begun to suppose that having him as a brother-in-law could be a good thing. And this was how he had repaid her. Well, she would never again be foolish enough to fall for his hypocritical actions. "I refuse to listen to another word," she announced, and turned on her heel to stalk toward the door.

"Oh, no you don't," her father said, catching up to her with surprising agility. He grabbed hold of her hand. "You will stand here and listen to reason."

His grip was firm, inescapable. It had stopped her in her tracks, but still she did not turn around. She said through clenched teeth, "I'm listening."

"That's better," he said, his voice becoming gentle. "You're a sensible girl, Lucinda. You are also a treasure."

Lucinda swallowed, but did not turn to face him.

In the same surprisingly tender tone, her father continued. "Do you really think I care only about selling you off to the highest bidder? You are the best, most clever young lady in London. I refuse to allow you to languish in a corner. You deserve far better. I will find you a man who appreciates you for what you are."

Lucinda stood quite still, clenching her eyes against the tears. She could not believe what she was hearing. "I know full well that you are ashamed of me," she countered, frustrated that her voice caught as she spoke. "You think it is a disgrace that I have no suitors. You are embarrassed to have a daughter with no marriage prospects."

"No." His voice was firm as ever, but now held more kindness than anger. "Your mother feels that way; I won't deny it. But whenever I think of you, my elder and more gifted daughter, it is never with anything less than genuine pride."

Lucinda tried to hold back a flood of emotions. Her father had never spoken to her like this before. She told herself he couldn't possibly mean what he was saying. This must be some trick James taught him. She allowed her doubts to pile up so she could find her voice. "I see James has been schooling you on the fine art of persuasion. You certainly are a fast learner." As vexed as she was, she still felt a spasm of guilt as she spoke. Never in her life had she been so rude to her father. What was happening to her? Her mind and her heart were in such a jumble that she could not control either one.

"Look at me, Lucinda." Her father tugged at her hand, urging her to turn and face him.

She turned reluctantly, embarrassed for him to see the tears in her eyes. But to her surprise, his expression was misty as well. "Lucinda, your mother and I are resolved to get you married—hold on," he added as she began to pull away again. "I see now that we have been going about it the wrong way. That is primarily because I have been allowing your mother to be in charge of this situation. Mr. Simpson has encouraged me to see the matter in a different light."

At the mention of James, Lucinda finally spared a glance in his direction. He was standing by the fireplace, surprisingly unobtrusive and yet watching them both intently. She did not know what to make of his expression. It was warm and inviting, eroding her efforts to harden herself against him. It was most unsettling. If only his eyes were not such a clear blue, the kind that easily drew a person in, encouraging you to believe him.

"Mr. Simpson told me what a different young lady you became today when you are doing something that truly pleases you," her father continued. "I should not have tried to discourage your interest in photography. I should have known from the beginning that only by allowing you to come into your own, and in your own way, could you really blossom. There are limits, of course, to what a young lady can and should do. But I have perhaps set those boundaries just a little too tightly."

He sighed a little as he said this, and Lucinda sensed the effort he was expending to admit these things.

"Papa..." It was all she could say. These revelations hit her so hard they overcame her ability to speak. Was her father truly having a change of heart? And was James the catalyst for it?

"Let me not to the marriage of true minds impose impediments," her father said gently.

Lucinda gave a small shake of her head—not because they were back to the subject of marriage, but from disbelief that her prosaic martinet of a father was actually quoting Shakespeare.

"The men on this list have something more in common than their bachelorhood or their position in society," he went on. "They are men that Mr. Simpson assures me have some life of the mind as well. It was wrong to try to put you in the mold of the debutantes who catch a man by their winks or a pretty turn on the dance floor. You are better than that."

"Do you really mean that, Papa?" Lucinda's mind was still reeling.

"Indeed I do. However, there is one caveat."

Lucinda grimaced. She should have known something of the kind would be coming. "And that would be...?"

"You have to give those other things a chance. Every man wants a wife he can take out confidently into public. I'm not saying you must be the belle of the ball, only reminding you that a good presentation in society cannot be ignored. You have always closed yourself off, rather than learning to make the most of your assets."

"Did Mr. Simpson tell you that, too?" She sent another glance at James. He merely gave her a look, both encouraging and sympathetic, that made her heart lurch. How did he keep doing that to her?

"I will be completely honest with you," her father said, drawing her attention again. "Here is what Mr. Simpson and I have been planning—no more, no less. He is going to personally pay a visit to each of these men. If they are amenable, we shall then arrange for the two of you to meet. We place no other expectations on you."

"We might begin with Lord Beauchamp's annual ball next week," James added. "Several of the men on this list will be there."

The mention of a ball only rekindled Lucinda's frustrations. She would rather face a tooth extraction than attend one of those soirees. She was no match for the beautiful and poised women who could laugh and dance and chat all evening with the gentlemen. "But is this really necessary, Papa?" she said, desperation returning to her voice. "You say I am being wasted, and yet I assure you my life is busy and full."

"Lucinda, listen to me. I know I am only your father and therefore completely unqualified to understand what is best for you." This bit of self-deprecating humor was so unlike her father that it immediately arrested Lucinda's attention. "Despite my vast shortcomings in this area, I am convinced you are not the sort of person who would be happy living alone. As independent as you are, you are also a nurturing soul. I should think your work at the school was proof of that. You need a husband to match wits with and a family to take care of."

When described like that, marriage did sound enticing. It brought back visions of Margaret and Tom. But was such a match really possible for *her*—a woman who never seemed to fit in anywhere? Of all the eligible bachelors in London, she could not imagine matching wits with a single one of them. Except for James, perhaps, she thought with a wry jolt, thinking back on the camaraderie they had shared this afternoon in the park. But no, he was a man she could never take seriously, and in any case he certainly was not eligible.

Her father was wrong; Lucinda was sure of it. But now that she understood the genuine care behind his edict, how could she keep rudely fighting him? The only solution seemed to be to go along with it for now, until, if he truly was seeking to find her a proper match, he would have to concede that it was simply not possible. Then, and only then, would he give up this plan. "Very well, you may introduce me to these men of yours," she said. "However, I wish it to be understood that I make no promises of any kind."

She half expected her father to object. But he merely nodded and said, "I suppose that's all we can expect from you for now."

It was a truce of sorts, and the relief on James's face was unmistakable. "I promise we will find someone amenable to you."

"I believe we are done here for now," Lord Cardington said briskly, his authoritative air returning. "Lucinda, will you accompany Mr. Simpson to the door?"

Lucinda led the way out, careful not to allow James near enough to take her arm. "I am still angry with you," she informed him, once they were alone in the hallway. "You should not have lied to me today."

"There was some dissembling going on," James admitted, "and for that I apologize. But please believe I would never do anything to hurt you."

The words were simple and direct, evincing such forthright honesty that Lucinda was almost taken in. Almost. She pointed a stern finger at him. "I accept your apology, but you are not off the hook yet. You must promise me that in the future you will always be completely honest with me."

He placed his hand on his heart. "Upon my honor as gentleman."

Lucinda tapped her chin. "Hmm. Not sure there's much collateral there."

"All right then, I swear upon my *dis*honor as the rogue that I am," James returned without missing a beat. "If ever you catch me deliberately lying to you, you may call for my head upon a charger."

"Ha! I shall hold you to that."

"As I prefer to keep my head attached to my shoulders," James said, placing a hand gingerly on his neck, "you may be sure that my word is my bond."

Despite herself, Lucinda found her anger abating, pushed away by a tiny flicker of amusement. It was just too difficult to resist James's brand of charm, especially when he was being ridiculous. "Did you really tell my father he should allow me more latitude?"

"I most certainly did. Furthermore, my intentions were entirely altruistic. Despite how it may appear at times, he truly does want the best for you. When I told him how you radiated confidence and assurance today, he said that's exactly what he wants for you *every* day. So I convinced him that giving you *more* breathing room—rather than less—was the best way to accomplish that."

"In that case I suppose I must be grateful to you," Lucinda said, feeling a bit sheepish.

"If you must." His eyes gleamed, and the familiar smirk returned. "I am also the one who got him quoting Shakespeare."

"You?" She shook her head in disbelief.

"Well you needn't act surprised. I am well acquainted with the Bard's work. I have found the ladies swoon when you speak to them in exactly the right way, and Shakespeare is very good for that."

"I should have known."

"Well, it worked on you. It at least got you to consider what your father was saying. But are you really so determined never to fall in love?"

"It is not *I* who determined it," Lucinda countered defensively. "It's just how things are."

"There's no reason why things cannot change, that's my motto. But then, I'm an incurable optimist." They reached the front hallway. "There is one more thing," he said, as he picked up his gloves from a side table and began to put them on. "Might I offer a suggestion?" He pointed to her gown. "Peach doesn't suit you at all." On the heels of his apology, this somewhat ungracious remark stunned her. But before she could decide how to respond, he added, "I suggest that for the Beauchamps' ball you find a gown the same color as the one you wore at Margaret and Tom's wedding. It was, as I recall, a bluish green, almost like a peacock feather. You looked so fetching in it, but I don't believe I've seen you in anything like it since then." With a wink, he put on his top hat and went out the door.

Lucinda stood in the hallway for a long time after he'd gone, thinking over his startling words. James had remembered a gown she'd worn more than a year ago. How had he noticed so many things about her that no one else had?

Or was it possible she was indeed making an impression on other people, but had merely been blind to the fact?

Margaret had helped Lucinda choose that gown. It was lovely—*too lovely*, Lucinda had thought. She'd felt very conspicuous in it. Perhaps she really was afraid to step away from the wall and be noticed. Perhaps she ought to open her mind to the idea that if she did so, there might be someone out there for her after all.

It was only when she heard the servants moving about in the dining room, laying the table for dinner, that Lucinda realized how late it was getting. As she hurried upstairs to change, doubts immediately began to assail her. This whole idea of finding a husband was preposterous. Why had she allowed James to talk her into thinking such a thing was possible?

Upon reaching her room, she rang for her maid and then sat down to await her arrival. She breathed deeply, trying to calm the turmoil of so many conflicting emotions. Then, as several minutes ticked by in the dim stillness, Lucinda suddenly realized she'd been forgetting what was, for her, the most vitally important question of all: what was God's will for her life? The Bible extolled the virtues of both being single and being married, so clearly there was not a single correct answer that applied to everyone. Lucinda had always assumed remaining unmarried was to be her fate, but now everyone else was trying to persuade her to think otherwise—and giving her valid reasons to do so.

Lord, she prayed, *I'm now thoroughly confused. Help me to know what I should do.*

Chapter 9

It took Lucinda until late into the evening to decide upon her next course of action. Now she tapped lightly on the door of her sister's bedchamber. "Emily, are you still awake?"

"Just a minute!" Emily's voice called out.

Eventually, the door opened. Emily was already in her nightdress, over which she'd hastily tossed a light cotton wrapper. Her hair was tied up in dozens of those little curling papers that Lucinda had always refused to use. At the moment they made her sister resemble Medusa.

"You're up late," Emily remarked, taking note of the fact that Lucinda still had on her dinner gown. "I thought you always went to bed early and got up with the dawn."

This came out more as a reproach than an observation, but Lucinda let it pass. "May I come in? I need to ask you something—that is, I need your help."

"You need *my* help?" Emily's eyes rounded as she considered this novel idea. She stepped back from the door and ushered Lucinda into the room.

Lucinda took a seat on Emily's bed while her sister closed the door.

"Did you have fun today?" Emily asked, joining Lucinda on the bed. "I thought you had enjoyed yourself, but then you looked so cross at dinner. I didn't dare say anything for fear you'd bite my head off."

Lucinda gave a thin laugh. "I thought you were being unusually quiet. I assumed it was because you were dreaming about James."

"I'm always thinking about James," Emily said with a wistful smile. "He's the handsomest, most charming—"

"Yes, yes," Lucinda cut her off. She didn't think she could bear hearing her sister enumerate—yet again—all of James's wonderful qualities. It had been tedious enough before, but now that she knew how easily James could hide subterfuge under his charm, it made her even more uncomfortable. She still was not entirely sure she could trust him. "I was not cross at dinner, merely perplexed and astounded."

"Perplexed and astounded? About what?"

Her sister looked at her with the wide-eyed innocence that was her trademark. She and James really were a pair, Lucinda thought. They each had their own way of misdirecting other people for their own aims. "To be honest, I'm astounded that you could keep a secret."

This brought out a giggle. "What do you mean? I am forever keeping secrets."

"I'm not speaking of all the times you manage to evade Mama so you can flirt with men at parties. I'm referring to something more important. You knew the outing in the park today was nothing more than a charade, trying to put me in a better frame of mind so I might be more willing to talk about getting married."

Emily's smile turned to a look of consternation. "How did you find out?"

"I had a little chat with Papa and James before dinner."

"You know it is only for your own good," Emily said hastily, as though trying to avert an expected tirade from Lucinda. "James said he was sure that in your heart of hearts you are longing for a husband. 'Doesn't every woman want to get married?' he asked me, and I said, 'Well, of course!'"

Lucinda tried hard to keep from grimacing. "I have no doubt that is exactly what you said."

"Please tell me you are considering it!" Emily beseeched. "If you and I both get married, Mama and Papa will be so content, and our lives will be settled, and both our dowries will be intact—"

"Hush," Lucinda said, holding a finger to her sister's lips. "Let me get a word in. As it happens, I told Papa and James that I would agree to meet these marriage prospects, but that I make no promises."

"Oh, that's wonderful!" Emily beamed, not even registering the second half of Lucinda's statement. She always did have a way of focusing only on what she wanted to hear. "James says he knows several men who are ever so clever and who therefore won't be threatened by you."

"Oh really? Those were his precise words, I suppose."

Despite Lucinda's disparaging tone, Emily was still bubbling. "He told me about one man—I don't remember his name, but James says he's just gotten back from a grand tour of Europe. He took a first at Cambridge, and he loves books, so I think it's a match made in—"

"Emily!" Lucinda broke in sharply. "Let me repeat: I make no promises!"

Emily stared at her like a wounded puppy. "You needn't get all huffy about it."

As aggravating as her sister was, Lucinda could never bear to quarrel with her for too long. So she said more gently, "However, I do agree that, for the ball next week, it would be a good idea for me to do all I can to put my best foot forward. That's where I need your help."

"How can I—oh, I see! You want me to help you dress for it!" As usual, Emily had leaped to conclusions, but this time she was correct. Her smile and enthusiasm returned immediately, for Emily was as changeable as the weather. "We shall have one made for you in the latest style, with a nice, low décolletage to emphasize your—" She paused and frowned as she considered Lucinda's less-than-ample bosom. "Well, there are special corsets to help maximize..." Lucinda reddened, but Emily galloped off in yet another direction. "I will also loan you my Clara to do your hair. Your maid just doesn't have the knack."

"One thing at a time," Lucinda cautioned. She wasn't sure she was ready for the curling papers. "Let's just start with the gown, shall we? Will you go with me tomorrow to find the right material? James said—that is, I was thinking—perhaps I should look for something near the color of the gown I wore to Margaret's wedding."

"Yes, that would be perfect!" Emily agreed happily. "James is right, as always. You know how many times I've told you that the drab colors you wear do nothing for your complexion."

"Yes," Lucinda murmured. "I know."

Emily bounded off the bed and went to a large wooden chest. "Something like this, perhaps..." She drew out a vibrant blue shawl made of fine silk from India. "Come on, then." She pulled Lucinda over to a full-length mirror and arranged the shawl artfully over her shoulders to mimic the cut of an evening gown.

As they stood side-by-side at the mirror, Lucinda saw clearly how a change in color really did make a difference in her appearance. At the moment she almost looked prettier than Emily, although it wasn't really a fair comparison since her sister wore plain cotton nightclothes and a head full of curling papers.

"She how lovely that looks on you!" Emily exclaimed. "You always insist that being wise and intelligent is more important than beauty. But I say, if you can be wise *and* make yourself prettier as well, why wouldn't you want to?"

It was precisely her sister's brand of logic. But Lucinda had no answer to it.

Emily put an arm around her and drew her close. "Oh, Lucinda, we shall both be married and we shall both be so happy."

Lucinda met her sister's gaze in the mirror. "Is that really all it takes to be happy? To be married?"

Emily's face scrunched in thought. "Well, the man must be rich, of course. And handsome."

Lucinda sighed. She knew her sister was thinking of James. He was handsome, there was no doubt about that. But Lucinda knew there would be no point in mentioning that James wasn't exactly rich, which was the reason her father now had all three of them doing his bidding. Not for the world would she trade her clear-eyed view of

matrimony with her sister's delusions. And yet, maybe
her life would be simpler if she did. No thought required.
Only happy ignorance.

No. There was more to life than that. Sooner or later,
Emily would find out this truth for herself. It would probably happen about the time she became mistress of a
house she had no idea how to run. Nor did Lucinda harbor any illusions that James would be any more practical
than his wife. She could only hope the servants wouldn't
steal them blind.

Emily placed her chin on Lucinda's shoulder in an
affectionate gesture, something she hadn't done since
they were children. "Lucinda, you put up this hard exterior, but I think you must be a romantic at heart. After all,
look at that school you've started. You believe women
who have known only poverty and vice can still find
their way to happiness."

"It's not the same thing—"

"Oh, but it is! If God can bring them happiness, why
not you? Why do you expect Him to work miracles for
others but not for you?"

"Getting married is no miracle," Lucinda protested.

Getting married to someone I loved would be.

The startling thought seemed to come from nowhere.
Or perhaps it had come from the depths of her heart,
for Lucinda could not deny the intense surge of longing that accompanied it. Had her shallow sister somehow hit upon something profound? Did Lucinda really
believe God could work miracles for everyone except
herself? It was not a question she was prepared to explore
just now.

Lucinda frowned at her reflection in the mirror.

"Emily, let's just concentrate for the moment on the miracle of making me presentable."

*

James whistled as he strode up the wide marble steps to the front doors of the building that housed the newly built racquet club. The massive stone edifice housed several excellent courts to meet the demand, for the game of "rackets" as an indoor sport was becoming popular with the gentlemen of London. James loved coming here; it was the perfect way to spend an afternoon. Despite the energy he expended he found the physical challenge always left him refreshed and invigorated.

Today his visit would do more than simply provide diversion. He was sure he'd see Myron Stonewell, one of his candidates for Lucinda. James figured the racquet club would provide an excellent atmosphere for a chat, allowing him to bring up the subject in a way that would appear casual and not put Stonewell on the defensive.

Finding himself alone in the changing room, he quickly got into loose-fitting clothes that were more appropriate for exercise. As he made his way down to the courts, he prepared himself for a good deal of ribbing from the other bachelors, for the announcement of his engagement had been in the *Times* this morning. Sure enough, his friends Chapman and Hopkins, who were in the middle of a game, stopped playing as soon as they saw him.

"Well, look who's here—the next man to put his neck in the noose!" Chapman said in a boisterous voice that immediately grabbed the attention of the other men in the cavernous room. Within moments everyone had gathered around James, including Ned Stover, the only married man in the group, and George Wilson, who was another candidate on James's list.

"You're a fine one to talk, Chapman," James returned. "I saw your announcement in the *Times* yesterday."

Chapman gave him a cheeky grin.

"It's hardly news that Chapman's got himself engaged," Hopkins said dismissively. "Everyone knows he's been chasing Miss Hallowell for ages. But you surprised us all, Simpson. We didn't think you'd ever get married."

"I'm not surprised," said Stover. "Not after that little tidbit in the gossip column on Monday. If you compromise a lady, there's always hell to pay."

"Not that you would know anything about that personally," Hopkins rejoined, giving Stover a friendly slap on the back. Stover responded with a shamefaced grin and a shrug.

"I want you all to know I had every intention of proposing to Miss Cardington," James said. "The events at Cremorne merely hastened things a bit."

This brought a round of disbelieving grunts from the other men.

"No, truly," James insisted. "She's a marvelous girl, from a well-connected family—"

"And rich," Chapman put in. "A fat dowry, I hear."

"Hope it's fatter than her mother," Hopkins said. "Good luck with her as a mother-in-law."

"That is why you will never get married, you uncouth rogue," James chided, poking the man's chest in a gesture of mock disapproval. "However, I am not marrying her mother."

"Happily for you," Hopkins said, unabashed.

"Where's Stonewell?" James asked, looking around. "He owes me a match today."

"You haven't heard?" Hopkins answered cheerfully. "We won't be seeing him for a while. He's off arranging his own marriage—by special license, no less."

"Special license?" This was unexpected news. "Why? And to whom?"

"Well," said Hopkins with a smirk, "it appears he and Miss Jane Abernathy have gotten to be more than mere acquaintances."

The other men snickered knowingly.

James groaned. He'd had no idea things between Stonewell and Miss Abernathy had progressed so far. It was more proof, he thought morosely, that his perception in *les affaires d'amour* had fallen into steep decline. Even worse, it meant he had one less prospect for Lucinda. But the next man on the list was standing right here, and there was no time to be lost. "Look, Wilson, I've got a favor to ask you. Are you going to the Beauchamps' ball next week?"

"I wouldn't miss the best event of the season." His brow furrowed. "What kind of favor did you have in mind?"

"Nothing too onerous—it's just that Emily's sister often feels left out at these events, and I'm trying to help her out. All I ask is that you allow me to introduce you to her, and that you spend a few minutes chatting with her."

"What's she like?" Wilson asked warily.

"Gawky," Hopkins declared. "And rather clumsy. Whatever you do, don't ask her to—"

"You stay out of it," James interrupted, giving him a small shove. Turning back to Wilson he said, "Lucinda is a wonderful young lady. Well bred, with excellent manners."

But Wilson had picked up on the lack of enthusiasm from the other men. "What's wrong with her, then? Is she plain?"

Hopkins snorted, but after a warning glance from James, stayed silent.

"Nothing's wrong with her!" James insisted. "I'll admit there are those who say her sister is the prettier of the two, but Lucinda is perfectly charming. She's intelligent, too. Isn't that more important than mere beauty? Just last week you mentioned how much you dislike having to carry on a conversation with some of the more vacuous young ladies of the *ton*."

Hopkins grinned. "Like Miss Emily, do you mean?"

"I suppose I deserve that," James said, fighting to keep his tone light. Hopkins could always be relied upon for a good jest, but at the moment James found this more of an aggravation than an attribute. "Don't forget that Emily is still young. She has a lot of potential. As does Lucinda," he added pointedly, once more aiming his remarks at Wilson.

Wilson looked unconvinced. "I'll have to see her first. I won't be trapped into wasting an evening with her if she doesn't interest me."

This wasn't going well, and James realized he should have gotten Wilson alone before broaching the subject. Now he would have to work harder to keep Wilson on the line. Remembering how the man's eyes had lit up at the mention of Emily's dowry, he said casually, "I understand Lucinda will bring well over twenty thousand pounds to her marriage."

"Really?" Wilson said, his attention piqued. But then he scowled. "It appears you want to do more than get me to chat with her. You can introduce me, if you like, but I warn you I have very high standards. Whoever I marry must be beautiful and graceful as well as wealthy and smart."

"That's an awfully tall order," Hopkins pointed out. "If you gamble on cards using those odds, I doubt you win much."

"Enough of this talking," James said. "I came here to play. Are we going to get this match going or stand about all day?" He'd gotten Wilson to at least consider Lucinda, and that was all he could do for now.

That afternoon, James played with more vigor than usual. The exercise was good, and it helped take his mind off his troubles, if only for a short while. He tried to shake off the feeling that he'd sold out Lucinda by resorting to mention of the dowry, even though he'd been vague about the actual amount. He justified his actions by focusing on the fact that even though it had sweetened the deal, Wilson was looking for more than just money. He was picky, that was all. Surely there was no reason why Lucinda could not meet the man's expectations— especially if Emily did her part to help Lucinda with her wardrobe and social skills. Unfortunately, Lucinda's cooperation was the most uncertain element in this whole mad scheme. As with Wilson, he'd won only her grudging acquiescence.

James slammed the ball hard, venting all his frustration on it. The ball flew past Wilson, easily winning James the match.

What did that woman truly want? James was still mystified. Her protestations against marriage did not entirely ring true. James was sure of this; it was not mere self-serving wishful thinking on his part. Perhaps if he could just talk with her alone, without any of her family around, he might be able to find out what was really going on in her head. Then he could tailor his efforts, and the whole enterprise might succeed much more quickly. And wasn't that also what his aunt had suggested from the beginning? The afternoon of photography in the park had helped move the plan forward, if somewhat haltingly. Perhaps another outing was in order.

*

"I'm sorry to be leaving you with all of this, Mrs. Cheadle," Lucinda said.

Mrs. Cheadle, the venerable matron who oversaw the day-to-day business of the school, waved away Lucinda's apology. "Don't you worry, Miss Cardington. The girls are nearly done with their lessons, and we'll be spending the rest of the day cleaning."

Despite Mrs. Cheadle's assurances, Lucinda still felt she had not done enough. During the past week there had been too many other demands on her time. She and Emily had spent several days shopping for material and deciding on the style of her gown. Later today she had an appointment with the dressmaker for yet another fitting. It seemed like such a waste of time compared to what she was accomplishing here.

"The girls know you have other things to attend to," Mrs. Cheadle assured her, shooing her toward the door. "They are grateful for any time you spend with them."

Even so, Lucinda left reluctantly. She was so wrapped up in her thoughts that she was stepping out of the school's battered little front gate by the time she saw James. Or rather, she saw the small crowd gathered around the wagon James had fitted up with his photography equipment. The driver, another "borrowed" servant of Lord Somerville's, was keeping an eye on the crowd, making sure they didn't get too close.

James was leaning casually against wagon, his arms folded. He must have been watching her as she came out. It was unsettling to realize he had been studying her without her realizing it. She really had to get her head out of the cotton wool it seemed to be wrapped in these days. But since the cause of her distraction was this push to get her ready for the marriage market, having James here wasn't likely to help.

He swept off his hat and gave her a bow. "Good afternoon, Miss Cardington. How are you today?"

She looked at him askance. "You are brave to bring your photography wagon into this neighborhood. Aren't you worried something will happen to it?"

"Not at all. Turner—" he jerked a thumb toward Geoffrey's servant—"is more than capable of keeping the riffraff at bay. And in any case, now we have your footman to help us as well." He indicated Peter. Lucinda had sent him out here to wait for her, and he was looking over the wagon with interest.

"You can't be intending to take photographs here," Lucinda said.

"No, but it wouldn't be a bad idea. There are writers, such as Mr. Dickens, who do an excellent job of depicting the squalor of these people's lives, but many still believe what he writes is pure fiction. Just the other day a gentleman said to me, 'If these descriptions Dickens has given us are true, we really must seriously look into it.' Perhaps if the public at large saw photographs of these places, they would be convinced."

"You're right," Lucinda said, warming instantly to the idea. "It might be easier to persuade people to take action if they had visible proof."

"It is a worthy goal. Today, however, I have other plans." James pointed overhead, where a few lazy clouds floated in the bright blue sky. "We are having one of our rare crystal clear days, and I plan to take a panorama of the city from the rooftop garden at Westminster Palace."

"Westminster!"

"Yes indeed. Parliament is not in session today, so Geoffrey pulled a few strings to allow me up there for a few hours. It should be quite exciting. Would you care to join me?"

Lucinda stared at him in disbelief. "Me?"

"You know this is a privilege afforded to very few people. It's a bit of a climb, but I'm sure you are up to it. At least you are wearing something sensible."

Lucinda looked down at the simple day gown she was wearing. She was always careful not to dress too elaborately when coming to the school. Even at home she favored simplicity. Only on formal occasions did she wear the wide, bell-shaped crinolines favored by so many ladies this season. The rest of the time she simply used a layer or two of petticoats to add fullness to her skirts. But the cut of her gown was irrelevant; she could not accept this invitation. "James, it's really tempting, but the truth is … well … I have a dress fitting in an hour, and Emily is meeting me there."

"A dress fitting?" James nodded in appreciation. "How wonderfully feminine."

Lucinda felt her face growing scarlet. James would no doubt take this information as proof she was putting forth an extra effort to look good for the Beauchamps' ball. Even if that were true, she did not want him thinking she had high hopes for how that event would go. "I do need new dresses from time to time," she pointed out.

"Of course you do," he said, dismissing the subject with a shrug. "Now, listen. This may be your only chance to see a place normally reserved only for peers. Besides, you know Emily is always late, wherever she goes. We should have plenty of time. Now, let's get going before we lose this good light." He beckoned her toward the wagon. "We'll just send a message to Emily telling her to meet us at your dressmaker's in an hour and a half. That should do it. You can send your footman, for you will have me to keep you safe and Turner here to act as the chaperone."

"I hardly think a chaperone is necessary," Lucinda protested. "That would imply..."

"Precisely," James answered smoothly. "And we all know how preposterous that is."

Lucinda raised an eyebrow, wondering if she ought to feel insulted.

James flashed her a smile. "In their eyes, my dear. That's all I'm saying." He gave her a wink that made her even more uncomfortable than his first remark had done. "I'm simply trying to get you to see that no one will take exception to our spending time together."

"Except perhaps Mama—"

"Miss Lucinda Cardington," James said severely.

"How many times have you insisted that you act independently of what your mother thinks? You cannot therefore use her now as an excuse not to do this." He motioned her forward. "Come along, then. The light is fading even as we speak."

It was tempting, on such a beautiful day as this, to think of climbing so high and having their own private view of the city. Still, Lucinda hesitated, unwilling to look too eager. "Will you allow me to coat the plates again?"

James laughed. "You think you are driving a hard bargain, Miss Cardington, but I assure you that is what I had in mind all along. You are the very best photographer's assistant a person could hope to have."

Swept up by his enthusiasm, she allowed him to help her into the wagon. But she could not resist saying, "You will not have me as an assistant for long, Mr. Simpson. One day I will be my own photographer."

"I don't doubt that for a moment," he replied cheerfully. "I would even sponsor your admission to the Photographic Society."

They dispatched Peter with the message for Emily. Then Turner clambered into the driver's seat and the wagon lurched forward, scattering the bystanders and a few dogs as it lumbered down the narrow lane.

Once they were under way, Lucinda began to have second thoughts. She reminded herself that she'd been fooled by James's dissembling before. Most likely he had an ulterior motive for coming out today, but she could not imagine what it was. She'd already agreed to meet the prospective suitors. If he thought he was going to get any more out of her, he was mistaken.

As the wagon turned the corner, she took another glance back at the school. Perhaps she ought to take this time to impress upon James the importance of what she was doing there. If only he could be made to understand how much it meant to her, maybe he would stop trying to pull her away from it.

Another tack could be to turn the focus of the conversation back upon him. What did he really want from life? Was he truly seeking nothing more than a life of ease and luxury, content to make no real difference in the world? For all his laughter and tomfoolery he seemed a decent man. As far as she had seen, James treated everyone—rich or poor, peers or servants—with the same kindness and affability. There had to be something worthwhile beneath his glib exterior. If there was, she was determined to find it.

Chapter 10

Lucinda looked up doubtfully at the imposing spires of Westminster Palace as James helped her down from the wagon. It would be quite a climb to get there, especially considering how much equipment they would need. "How do you plan to get your chemicals, work table, and dark tent all the way up to the roof?"

"Actually, the bulk of it is already there." James went around to the back of the wagon, where the driver was already opening the doors to the storage compartment. "Thank you, Turner," he said, as the man handed him the large wooden box that held the camera. He motioned Lucinda toward him. "I will need you to carry the tripod, if you think you are up to it."

She nodded, and Turner gave her the tripod. Although it was made of sturdy wood, it did not seem overly heavy. "I believe I can manage. But how is it you already have the rest of the equipment up there?"

"Earlier today I came here with Bertie—he's the newest member of Lady Thornborough's staff. He and I carried up the needed items, along with another lad we found who was very willing to do it in exchange for a shilling. Bertie is still up there, watching over everything."

"Are you saying you are going to climb this twice today?"

"Yes, the things I do for art." He shifted the bulky camera in his arms. "This is the only thing I did not want to leave with Bertie. It's not that I don't trust him. It's just that the camera is simply too precious to leave out of my sight."

To Lucinda's surprise, James told Turner to stay with the photography wagon and wait until he sent down Bertie with more instructions. "I thought Turner was supposed to act as our chaperone," Lucinda said, more to tease James than out of any real concern.

"I won't tell anyone if you won't," James responded with a cheeky grin.

The long flight of stairs presented a challenge, especially with the extra weight of the tripod she was carrying. Lucinda quickly found herself growing warm and out of breath. She had no idea how James was managing to carry the camera on this—his second trip of the day—without appearing too taxed. He was breathing hard, to be sure, but moving rapidly.

At one point they did pause to rest. "We're about two-thirds of the way up," James told her. "Nearly there." But they did not linger long. James began moving swiftly up the stairs again. "Come on, we've got to get this light."

Lucinda took off gamely after him, although in truth the tripod was feeling much heavier now than it had done at the beginning of the climb. Over the next few flights the gap between her and James widened. "I'm surprised you came to get me if you were so concerned about missing the light," she said between gasps.

James sprinted up the last few steps and opened the door that led out to the roof. He carefully set down his camera and waited for Lucinda to catch up. With a final push, she took the remaining stairs and stepped out into the open. Immediately a stiff breeze brushed her face, as refreshing as a glass of cool water. James took the tripod from her and set it aside, then led her over to the railing. "I did not want you to miss this. I knew you would appreciate it more than anyone else."

It was an exhilarating sight. All of London—the streets and the landmarks and the inimitable River Thames—laid itself out like a large, living map. "What a dilemma I am in," she said. "How can I catch my breath when this view wants to steal it away again?"

"Nicely put." James's blue eyes twinkled. "I always knew there was poetry in your soul."

James's smile was so vibrant and welcoming that it was absolutely irresistible. Now Lucinda found herself smiling back, her heart light, glad she had not turned down the opportunity to come here.

"Thank you for coming," he said. He removed his hat, and a gust of wind ruffled his hair. As his gaze held hers, Lucinda realized more powerfully than ever before just how handsome this man was. She was thankful she had the excuse of the vigorous exercise and the dramatic view to account for her flushed face and shortness of breath.

James rubbed his hands together briskly. "Now then, let's get to work, shall we?" He turned her attention toward another area of the rooftop garden. His photographic equipment was arranged neatly, and on the ground next to it lay a boy who was fast asleep. Lucinda guessed him to be about twelve, although he looked small and very thin for his age. On a cloth nearby were some food wrappings, a few chicken bones, and an apple core—evidence he had eaten a hearty lunch before dozing off.

"Looks like we caught Bertie lying down on the job," James said. "Ho, there, Bertie!"

The boy awoke with a start. Seeing James, he scrambled to his feet. "I beg your pardon, sir," he mumbled quickly, giving James a little bow.

"Clearly we feed you too well," James said, but there was a smile in his voice. "Have you been keeping watch over the equipment like I told you to?"

"Oh, yes, sir!" Bertie said, but he threw a quick glance behind him as though to double-check that everything was still there. "No one has been up here since you left—I'm sure of it!"

James crossed his arms as he looked askance at the boy. "I think a whole army might have come up here and you wouldn't have known it."

Lucinda could see he was merely teasing the boy, but Bertie answered solemnly, "I don't think so, sir. If they had, they'd have taken those last two meat pies for sure."

"Good point," James said with a laugh. "Although I do think their lordships have more sophisticated ways of stealing from people. Now help us set up this camera equipment."

Bertie did not hide his surprise at seeing Lucinda. He turned to James. "You said you was bringing an apprentice here today."

"So I did. Bertie, this is Miss Cardington."

"How do you do," she said.

Bertie gave her an ungainly little bow, but said nothing, and Lucinda had the sense he was unsure how to act.

She did not think he had been a household servant for very long. He soon relaxed, however, when James set him to work assembling the tripod. He must have done it before, for his small fingers nimbly attached the pieces together. In the meantime, James arranged the chemicals and plates in the order he would need them.

Lucinda marveled as she watched the two of them working. "I think Bertie is the real apprentice here," she observed.

Bertie looked proud. "Do you know Mr. Simpson can actually capture pictures onto those glass plates? I wouldn't 'ave believed it if I ain't seen it for meself."

"It is astounding, isn't it?" Lucinda agreed.

"Bertie has been a tremendous help to me," James said. "Very soon I will allow him to do more than merely carry the equipment." He took a coin and a folded piece of paper from his pocket and handed both of them to the boy. "Today, however, I need you for another important task. Go on down now. Come back in an hour's time, and bring another lad with you to take this equipment down. Tell him there'll be good money in it."

"Yes, sir!" Bertie replied.

"And if anyone gives you trouble, show them this letter of permission from Lord Somerville, and tell them they can also verify it with the sergeant-at-arms by the door."

"Yes, sir!" Bertie said again. If he was disappointed at not being able to stay and watch the photography process, he didn't show it. He pocketed the coin and the paper, scooped up the remains of his lunch, and headed for the staircase. Before long they could hear him whistling as he went down the stairs.

"Did you say he was a member of Lady Thornborough's staff?" Lucinda asked. "He seems awfully young."

"He's been with us for about a month. Cook found him scrounging in the back alley for scraps, desperate for something to eat. The poor boy was on the point of starvation—even thinner than he is now, if you can believe it. He's an orphan, and had nowhere to go, so my aunt decided to take him in. He helps the housemaids with the early morning chores, and then goes off to one of the ragged schools so he can get a bit of learning."

"That's commendable," Lucinda said. "But isn't Lady Thornborough worried about having such a person in the house? So often the boys on the street become experts at thieving."

"It did concern her at first," James acknowledged. "But Bertie had not been an orphan for long. His mother had died only a month before, and there hadn't been time for the streets to harden him completely. I convinced my aunt that Bertie is an honest soul, and this has proved to be true. He's so grateful to have a roof over his head that he works very hard, doing whatever is asked of him without complaining."

"Including the job of transporting heavy equipment and chemicals up and down hundreds of stairs?"

"Well, I give him extra money for that. Besides, he thinks it's far more exciting than hauling coal and ashes up and down the stairs at my aunt's house."

"I see you are a philanthropist after all," Lucinda teased. "Despite what everyone says. Including you."

James held out his hands in a gesture of humility. "I'm not trying to save the whole world. Just a small part of it that I can reach."

Lucinda laughed. "You may throw my own words back at me. In this case, I am glad of it. I think you care far more for your fellow man than you care to admit."

He gave a sad little smile. "To be honest, I felt sorry for the lad. I know what it is like to lose one's mother at such a tender age."

A look of genuine sorrow crossed his face, and Lucinda's heart gave a little tug at seeing this crack in his usually carefree exterior. "I'm so sorry," she said. "When did she—"

"Enough of this idle chatter," James said brusquely. "Let's get started. There's no time to be lost." He picked up one of the glass plates and held it out to her. "I believe you said you wanted to do the first coat?"

*

Lucinda eyed him curiously as she accepted the plate, and James regretted that he had allowed her to see the hurt he still felt over his mother's death. He never shared that information with anyone, so why had he done it now? It must have been because she'd praised him for helping Bertie, giving him far too much credit for such a simple act. Or maybe it was because Lucinda's unrelenting earnestness was beginning to rub off on him. He could not allow that to happen. It was a discomfort he could do without.

Deliberately he set those thoughts aside and concentrated on his primary reason for being here. He had a photograph to take. He handed Lucinda the bottle of collodion solution and watched as she poured it slowly onto the glass plate. "Excellent," he said, as she carefully tilted the corners so the solution would cover the surface evenly. "I believe you have mastered that step. Are you ready for something new?"

"Indeed I am." Smiling with pride, Lucinda set the plate on the drying rack. They would have to wait for this coat to dry before proceeding to the next step, but that would not take long on this warm and sunny day.

"Well then, while the plate is drying, I'll show you how the camera works."

Lucinda gave a tiny chirp of delight, which James found amusing and utterly charming. He enjoyed these moments when her stiff reserve fell away. She was more like her sister then, except she retained a touch of maturity that was pleasantly appealing—and something Emily's personality could benefit from.

She listened attentively as James pointed out the function of the camera's various parts. He'd not been able to do this during their trip to Hyde Park because he'd been forced to spend so much of his time mollifying Emily. Now they were free to go over everything in detail. "The lens slides into this slot up here in the front," he explained, pointing to the place. "At the moment I have what's called a single doublet lens—those are good for landscapes."

Lucinda nodded in understanding. "The two-doublet lenses are good for portraits."

"I see you've been retaining the information from all those photography books you purloined," he said appreciatively. "In that case, you are probably familiar with the fact that the camera is actually made up of two wooden boxes, one that fits inside the other." Lucinda nodded, and James continued, "You set the focus by sliding the two boxes back and forth. The scene appears on the ground glass here. It's upside-down, which does take a bit of getting used to." He pointed to the slot where the glass was inserted. "You have to be under this cloth to see the picture." He pointed to a black drape that was attached to the camera at the opposite end from the lens.

"May I try setting the focus?" she said hopefully.

"You certainly may." James could not help from grinning as he said this. "However, I believe you will find it easier if you remove your bonnet first."

"Oh yes, I see what you mean." She reached up to untie the ribbon beneath her chin, then lifted the bonnet from her head. Amazingly, she began to blush a little as she did so, looking for all the world as if she felt she were disrobing in front of him. Her expression, far more than her movements, suddenly made the act seem quite sensual indeed.

Her hair was pulled back in a neat bun, although a few wisps snagged on the bonnet and became dislodged, dancing gently in the breeze. Lucinda set aside the bonnet and tried self-consciously to tuck the loose strands behind her ears. "It does seem strange to be outdoors without my head covered," she said.

James thought she looked better without all the distractions of flowers and ribbons. "I won't tell a soul," he promised. Nor, he thought with a smile, would he tell anyone how he'd spent a portion of this afternoon admiring the view of her waist and backside as she bent over to duck her head under the cloth.

Feeling a sudden pang of guilt, James forced himself to take hold of his thoughts. Even he knew better than to dwell for too long on the very fine attributes of his future sister-in-law. He only wished he might have noticed them sooner. Why in the world hadn't he? He purposefully shifted his attention away from her hips and onto her hands instead, which he gently guided to the handles on the side of the camera. "Use these to help you set the focus. Go ahead and practice with it. Do you see how the focus shifts as you move the boxes in and out? I've set up the shot so that the dome of St. Paul's Cathedral will be the focal point. Do you see it?"

"Yes, and it's wonderful!" she cried, her voice muffled from underneath the cloth. She spent a few more moments moving the focus handles. Although he could not see her face, everything about her posture told him she was alight with pleasure. "I think I've got it!" came the muffled voice once more. Then she pulled her head out from the cloth and stood up, exclaiming, "This will be a wonderful photograph!"

In that moment, James finally admitted to himself that this was the real reason he had brought Lucinda up here. He had wanted to see that look on her face again— the way her eyes lit up and her habitually serious expression fell away. Most women would find this tedious, and the handling of all those chemicals to be distasteful, but for Lucinda it seemed nothing but pure delight. "I think so too," he said, drinking in her bright smile. "The day is, in fact, turning out perfectly."

James reached into his coat pocket and brought out the small notebook he'd been using to record the details of all his photographs. He wrote down the time of day, weather conditions, lens type, and exposure time. Double-checking his notes he said, "I believe we will need two minutes."

He looked up to see that Lucinda's smile had faded. She was staring at the notebook. No doubt she recognized it as the one she had returned to him on the day she discovered the list. Well, there was no avoiding the fact that James had been tasked to find her a husband, and that Lucinda knew it. "Thank you for returning this. The notes I made in here are indispensable."

She made no reply. The memories brought on by the sight of the notebook threatened to cast a pall over the proceedings, but James refused to allow it. He said brightly, "I believe the plate is dry. And look, the clouds are cooperating by staying out of our path. I will just check the focus one more time." He put his head under the viewing cloth. He had been prepared to compliment Lucinda no matter what the focus looked like, but he was happy to see she had done a very good job. He pulled out his head and straightened. "It's perfect!"

Tentatively, her smile returned. "Are you sure?"

"No doubt in my mind." He picked up the glass plate, which was now dry. "I'll just go and apply the silver nitrate—unless you'd like to try it again?" He extended the plate toward her.

"Perhaps I should pass on that today. Mama will have a fit if I ruin another gown."

James grinned, remembering the lovely spectacle she'd made as she'd held that dripping plate at Hyde Park. He ducked under the dark tent and quickly completed the preparations. When he re-emerged, he found Lucinda leaning against the railing, looking out dreamily over the city. The breeze lifted and played with the loose strands of her hair.

"Here we are," James said. Lucinda turned to watch as he took the frame over to the camera. "Now, I shall take out the ground glass, and drop the frame into its place, like so...and then I will remove the dark slide, which will expose the negative to light coming through the lens." When this was done, he pulled out his pocket watch. He waited until the second hand was where he needed it to be before lifting the cap and beginning the exposure. "And...now." He pulled away the cap.

While he was counting the exposure time, Lucinda surveyed the city once more. The Thames was busy with boat traffic, and an endless tide of carriages moved along the wide thoroughfares. "How vast London is," she murmured. "So full of opportunities and ideas. 'The very forge and working house of thought,' Shakespeare called it." She sighed. "How small my world seems in comparison. And how much smaller my parents wish to make it."

Her words were painfully sad, and this bothered him. Lucinda was a serious person, but he did not think it was in her nature to be morose. "Lucinda, I promise you that when I am your brother-in-law, I shall fight to make sure your world is as wide as you want it to be."

She turned to face him. "Will you really? And how will you do that? My father will tell me I should focus more on finding a husband than on photography. And then when I get married... *if* I get married..." She shook her head.

"Marriage does not have to be the end," James insisted, hoping for his own sake as well as hers that this was true. "We'll find you a husband who will allow you to pursue your goals and dreams. In fact..." Here was the opportunity he'd been looking for to tell her about Wilson, and yet now, for some reason, he did not want to do it. He wished they might have spent this lovely afternoon discussing anything but marriage. Sternly he told himself he had no choice. All their futures were at stake. "In fact, there is an excellent candidate that I want you to meet at the Beauchamps' ball. His name is George Wilson. He told me himself he wants a woman who is intelligent and well read." James didn't mention the rest of Wilson's requirements. Surely once the man got to know her, he would see how beautiful she truly was.

Lucinda said nothing. A look of pain darted across her eyes, and she dropped her gaze to the watch in James's hand. "Is the exposure time up?"

James glanced at the watch. "One more minute. Lucinda—"

"I would prefer not to discuss the husband hunt today, if you don't mind." Her voice was brittle. Harsh, almost. Brooking no argument. Then she added matter-of-factly, "Is everything ready to fix the plate once you remove it from the camera?"

"Good point," he acknowledged, deciding it was better to allow her to shift the conversation back to the task at hand. He made a show of double-checking his materials, although he knew everything was in order. When the exposure was complete, he put the lens cap and dark slide back in place, then withdrew the frame from the camera. "This won't take long," he told her, and went under the dark tent to wash and set the plate.

As he worked, he brooded over the direction their conversation had taken. Today's outing was supposed to provide an opportunity to get her to open up, but he'd been successful only to a point. When it came to discussing her future, Lucinda was still firmly ensconced in her defensive fortress. Well, he'd just have to keep trying.

"Did it turn out all right, do you think?" she asked when he came back out again.

He shrugged. "It's difficult to tell. I'll know for sure when I make the print."

"Might I—that is, would you show me how to make prints sometime?"

"I would love to," James said, his heart lightening a little. At least she wanted to see him again. Surely this was a good sign. "Lucinda, I'm sorry if I caused you any distress earlier."

Her expression was neutral, or more precisely, stoic. "I understand. You are just doing what my father tells you to do."

She was right, of course. James couldn't deny it. He turned and began to pack up, beginning with placing the various chemical bottles into a packing crate.

"Were your parents happy, James?"

Startled by this question, he stood up and turned around to find she was watching him intently. Was this, then, what Lucinda wanted most in a marriage? That elusive thing called happiness? "I never doubted that my parents loved each other." It was not a direct answer, but at least it was honest.

"What was your father like? Mama says he was a wastrel."

It was a fairly blunt statement. James had no idea where this conversation was going, but if she wanted to talk, he would oblige. "I suppose that's an accurate assessment on the surface of things." He was well aware that his father's exploits had provided endless fodder for gossip. Hard drinking and irresponsible living had ended the man's life much too early. Over the years, James hadn't bothered to correct the inaccurate things that had been said about his father. But now—with Lucinda, at least—James found himself wanting to set the record straight. "It's not the whole story, however. Did you know my father was a soldier in the Napoleonic wars? He was wounded severely, almost to the point of death."

"I didn't know," Lucinda said. "He must have been terribly brave."

"He received the special medal awarded by the king to all the soldiers who fought in the Waterloo campaign. Trouble was, my father never felt he was entitled to it."

"Why not? If he fought at Waterloo—"

"That's just it. He never got to Waterloo. He was wounded at the battle of Quatre Bras two days before. He was evacuated to a hospital in Brussels. By the time he regained consciousness a week later, Napoleon had been defeated and the war was, for all intents and purposes, over."

"Even so, how could your father think he had not earned the medal?"

"My father once told me that he spent most of his life on the mere fringes of victory. Quatre Bras was the first of many such instances. He was just nineteen years old, and like all young men his head was filled with the glories of war. He'd already met my mother by that time, and she'd fallen in love with this dashing soldier and his scarlet and gold uniform. They were married, and she accompanied him as far as Brussels, as many women did in those days. It was quite the time, you know. Brussels was taken over by the officers and soldiers and all their women, and there were endless parties and feastings. Then came the inevitable time when they actually had to go and fight."

Lucinda nodded sadly. "I imagine his dreams of glory vanished at that point."

"Yes. His division was young and inexperienced. They were badly mauled by the French, overrun while they were still trying to organize themselves into that square configuration they used for battle. It was chaos."

He could see Lucinda shiver as she imagined the scene, but he felt compelled to finish his story, painful as it was. "My father was lucky to survive. Many were killed, including two of his dearest friends, men he had grown up with."

James set the last of the bottles into the crate. The rest of the packing could wait until Bertie came. He walked over to Lucinda. "You asked if my parents were happy. I don't think they were, but it was not for the reasons you may think. They were in love, but you can also see how the war was devastating for both of them. When my mother received news that they'd gotten my father to the hospital in Brussels, she went there instantly and spent day and night by his side. She tended him and the other soldiers in any way she could. The wound in his leg had festered and he had a raging fever. They were sure he was going to die. But my mother prayed."

James could see his statement took Lucinda's interest, as he intended it to. This was what he wanted to share with her, that his mother had been a woman of strong faith, just as Lucinda was. "My mother told God in no uncertain terms that she was not returning to England without her husband. Some might call that more of a command than a prayer, but it seemed to work. Not too long after she sent up that prayer, his fever broke."

"Your mother sounds like an admirable woman."

"She was indeed." James felt his heart constrict a little at the memory of her. "She was honest and kind and good."

"I still don't understand how this event should have made your father consider his life a failure."

"After they returned to England he left the Army. He didn't have the heart for it, and my mother was terrified for him, too. So he sold his commission and decided to get into business. Over the years he tried a number of things, but nothing ever panned out. Then a series of bad investments bled away what little money he had left."

"How terrible."

She was looking at James with pity, something he normally could not abide from anyone. But if it could help Lucinda take her mind off her own troubles, he would endure it. "I believe it was a relief to my father when it became apparent that Sir Herbert Thornborough would have no sons and I would therefore end up inheriting Rosewood, the estate in Kent. I was fourteen when my mother died, and my father felt it was the perfect time to pack me off to Aunt Thornborough's home and allow her to unofficially adopt me. At the time I was resentful, thinking he was abandoning me. Now I see that he simply felt he had nothing left to offer me. Aunt Thornborough was of the same opinion. She had never approved of his marriage to her niece."

"Is that why there always seems to be this little tug-of-war between you and your great-aunt?" Lucinda asked.

James nodded. "I love her dearly now, but it was difficult at first. She was determined that I should not grow up to be like my father, and so I rebelled and did all I could to be exactly like him."

"Aren't you still doing that?"

"I know it must appear that way. However, I have begun mending my ways. I don't want my life to be a series of might-have-beens."

They were lofty sounding words, but he wanted to believe them. He wanted *her* to believe them. "My mother prayed for my father every day of her life. He was often too distracted by his problems to give her the attention she deserved, but I'm sure he cared for her deeply. It was only after her death that my father truly went off the rails, as they say nowadays. She had been his anchor. On the heels of his failures, as well as losing her, I can easily see why he descended into a ruinous cycle of 'eat, drink, and be merry, for tomorrow we shall die.' So you see, Lucinda, it does not always follow that true love leads to happiness. There must be some other ingredient. I don't know what it is, but I am doing everything I can to find it."

If she had wanted honesty from him, she certainly got it today. She said nothing, but continued to search his eyes, pondering his words. It was greatly to her credit, James thought, that she did not immediately speak some banal and useless sentiment, the sympathetic-sounding drivel that comes so easily and means nothing.

"I may have misjudged you," she said at last. "I—"

She was interrupted by the sounds of voices coming from the stairwell. Bertie was returning, and he had brought someone with him, just as James had instructed.

Lucinda hastily reached for her bonnet. "Thank you for this day," she said. "You've given me plenty of think about."

Immediately James began to regret having shared so much. His goal was supposed to be softening Lucinda to the idea of marriage. Why, then, had he spoken about his own life?

Because she'd asked. Something Emily had never done. Emily loved him for his surface charms, and he was content to leave it so. Conversing with Lucinda was a different matter altogether.

He briskly set about directing the boys on how to complete the packing. As he did so, Lucinda finished tying her bonnet and returned to the railing, taking in the view for one last time. When all was ready, James sent the boys down first while he and Lucinda followed after.

As they were descending the stairs, he held Lucinda back for a moment and allowed the two boys to get well ahead of them. "Please don't share with anyone the things I told you about my parents," he said. "Emily and I will have this discussion at some point, but I don't feel the time is right just yet."

She looked at him in surprise. "You haven't told her these things?"

James gave a dry laugh. "You must wonder what we find to talk about. Well, it isn't the deep things of the soul, I can tell you that."

Her eyes narrowed as she gave him a thoughtful look. "I'm beginning to suspect that despite your outgoing nature you are in fact a very private man."

"Shhh," he said, holding a finger to his lips. "Don't tell anyone, or I shall lose my hard-won reputation as a shallow and lightheaded dolt."

Lucinda smiled at his joke. "I understand."

As they proceeded once more down the stairs, James reflected over all that had passed, marveling again at all the interesting facets this woman possessed. She kept insisting she would be content if only she could carry out her plans to live alone, but today James had seen this was not the whole story. Her yearning for something more was palpable. Perhaps she did understand a man like James, but he could not help but wonder how well she understood herself.

Chapter 11

W ell, where is she?" Wilson asked.

They had been at the ball for nearly an hour, but there had been no sign of the Cardingtons. It was not like them to be so late. "Perhaps something came up," James suggested.

Wilson frowned and handed his empty glass to a passing waiter. "Well, I do not intend to stand around and wait. I'm off to the card room. You may come find me if they ever get here."

"Wait," James said, taking hold of Wilson's arm as he turned to leave. "There they are now."

The entire Cardington family was, in fact, standing at the top of the stairs that led down into the Beauchamps' massive ballroom. At a glance James could see that both Lord and Lady Cardington were out of sorts, although they attempted to disguise it with stiff, cheerless smiles as a footman announced their arrival. Lady Cardington was fanning herself furiously. Emily, too, could not hide her agitation, although it dissolved into a genuine smile the moment she saw James. She waved and immediately began to descend the stairs.

Once Emily had broken away from her family, Lucinda came into view. She stood very close to her mother, as though she were substituting that large lady for one of the walls she always tried to prop up at parties. Her stiff demeanor displayed her clear desire to be anywhere but here. There was nothing unusual in either of those things, but tonight there was one very great difference. Tonight, despite her evident unease, she looked... well, *beautiful*.

Her gown of deep bluish green suited her perfectly and was a welcome change from the pale colors she usually wore. The style of her hair had changed, too. Normally she wore it pulled straight back and free of frills, but tonight there were soft curls expertly framing her face and giving it a fuller and softer look. Her gown's neckline was by no means the most daring in the room, and yet it was surprisingly lower than she usually wore. In the past James had surmised the purpose of her modest gowns was to disguise a thin and bony frame; now he saw how mistaken he'd been. Her delicate neck curved gracefully to slender shoulders that still evinced a softness despite her arrow-straight posture. Tonight, Miss Lucinda Cardington could hold her own against any woman here. James stared at her, transfixed.

Wilson broke into his thoughts. "Is that Miss Cardington?"

James suddenly found his mouth had gone very dry. "Yes."

Emily was by now halfway down the staircase, but she stopped short, turned around, and hurried back up the stairs to take hold of Lucinda's hand. James could see her urging her sister to come with her, and Lucinda's hesitant query to her parents. Lady Cardington took one look at James and, seeing Wilson beside him, practically pushed Lucinda to follow Emily.

James knew he ought to at least try to meet them half-way, but he was too spellbound to move. He also found he enjoyed watching Emily pull Lucinda along like a recalcitrant five-year-old.

"Here we are at last," Emily said, breathless as they reached James.

"Good evening." James took both the ladies' hands by turns and bowed over them. "May I say you both look stunning this evening." He met Lucinda's gaze. "Absolutely stunning."

Lucinda's eyes widened a little, but she said nothing.

"It took us forever to make Lucinda's hair just right," Emily said petulantly. "Then our carriage wheel broke on the way here—can you imagine?"

"Well, you are here now, so you may leave all your worries behind," James assured her, wishing to get both of the sisters into a more pleasant mood. "And"—he tapped Emily's nose gently, which drew out a smile—"you will be happy to know you haven't missed any of the dancing."

"Thank goodness!" Emily exclaimed. "I shall be able to dance away the evening with my betrothed after all!"

Beside her, Lucinda stiffened. Judging by her expression, she had no expectations of enjoying herself this evening. She was also steadfastly *not* looking at Wilson. James decided it was time to rectify that. "Mr. Wilson, I should like to introduce two of the most charming ladies of my acquaintance: Miss Lucinda Cardington and Miss Emily Cardington."

As they murmured the requisite niceties, Wilson scrutinized Lucinda with mild curiosity, sizing her up from head to foot. Certainly he could find nothing to dislike, James thought. True, she was beginning to redden a little as Wilson studied her, but even so she had never looked better.

"How odd that we've never met before," Emily declared. "Are you newly arrived in London, Mr. Wilson?"

"Indeed I am. I finished my studies at Cambridge last year and just completed a tour of France and Italy."

"How wonderful!" Lucinda said. "I should love to visit those countries someday."

Wilson shook his head. "For my part, I'm glad I'm home. If my tour showed me anything, it's that England is, and always will be, the greatest nation in the world."

He said this with such smugness that Lucinda frowned, drawing a crease between her eyebrows.

"Rule, Britannia!" James tossed out gaily, attempting to draw Wilson's attention away from Lucinda's darkening expression. He could guess what she was thinking: that it was a crime to dismiss two countries so rich in history and culture with a few offhand words.

"How astute," Lucinda said drily. "And what do you intend to do now that you are returned to this paragon of nations?"

"Do?" Wilson said, giving her a blank look. "Why, be a gentleman, of course. The usual pursuits."

"Is that what your studies at Cambridge qualified you for—the important occupation of being a gentleman?"

Now the edge in her tone was unmistakable. It was

also highly unusual. James had never seen her so forward in polite company, especially with someone she'd
just met. "You two have something in common," he
broke in quickly, hoping to smooth things over. Turning to Lucinda he explained, "Wilson has just joined the
London Photographic Society."

Unfortunately, this produced the opposite effect of what
James was hoping for. "You are not thinking of joining, I
trust," Wilson said to Lucinda in a disparaging tone.

Lucinda looked as though she'd been stung. "Why—
why shouldn't I?"

"The chemicals are dangerous and the procedure is
far too complicated. It's no pastime for a proper lady."

James recoiled at these words. Lucinda, who might
have reasonably been expected to do the same, instead
lifted her chin and went on the attack.

"I suppose you think a proper lady does little more
than make social calls or attend soirées," she said frost-
ily. "I'll have you know I have more important duties.
I spend many days at the Caring House school, helping
less fortunate ladies improve their lot in life."

"Admirable," Wilson said, in a tone that showed no
genuine interest. "What sort of ladies?"

"Prostitutes, actually."

She said the words distinctly, even lifting her voice
a little. James was pretty sure she did it on purpose,
just to nettle the man. It had the added effect of grabbing the attention of everyone within hearing—and there
were a good many. Dozens of people paused in mid-
conversation to turn and look in their direction.

"Former prostitutes, I should clarify," Lucinda continued, still speaking loud enough for those around them

to hear. "And a few who were on the verge of such a dire fate, faced with no other choice for survival, but whom we managed to rescue in the nick of time."

James was stunned by Lucinda's sudden boldness. She must have surprised herself as well, for he saw her eyelids flutter briefly, as though she couldn't believe her own actions. But then her fists clenched and she pulled herself up even taller. What had gotten into her? Had she changed her personality along with her gown?

No. She was simply displaying it to the public at large, along with her delicate collarbone—to which James's gaze was irresistibly drawn as her breathing became noticeably faster. He'd once jested that she ought to stand up for herself; he never expected her to take it this far. Now he was torn between the thrill of watching her shed her habitual reticence and dismay that she had chosen the worst possible time to do it. She was inviting public censure and sabotaging any chance she might have with Wilson, or any other potential suitor, for that matter. His worry increased as he realized this might even be her goal, to thwart her father's wishes in any way possible. Perhaps she really did prefer to remain unmarried. It would be an enormous pity if it were true, for Lucinda Cardington had more to offer than anyone here realized.

Suddenly the silence was replaced by a ripple of murmurs. James heard a woman declare in a nasty stage whisper, "She should know all about such women, what with all the nights she spends at Cremorne Gardens."

James tried to discern where that remark came from. He suspected the culprit was one of three ladies who had opened their fans and were staring over them at Lucinda with wide, shocked eyes.

"Scandalous," another voice agreed.

Wilson turned an appalled glare upon Lucinda. "How much time do you spend with such people?" he demanded. "What's all this about Cremorne Gardens?"

"Oh, listen, they've struck up a waltz," Emily broke in with forced brightness. "Let's dance." She took hold of Wilson's and Lucinda's arms and practically dragged them to the dance floor. James had no choice but to follow. At least it got them away from the knot of hostile onlookers.

"What are you doing?" Lucinda hissed into Emily's ear.

"Just remember what I told you, and you'll be fine," Emily fired back in the same tone.

"You cannot expect me to dance," Wilson protested, endeavoring to pull away from Emily's clutches. "This is most improper."

Emily turned on him. "Mr. Wilson, if you rudely abandon my sister here on the dance floor, you are no gentleman," she said vehemently. "If you truly value your honor and integrity, you will show your good breeding by dancing with her."

Wilson stared at her, seemingly caught off guard by the authority in her tone. James, too, found himself in awe that Emily could suddenly draw up such a commanding presence. *Both* Cardington sisters were showing new sides of themselves tonight.

Wilson did not speak for several moments, clearly weighing his choices. At last he said tersely, "Very well." He bowed stiffly to Lucinda and offered up his arms for the dance.

Lucinda looked about to refuse, but Emily gave her a shove in the small of her back, pushing her into Wilson's arms. Both Lucinda and Wilson took up their positions for the waltz as though they'd rather be touching a snake. They had not danced more than a few steps before it became apparent that Lucinda—a poor dancer in the best of circumstances—was not anywhere close to being in step. James watched them with growing dread, knowing there was no way this could end well. His husband-hunting business was poised to record its first colossal failure, and he had better start thinking now about how to pick up the pieces.

*

ONE-two-three, ONE-two-three…

It was no use. Lucinda stumbled as her feet refused to keep time with the measure. Nor could she give it the concentration required, for she was too busy marshaling her thoughts, trying to figure out what had just happened.

She'd been truly hurt by the comments she'd overheard from the other women. She'd mistakenly thought they understood what she was trying to accomplish at Caring House. Perhaps they had—once. Now, thanks to that one night at Cremorne, no one saw her as a woman doing Christian charitable works. She was perceived as some kind of strumpet who preferred the company of base people.

Well, perhaps she *did* prefer such company, Lucinda thought with a surge of defiance. At least they told you to your face what they were thinking. Here it was all whispers behind fans, just audible enough to convey disapprobation without having to own up to it personally. This was why so-called refined society always seemed to chafe at her soul. At least Mr. Wilson had not prevaricated about his opinion of her, which was the only tiny point in his favor.

Everyone would think she had deliberately sought to goad Mr. Wilson. But that was not the case at all. She had merely spoken freely and honestly about something that was vitally important to her. It was, perhaps, the first time she'd ever done so in such a public manner. But if the events of the past two weeks had shown her one thing, it was that she had to start speaking up. She could no longer afford not to. Any chance at future happiness depended on it. They were all trying to marry her off, but Mr. Wilson's pompous, condescending attitude had plainly shown he was not the man for her. She hoped it would go a long way toward confirming for her family what she knew too well already: there *was* no man for her.

ONE-two-three...

Mr. Wilson's hand gripped hers tightly, and the pressure of his other hand on her back was truly unsettling. After the second or third misstep he began practically pushing her around, as though willing her by sheer force to follow his lead. It seemed a perfect indicator of his personality. How could James have possibly thought this man would be a good match for her?

Despite being an experienced man of the world, James must retain a good bit of naïveté if he thought everyone shared his empathy toward those less fortunate. She would have to correct that misunderstanding, and give him a piece of her mind in the process. He was watching them right now, and Lucinda tried to send a look in his direction to show how angry she was, but this only had the effect of making her stumble and lose her step once more.

They stopped so abruptly that another couple ran right into them. Sending glares sharp as knives toward Lucinda, they gathered themselves and moved far away before resuming their dancing.

Mr. Wilson's grip tightened. "Shall we try again?"

Lucinda felt a blush of shame rising. She was out of her element, and furious for being pushed into a situation that made her look like such an incompetent fool. She could almost feel the sniggers of those around her. But she could not admit defeat. Gathering her courage, Lucinda nodded, and they began again.

ONE-two-three...

She had no trouble playing waltzes on the piano; why could she never dance to them? Why did she invariably lose all sense of the meter, along with her balance and coordination? In desperation, she decided to try Emily's method. She closed her eyes and forced herself to think about nothing except the music and the feel of her partner's lead.

Suddenly it was not the floor she felt under her shoes, but Mr. Wilson's foot. His face twisted in pain as he visibly suppressed a groan. He must have decided he'd had enough, for he pulled her away from the throng of dancers and said, "Perhaps you would care for some refreshment?"

It was the only dignified way out, and she was happy to take it. Surely once he had deposited her at the punch table in the company of her mother or some other matron, he would make his excuses and leave.

Except...he didn't. He secured glasses of punch for both of them, and then remained standing next to her as she drank. Was he still even remotely interested in her? Surely not. It was too revolting even to contemplate. And yet he kept...looking at her. Eyeing her up and down, from all angles. She could imagine his thoughts, weighing the possible benefits of acquiring an item versus the drawback of its flaws.

"I apologize for my clumsiness just now," Lucinda said, speaking mostly to fill the silence between them and to ward off the disturbing sensations from his scrutiny. "I'm not feeling my best this evening, and it is dreadfully hot in here."

Mr. Wilson's mouth widened into something that was probably intended to be a reassuring smile. "I understand. At times, a new or unexpected situation, such as meeting someone extraordinary, can be overwhelming to one's senses."

There was, of course, no polite response to that remark. Lucinda held her tongue and began to scan the area around them, hoping to see someone she knew, looking for any pretext to leave this overbearing man. At this point even her mother would provide a welcome excuse, but she was on the other side of the ballroom chatting with James and Emily. Lucinda sent an imploring look in their direction, which James met with a sympathetic smile. When he tried to break away, however, Lady Cardington took hold of his arm and kept prattling on. She probably thought she was generously giving Lucinda and Mr. Wilson an opportunity to get to know each other. Well, Lucinda decided, she was getting to know Mr. Wilson far better than she cared to.

Mr. Wilson emitted a small cough to regain her attention. "Miss Cardington, I believe we may have gotten off on the wrong foot."

Lucinda stared at him. Was this a cruel joke at her expense? She could not tell for sure; his expression seemed perfectly earnest.

"I would like to offer you a friendly word of advice. You will no doubt think me forward for speaking so candidly, as we have only just met. However, I don't believe in obfuscation." This was offered up with the air of an apology, although he looked more self-satisfied than sorry. "I suggest you consider spending less time with your charitable works and more time developing the skills required of a lady." Seeing she was about to protest, he held up a hand. "I believe that if you were to follow such a course of action, you would soon find yourself so much more at ease and content that you will wonder why you did not do it sooner."

Lucinda was nearly smothered by a wave of disgust. Why was everyone so interested in *improving* her? And why did they persist in couching it as counsel given for her own best interests? She could not resist demurely batting her eyelashes in an imitation of Emily. "It's such a daunting task, Mr. Wilson. Where do you suggest I begin?"

He smiled, too pleased with himself to register the sarcasm in her words. "I recommend you seek out the services of Monsieur le Beau. He is an excellent dancing master who has been able to help even the most tone-deaf and uncoordinated of ladies."

Lucinda's mouth dropped open. Mr. Wilson would probably take this unladylike response as further proof of her lack of refinement, but she didn't care. She was stupefied by the insult that he had tucked so deftly into his "advice."

He was once more studying her closely, his eyes narrowing. "I sense some hesitation on your part. I have concerns myself—I can't deny it. Shall we make an effort to meet in the middle? I'll overlook your past indiscretions if you will set yourself to following my advice. I am certain you will grow more comfortable in my presence as your confidence improves."

The room was more than close; it was suffocating. Lucinda was sure that whatever had been roiling inside Mount Vesuvius before it erupted over Pompeii could not equal what she was feeling right now.

James and her family were finally on their way over. Perhaps they might all like to discuss the ways they might groom Lucinda into someone worthy enough to marry this ideal man. Well, she would not stand for it. She was discovering that she could only be pushed so far before sheer survival instincts kicked in. "What a privilege it has been to meet you, Mr. Wilson. You have opened my eyes to a number of things in my life I must correct."

His eyes lit up with satisfaction and he placed a hand over his heart. "I am honored to have you receive my advice so willingly."

Lucinda worked to suppress the gagging feeling in her throat. "I do not say that. In fact, I will take up no more of your time, for I know I shall only disappoint your expectations. In accordance with my high station in life, I have tried very hard to lessen my concern for those who are poor and underprivileged. I find, to my chagrin, that I simply cannot do it. I regret to say I simply have no time to seek out Monsieur le Beau, for I do shamefully persist in spending my days trying to render help to those who desperately need it. Good evening to you, sir."

She turned, intending to stalk away proudly, held high, salvaging whatever dignity she had left. Instead, she ran headlong into the dowager duchess of Coventry, spilling the entire contents of her punch glass right down that venerable old lady's fine silk gown.

*

By the time James and the others reached the scene of the altercation, Lucinda had raced off in the direction of the ladies' retiring room. Her sister and mother hurried after her, as several ladies who'd been standing nearby tried to calm the irate dowager.

James caught up with Wilson just as he picked up his hat and began heading out the door. "Wilson, wait!" he called out. "What happened back there?"

Wilson turned, his face red with rage. "Didn't you see it? Everyone else in the ballroom did."

"Only from a distance. It looked like you and Lucinda were arguing, and then she turned and ran into the duchess."

"*We* were not arguing," he sniffed. "*She* was arguing with *me*. I have never in my life met such a rude, ill-bred, and headstrong woman."

James found it hard to imagine any of those adjectives applied to Lucinda. Except for perhaps *headstrong*, a wholly new quality which she was lately showing with increasing frequency. He followed as Wilson continued down the steps and signaled for his carriage to be brought forward. "I don't know what got into her," James insisted. "I've always found her to be quiet and pleasant. Did you say something to put her off?"

"Me?" Wilson replied indignantly. "Certainly not. I was only trying to help her. And what's all this about a school for fallen women? Why didn't you tell me about that?"

"I believe I did mention she was involved with charity work."

Wilson's brow furrowed. "It's one thing to contribute to charity, or even to visit schools for orphaned children. But to actually spend day after day with *prostitutes*? How could a well-bred young lady even think of such a thing? It's evident their low manners have rubbed off on her. Maybe even their morals too, to judge by what those women were saying."

"It's nothing but pure gossip and lies!" James said vehemently. "Lucinda is the most upright, God-fearing person I know."

"I can tell you that is certainly not how she presented herself tonight. All the money in England wouldn't persuade me to align myself with such a woman." Wilson got up into his carriage. "Good night."

As the carriage pulled away, James just stood there, berating himself for having even considered Wilson to be a viable candidate for Lucinda. He could not possibly have shown worse judgment, and if he were honest with himself he owed Lucinda an apology.

"What a miserable night this has been," said a voice behind him.

James turned to see Lord Cardington. The old man looked cross and confused. "I battled one setback after another to make it here this evening, only to have my daughter publicly humiliated. What happened? Did Wilson tell you?"

"Only that they did not get on well," James hedged, unwilling to cause the man any more grief.

"So I gathered from the duchess—in between shrieks about how her costly gown was ruined." Cardington pulled a handkerchief from his pocket and wiped his forehead with it. "So I suppose we may scratch Mr. Wilson off the list?"

"It appears that way, sir. But perhaps it's for the best." James was speaking truthfully. He knew Wilson could grate on people, but he had no idea Lucinda's reaction would be so violent. He could never live with himself if he thought he'd made Lucinda miserable just to keep his promise to get her married. He had to find her a husband she could love and respect. Problem was, he was fresh out of ideas.

"Well, I suppose I must go see about the ladies," Lord Cardington said with a heavy sigh. "Come to my house tomorrow, Simpson, and we'll discuss what's to be done next. The women will be out on their calls, so we'll be able to talk without interruption."

"Yes, sir," James said, with a sinking heart. "I'll be there."

Chapter 12

James sat in Lord Cardington's study, tapping his fingers along the arm of a leather armchair. The butler had informed him Lord Cardington was detained by business at the House of Lords but had sent word asking if James would wait, as he would be home shortly. James had been only too glad to sit here for a while. Having more time to think over his list would be helpful, since he had gotten nowhere with it last night. He'd been too busy worrying about Lucinda.

Gradually it dawned on him that faint sounds of music were coming from somewhere in the house. This surprised him, since Cardington had said none of the ladies would be home this afternoon. "Jennings, is that a piano I hear?" James asked, when the butler entered with a silver tray bearing brandy.

Jennings's face remained inscrutable as ever. "Yes, sir, I believe it is."

James picked up the proffered glass. "I thought the ladies were gone out on calls?"

"This is normally their day for it," the butler acknowledged.

"But clearly someone is here," James persisted. He was sure it was Lucinda. No one else in the family could play that well.

The butler looked distinctly uncomfortable. "That would be the elder Miss Cardington."

"Why did she not go out today—do you know?"

Again, Jennings hesitated. It was not right for a servant to indulge in gossip of any kind, and Jennings seemed determined to uphold that rule. Yet James was too intrigued to let the matter rest. "I suppose you've heard I'll be her brother-in-law soon."

"Indeed I have, sir, and I wish you joy."

"Thank you, Jennings. And since I am practically a member of the family, I'm sure it is proper for me to ask after Miss Cardington's health?"

At last he had hit upon the right tactic. Jennings said, "It's very kind of you to show concern, sir. I believe Miss Cardington is suffering from a headache."

So that was her excuse. Of course, after last night's fiasco, James could well believe it was true. He'd never seen anyone look so humiliated as she was, standing frozen in shock with punch splattered all over her and Lady Coventry, and dozens of people staring at them both with a kind of horrified delight. His heart went out to her, especially as he felt so terrible about introducing her to Wilson in the first place. Perhaps now would be a good time to speak to Lucinda privately and try to make amends.

Jennings withdrew, and James leaned back in his chair and took a sip of brandy. He wanted to allow the butler time to get down the hall so he would not see James making his way to the parlor. He was also enjoying the music, for Lucinda played wonderfully. It did seem implausible that a person with a headache would want to play the piano. Even when played well, surely loud music would only aggravate the pain rather than soothe it. James suspected she'd stayed home today in order to avoid facing other women, all of whom would offer either pity or barely disguised mockery. Who could blame Lucinda for not wanting to subject herself to that?

It was an odd feeling to know he was alone in the house with her. Except for a dozen or more servants. He began to reconsider his plan to go and speak to her. As he had pointed out to the butler, he was almost a member of the family. But the wedding was still months away, and in the meantime it would be a breach of etiquette for Lucinda to receive a gentleman alone. In any case, he reminded himself, Lord Cardington was due back anytime.

In the end, none of these considerations could sway him from his desire to speak to Lucinda, if only for a few minutes. He owed her that apology, and putting it off could only make things worse.

He set down his glass and stood up. Cautiously he opened the door and peered into the hallway. No one was about. He made his way to the parlor, easily drawn there by the strains of beautiful music. James did not know what piece Lucinda was playing, but he could tell she was putting her whole soul into it. The melody was soft and gentle, filled unmistakably with longing and heartache. For James, it was indisputable proof there was romance in Lucinda's soul—and it was both rich and profound.

He could sense it in the way her heart was pouring out through her fingers.

At the parlor door he paused, just listening. Strange, how the melody touched him. For the first time in his life, James could *feel* the passion in the music. He'd always been able to dance easily, moving smartly to the measure, but never before had music actually penetrated his soul. It suddenly put him in mind of his cousin Ria. They had grown up together, and James could remember so many times when she'd attempted to describe the deep connection she'd felt to music. He'd never been able to grasp it. Now he was beginning to understand what Ria had been trying to share with him all those years ago.

Quietly he opened the parlor door. Lucinda did not hear him; her attention was focused on the keys, which she caressed with long, delicate fingers. This was a piece she knew by heart, for there was no sheet music on the piano. She was striking each note as if her very life depended upon it. Her slender form seemed barely to occupy the stool as she swayed with the melody. He had seen her play before, but never like this.

The sight of her playing so passionately set off a round of dizzying sensations. Who was this woman? What depths of emotion was she keeping hidden from everyone around her? And how had he been stupid enough to miss it? James had always thought Emily's fuller figure was more appealing, but now as he saw Lucinda's slim waist, her elegant neck, and the way she leaned toward the piano like a lover, he realized she had a willowy beauty that everyone had too easily overlooked. Including him.

How could someone who obviously felt the music as

she did be so ungainly on the dance floor? James could not reconcile it. He could only watch in fascination as her fingers moved lithely over the keys. The song crested and crescendoed, then began a slow sweep downward toward an ending so hauntingly beautiful that James was left breathless, deeply moved.

Lucinda took a deep, shuddering breath as the final notes dissolved into silence. Her hands rested lightly on the keys, as though she were drawing strength or comfort from them. James drew a hand across his eyes, mostly to assure himself they were dry. As touched as he had been, it would not be right to reveal it. He had just witnessed a part of Lucinda that she never showed to others; she might feel in some way violated if James let on that he had seen it. He tiptoed backward out of sight, took several seconds to be sure he had regained his own composure, and then strode in noisily as though he had just arrived. "Why, hello, Lucinda," he said cheerily. "Was that you playing just now? It was wonderful!"

Lucinda turned so sharply on the stool that she nearly fell off. Somehow she managed to catch herself and rise to her feet. Hastily she wiped away a few tears, along with the wistful, faraway look that had so beautifully softened her features. Now there was only cold annoyance. "What are you doing here?"

The pain in her voice stabbed at his heart, but he did not think she would be helped by any show of pity. So he pasted on a teasing smile and answered, "I was drawn irresistibly by the music, just like Ulysses to the Sirens' call. I ask only that you do not dash my ship against the rocks."

She frowned. "I ought to do just that."

"You would no doubt be justified. But please, allow me to apologize first."

"Apologize?" She repeated the word stiffly.

"I was wrong to try to pair you with Wilson. You are too good for him."

Lucinda did not reply. Her look was still severe, but she was also trembling a little.

"I promise you that in the future, no matter what happens I will never try to force you into the company of such a man."

She took a deep breath, and James could see she was slowly regaining her composure. "Of such a *boor*, you mean."

He nodded and grinned. "Of such a *boring* boor."

"And conceited, and pretentious, and controlling, and—and—"

She sputtered to a stop, her fists clenched. But James was happier to see her angry than in anguish. "And, being a good Christian, you cannot complete that sentence," he supplied. "But don't think Wilson underestimates you. After all, he told me you were rude, ill-bred, and headstrong. If I were you, I should take that as the highest praise."

A gleam of triumph briefly lit her eyes, giving James hope that he was getting Lucinda past the hurt. But then she leveled a hard look at him. "Do you have any idea what I went through last night? The mortification?"

"I know you are angry and embarrassed, but I think you should try to see the events in a different light. You stood up for yourself, Lucinda, and for that you should feel very proud." James waited a moment for that to sink in before adding, "I'm sorry the dowager duchess got caught in the crossfire, but—" He shrugged. "I daresay a woman who has survived three husbands, a house fire, *and* highway robbery can recover from getting a bit of punch on her gown."

Lucinda's lips finally parted in the smallest fraction of a smile, although he could see it pained her to do so. "You are forever making jokes."

"Indeed I am." He winked. "I was born to speak all mirth and no matter."

He knew she would recognize the quote from *Much Ado About Nothing.* She did. With another tiny smile she said, "Without question you were born in a merry hour."

James put a hand to his heart. "No, sure, my mother cried." He pointed upward, as though toward the heavens. "But then 'twas a star danced, and under that was I born."

At last a spark of warmth began to ease the pain in her expression. James sensed that if he was ever to be forgiven for his part in having caused that pain, this might be the moment. "Do you want to know the real reason why I am so completely useless at doing anything of a serious nature?"

She took the bait, regarding him with curiosity. "Indeed I would."

James stepped back and opened his arms wide in a theatrical gesture. "Well then, I will tell you. Do you know what year I was born?"

"No, but I think I can figure it out. What age are you now?"

"I'll save you the trouble. I was born in 1816. The year without a summer."

Her brow crinkled. "The year without a summer?"

"It has been given that name because the weather

stayed unseasonably cold, even extending into summer." Using exaggerated gestures to punctuate his words, he intoned, "The seasons were out of course. It snowed in July. The crops failed. Great misery overtook much of Europe and North America. There were *dire* predictions that soon the sun would be *extinguished*, leaving the world in utter *darkness*."

She looked at him warily. "Are you telling me the truth?"

"Would I lie?" Seeing her mouth quirk into a wry smile he added hastily, "Wait—don't answer that. But have you ever read Lord Byron's poem 'Darkness'? It begins, 'I had a dream, which was not all a dream. The bright sun was extinguish'd, and the stars did wander darkling in the eternal space.'"

"I have read that poem! But I never knew its history."

She was engaged now, and James was glad to see it. Anything to get her mind off her troubles. "Byron wrote that poem in July 1816, the same month I was born. When I entered the world on the seventeenth of July, it was a bitter cold day. Frost covered the hard ground and an eerie gloom had settled everywhere. It affected my mother greatly. She was in her own sorrowful fog, despite the safe delivery of a son."

"I have heard that women sometimes go into a deep depression after giving birth."

"True, but I believe there were other causes. She was worried about my father's growing despair after the war. They must have felt their lives were as out of joint as the seasons, for nothing my father put his hand to seemed to work out. The weather returned to normal the following year, but my mother's melancholy remained. By the time

I was a young boy I realized my job in life was to coax smiles out of her. It wasn't long before I became a master at it."

He'd also become a master at hiding his own sorrows in the process, but this was not something he was ready to share. So he put his index fingers at either end of his mouth and drew it into a silly grin. "And now, my whole life's mission is to cheer up any and all distressed ladies. Yourself, for example."

Lucinda laughed. "I can believe that. It's hard to be sad about anything when you're around."

"You have hit upon it, me bonnie lass," James replied, choosing, for no particular reason, to speak in a broad Scottish brogue. "It has been my calling ever since to make people merry. Are ye feelin' better then?"

She nodded, her smile coming more easily now, whereupon James broke into a little jig. How pleasant she looked when her face was softened by laughter. All women were more appealing when they were smiling, and none more so than Lucinda. He paused to catch his breath, asking himself yet again the frustrating question that had been plaguing him ever since he'd taken up this mad task of getting Lucinda married: why was no one else ever allowed to see what a perfect companion she could be? She was intelligent and lively and kind, her gentleness delightfully seasoned with just a dash of dry wit.

She idly traced a finger along the top of the piano. "Do you know the Bible says, 'A merry heart doeth good like a medicine'?"

"Och," James said, returning to his Scottish brogue. "I'm in trouble, then. If the Right Honorable Geoffrey

Somerville hears I've actually done something godly, he'll be expecting more out of me. Then I'll be done for, for there's no way I could keep it up."

Lucinda shook her head. "I think you undervalue yourself."

James pointed a finger at her. "That, my bonnie lass, is the pot calling the kettle black."

Her smile wavered. "What do you mean?"

James dropped the brogue. "I heard you play just now. You *feel* the music. Every detail of it. The pitch, the tone, the melody—and whatever else music is made of. It's the most lovely and passionate playing I've ever heard."

Lucinda began to shake her head again, this time to deny the truth of what he was saying.

James stepped forward and took her hands, looking at her earnestly until she returned his gaze. "I've heard hundreds of performances, from concert pianists to debutantes at dinner parties. No one—no one—plays like you do."

Red began to tinge her cheeks. Gently she withdrew her hands from his. "Thank you," she whispered. "But you needn't feel obligated to compliment me."

"I speak from the heart! Not from obligation. Don't sell yourself short. Hearing you play just now does raise two important questions in my mind, though. The first is, why don't you play with that kind of feeling when you are performing for others?"

"Oh, I couldn't! They would think..." She faltered.

"What would they think?" James pressed.

"They would think me ridiculous." The words came out small and soft, as though she were ashamed to speak them.

"No. They would only admire you. Laud you to the skies, even."

She must have felt it would be fruitless to argue the point, for she merely said briskly, "And your other question?"

"I want to know why someone who feels and understands the music as you do can be so completely hopeless at dancing to it."

Lucinda flinched. "Tell me, do you always follow up a compliment with an insult?"

"I'm only trying to help you," James insisted. "I believe you could dance as beautifully as you play, but something is preventing you."

"You're wrong!" she said vehemently. And, as if unwittingly making her point, she took a step back and immediately tripped over the piano stool. She would have fallen to the floor if James had not dashed forward and caught her around the waist. Reaching instinctively for something to grab on to, she threw her arms around his neck. Carefully he lifted her up. He kept hold of her even after he had set her on her feet, savoring this opportunity to study her up close. The flecks of green and gold sprinkled in her hazel eyes seemed different each time he looked in them, as though her eyes never could settle on one color. He was also surprised to discover how soft she felt in spite of her slender frame. She was taller than her sister, and James marveled at how well she fit into his arms.

She began to wriggle, trying to get free. "I'm fine," she protested. "You may let me go."

"Easy," James said, releasing her but keeping his hands poised, as though he were soothing a skittish filly. As soon as there was a gap between them, the tension visibly released from her shoulders. And that was when

James realized why Lucinda could not dance. It hit him like a thunderbolt, although he ought to have known it all along. "It's your discomfort around men that does it!" he proclaimed.

She straightened her dress and reached up to check her hair. "Don't be ridiculous. I'm always around men. You know that."

"I don't mean discussing politics with old men in dusty libraries," James countered. "I mean you become embarrassed if you are in personal contact with someone. When it becomes a question of male and female."

"You don't know what you are talking about—"

James cut her off by taking hold of her again, wrapping an arm around her waist and drawing her close. "I think I do," he said in her ear. "What happens to you when a young man holds you like this?" He was shamelessly taking advantage, but he couldn't seem to resist this urge to hold her. It was amazing, really, how good it felt.

He expected her to draw away again, and no doubt she should have. But she didn't. In fact she grew very still, although her breathing quickened as her gaze locked on his. She lifted an eyebrow. "Young?" she repeated, with an unexpected burst of that dry wit he was beginning to adore.

"Don't try to change the subject!" he commanded with a laugh. "I'm not so old as that. More important, I'm young in all the ways that count." Her eyes widened and she tried to step back, but James held her tight. "You can do this, Lucinda. You have nothing to fear from a man on the dance floor. The vast majority of us don't even bite."

"Don't they?"

"You are trying to joke your way out of this. Although I heartily approve of the tactic, I shall not allow you to do it." He adjusted one hand on the small of her back, and lifted her left hand, as though they were preparing to waltz. "Now, let's begin. I want you to close your eyes and hum a waltz."

"Closing my eyes will only make things worse, I assure you."

"All right then, leave them open. But start humming. Here, I'll help you." He launched into his favorite waltz. After a brief hesitation, Lucinda joined in. She was standing as stiff as a rail in his arms, but the moment she began to hum a tune, he felt her soften. The music was having its effect. "That's right. Just forget I am even here," he urged.

"Well, that's rather difficult—"

James put a finger to her lips. "Just do it," he commanded softly. She nodded, although he could see doubt in her eyes. "*Enjoy* the music, Lucinda," he urged. "Feel it, in your bones, the way you did earlier when you played the piano." He reached again for her hand, feeling a burst of pleasure as it slipped easily into his. She wanted to do this! She was going to trust him to take her into uncharted waters. Whatever happened, James was determined not to fail her. He began to rock back and forth, starting with barely any movement at all, then gradually increasing, gently coaxing Lucinda into movement. "That's it," he murmured, as she tentatively followed his lead.

She kept her eyes fixed on his as they traced a small circle in the center of the room. Although he caught the occasional flicker of uncertainty there, it seemed as though she was willing herself to trust him. Her lips parted slightly, her front teeth briefly tugging at her bottom lip in an artless gesture that was undeniably appealing.

They were moving easily now, but James hardly

noticed. He was entirely caught up in the way she was watching him. In fact, they must have circled the room several times before James realized that neither of them was humming anymore. There was only the gentle swish of her gown and the soft tread of their feet upon the floor. They were moving in perfect harmony, hearing precisely the same music in their heads.

Lucinda's eyes flickered and her head tilted back slightly. She appeared completely transported by the dance. Her mouth opened to a smile and a small sigh escaped her. And that's when a thought crossed James's mind that was more dangerous than any yet: *Lucinda is beautiful*. Not just pleasant, or passingly pretty. From her soul to her soft brown hair, inside and out, she was the most beautiful woman he had ever known. All those photographic chemicals must have addled his brain after all, for it was now filled with all sorts of thoughts about his future wife's sister that any sensible man would never allow to lodge there.

He stopped. Their sudden lack of movement brought Lucinda's eyes wide open again in surprise. As her gaze shot around the room, assessing where they were, James realized they had drifted very far indeed from the point where they had begun.

"We were dancing, weren't we?" she said in wonder.

"Yes," he replied, though he could barely trust himself to speak. "We were." Reluctantly he removed his hand from the small of her back, although he could not yet bring himself to let go of her hand.

"Thank you," she said softly. "I don't know why I can't dance like that with other men. With you it was... easy."

Lucinda was always so truthful, so sincere, that it pained him to see how she was looking at him. He was in no way deserving of her trust, and yet she had given it to him. "Perhaps it was because you were listening to the music inside you. Inside here." He lightly placed a forefinger just above her heart. It was edging on indecent to do so, but she didn't object. She just kept looking at him, and beneath his hand he could feel her heart pounding wildly.

Around them, the stillness seemed to settle, even as specks of dust floated in the sunshine coming through the window. James could not seem to move. He really should not be so intensely attuned to the allure she did not even realize she presented. Without question he should not be touching her at all, let alone in a private room. And yet she remained tantalizingly close. She must be, as he was, either unable or unwilling to move away. One hand remained in his, cool and soft. Its light, gentle touch sent powerful sensations through him. They were both watching each other intently, and he felt, right down to his core, the moment their gazes dropped to each other's lips. What kind of a man was he, to be giving serious consideration to such a clearly wrong action? He was either a cad or an idiot. Most probably he was a good mixture of both, because slowly, deliberately, no longer caring to resist, he closed the distance between them and kissed her.

A thrill shot through him the moment their lips touched. He felt her startled reaction too, but she did not pull away. She leaned into him, her motion signaling she wanted this as much as he did. He settled in for a proper kiss and discovered she was...delicious. She must have the habit, as many did, of chewing on a clove for fresh breath. The sharp, delectable tang lured him in for more, and he deepened the kiss, urging her to open to him. She did so, tentatively at first, but then with more confidence, just as she had followed his lead when dancing. How could anyone think this woman was not kissable? It was sheer bliss. Never had the taste of a woman's lips, the feel of her in his arms, moved him so powerfully. He held her tightly, wanting this moment never to end.

Lucinda was the first to come to her senses. Her hands came up to his chest, and he could sense her grabbing for the sanity they had both been willing to throw aside. She pushed him away, breathing heavily. "Oh, my Lord, what have we done?"

She spoke in a low hiss, casting a worried glance at the parlor door. James turned sharply to follow her gaze. The door was open, and anyone in the house might easily have seen or heard them. James went quickly to the doorway and was relieved to see the hall was empty. If the Cardingtons had seen that kiss, they likely have murdered him then and there. What had he been thinking? Clearly, he hadn't been.

He turned back to Lucinda, steeling himself, expecting her to begin hurling indignant invectives, which she had every right to do. But she seemed too horrified to speak. It had probably been her first kiss, James realized. How on earth was she supposed to react? He saw her fighting to catch her breath, to calm the confusion that must be coursing through her, and felt more of a cad than ever.

He held out his hands in placating fashion. "Lucinda, please forgive me. I don't know what came over me. Something about the moment, the dancing—"

"No!" she cried. "Don't try to explain it away. There is no excuse for what we did, and I am so ashamed." She raised her hands to her cheeks, which were bright red. "If my sister knew of this, it would break her heart. She loves you, you know. In her own flighty, silly way, she truly loves you. You cannot betray her!"

Her voice broke as she tried to stifle a sob, and the sound of it piled even more guilt on top of what James was already feeling. When he became engaged to Emily, even given the unfair circumstances, he swore to himself he'd be faithful to her. But could he truly uphold that vow if he could be so easily distracted by another woman? And not just any woman, but her sister. Even now, with her so distraught and his own guilt rising, he could not deny that the kiss they had just shared had been more wonderful than any he could remember.

James had always thought his mother's melancholy had driven his father to seek the company of other women. But what if she had been miserable *because* he had gone after other women? What if James turned out to be no different? Would sweet little Emily live in misery all her days because of him?

His fists clenched as frustration overtook him. He had to get hold of himself. His course was set, and the sooner this episode was put behind them—if indeed, it ever could be—the better. "I will be a good husband to her. I swear it." He tried to put conviction into those words, yet they sounded hollow.

"You must keep that promise," Lucinda said. It sounded more like a desperate plea than a command.

Once more the room settled into silence, but this time there was nothing warm or magical about it. There was only the chill of disappointment and regret. Everything James had been forced to strive for during these past few weeks now hung precariously in the balance.

"I think you should leave now," Lucinda said at last. "Papa will no doubt look for you in his study when he comes home. Good day."

It was a dismissal, as cool and calm as she could make it. She was striving for normality. Trying to sound as though she'd been unmoved by that kiss, when James knew beyond a doubt that nothing was further from the truth. She was pulling back into her protective shell. He'd drawn her out for a few precious moments, but in doing so he had only hurt her deeply. There could be no way his continued presence here could make it better, so he nodded and turned away.

When he reached the doorway he hesitated and looked back. Lucinda was standing by the window, staring intently out—probably so she wouldn't have to watch him leave. Her hand reached up and touched her lips, as if remembering. The look on her face was utterly forlorn.

He wanted to do something, say *anything* that might make things better. But it was clear that words would accomplish nothing. It was time for him to leave, to set his own life in order, to show her by his future actions that he could be an honorable man.

Chapter 13

Lucinda sat in the small garden and stared, unmoving, at the orderly row of blooms and shrubs lining the gravel walkways. They exuded a peacefulness which she had hoped might ease her unsettled heart. She'd been there for an hour or more, watching the sun's rays gradually light the rose bushes along the far wall. It was a quiet morning, and unusually cool for summer. The scent of flowers mingled comfortably with the aroma of baking bread wafting out from the kitchen.

Inside the house, the servants would be preparing breakfast and setting the house in order for the day, bustling quietly about their assigned tasks. But here in the garden everything was still, unmoving but for the gentle swaying of the leaves and the flights of a few birds. It was the perfect place to think.

For the past twenty-four hours she'd been reliving that dance with James—and the alarmingly passionate kiss that had followed. He'd been right about the reason for her awkwardness on the dance floor. Lucinda had never fully realized or admitted it to herself before yesterday, but her intense embarrassment around men—bordering on fear, really—had literally been a stumbling block for her. So why had it been so easy to dance with James? Her initial discomfort had evaporated within seconds of being in his arms. For once she had danced without tripping over her own feet. He'd made her feel confident and beautiful.

And desirable. Never had she imagined that a kiss could be so wonderful, so wholly captivating. His kiss had ignited a fire within her so intense it burned there still. This was deeply troubling. How could a man kiss her like that when he was engaged to someone else?

Perhaps it was because James wasn't in love with Emily. Lucinda never believed he was. She knew he'd been trapped into the engagement. James was an inveterate ladies' man; he'd never made a secret of it. What had passed between her and James had felt at the time like a very special connection. But she had, admittedly, no experience in such matters, whereas James had flirted with countless women. Lucinda was just one more on a very long list.

Surely this could only bode ill for Emily. Although he'd sworn to be a good husband to her, how could he be, if he still seized an opportunity to kiss another woman?

Lucinda tugged at the branch of a nearby rosebush, bringing one of the blossoms close enough to inhale its scent deeply. She had to forget that kiss, of course. But how could a person forget such a thing? She must summon up everything she knew about James to convince her it had meant nothing to him. Perhaps in that way she might be able to erase the memory of the one and only time a man had made her feel like a woman to be desired...

"I beg your pardon, Miss Cardington."

Startled, Lucinda abruptly let go of the rosebush. A shower of petals fell as the branch snapped back into place. She turned to see Peter, the footman who always accompanied her on her trips to the school. He tipped his head deferentially.

Brushing away the petals that had fallen in her lap, Lucinda stood up and briskly smoothed her skirts. She did this primarily to snatch a few more seconds to collect herself, hoping the footman had not caught the gleam of a tear in her eye. She cleared her throat. "Yes, Peter, what is it?"

"Mr. Jennings is making up a list of work assignments, and he asked me whether I would be staying at the house today or accompanying you on errands."

"Why did he ask? Does he have work for you to do?"

"Mr. Jennings never runs out of work for us footmen to do," Peter said with a hint of a grin. "But I reminded him as how her ladyship strictly commanded that my duties to you come first. And I was sure you'd want to go out, as it is your usual day to give lessons at the school."

"Actually, I—"

She paused. In truth, she had not planned to go out. After the sinful thing she had done, her heart would fail her if she were to look upon the faces of those women who trusted her integrity and virtue. The newspaper had accused her unjustly after the Cremorne Garden affair, and that had been scandal enough; what would have happened if anyone had seen her kissing her sister's fiancé? It was that very thought that was keeping her stomach tied up in knots. She hadn't felt this kind of queasy unearthliness since the day she was presented at court and made herself sick with worry that she'd trip in front of the Queen. That blunder might have been reparable, but what had happened yesterday was not.

"It is Wednesday, after all," Peter added unnecessarily, perhaps to fill the void left by Lucinda's silence. "You always go to the school on Wednesdays."

He seemed almost to be entreating her to go. The hopefulness in his voice was so unmistakable that it finally began to penetrate the fog of Lucinda's misery. She had to wonder what mundane chore Mr. Jennings had been planning for him if he was so keen to get away. It must be something like polishing the silver or assisting with inventory.

On the other hand, this show of enthusiasm from her footman might actually be genuine. His attitude had changed drastically since the day he'd first been assigned to go with her on these trips. Although he'd been a dutiful servant and never complained, Lucinda was sure he'd initially thought it beneath him to spend days in the rough, dirty parts of town instead of wearing his fine livery and serving the refined guests that visited the Cardington home.

Even so, Lucinda was aware that having him escort her often left the staff feeling short-handed. "Are you sure Mr. Jennings can do without you today?"

"Oh, yes, miss," Peter said with confidence. "He's got Tim and Johnny, and there's no formal luncheon planned, so they won't need me to serve."

He was so earnestly eager that it lifted Lucinda's heart a little. "Why, Peter, I do believe you enjoy going to the school now."

"Indeed I do, miss," he said with a smile. "It's such an admirable thing you're doing, helping those ladies to a better life. When I think how low and miserable they was, and what outcasts they was before your kindness lifted 'em up, why I couldn't be prouder."

Peter's words brought a tiny lump to Lucinda's

throat. He was right; her works at the school were honorable. Yesterday's terrible misstep did not change that fact. If she had taught her students that the sins of the past could be forgiven and that with God every day was a new beginning, then she ought to believe it about herself as well. She plucked a rose petal from her sleeve. "All right, Peter. I believe I shall go to the school today."

Although a servant was not supposed to show strong emotions, Peter did not even attempt to hide his joy. "Very good, miss. I'll just go and tell Mr. Jennings, and I'll be ready when you call for me."

He strode off rapidly, nearly bouncing up and down with a zeal that Lucinda found infectious. She allowed herself a tiny smile. Yes, it would be far better to put her energy into helping others rather than to brood over herself. It would not solve all her problems, for her heart was still in an upheaval, and she worried about what lay ahead. But the weight of her troubles lessened as she remembered what those women at the school had overcome. God had helped them; surely He would help her. *Charity covereth a multitude of sins. Charity never faileth.*

I have been entreating the Lord's forgiveness all morning, she thought, *when the Bible says plainly that if we confess our sins, he is faithful and just to forgive us.*

Her own step was a little lighter on the stairs as she went up to change into a gown more suitable for going out.

*

"James, are you listening?" Emily paused on the path and pouted up at him. "I don't think you've heard a word I've been saying."

"Of course I'm listening, my darling," James assured

her. "The, ah…" What had she been talking about, anyway? He fought to bring his attention back to the woman beside him. This outing to Hyde Park had become a daily ritual, and he had been doing his best to make the usual small talk. Today, however, his confusion over what had happened with Lucinda made him unnaturally tongue-tied. Having his future mother-in-law trailing along behind, out of earshot but not out of eyesight, was another novelty that added to his discomfort. His distraction must have been apparent, even to someone as self-absorbed as Emily. James decided to take the route that always worked. "The truth is, how can I think about anything when you look so luscious in that frock? And is that a new bonnet?"

"James, you sweet-talking fraud," Emily chided, although she beamed with delight. Vain creature that she was, she always accepted compliments of any kind. "I was saying that even though the wedding is some months away, it isn't too soon to begin planning the details of our wedding feast."

Right. The *wedding feast.* Which would be followed by the *marriage famine* unless they got Lucinda married. "I agree this is of the utmost importance," he said, trying to sound casual although he thought the pressure on his heart would crush it. "However, shouldn't we also consider what we shall do about Lucinda?"

Emily's pout returned. "Everything has been about *her.* It ought to be about *me*—about *us.* We're the ones getting married, after all."

"Right you are, my love," James said soothingly. "However, the sooner we can get Lucinda engaged, the sooner we can concentrate on us."

Lord knows I need to, he added to himself. Once

Lucinda was securely set on another man's arm, perhaps then he would be able to forget what had happened between them. No, he thought to himself with chagrin, he could never forget it. Who could forget a kiss that was so powerful in its pure sincerity? For the hundredth time he reminded himself sternly to keep his mind focused on Emily. She was to be his wife, after all. He was duty-bound to give her his love and attention. Even if she did behave like a spoiled child sometimes.

"But how are we to get Lucinda engaged?" Emily whined. "I believe she deliberately tries to scare off any man who comes near her. Her actions toward Mr. Wilson are clear proof of that. I believe she detests men."

James thought once more of the way Lucinda had returned his embrace with such innocent fervor, how natural she had felt in his arms, and what her body pressed against his had done to him. He swallowed hard. "I can assure you she does not detest men." His words came out in a rasp, and he was thankful Emily could not perceive the wry conviction behind them. If Lucinda had responded to James that way, surely there must be other men who might also garner such a reaction? The thought did not exactly fill him with delight, but he clung to it anyway. "I will find her a suitor, I promise you. I am not at the end of that list yet." In truth, he was. He had not been able to persuade any of the other men on the list to even give Lucinda a chance. But he could not admit this to Emily or her parents.

"Lady Thornborough sent me a present yesterday," Emily announced.

"Did she?" he said with genuine surprise. "How kind of her. What was it?"

"It was a book." Emily pulled a face. "A copy of *Mrs. Beeton's Book of Household Management*. Do you think she's trying to tell me something?"

James couldn't help but be amused at his great-aunt's brutal honesty. "Clearly she wants to ensure you are prepared to take on your duties as a wife. Have you begun reading it?"

Emily wrinkled her nose. "Such dry, dull stuff."

"It is important, though. You will need a firm grasp of those things once we are married."

"But that is such a long way off."

"It didn't seem so far away when you were discussing the wedding breakfast." This was true, but it was not something James should have pointed out if he wished to keep Emily in good spirits. Seeing her expression turning sour again, he lifted her chin gently and said, "Never mind that now. We shall discuss everything in due time. I promise we shall make plans for a wedding feast so grand it will rival the Queen's."

"Oh, James!" Emily said with a giggle.

It bothered James that his fiancée had to be coddled like a child. It put him in the distasteful position of being the *adult*, including all the serious-mindedness that went with the job. It was something he had carefully avoided for years, and now he was paying dearly for it. He pulled out his watch to check the time. "And now, my dearest, we really should be getting back. It's nearly half past four, and I can bet your poor mama is desperate for tea."

Emily didn't even spare her mother a glance. "If she's tired it's her own fault, since she's so adamant about following us everywhere. Can't we stay out a bit longer?"

"No," James said firmly. "I must go. Have patience, my love. I will see you again on Saturday evening."

"Not until Saturday?" Emily protested.

"Time speeds on wings until we shall meet again," James promised. "In the meantime, I will go and have a chat with the man I believe will be an excellent candidate for Lucinda."

"You've found someone?" Emily said hopefully. "Who is it?"

"It's a surprise," James said, because he had no idea who it was. But he had three days to come up with someone. Surely in all of London he could manage that.

Emily tugged him forward, drawing him behind one of the larger bushes in the curve of the path. "Mama can't see us now," she whispered, taking hold of his coat lapel and pulling him closer, bringing her lips within an inch of his. "Kiss me quick, before she catches up to us."

Her mouth was as full and sweet-looking as ever, yet James found it not nearly as tempting as it had once been. He granted her request, but kept the kiss neat and perfunctory. He felt like a despicable rogue as he realized the memory of his kiss with Lucinda was still foremost in his mind.

"What was that?" Emily said crossly. "That was no kiss."

"We must maintain propriety," James said. He stepped back in order to put a more honorable distance between them, and then brought her hands up to give them a chaste kiss. "Soon, my dear, we shall be able to give our love free rein. But not today."

She gave him a sultry smile and leaned forward, placing her cheek against his. "I am really looking forward to that day," she whispered.

"Why you little minx," James responded playfully. But he frowned to himself as he led Emily back to the path.

On those rare occasions when he had thought about marriage, James certainly never envisioned having a foolish young woman like this as his bride. He had long ago made up his mind that when he did marry he would fully carry out his duties as a husband—far better than his own father had ever done. But one thing he had not counted on was having a wife who might never be mature enough to understand and carry out her responsibilities as well.

There was no doubt that under the circumstances he was doing the right thing. But his dread over the impending marriage grew with each passing day. At times it felt like these new responsibilities were going to drain every ounce of *joie de vivre* he had left.

*

Once he'd returned to the welcome solace of his club, James brooded for well over an hour in his favorite chair. There was no way around it; he still had to find a husband for Lucinda. Just at the moment this task was, for more reasons than he could catalogue, the very last thing on earth he wanted to do.

He'd been so caught up in his thoughts he hadn't even realized the chair at the opposite end of the room—the one normally occupied by Daniel Hibbitt—was empty. He was made aware of it with a jolt when he heard a door at the far end of the hall slam shut and Hibbitt's gruff shout to the attendant to bring him some brandy. "A bottle of it!" he commanded, and came stomping into the room with more noise than an army of Hessians.

He dropped into his usual chair, and without a word he opened his newspaper and promptly disappeared behind it. Ignoring James was normal for Hibbitt, but his highly agitated manner was not. It was unlike him to cause a commotion. Now, as the pages of his newspaper snapped angrily, it was clear something was amiss.

"Is something the matter, Hibbitt?" James inquired.

"Why can't I be left alone?" grumbled the voice from behind the newspaper.

Assuming this barb was aimed at him, James shrugged and prepared to say no more. But then Hibbitt lowered the paper and said, "Why can't she just leave me alone? All I want is peace and quiet, but I'll never get it so long as my mother is living."

Now James understood. Hibbitt must have just returned from a trip to the country to visit his parents. He was always out of sorts when he came back from these visits, although today he was in a fouler mood than usual. Apparently this was due to something his mother had done, which at this point in his life James found completely unsurprising. "Women do have a tendency to interfere with perfectly laid plans," he agreed. It was a normal sort of quip for him, but today it reflected a hard truth.

The attendant bustled into the room and set down a decanter and a glass on the table next to Hibbitt's chair. Tossing the paper aside, Hibbitt reached for the brandy and poured himself a glass. Seeing the empty glass next to James's chair, he brandished the decanter to indicate an offer. This was a rare act of generosity on his part— another signal to James that something was wrong. James crossed the room and took the chair next to Hibbitt as the man leaned forward to fill his glass.

"I try to tell her I'm perfectly content," Hibbitt said, speaking in a low growl as if talking to himself. "But she won't listen to reason. She goes on and on about how the long and illustrious Hibbitt family lineage is teetering on the brink of the abyss and it's all my fault and why am I determined to bring her such misery." He paused just long enough to drain his glass in one gulp. "It's emotional blackmail, that's what it is."

James had never heard so many words coming from the club's hermit at one time. It was enough to make him forget his own problems for a moment and stare at Hibbitt in fascination. In truth, he knew little about the man, other than that his family lived near London and Hibbitt was heir to his father's baronetcy. "Your mother's concerned about your family lineage? How so?"

"How do you think?" Hibbitt returned. "I'm supposed to get married and begin producing sons immediately. I see no need to hurry—after all, my father is still hale and hearty, and I have no intention of filling a grave anytime soon. Yet my mother is certain the Hibbitt family tree is already as good as extinct."

"She wants you to get married? To whom?" So far as James could tell, Hibbitt had no interest at all in the gentler sex. The man was gruff and terse and had few social graces. If he wasn't in his chair reading, he was over at the headquarters of the Royal Scientific Society. James had no idea what went on over there, but he imagined the members spent their time conducting all manner of experiments and then presenting dry research papers to one another. The man was positively made for bachelorhood.

"That's the problem!" Hibbitt moaned. "I've got to find someone."

Hearing this, James began to consider Hibbitt's dilemma with more than mere sympathy. Had the answer to his predicament been in front of him all along?

James wasn't about to leap to any conclusions. All his efforts so far had only brought Lucinda embarrassment and heartache. He was determined to consider any future actions very carefully in order to keep from causing her any more pain. That woman deserved the best, and he was going to do everything in his power to get it for her.

He took a moment to study Hibbitt closely. Before today, James would have thought him too old to take a young wife. His face had furrows, and there were splashes of gray on the jet-black hair at his temples. But now he realized the furrows in Hibbitt's face could be attributed to his dour expression rather than to age. "How old are you, Hibbitt?"

Hibbitt frowned, deepening the furrows. "Just had my thirty-third birthday. That's what brought on this latest tempest from Lady Augusta Hibbitt."

"Why, you are younger than I am," James said in surprise. "I'd never have guessed it."

"Because of the gray hair, do you mean?" Hibbitt answered, tapping one of his temples. "You may thank my dear mother for that." He began to speak in a high-pitched voice that was no doubt intended to imitate and mock his mother. "You're middle-aged, now Daniel! You must get married soon, or else you'll be too old and then *no one* will marry you! And even if they did, you'll never manage to have any children!" Hibbitt slammed his glass down on the table, then eyed James frankly. "I ask you, Simpson—speaking man-to-man, that is—how does one assure one's own mother that one's essential parts are still in perfect working order?"

James laughed outright. "Hibbitt, you old devil. I never knew you had it in you."

A glint appeared in Hibbitt's eye. "I'm discreet, Simpson. Not oblivious."

"I see," said James, marveling. Clearly there was more to this man than he'd realized. "Discreet in what way, exactly?"

Hibbitt leaned back in his chair and sighed. "There was an opera singer. I will not tell you her name, for as I said, I am discreet. She's very talented. That idiot of an opera manager keeps her relegated to the chorus, but she is capable of far more. I was so impressed with her that I made her acquaintance one night after a performance. For over a year she was most amenable to receiving my attentions."

James listened in fascination. Now that Hibbitt had actually begun to converse, it seemed he had rather a lot to say. It was like a dam had broken.

"Several months ago she caught the eye of a certain earl," Hibbitt continued. "Naturally, she decided he would make a better patron. Certainly a loftier one." He shrugged. "So that was that."

"Hibbitt, I am in utter amazement," James said, still trying to assimilate this information. Now that he thought about it, he realized Hibbitt was indeed a regular at the opera. And yet James had never seen him socializing with any of the well-to-do patrons. He always arrived at the last minute, sat alone in his box, and looked as though he was actually paying attention to the performance. He always left immediately after the curtain fell—which James now realized was because he had gone to meet his ladylove, probably in some out-of-the-way restaurant. Discreet, indeed. "You don't seem too torn up over the affair," James observed.

Hibbitt shrugged again. "She's happy, and perhaps

the earl can use his influence to get her the better roles she deserves. And now it keeps me from the messy business of having to break off our liaison. I could not have married her—that would have killed my mother for sure." Hibbitt's expression, which had lightened a little in remembrance of his former flame, now turned morose again. "Which actually brings me back to my current problem. Today my mother told me she's dying."

"I'm sorry to hear it," James said earnestly. "It's no easy thing to lose one's mother, under any circumstances."

"Bah," Hibbitt said with a wave of his hand. "I don't believe her for an instant. But what am I to do? She's got everyone else believing her ruse, including my father, and now she says her dying wish is to see me properly married."

"Are you sure it is a ruse?"

Hibbitt scowled. "She'll outlive us all."

"I see." James considered this. "So that is what you meant by 'emotional blackmail.'"

"Precisely." He ran a hand through his hair in frustration. "I'll be forced to give in, of course. I can't exactly accuse her of lying about such a thing."

"Marriage might not be so bad," James said. "There are advantages."

Hibbitt gave a disbelieving grunt. "You would say that, since you're heading that way yourself."

"You know about my engagement?"

Hibbitt pointed toward the newspaper. "I read all about it. Big wedding next May. How they got you in their trap, I don't know." He lifted a finger as though remembering something. "Oh, wait, I do know." He grinned, although for a man unused to smiling it came out as more of a twisted grimace. "Once it got in the papers that they'd caught you at Cremorne with the Cardington sisters, I figured you were done for."

"But I am happy about it," James insisted, trying to look as though he were. "Tell me, Hibbitt, if you had to—that is, if you were to seriously consider getting married—what kind of wife would you be looking for? Under ideal circumstances, I mean."

Hibbitt frowned and poured himself another drink. "All I want is someone who'll leave me in peace. But I suppose that's too much to ask."

James leaned forward in his chair. "Listen, Daniel. Can I call you Daniel?"

Hibbitt shrugged. "One name works as well as another."

"As you know, I'm engaged to Emily. But her father is anxious to get her sister Lucinda settled also."

"The plain one?"

James flinched. Now that he'd seen all the ways in which Lucinda was in fact quite beautiful, it pained him to think others still thought disparagingly of her. "You've seen her?"

Again the shrug. "At the opera. Second box, stage left."

"That's right. I've sat with them several times, and I can tell you they enjoy the opera immensely, just as you do."

Another grunt showed Daniel didn't believe this for an instant. "Nobody cares about the opera. It's the most beautiful music in the world, but everyone treats it like so much background noise. They are more interested in showing off their finery to everyone else."

"That is certainly the case for most people," James conceded. "But Lucinda is different. I've seen how she hangs on every note." That wasn't exactly true; during the performances James had spent more time whispering with Emily than observing Lucinda's actions. But from what he knew of Lucinda, it was a pretty good guess. "She cares nothing for all that see-and-be-seen nonsense."

"How novel," Daniel said dryly. But James could see his interest was increasing.

"Furthermore, she's talented in her own right. She plays the piano beautifully."

"Really?" His eyes narrowed. "Can she sing? There's nothing worse than a woman who is even slightly off-key."

"She sings like a lark," James assured him. Remembering Daniel's involvement with the Royal Scientific Society he added, "She is also well read and prefers to discuss science or literature rather than fashions or the latest gossip."

Daniel still looked unconvinced. "I don't know. After all, she's not much to look at, is she?"

So they were back to that. In Daniel's eyes, Lucinda would pale in comparison to a beautiful opera singer. How easy it was to judge by outward appearances. James had been guilty of it too, and now it haunted him. "She is a perfectly lovely woman," James insisted. "She has a quick mind and an engaging sense of humor. She's honest and kind. Conscientious, too. She'll keep your house well."

"You seem awfully enamored of her," Daniel observed. "I wonder you didn't get engaged to her yourself."

Although Daniel had spoken in jest, the comment hit James like a blow to the gut. If he'd had two ounces of common sense, he would have begun courting Lucinda long ago. Perhaps they might even have been engaged by now. Then this entire mess with Emily would never have happened. He would not be trying to find a suitor for Lucinda when now he would gladly fill that role himself.

But that was all water under a very slippery, very dangerous bridge. One that James had no choice but to cross. He sat back and eyed Daniel as though he were considering a new thought. Purposefully keeping his tone light, he said, "Don't think marriage to Lucinda hasn't crossed my mind. But I'm not good enough for her." That was a solid piece of truth, James reflected sadly. "But Daniel, now that I think it over, perhaps you are not the right person for Lucinda either."

"What?" Daniel's bushy eyebrows shot up. "Why not?"

"Lucinda is the epitome of kindness, and yet there are times when she can be brutally honest. She has no tolerance for pompous, vain, or self-important people."

Daniel looked offended. "And you think I am such a man?"

"Not at all," James said appeasingly. "However, as a future baronet you do have a certain place in society to uphold. I'd hate for you to put that at risk; for you see, Lucinda has a number of interests, including heavy involvement in charity work, that some people might object to."

Now Daniel looked confused. "Why would they object to charity work?"

Now was the time for James to test Daniel's real suitability. If the man objected to Lucinda's school, James would not even consider introducing them. He would not allow Lucinda to be hurt that way again. "She spends a lot of time at a place called Caring House. It's a school and a home for women who are trying to better their lives."

Daniel shrugged. "Sounds admirable."

"It's a home for *fallen* women."

"Prostitutes?" Daniel's eyes widened, but it seemed more from interest than shock.

James nodded. "There are some of the better society folk who find her daily contact with those women to be offensive. As though their low morals or rough ways would somehow rub off on her."

"Yes," said Daniel, considering. "I see what you mean. I daresay my mother would not be overjoyed."

"Precisely. So you see, it probably wouldn't work out—"

"When can I meet her?"

James stared at him, mouth agape. "I beg your pardon?"

"I promised my mother I'd marry a lady from a good family. But at the same time, I refuse to settle on some insipid hothouse violet who wants to cling to me all the time and knows nothing of real life. I want a woman who isn't afraid to get out and see firsthand what's going on in this city." A gleam lit his eyes. "If Lucinda has spent time with these women, learned their histories, I daresay she's got some interesting stories to tell."

"Well, yes, I suppose that's true—"

"So when can I meet her?"

James hesitated, reluctant to answer. He could not believe he'd been trying to talk Daniel *out* of the idea, nor that this approach had in fact only fueled the man's interest. But his reluctance had nothing to do with Daniel's suitability. In fact, Daniel and Lucinda might well be perfect for each other. Unfortunately, that was exactly the trouble.

He could not forget how surprisingly right Lucinda had felt in his arms. And how eminently kissable. Even now, the memory sent a fresh rush of desire through him, a deep yearning to hold her again. What would happen, he wondered, if Daniel kissed her? Would Daniel's reaction be just as strong?

Don't go down that road, he warned himself. Whatever might happen between Lucinda and Daniel would be none of his affair. He ought to be hoping things went well. It would certainly make Daniel want to marry her, and that was the goal, wasn't it? Yet when it came right down to it, James found himself fervently wishing the magic he and Lucinda had shared during their silent waltz was unique, never to happen again.

It was not a charitable sentiment. It was more akin to jealousy, and he had never in his life been a jealous man. To suddenly find himself dealing with it at this stage of his life was unexpected and unnerving.

James, you must forget her, he told himself sternly. *You must commit yourself to Emily and love her properly, and all other feelings be damned.*

Or else he would be.

Daniel was still looking at James expectantly. "Well?"

Forcing his resolve firmly into place, James said, "The Cardingtons are holding a dinner party on Saturday. I can probably get you an invitation."

"Excellent," Daniel replied, and promptly poured them both another glass of brandy.

Chapter 14

Lucinda came down the stairs to the main floor of the
school. She and Mrs. Cheadle had just completed a
review of the school's finances, made a list of items that
were needed, and inspected the bedchambers to be sure
the ladies were fulfilling the requirement to keep their
rooms clean and orderly. As there was nothing more for
Lucinda to do today, she made her way to the school-
room, where she knew her footman would be waiting
for her.

Peter was standing near the front door, alert as a senti-
nel keeping guard. He had been extra diligent and watch-
ful ever since the day Bill had shown up and caused a
disturbance over Kate. Peter had not been present at the
time because Lucinda had sent him out on an errand, and
yet he still berated himself soundly for not having been
there. He was growing increasingly protective of the
students.

Lucinda was surprised to discover Kate was also in
the room. Everyone else had been sent out on various

errands or to the shops where they were learning their new trades. "Hello, Kate," Lucinda said. "Shouldn't you be off to the milliner's?"

Kate dipped her head respectfully. "Yes, Miss Cardington, but I still have a few minutes, and there is something I should like to speak to you about first."

Peter cleared his throat. "Something *we'd* like to speak to you about."

"We?" Suddenly it dawned on her that Kate was standing very close to Peter. So close, in fact, that they were nearly touching.

Kate was beaming. "Miss Cardington, there is a lovely verse you taught us here at the school, when we were so discouraged of ever finding our true place in life: 'Delight thyself also in the Lord, and he shall give thee the desires of thine heart.'"

Peter reached out to take her hand, and she turned her smile on him, her eyes shining.

Merciful heavens. Dumbstruck, Lucinda put a hand to her heart. It was a lovely verse, one of her favorites. But she had never imagined it coming to pass in this way. No wonder Peter had become so enthusiastic about accompanying her to the school. Why hadn't she seen this before? How had she not noticed?

Because love used to be the last thing on my mind, she thought miserably. *Now it is everywhere. Inescapable.*

Everyone around her was falling in love, while she—

"Miss Cardington?" Kate said hesitantly, watching her with concern.

"Perhaps you are thinkin' it's wrong," Peter put in hastily. "But I say we can't help who we fall in love with."

Lucinda put out a hand. "Please don't say any more."

Finding her legs dangerously unsteady, she sank down onto a bench. Really, she should not be surprised at this match. Falling in love was only natural—for everyone else. Peter was a handsome man, which was why her mother had hired him in the first place. Kate was beautiful and capable, and she was unusually tenderhearted, given the sordid details of her past. If two such people had found love, Lucinda ought to be joyful for them. Yet the sight of their interlocking hands felt more like a blow, like she was about to lose an ally. She'd come to depend on Peter. She would hate to lose him, which was precisely what would happen if this was taken to its logical conclusion. "You know my mother forbids her servants to marry," she said flatly.

"Yes," said Peter.

"You do intend to marry, don't you?"

"Of course!" Kate exclaimed. She came over and knelt down, peering earnestly into Lucinda's eyes. "We want everything to be honorable, and we would love to have your blessing. We plan to be married within the month, if we can manage it."

"But...you..." Lucinda stammered, still trying to grasp all this information. "You were going to work at the milliner's shop."

"I still intend to," Kate said firmly. "Mrs. Downey can have no objection to my being married, so long as I keep to the hours she sets for me."

"But, Peter, what will you do?" Lucinda protested, turning her gaze back to her footman. "You know you'll be out of a job the moment Mama finds out you are getting married."

"Does she have to find out?" Peter asked.

Lucinda stared at him in astonishment. "You want me to lie to my own mother?"

"Not *lie*, exactly. A secret perhaps, but not a lie. After all, she's not likely to ask you out of the blue whether I'm married, is she?"

It was difficult to refute that kind of logic. For some reason it brought to mind James, for it was just the sort of thing he'd say. She tried to push that troubling man from her thoughts. "But Peter, even if I say nothing, Mama is bound to find out anyway. After all, the two of you have to live somewhere, and you can't exactly make your home on the servants' floor."

"There's a room to let near the milliner's shop," Kate said. "It's tiny, but it's respectable enough. I shall live there, and Peter will come whenever he can."

"But you might only see each other once a week! What kind of life is that?"

"It wouldn't be permanent," Peter insisted. "It's only until I can find another position."

"Why are you in such a hurry to get married?" Even as Lucinda asked this question, a possible answer came to mind. Her eyes dropped to Kate's stomach.

Kate straightened and set a hand against her slender waist. "It's nothing like that," she assured Lucinda. "Peter has been a perfect gentleman. We are going to wait until we are married."

"Then I still don't understand why you feel the need to rush into this."

"It's because of what happened last week with Bill Nelson," Peter said. "I'm going to make sure it never happens again."

"Oh, I see." She could literally see it, too, in the way

Peter's stance was now fierce and protective. Ready to guard the woman he loved.

"Kate and I have agreed that the past is behind her. We will never mention it again. But she cannot move on while this beast keeps trying to drag her back to the gutter." Peter put his arm around Kate, drawing her close. "If I make her my wife, Bill will have no more claim over her."

"But surely that is not the only way to address the problem."

"It's not." Peter held up a clenched fist. "I was fully prepared to take care of it in a very different way."

Lucinda's mouth dropped open. She had never in her life imagined that this well-mannered footman could become a man bent on violent retribution.

Kate gently took hold of Peter's hand, caressing it until it relaxed. "I persuaded Peter that trying to fight Bill would only be wrong. I told him when we begin our new lives together, our happiness will be sweeter than revenge—which in any case is for the Lord to mete out, isn't it?"

"Yes," said Lucinda, still stunned by this news. Everything around her was changing, shifting, sending her off-balance. "Do you really love her, Peter?"

"More than anything in the world." He turned his gaze to Kate, lightly touching her cheek.

The sight of this tender gesture sent another queer feeling across Lucinda's stomach. This time, however, she tried to ward it off by standing up and saying briskly, "I suppose when you said you had something to ask me, it was that I keep your marriage a secret from my parents."

"Well, yes, but we also wanted to ask you if you would do us the very great honor of attending the wedding," Peter said.

"I—I beg your pardon?" Lucinda was unable to conceal her dismay. She'd played bridesmaid at too many weddings already. She wasn't sure she could endure another one.

Misunderstanding her hesitation, Peter said, "I know it's acting above my station to ask, but it would mean ever so much to us. And you have taught us from the Bible that we are all one in Christ."

Now Lucinda was truly amazed. "Why, Peter, you were paying attention to my teachings?"

He smiled and shrugged.

"And you have changed my life," Kate said. "When I think of where I would be today if not for your kindness..." Her eyes teared up.

Impulsively, Lucinda hugged her. "Of course I'll come. I would be honored."

*

Lucinda spent the long carriage ride home mulling over the day's confounding turn of events. She'd always believed these women could set aside their past ways and go on to lead respectable lives. It was the whole purpose of Caring House. But she had never really thought for them in terms of marriage, because few could get past the stigma of being a fallen woman. That Kate had done so was surely a testament to the power of God's saving grace.

She wished only that she was not forced to keep their marriage a secret. She reflected, as she had done countless times, that if she were mistress of her own house she would not have to abide by her parents' overbearing rules. Perhaps she might even have offered employment to both Peter and Kate.

But for now it seemed to be the only answer. She and Peter had agreed never to speak of this when they were at her home. They could not afford even the slightest chance of anyone overhearing. If her mother saw her having a friendly chat with the footman, she would be appalled and possibly suspicious. Neither would be good.

Lucinda's frustration mounted as the carriage drew closer to her house. Life there was so confining that at times it felt like a prison. She desperately wanted the freedom to make her own decisions and live her life as she saw fit. All this talk of marriage today reminded her that if she gave in to her parents' demands she could move out of their house that much sooner. After the lovely scene Kate and Peter had presented, marriage did seem tempting. Now that their secret was known to Lucinda, Peter had made bold to kiss his betrothed goodbye before they'd left the school. At the sight of it, Lucinda's mind had flooded with memories of James. It made her heart ache, for now she knew firsthand just how wonderful a man's caresses could be . . .

Lucinda pulled herself quickly from that train of thought. She should not be lapsing into such daydreams—and certainly not about James. She had to forget that ill-advised interlude and remind herself of the risks marriage presented. A husband of her father's choosing might well turn out to be an arrogant, overcontrolling ogre like Mr. Wilson. Then her life would simply go from bad to worse. When she thought of that, she could take some comfort in the fact that after her disastrous run-in with Mr. Wilson, no one was likely to want to marry her anyway. Not for any kind of dowry. What had happened between her and James was an anomaly she could not account for; she knew only that dwelling on it could bring nothing but pain.

The carriage came to a stop, and Peter helped her down. Everything about his demeanor was flawlessly correct. He was carrying out his part of the plan. Once more Lucinda marveled at how much he was willing to give up for the woman he loved. Was this kind of devotion perfectly romantic or utterly foolish? Lucinda was in no position to answer that question. She could only wish them the best and pray they found the happiness they sought.

Heaving a great sigh, Lucinda went into the house.

And because the day had not been trying enough, her sister was in the foyer waiting for her. "There you are!" Emily squealed, practically pouncing on her the moment she entered the house. "I have wonderful news! It's about the dinner party!" She was very nearly jumping up and down with excitement.

Praying for strength, Lucinda freed herself from her sister's grasp and began untying her bonnet. She'd just done her best to set aside thoughts of James, and now her sister's talk about the dinner party brought back all her dread of seeing him again. How would she react? What would she say? Her sister's naïve joy only added to her guilty burden. "Emily, if this is about some shawl or fan you've just purchased, I'm in no mood to hear about it. I'm sure James will think it's lovely, so let's just leave it at that, shall we?"

"Oh it's not that," Emily replied with a laugh, her enthusiasm not the least bit dampened by Lucinda's acrid response. "It's even better! James has found a gentleman who wants to meet you! His name is Mr. Daniel Hibbitt, and one day he will be a baronet! James says Mr. Hibbitt is keen to get married and that he will be a perfect husband for you." She gave Lucinda's arm a happy squeeze. "Isn't that wonderful?"

Lucinda stared dumbfounded at her sister, as irritation turned to shock, and then to pain. Clearly, James had wasted no time returning to the business of finding a husband for her. This indicator of his thoughts about what had happened between them—which is to say, that he had thought nothing of it at all—only sent another jab at Lucinda's sorely battered heart. Rallying, she reminded herself that Emily was notorious for placing her own words into other people's mouths. She had a true gossip's talent for that. "Did James really say Mr. Hibbitt would be 'perfect' for me? In so many words?"

Emily's forehead scrunched a little. "Well, it was something like that." She gave a little shrug. "The point is, Mama has issued Mr. Hibbitt an invitation, and he's coming here Saturday night! Then we shall both have a beau, and we can begin planning for next May!"

"You are jumping to unwarranted conclusions," Lucinda scolded. "I don't even know the man, and I have no intention—"

"No arguments!" Emily interrupted. "Do you know what time it is? Mama is livid that you stayed so late at the school today. If she discovers us lingering here instead of dressing for dinner we will both get an earful." She wrapped her arm around Lucinda's and lowered her voice to a confidential whisper. "This is your chance, Lucinda. You know you want to get out of this house and away from Mama's domineering ways. Don't you see? The sooner you get married, the sooner you can live the life you want to live."

There were times when her sister astonished her.

Hadn't she just echoed the very thoughts Lucinda had been thinking only moments before? Emily began urging her up the stairs, and reluctantly she complied. She was still smarting over James's cavalier attitude, that he could be passionately kissing her one day and pushing her into someone else's arms the next. It was a timely if brutal reminder not to put her trust in people, but in the Lord. Just as Kate and Peter had done.

The sound of her footsteps on each stair tread suddenly brought to mind another of her favorite Scriptures. *A man's heart deviseth his way, but the Lord directs his steps.* Had she truly been allowing Him to direct her steps, or had she been vacillating between half-heartedly doing what others told her to do and then chafing against it? She'd already asked the Lord for answers; now it was time to get adamant about it. *Believe* and ye shall receive.

By the time they reached the first landing, Lucinda had made her decision. It was an idea so daunting, so incredible, that it thrilled her soul. What was truly the desire of her heart? To be comfortable in her own skin; to be confident at *all* times, including situations that had stymied her in the past. If this Mr. Hibbitt really was amenable to the idea of courting her, then let him try. *He* was the person on audition here, not her. He would either meet her exacting standards or he would not. If not, then there was a better way, and the Lord would help her find it—and overcome any obstacles along the way. Somehow, some way, she would be victorious.

As James and Daniel approached the large parlor in
the Cardingtons' home, they could already hear
Lady Cardington's piercing voice. It rose easily among
the general hubbub of the two dozen guests chattering
in the room. James could not resist turning to Daniel and
saying, "Welcome to the lion's den, my friend."

Daniel gave him a scowl. "Aren't you supposed to be
egging me on?"

"Ah yes, good point." James spoke with a jovial air, but
his heart was not in it. Too many things weighed on his
mind. He was hoping that once he saw Lucinda, the dream-
like quality that had kept her continually in his thoughts
would be broken. Memory could play tricks on a person,
exaggerating the impressions of an event all out of proportion. Surely when he saw her again he would not feel that
same irresistible draw. It would be the proof that one fascinating kiss had been a mere fluke. Tonight Lucinda would
be as she'd always been—pleasant enough, and nothing
more. James wanted that to happen. He *needed* it to happen.

"James, you're here at last!" Emily attached herself to his arm as soon as he and Daniel entered the room. "It's been ages. I thought you'd never get here."

James patted her arm and absently gave her a suitable greeting. But he was scanning the room, searching for Lucinda. It took no time at all to find her, even though there were at least a dozen people between them. James waited for the grip around his heart to lessen with relief, reassured that everything had returned to normal. Instead, his heart mutinied, leaping at the sight of her. Tonight her gown was a vivid blue. A delicate ivory cameo hung on a silk ribbon around her neck. She had not attempted the frivolous curls she'd worn for the Beauchamps' ball, but neither had she kept her usual, unadorned style. Tonight her hair was arranged in elegantly coiled braids and decorated with two white silk rosebuds. The overall effect was deceptively simple, yet dazzling.

The memories that had overrun his thoughts for days were not the product of some illusion. His attraction to her was very, very real.

And he was in serious trouble.

Her eyes met his, and although that familiar blush began to stain her face, she had the same the fierce determination in her eyes that he'd seen on the day she had tossed a drunken troublemaker onto the street.

She was sandwiched between her parents. Her mother was in busy conversation with Mrs. Paddington, an ugly post of a woman. Those two were always together at parties, and always gossiping—as they undoubtedly were now. They turned their heads in unison and looked—not at James, but at Daniel. Sizing him up, no doubt. The

man had been such a successful social hermit that not
even the most notorious gossips had gotten much of a
look at him. Daniel would be held under a magnifying
glass tonight.

Lord Cardington steered his wife and daughter over
to where James and Daniel were standing. "Mr. Hibbitt,
it's a pleasure to see you again," he said, shaking Daniel's
hand. "It's been what—four years?"

"At least that long, sir. I don't get out to these kinds of
events very often."

And I know why, thought James, as he observed
the way Lady Cardington was scrutinizing the newest
potential suitor for her daughter. James had been doing
his level best to avoid the marriage brokers himself,
despite the fact that he had not eschewed society. Daniel
had tried the opposite tack. In the end neither of them
had succeeded. Mothers will have their way.

"It's very kind of you to have invited me," Daniel
said. His gaze flicked back and forth between Lucinda
and Emily, and James braced himself while Daniel made
the inevitable comparison. But Daniel seemed to be
studying both sisters with equal interest.

"We're so glad you could join us!" Lady Cardington
enthused. "Mr. Hibbitt, may I present my elder daughter."

"A pleasure, Miss Cardington," Daniel said. He was
doing his best to be sociable, but James could tell it was
costing him. Despite his frank appraisal of the sisters, his
discomfort at being here was evident. A small bead of
sweat appeared at his temple. No doubt he was wishing
he was back at the club with his pipe and his newspaper.
And yet, his gaze kept returning to Lucinda. Was he lik-
ing what he saw? It was impossible to tell.

"My daughter will be playing for us after dinner," Lady Cardington informed him. "She's very accomplished and has a lovely voice."

"So I have heard," Daniel said. "I am most anxious to hear it."

"She has arranged an eclectic program," Lady Cardington said proudly. "Mr. Hibbitt, perhaps you will be so kind as to escort her down to dinner? Then she can tell you all about it."

"It would be a pleasure," Daniel said.

He offered his arm to Lucinda, which she accepted with a cordial smile. So far she hadn't said a word beyond a few polite responses, and her face was tinged with its usual red patches. Even so, something about her had changed. Her manner was quiet, but not reticent. She seemed absorbed in making Daniel's acquaintance, meeting his gaze without a hint of shyness. She barely cast a glance at James as Daniel led her out of the room.

Past experience had taught James that there were two very opposite ways a lady could react if she was interested in him. Either she would launch herself at him, doing all she could to attract his notice, or else she would be so shy that she purposefully avoided speaking to him. With this second sort of woman, James perceived their interest by the sidelong glances they stole at him when they thought he wasn't looking. Lucinda would surely fall into that second camp, and yet she had sent James no furtive glances. In fact, she seemed to have dismissed his presence without a single thought.

Emily tugged on his arm impatiently. He pulled his eyes away from Lucinda and fell in line with the other guests going down to dinner. If Lucinda had set aside

the remembrance of their romantic encounter so effortlessly, then it was all to the good—wasn't it? James
desperately wished his heart would be at ease with the
obvious answer to that question. For the first time in his
life, a woman who had kissed him was casually rejecting
him. It was a set down that hurt, no matter how much he
deserved it.

*

As subtly as she could, Lucinda had been taking deep,
calming breaths from the moment she'd seen James enter
the room. Even so, her hand had trembled a little as she'd
accepted Mr. Hibbitt's arm. She prayed that James had
not seen it. Under no circumstances would she allow him
to sense her discomfort.

Mr. Hibbitt seemed a very reserved kind of person,
but his manner toward her had been reasonably friendly,
and Lucinda considered that a good beginning. "My
mother will do all she can to throw us together this evening," she told him quietly, as they followed her parents
toward the dining room. "Perhaps I should apologize in
advance for her unsubtle ways."

He shrugged. "I have no objection to directness. In
fact, I prefer it."

"You do?"

"Why do you think I spend so little time at events like
these? I cannot abide all the pretense and drama, people
saying one thing when they mean quite another. If I want
play-acting, I go to the theater."

"How very sensible." Lucinda gave a tiny sigh. "I
wish I were free to do the same."

He raised one thick eyebrow. "You mean to say you

have no taste for these elegant soirees?" The sarcasm in his words was unmistakable.

"Good gracious, no. They used to scare me to death."

"And now?" he queried, catching her use of the past tense.

"Now they bore me." Lucinda noted with great satisfaction that her words came off assured and had a ring of truth. It was a tiny step forward for her. *Trust in the Lord...* She was still nervous, as her shakiness attested to, but even that was diminishing. "For the time being I must be obedient to my parents' wishes. Once I am married, I shall do as I like."

Again the eyebrow twitched. "Are you sure? Won't you then be subject to your husband's dictates?"

"Must I be? I would hope we could be on more equal footing." If Mr. Hibbitt wanted directness, she would give it to him. She fully expected to chase him away with her frank talk of marriage when they'd only just met.

To her surprise, he gave a small grunt of approval. "And I would want a wife who not only speaks her mind, but has the intelligence to make good decisions."

Lucinda felt a small part of her relax, and the fire in her cheeks began to cool. *This isn't so bad after all,* she thought. Everyone took their places at the table, and Lucinda dropped smoothly into the chair as Mr. Hibbitt held it for her. That was a small victory, too. For the first time in her life Lucinda had no fear that she would spill her wine glass or drop food in her lap. She would chat with this Mr. Hibbitt in order to find out more about him, and she would not hesitate to give an honest opinion on any topic.

Somehow she knew, without even looking in his

direction, that James's eyes were upon her. She decided it would be foolish to avoid his gaze. That would only show him that his actions still hurt her. So she turned her head and looked at him directly. There was no denying the way her heart picked up its pace when their eyes met. A lump tried to form itself in her throat, and she forced herself to take a few more calming breaths. There was something unreadable in his normally open expression. A question, perhaps? Longing? Lucinda's heart stuttered. That was ridiculous. After all, he'd wasted no time pushing another man in her direction.

Still looking at James, she said coolly, "Mr. Hibbitt, I am so glad Mr. Simpson has prevailed upon you to join us this evening. I can't imagine what I would have done otherwise."

*

As Lucinda had expected, she made it through dinner without any mishaps. She was thankful her mother had placed James at the opposite end of the long table, so she was not obliged to converse with him. That might well have been more than she could handle. She noticed he frequently sent glances in her direction, but she carefully kept the focus of her attention at her end of the table.

Mr. Hibbitt's terse, straightforward speech was very different from James's florid style, and Lucinda found it easier to keep her bearings. They discussed their favorite operas and composers, and found they had a lot in common. He had even listened with interest as she'd described her work at the Caring House. Unlike Mr. Wilson, he'd not shown any dismay at her involvement in it. This made her like him even more.

After dinner, once the gentlemen and ladies had reconvened in the great parlor, Mr. Hibbitt appeared content to find her again and resume their conversation.

"Attention, everyone!" Lady Cardington called out. "Please find a chair. Lucinda is going to play for us."

"Shall I assist you?" Mr. Hibbitt asked. "Turn the pages, perhaps?"

"Thank you, but that won't be necessary. My sister will be doing that honor. We don't trust her to sing or play in public, but she is proficient enough to turn the pages."

"Well then, I shall go and find a seat." With a small bow he left her and made his way across the room to take a chair next to James.

Lucinda sat down at the piano and double-checked the arrangement of her music. Emily joined her and, leaning in, said softly, "Well, what do you think? Mr. Hibbitt seems very nice, in a gruff sort of way. But you two seemed to find plenty to talk about. I'm so happy for you!"

"I told you not to jump to any conclusions," Lucinda warned. "An hour's acquaintance is not nearly enough time to get to know someone."

"Nonsense. I knew James was the man for me the minute I met him."

The more fool you, Lucinda thought, but said nothing. All eyes were upon her now, and it was time to begin.

The room fell silent as Lucinda placed her hands on the keys. She closed her eyes, reaching again for one of those calming breaths, but instead something very different happened. The smooth ivory under her fingers, plus the quiet of the room—this room where she and James had been alone together—brought back the memory of James's lips on hers with a forcefulness that made her gasp. She jerked her hands from the keyboard as if they'd been burned. She glanced quickly toward the audience and saw both Daniel and James watching her intently.

"You're not getting stage fright, are you?" Emily whispered.

"Certainly not," Lucinda hissed. She had to forget those memories at all costs, and forge new ones to replace them. With deliberate care she repositioned her hands on the keys, silently counted to three, and began to play.

The first piece was one she knew well, and it was a good choice. She played almost without thinking, her fingers knowing exactly what to do. It was a peaceful song, one she often played when she was distressed. She gave herself wholly to the melody, and before long her mind began to fill with beautiful images—a placid lake, a flowering meadow, a walk in the countryside at dawn.

It was only as she finished the piece, sighing in contentment as the notes gently drifted away, that she realized she had forgotten about the other people present. The room filled with applause. Everyone was murmuring in appreciation, and Lucinda felt her confidence soar. She could not resist glancing over at James. The heat of his admiring gaze sent a tingle through her, right down to her toes. Whatever else she might think about him—and her feelings were definitely all over the map—she was glad he had challenged her to perform in public without reservation or self-consciousness. For the very first time, she had done it.

Smiling in triumph, she began the next piece. It was a spritely number which, at this precise moment, completely matched her mood. She played a half dozen pieces in all, and when it was over she found herself surrounded by many who came up to compliment her. When Mr. Hibbitt reached her he said, "That was excellent, Miss Cardington. I've never heard such accomplished playing outside of professional performances." Over his shoulder, Lucinda could see her father beaming and her mother looking as though she might burst from pride.

She gave Mr. Hibbitt a poised smile. "Thank you. You are too kind."

"Daniel isn't the least bit kind," James said, reaching them in time to hear these comments. "If he gives a compliment, he really means it."

Mr. Hibbitt sent James a withering glance. "And I counted you among my friends."

"Did you? I'm surprised to hear it," James retorted. "But I am overjoyed nonetheless."

"Don't let it go to your head," Mr. Hibbitt growled. "The status is not necessarily permanent."

Lucinda couldn't help but smile at this good-natured sparring. It pleased her to see there was a sense of humor underneath Mr. Hibbitt's taciturn exterior.

"I'm thirsty," Emily announced. It was said to no one in particular, but since she had firmly affixed herself to James's arm it was clear she expected him to address her problem.

Lucinda could see James fighting the urge to roll his eyes. With some reluctance he said, "Let's go find you something to drink." Emily's pout turned to a sunny smile as he led her away.

Daniel shook his head. "Poor fellow," he muttered, then seemed to recollect himself. "I'm sorry. That was tactless of me. I'm sure you've gleaned by now that I'm ill-suited for good company."

"No need to apologize." Lowering her voice she added, "I agree with you, as it happens."

"I'm not surprised. There never is any love lost between sisters. I've got four of them, so I should know."

"Good heavens! Four?"

He nodded. "Three older, one younger."

"I can just imagine what a household that must have been."

"It was very . . . loud."

His gray eyes held a touch of mirth, and Lucinda noticed they were handsomely set off by the gray at his temples. The man also had a certain measure of charm, when he chose to use it. She had the sense that he had dusted it off for tonight's party.

"I was the only son," Daniel went on. "Therefore, in order to survive I had to become adept at reading my sisters' moods and learn how to stay out of their way when they were in a temper. It served me in good stead, I assure you. Tonight I could tell Miss Emily was green with envy while you were playing."

"Emily was envious of me? I hardly think so," Lucinda said with a shake of her head. "She's too well aware that everyone admires her far more than me."

"Precisely. Therefore she was exceedingly put out by all the attention you were getting."

"It will pass. It always does." Even now as Lucinda glanced across the room she could see Emily laughing at something James said as he handed her a glass of champagne. They looked like the ideal couple, so handsome and so in love. At least, Emily was in love. James wore his usual smiling expression, which Lucinda was beginning to suspect was a mere mask. He only appeared to be an open book. He was, in fact, a difficult man to read.

Daniel, too, had followed her gaze. "She does seem very changeable. That's why I don't envy James one bit. Such women are beautiful, but time-consuming. I prefer someone more stable."

"James would be better off with such a person himself. That's why it's such a shame that—" She cut herself off. She had no idea how much Daniel knew of the real story behind the engagement. So she finished by repeating something her footman Peter had said. "Well, one cannot help whom one falls in love with."

"*She* is smitten, at any rate," Daniel agreed. He lowered his voice and said, "Miss Cardington, James told me what happened that night at Cremorne Gardens."

"Did he?" Lucinda found her anxiety returning. "My sister was foolish, but she is essentially a good girl. It would be devastating to our family if she was publicly accused of having low morals."

"I assure you, James told me everything in the strictest confidence, and I intend to honor the trust he placed in me."

Lucinda glanced around to make sure they were not being overheard. Most everyone else had moved toward the other end of the room—including her mother, who seemed to have sense enough to realize that if Lucinda and Daniel were to get anywhere, it would happen much faster without her interference. A group of people were clustered around James and Emily, laughing and absorbed in some tale James was telling. Once more Lucinda reflected that they were admirably suited to the role of being the center of attention, the life of the party.

Lucinda had always been the type who stood quietly in corners, unnoticed. Except tonight there was a difference. She was neither alone nor unnoticed. She was holding a conversation with a man who seemed to be taking a genuine interest in her.

He was looking at her now with some earnestness. "James told me about that night at Cremorne because he wanted me to know exactly why you were there. You were trying to save your sister's reputation—as James is now by marrying her." He sent another concerned glance over at James. "It's a laudable act. I hope he'll be happy."

"One might also put it down to sheer self-preservation. Did he tell you the other half of the agreement he made?"

"Yes."

His unhesitating response surprised and impressed her. "Did he?"

"He said his duty is to find you a husband. He said Emily's dowry hinges upon it."

Knowing Daniel was aware of these facts gave rise to some doubts in Lucinda's mind. Their interaction this evening had gone well enough, but she still knew little about him. Was he just another in a long line of impoverished gentry seeking to marry for money? If so, they might as well get that out in the open right now. "Did James also tell you that I come attached to a sizable dowry?"

She fired this at him with the force of an accusation, but he didn't even flinch. "That makes no difference to me. I have plenty of money."

"Do you really? Even with four sisters to provide for?"

"All that has been settled already," Daniel said casually. "My father is a conscientious man, and the estate at Highgate is doing well. Two of my sisters have made excellent matches with well-connected families. The third is happily engaged to a prosperous cotton merchant, and the fourth appears content to stay at home and help my mother."

"I see. And so that leaves only you unaccounted for."

"Yes. And I—" He paused. "Well, the truth is, I would prefer to be left alone."

Once again, the man's forthright answer took Lucinda by surprise. He seemed to be implying that he had no intention of getting married. *Good,* she thought. They were even on that score. "So would I," she declared.

"Then we are two of a kind. We both prefer our lives the way they are, and yet we are being pressured by our families into marriage."

"Are you being pressured, then?"

"Good Lord, yes," he said with a grimace. "You are not the only unfortunate soul contending with a formidable mother. In fact, I will lay odds that mine is worse."

Sending a glance toward her mother, who was watching their conversation from afar with rapt attention, Lucinda couldn't help but give a small laugh. "Then I feel sorry for you. And are any of your sisters like mine?"

Daniel's gaze rested once more on Emily, who at this point let out a rather unladylike squeal of delight in response to something James was saying. "No, thank God."

Lucinda winced in amusement. "You don't mince words, do you?"

"Not unless it is absolutely necessary."

The unapologetic honesty this man displayed was refreshing, not the least because his views were thus far entirely in line with her own.

Unfortunately, their talk of mothers must have set off some silent call to draw hers toward them. With a sinking heart, Lucinda saw her mother moving in their direction. "This might be one of those times for mincing words," she told Daniel.

Lady Cardington swept up to them, wearing an expression of smug pride. "Mr. Hibbitt, did you enjoy Lucinda's little performance?"

"It was delightful," Daniel said smoothly. "I don't know when I've heard better."

"I do hope you will join us in our box at the opera next Thursday. It's the London premiere of Verdi's newest opera! It's called 'La something-or-other.'"

"*La Traviata*," Lucinda supplied. "But, Mama, you know I do not wish to attend. I have told you my objections to it—"

"*La TRAH-vee-AHHH-ta*—yes, that's it!" Lady Cardington broke in, pronouncing the title with a horrifying Italian accent. "You see, Mr. Hibbitt, my daughter is superbly knowledgeable about all things musical."

"But, Mama—"

"You do not like this opera?" Daniel asked Lucinda, seeing through Lady Cardington's attempts to cover her protests. "But you can't have seen it yet. This will be the first time it plays in England."

"The scandal precedes it," Lucinda said brusquely. "I know that the main character, Violetta, is a wealthy courtesan. Surely it only romanticizes prostitu—"

"It's just a story!" Lady Cardington interrupted. "You know how the Italians lean toward the risqué. What's more important is the wonderful music!"

Lucinda knew full well that her mother cared not a

whit for the music; she wanted only to put pressure on Lucinda to go. There was also hint of desperation in her tone. No doubt she thought Lucinda was going to lose her one chance at snaring Mr. Hibbitt. She might be right on that score; his frown deepened, and Lucinda wondered if she'd just made her first faux pas of the evening.

"You have often said how much you love the music of Signor VAIR-di," her mother continued to press, pronouncing the maestro's name with an atrocious accent. She turned to Mr. Hibbitt. "Do you enjoy Verdi's music, Mr. Hibbitt?"

"Indeed I do," Daniel confirmed. Seeing Lucinda about to protest once more, he said hastily, "Miss Cardington, perhaps you should withhold judgment until you've seen the production for yourself. I had an opportunity to attend its Paris debut last year, and I can tell you it is magnificent. Verdi grows more assured with each new opera he composes. This latest is admirably complex and sophisticated. Several of the arias will utterly astound you."

"But—"

Daniel held up a beseeching hand. "Based on your objections, I assume you are aware that *la traviata* means 'one who has strayed.' However, given what you've told me about your work with fallen women, I would think that you, of all people, would sympathize with poor Violetta. Especially since most of the opera revolves around her attempts to give up that lifestyle for the sake of true love."

"Well, I..." Lucinda paused, uncertain. She had not considered the matter in that light. It brought to mind a picture of Kate and Peter standing hand in hand, looking so determined to make a better future for themselves. There was probably not the least correlation between their lives and what would be portrayed in *La Traviata*, and yet still she hesitated.

Warily she surveyed Mr. Hibbitt, trying to discern if he was somehow mocking her. But he looked sincere. His eyebrows lifted slightly, as if in challenge. "I'm sure you would agree it is a terrible thing to pass judgment based on preconceived notions. It is even worse for the poor soul who must bear the brunt of it."

"That is a valid point," Lucinda conceded. What a shrewd debater this man was. She felt a warm glow rising once more to her cheeks, not only because of the way Mr. Hibbitt was scrutinizing her just then, but also because she saw James once more approaching them. Somehow he had managed to disengage himself from Emily.

"Wonderful! That's settled then!" Lady Cardington trilled.

"Is everything really settled so quickly?" James asked, reaching them in time to hear this proclamation. "When's the happy day to be?"

"Next Thursday," Lady Cardington said.

James's smile seemed to freeze. "I beg your pardon?"

"We were discussing the opera, nothing more," Lucinda said tartly.

"Oh, I see. How foolish of me to leap to conclusions."

She leveled a look at him, wishing she did not have cheeks that exposed her true feelings like signal flares. "Yes, indeed. Very foolish."

James cleared his throat, looking for once like he was at a loss. This passed quickly, however. He clapped his hands together, and his mouth broadened into a smile—

that beautiful smile that had the most alarming effects on her. "Are we discussing *La Traviata*, then? I must say that after all the scathing things I've read about it in the press, I am really looking forward to it..."

And once more, in that effortless way he had, James commandeered the conversation, keeping it moving at a rapid pace right up until the end of the evening.

Much later, when Lucinda was finally alone and able to reflect on the night's events, she found herself thinking far too late into the night about James. She was trying futilely to piece together his true feelings. It bothered her beyond measure the way he'd implied she might meet a man and get engaged to him in the same evening. Did he really think she could be dispatched so easily? Even though she knew by now she could not trust a thing James said or did, she would have given anything if he had not looked quite so happy at the prospect.

Chapter 16

"I think Miss Cardington will do just fine," Daniel informed James, as the two of them strolled along the wide thoroughfare. The weather was mild, so they had decided to walk the mile or so that lay between the Cardingtons' home and the club.

The well-lit street was bustling, despite the late hour. The city never really completely retired for the night. Tonight James had an idea that he would be among those who stayed awake until the glaring gas lamps were finally outdone by the rising sun. He would be thinking about the woman who had captivated him all evening.

How lovely she had looked in that sumptuous gown. Its neckline, cut similar to the gown she'd worn to the Beauchamps' ball, invited admiration of her fine, slender neck and delicate shoulders. And when she had played for them, she had given herself to the music just as James had seen her do on that glorious morning when he had kissed her. Her lips had parted, and her small, perfectly rounded breasts had lifted as her breathing had increased—sending out an unconscious invitation, a woman to be sought and claimed. "She'll do *fine*?" It came out as a rasp, and James paused to collect more air in his lungs. "It seems to me if you are contemplating marriage you ought to be more excited about it. About *her*, I mean."

"Simpson, you know I'm not the least bit excited about marriage," Daniel said curtly. They stopped at a corner, waiting while a hackney cab rattled through the intersection. "I am resigned to it, however," he continued, once the road was clear and they began to cross it. "If it makes you happier, I will say that on the whole I was pleasantly surprised by Miss Cardington."

"You were?" This, at least, was something.

Daniel nodded. "She is a sensible woman, and I believe my mother will approve."

"Well, that *is* the most important thing."

Daniel ignored the barb. "Also, I am glad she has so many interests. She will keep busy with her projects, and I will be free to pursue mine. We can leave each other to our own devices."

"It does sound ideal," James agreed drily.

"Don't try to criticize me," Daniel returned. "You knew from the beginning what I would require in a wife. In fact, the only problem I can see is that I don't much care for the rest of her family. Her mother is annoying, and her sister is very pretty, but—" He shot James a look. "Are you sure you want to marry her?" Before James could reply he said, "Oh, that's right, you have no choice. Well, it's on your head, then."

"It certainly is," James assured him, injecting as much conviction into his words as possible. "Emily is a fine

creature, and I am sure she'll make a good wife. She's..."
He searched for the right word. "...pliable. Since she
has no ideas of her own in that pretty head, she'll accept
whatever I choose to put in there for her."

"That is a benefit," Daniel acknowledged. "Miss
Cardington certainly has her own opinions. On some
things she is rather...intractable."

"She'll soften up as she gets to know you. She did
for me."

This was a poor choice of words. Daniel paused under
a street lamp and turned to stare suspiciously at James.
"Are you that much of a scoundrel, then? Did you manage to get Lucinda alone in a dark corner, as you've no
doubt done with her sister?" An undertone of disgust and
possibly anger lay beneath his words. "Because if you
have, we can call this whole thing off right now."

"Don't be ridiculous," James said, striving for a deliberately dismissive air. "Emily is the only one I've ever,
ah, met in a dark corner." Technically, this was true. He
had kissed Lucinda in the middle of a broad, sunlit room.
If ever his ability to speak half-truths had come in handy,
it was at this moment. He was not going to risk malign-
ing Lucinda's character over one kiss, especially when he
was the one who had instigated it.

"Good," Daniel said with a curt nod. "I'd hate to think
Miss Cardington has been compromised. I don't want
any surprises."

"Trust me, those two sisters are pure as the driven
snow."

"Both of them?" Daniel asked incredulously. "Come
on, James, you can be honest with me. We may be broth-
ers-in-law soon."

"Miss Emily's virtue is absolutely intact," James insisted. "Despite my roguish reputation, I only dally *in that way* with experienced women. I have never in my life deflowered a virgin. I'm saving that for my wedding night."

"Quite right," Daniel agreed. "Glad to hear it."

What a pair of hypocrites we are, James thought, as they proceeded once more down the street. It was the first time his attitudes toward women had ever struck him that way. But these days he seemed to be looking at a lot of things differently.

Daniel's less-than-glowing evaluation of Lucinda troubled him. The man was actually looking forward to *not* spending time with her! And yet, perhaps when he got to know her better he would see her as James did and know, as James did from personal experience, just how electrifying her kisses could be. Unfortunately, that thought troubled him even more.

*

"He will do, I suppose," Lady Cardington said. "I had hoped for at least one of my daughters to marry into the peerage, but Mr. Hibbitt will be a baronet someday, and that's something."

Lucinda squeezed her palms together in irritation. The four of them—Lucinda, Lady Cardington, Emily, and James—were riding in an open carriage in Hyde Park, enjoying the afternoon sunshine after the morning's rain. The others were enjoying it, at any rate. As for Lucinda, her head ached and she was exhausted. She'd lain awake all night, tossing and turning, unable to fully accept this idea that Daniel Hibbitt actually seemed inclined to begin a courtship with her. She could find no real objection to the man, but she resented the shallowness with which everyone seemed to be approaching the situation.

"Take heart, Lady Cardington," James said. "I'm ninth in line to a small earldom through a cousin once removed. It might happen yet."

"Oh, James," Emily giggled. "You're so droll."

"I really wish you would not speak as though Mr. Hibbitt and I were engaged," Lucinda said crossly. "We are not. We've only just met."

"It's just a matter of time," Lady Cardington insisted. "He was completely enamored with you, I could tell."

"And just how do you glean that, Mama?" Lucinda's tone verged on rude, but the day had grown uncomfortably warm and the throbbing in her head was making conversation virtually unendurable.

"Why, he couldn't take his eyes off you when you were playing the piano, and he never left your side all evening." She pulled out a voluminous handkerchief and began to dab at beads of sweat sprouting on her face and neck, giving Lucinda what she must have supposed was a knowing grin. "It has been a year or two since I was a debutante, but I can still spot the signs of a man who is falling in love."

"Mama, please!" Lucinda did not want to discuss this at all, and certainly not in front of James. "There is a gentleman present."

"I beg your pardon—I am no gentleman," James quipped, galling her with a wink.

Emily giggled again. "James told me he and Mr. Hibbitt had a nice little chat about you after the party." She turned to him for confirmation. "Isn't that right, James?"

James tugged a little at his cravat. "Yes, well, I believe he was favorably impressed. There is no doubt that marriage is on his mind."

Some brief look crossed his face as he said this. In any other circumstance Lucinda would have put it down to pain. It prompted a worry that he was hiding something. "Did Mr. Hibbitt expressly say he was contemplating marriage to *me*? Or are you just trying to be nice?"

James shook his head and said softly, "My dear girl, I have told you before that you really do undervalue yourself."

His eyes locked on hers. Lucinda felt every part of her go still, except for her heart, which lurched into an unsteady pace. For a fraction of a second his gaze dropped to her lips, and she shivered, despite the heat. That one brief glance was enough to bring back every vivid memory she'd been trying to forget. She could feel the heat of his lips against hers and the way her entire body had come alive with pleasure when he'd held her. She could feel it as surely as if he were holding her right now. Dear Lord, why did she persist on wanting something so improper and out of reach? And why did James look as though he, too, were thinking the very same thing?

"It's no surprise that Lucinda undervalues herself," Lady Cardington said. "She has been feeling the lack of a suitor. How fortunate that we have found this Mr. Hibbitt. At last there is a gentleman who can see her good qualities."

And just like that, the moment was broken. James looked away, and Lucinda was hit by a dose of reality that washed over her foolish fancies the way an outgoing tide draws the sand.

How had Mama and Emily not noticed what had just passed between her and James? They were blissfully blind, being now fully launched into a discussion of all the details they'd gleaned about the Hibbitt family's wealth and lineage, speaking as though the banns had been read and the wedding date set. Lucinda could not bring herself to protest. She was still too shaken by the idea that James might not have forgotten the power of their kiss after all. That he might be remembering it with the same longing she did.

She could see nothing of his thoughts now, however. He leaned back in his seat with the politely indulgent and distant expression he wore whenever he was around Emily. Lucinda hated to see it. She preferred him fully engaged, such as whenever they talked about photography, or when he asked her questions about her work at the school. Or that hour on the rooftop of Westminster Palace when he'd shared a tiny bit of his life's story. Or even when he was gently teasing her into overcoming her fear of dancing. Surely that was the real James Simpson. It troubled her to see this façade he'd adopted for her family when she'd had such tantalizing glimpses of a better man behind it.

She did her best to appear as though she was paying attention as her sister prattled on about what Lucinda ought to wear to the grand debut of *La Traviata*. In truth, she was expending all her efforts in the single task of trying *not* to show just how intensely she was thinking about the man seated opposite her.

Chapter 17

The second act was drawing to a close, and Lucinda did not think she had ever been so mortified. Everything about this evening had drained away all the delight she usually took in attending the opera.

Never before had she felt so trussed up for public display. The box seated just six people, and with Daniel Hibbitt joining them tonight, it was filled to capacity. Daniel had taken a chair in the back row with Lord and Lady Cardington, leaving James to sit up front between the two sisters. But one glance around the theater showed Lucinda that every tongue had already been set to wagging, making assumptions about her and Daniel. At the first intermission he had gone outside with her father for a smoke and a friendly chat, and Lucinda had no doubts about what they'd discussed.

Adding to her discomfort was the agony of sitting so close to James. Every nerve in her body thrummed from his presence, mere inches away from her. She was painfully aware—for she had seen it from the corner of her eye—that Emily's hand had reached out to grasp James's, and that he had held it resting gently on his leg. His leg! When he began to caress the back of Emily's hand with his thumb, the gesture was so intimate that the mere sight of it took Lucinda's breath away. Emily let out a little sigh of pleasure, which sent a stab of pain into Lucinda's heart.

Trying desperately to take hold of her thoughts, Lucinda set her attention toward the action onstage. The scene unfolding there was equally distressing. The heroine, Violetta, had given up her one chance at happiness, choosing instead to leave her lover, Alfredo, and return to her life as a courtesan. Not knowing she had done this solely to preserve his family's honor, Alfredo hurled invectives at her, demeaning her and throwing money at her feet to "pay" for her services. Violetta, although mortally ill and heartbroken, was stoically bearing up under all of it.

"Isn't it wonderful?" Emily exclaimed as the curtain came down for the second interval. She took hold of James's arm, which she had only just let go of in order to applaud enthusiastically. "It's so romantic!"

"What on earth is romantic about it?" Lucinda demanded. She knew her harsh tone reflected more than her dismay at the opera, but she did not attempt to curb it. "Here is a fallen woman who tries to reform, and yet she is forced back to her old ways because of the prejudices society holds against her."

Emily looked incredulous. "I don't see it like that at all. I think she is so noble! She is willing to sacrifice everything for the sake of her one true love."

"Do you really think that?" Daniel asked, leaning forward eagerly in his chair. "Because I do, too. And what about that fascinating interplay between Violetta and Alfredo at the end of the first act? He is wooing her, but she is desperately afraid of falling in love. It is both tender and passionate, expressing the pain of not being loved and the fear of abandoning oneself to love. It is at once regret and desire."

"So, Mr. Hibbitt, you *can* talk!" Emily teased, giving him an approving smile. "Yes, I see exactly what you mean. In the beginning I was rooting for Violetta to fall in love with Alfredo, but now I feel terribly sorry for her because she is getting just what she was afraid of."

Daniel's eyes lit with admiration. For the first time, it seemed, he was warming toward Emily. This only increased Lucinda's frustrations. Of all the things that might cause him to like her sister better, it had to be this misguided idea about romance.

"Emily, I'm surprised you even noticed what the opera was about," Lucinda said curtly. "I've never known you to pay attention." *Especially tonight,* she added silently to herself, remembering how shamelessly Emily had reached for James behind the cover of her open fan.

"It's true, I don't always pay attention," Emily said, with the air of a confession. "But this opera is different. It's so thrilling! So passionate!" She turned to gaze lovingly toward James. "Perhaps I am viewing things differently now that I have found my own true love."

Lucinda fought back several caustic remarks, which seemed to burn like bile in her throat. Instead she said evenly, "Did you ever stop to consider that if Violetta had only been accepted into 'polite' society, her 'sacrifice' would not have been necessary?"

"Oh, that could never happen. Everyone knows that."

Emily spoke as though Lucinda had just said something completely outlandish. "Once a woman has been under the protection of another man—"

"Let's dispense with the euphemisms," Lucinda cut in. "You mean, once a woman has taken a lover?"

"Oh, heavens!" Lady Cardington opened her fan and flapped it vigorously. "Such talk, Lucinda. You ought to know better."

Lucinda pointed an accusing finger toward the stage. "How can we see an opera like this and not talk about it?"

"Mr. Hibbitt, I agree with you that the music is magnificent," Lord Cardington said, joining in the fray in an obvious attempt to smooth things over. "I can't recall an opera where the baritone had his own aria. What a treat! I'm a baritone myself, you know."

Lady Cardington stood up. "Let's go downstairs. I must have some refreshment, or I shall never survive the last act."

"I don't think poor Violetta will survive it either," James observed.

"I do hope you are enjoying the music, at any rate," Daniel said, taking Lucinda's arm as they made their way through the jostling crowd. "It is utterly transcendent."

"The music is lovely," Lucinda agreed, although she said it largely to allow the matter to rest. Many glances were turned in their direction, everyone watching this newest society "match" with interest. It worried her, but at the moment there was nothing she could do about it. She could only bear up under the scrutiny and listen with polite attention as they drank their champagne and Daniel compared the merits of tonight's soprano with the woman he had heard sing the role in Paris.

It was a relief when Daniel and Lord Cardington went outside for another quick smoke. Then Lady Cardington and Emily went off in search of the ladies' retiring room, leaving Lucinda alone with James. There were people milling all about them, and yet when James led her over to a quiet spot by the wall, it suddenly felt very intimate.

"Are you feeling better?" he asked, as she finished her champagne.

She sighed. "I keep telling myself I ought not to get so upset by a mere opera."

He said gently, "And yet you can't help it, can you?"

She shook her head. "My heart breaks when I think of the struggling women at my school, how they will never be able to lose the taint of the things they have done, while these people—" She lifted her empty glass to indicate the glittering crowd. "They will enjoy this story about a courtesan who sacrifices herself. Then they will go on about their lives, smug and secure regarding their own place in the world."

"It is a shame, I agree. God might forgive and forget, but it's much harder for people to do so."

This was an insightful statement coming from James. "How perceptive of you to see things from a spiritual point of view."

He gave her a rueful smile. "Perhaps you forget what my cousin Lizzie has been through. In the eyes of society, the respectable life she lives now can never erase the mistakes of her youth."

Lucinda nodded. "No wonder you understand. Sadly, I don't think Emily does," she added, thinking back to her sister's remarks. "I'm sorry she spoke so cruelly about how women can never be accepted once they have strayed."

He waved away her concern. "She was only repeating drivel she's heard. I doubt she'd ever think of Lizzie in that light."

"I certainly hope Mr. Hibbitt doesn't harbor such an unforgiving opinion."

"Do you like Daniel, then?" James asked. The question sounded casual, but Lucinda saw his shoulders tense as he spoke.

"Well, I . . . I didn't mean . . ." she floundered.

"Because I think he likes *you*—despite your provocative ideas about social equality."

"I suppose you want me to marry him." She gave a sour laugh. "Of course you do. You introduced us, after all—"

"Lucinda." James spoke her name softly and urgently. He reached out as if to take her empty glass, but grasped her hand along with it. "I don't want you to marry against your wishes. I want you to marry a man you love. A man who loves you."

She searched his face. "Do you really mean that, James?"

"I really am exceedingly cross with you, Miss Lucinda Cardington," he said, as though he had not heard her. "I used to be content in my selfish ways, but you have gone and changed all that. At this moment, your happiness is the only thing I care about."

"My happiness?" she repeated, intensely aware that his two hands were still wrapped around hers, spreading heat to every part of her body.

"Yes." His eyes were fixed on her. "If only I could tell you—"

"Here we are!" Emily said, coming upon them so suddenly that Lucinda jerked back. Feeling a ridiculous surge of guilt, she pulled her hands away. She had completely forgotten about the champagne glass that was still lodged between her hands and his. It fell to the polished marble floor and shattered with a noise that could surely be held throughout the large foyer.

"Lucinda, why must you always be so clumsy!" Emily scolded.

"I thank you for your sympathy, but you may keep it to yourself," Lucinda snapped, overcome with embarrassment and furious for having once more made a fool of herself. Instinctively she bent down and tried to gather up what pieces she could.

"Never mind that!" Emily said impatiently. "The attendants will clean it up."

Lucinda kept working, unwilling to rise or look at anyone directly. But James bent down until he was at her eye level. "I'm afraid Emily is correct," he said gently. "Much as I hate to admit it."

He took hold of her elbow and gently coaxed her up, his nearness sending riotous signals through her body. As soon as she was upright, his hand fell away, but she dared not look at him. She felt dazed and disoriented, wondering how it was that James's touch always felt like a firebrand.

She found herself face to face with Daniel, who was studying her with concern. "Are you all right, Miss Cardington? The glass didn't cut you, did it?"

Even as he said this, he shot a glance toward the staircase, which most of the crowd was now ascending in a great, multicolored river of movement. Lucinda could see how eager he was not to miss any of the performance. "I'm fine," she said, giving the commonplace answer she knew they all wanted. She opened her hand and allowed the few shards of glass to drop back to the floor, where they joined their fellows with a reproving tinkle.

"Then perhaps we might return to our seats? The third act is about to begin."

"So it is," she heard James mutter from behind her, as she accepted Daniel's arm and allowed him to escort her toward the stairs. "So it is."

Lucinda had no recollection of how she got back to her seat, nor of what was said before the curtain came up. She only knew that before long she was drawn fully into Violetta's final sad moments as they played out on the stage. Finally seeing beyond Violetta's social predicament, Lucinda felt instead the agony that comes from loving the wrong person at the wrong time. And when the opera reached its heartrending conclusion, drawing gasps and moans from the audience, Lucinda was free to shed tears without question.

Chapter 18

It was with a great deal of happy anticipation that James turned onto Regent Street, toward the corner where Lucinda had said she would be waiting for him. The note she'd sent last night, asking if he could come here this afternoon, was still in his coat pocket. He couldn't bear to lay it aside, nor even to burn it as she had asked. The neat, unembellished handwriting, comprising four evenly spaced lines on simple cream paper, was so exactly like her personality that the note was practically an illustration of the woman herself. Keeping it with him was almost as good as having her nearby.

He could not imagine why Lucinda would ask for such a peculiar way of meeting, nor why she had entreated him to come alone and tell no one where he was going. He only knew she wanted to see him again, and that was enough for him. Two weeks had passed since the opera, and he'd not caught even a glimpse of her. He'd had only Emily's reports that Lucinda and Daniel were, in her words, "getting on famously." But Emily's assessment of any situation was never entirely trustworthy, since she was inclined to see only what she wanted to see.

From Daniel he could get precious little information at all. It seemed Lady Hibbitt really was in some sort of decline, for Daniel was spending much of his time at the family estate outside London. If it was true that his mother was dying, Daniel could very well hasten an engagement with Lucinda. Although James had been responsible for the match, he now found himself hoping it would not move forward with any great speed, if at all. It was entirely selfish of him, but he wanted to spend as much time with her as possible before marriage claimed them both and made such meetings impossible. And if the very proper Miss Cardington dared to send him a secret note, which was contrary to all the rules of etiquette, then perhaps she felt the same way.

He spotted her instantly, even though the shop-lined thoroughfare was bustling with people. She was standing outside a silversmith's shop on the next corner. She continued to study the wares in the window, but he knew she was conscious of his approach. As soon as he reached her, she turned and gave him a smile that made his heart twist. "Hello, James." Her gaze flicked away briefly to ensure no one was close enough to hear them. "Thank you for agreeing to meet me here on such short notice."

"I would do anything for you, Lucinda. Anytime. You have only to ask." The words came out glibly enough, but for once he was completely serious.

"That's a dangerous promise," she teased. "It could get you into all sorts of trouble."

"I sincerely hope it does." He couldn't help but grin, for he was heartened by her playful response. When last he'd seen her, entering her family's carriage outside the opera house, she'd looked downright despondent. "I hope you will let me in on the reason for this charming secret public rendezvous? I confess I'm highly intrigued."

"Yes. Well, you see..." Two stiff-looking matrons strolled past, and Lucinda waited until they had gone inside the shop before continuing. "It's about a wedding."

"A wedding?" He nearly choked on the words. "Has it come to that already?"

She said hastily, "Not for me, of course."

James relaxed a little, feeling as though he were regaining his breath after having the wind knocked out of him. "Whose wedding, then?"

"It's Peter, my footman. He's getting married to Kate Darby, one of the girls at my school. The wedding is to take place tomorrow morning."

"Oh, I see." In truth, James was puzzled over her need to relay this information to him, and in such an unusual way. But then, as he considered the ramifications of such a match, he began to understand. "Are your parents aware of this happy development?"

"No!" Lucinda looked around furtively, as though any of the passersby on the busy street might be spies sent by her parents to eavesdrop. "They mustn't find out. Peter would be dismissed immediately. My mother strictly forbids the servants even to have followers, much less to get married."

"I don't know why people continue to cling to these heartless rules. My theory is that if servants were married they might be happier and far less troublesome. It's just a theory, however. One that's not likely to be tested anytime soon."

"Certainly not by my parents," Lucinda agreed. "Their rule is in place and I cannot change it. Therefore Peter and Kate will have to marry in secret. Unfortunately, it also means they will be separated once my family leaves for the countryside—which I have just learned this morning is sooner than we expected. Mama says she can no longer abide the heat and will be returning to our estate in Hampshire next week. She insists Emily and I go with her."

"You're leaving?" James could not hide his disappointment.

"Emily was violently upset at this news, as you can imagine. She does not want to leave London—or you. My mother has consoled her with a promise of a very large house party to take place next month. You will be invited, of course."

"Naturally I shall drop everything and be there." He added with forced casualness, "Are you sad to be leaving London?"

She hesitated, and her smile wavered. "A little. There are still so many things I'd like to do here."

"Such as?"

"Well, there's the school, and . . ."

James held his breath. "And?"

She didn't answer, but her gaze held his. James had the impression a million things were passing between them unsaid, moving as swiftly as the people hurrying past on the street. When she did finally speak, it was to say brusquely, "There is one benefit to all this hullaballoo over leaving London. I have cajoled my parents into allowing me two weeks at Tom and Margaret's home in Lincolnshire."

"That's wonderful," James said. He knew she'd purposefully changed the subject, but at the moment he thought it best not to object. "I've sorely missed them, especially after all the excitement they caused last year. You must send them my love."

"I shall. In the meantime—"

She paused as the silversmith's shop door opened and the two old ladies they'd seen earlier now exited the shop. They seemed surprised to see James and Lucinda still standing there, and one of the ladies raised a suspicious brow. James pointed to a snuff box in the window and said, "I don't know, Miss Cardington. It does seem nice, but I cannot make up my mind about it. What do you think?"

Lucinda put a finger to her chin, as if thinking. "I have my doubts about the gold trim. That silver one next to it seems more elegant, less gaudy."

"Yes, I see what you mean..."

Sufficiently satisfied, the two ladies turned and resumed their own conversation as they made their way up the street.

"I really cannot stay here much longer," Lucinda said. "So I shall get to the point. Peter and Kate will be separated, because he must go with my family to Hampshire and she will have to remain here in London."

"That's terrible. Is there no way he can stay here?"

"They both feel it is best for now, until Peter has time to find other employment. In the meantime, I thought they would enjoy having a photograph taken of them together. Something they could each have a copy of to help ease the pain of their separation."

"Oh, I see," James said. "And you would like for me to be the photographer."

"Would you mind terribly? I know it's asking rather a lot, and on such short notice too, because we would need to do it tomorrow morning."

She looked apologetic, as though she were imposing on him, when in fact she was offering him something he very much wanted. It was another opportunity to see her privately—or at least, without any of her family around. Coming up easily with a reassuring smile, he said, "My dear, nothing could make me happier."

"And I presume I need not mention that you must not tell Emily about this? I know she would never be able to keep the secret, even supposing she was willing to."

"No," James answered joyfully, "I will not be telling Emily."

*

Lucinda instructed the driver to take the long way home. A lengthy ride through the city streets in a closed carriage was just about the only way for her to find time alone. Obtaining permission to be away during one of their at-home receiving days had been difficult, but she'd managed by pleading a desperate need for a new bonnet. Both her mother and sister had agreed that was very sensible; indeed, they were far too concerned about her appearance these days, and all because she finally had a suitor.

Yes, there could be no mistaking Daniel Hibbitt's intentions. He'd made a point of seeking her out at public events, as well as visiting their home. She had the impression he'd been pleased at her openly emotional response to the last act of *La Traviata*, thinking she'd really connected with the opera. Lucinda would never let him know—nor anyone else, for that matter—what had truly been on her mind.

She'd agonized over whether to arrange today's meeting with James. Their brief conversation at the opera still troubled her. In retrospect she was thankful that Emily's sudden arrival had ended it, for she suspected James was going to say something that could only fan the wrong sort of flames. In the days since then, Lucinda had tried to tell herself it was foolish to imagine James was harboring any romantic feelings for her, but after the way he'd looked at her today she was not so sure. He'd been egging her on, wanting her to say she was going to miss him. This was James, however, and it was always impossible to tell whether he was serious or joking. But if she was right about the way they were beginning to care for each other, she was equally sure it was not something they could ever speak of, much less act upon. Only heartache could lay down that path.

Now that the meeting was over, Lucinda was glad she'd done it. She had been strong enough to keep the conversation out of dangerous territory. Peter and Kate would have their photograph, and that made Lucinda very happy. Of course, in order to get the photograph she would have to see James again, something she could not deny she wanted, despite the risks. Was it wrong to be so altruistic and so selfish with the very same act?

She was still mulling over that question when she finally arrived home and made her way to the parlor, where she knew her mother and sister would be waiting for her.

"Lucinda, there you are!" Emily said as soon as she entered. "We've been waiting for ages!"

Lucinda saw with some surprise that Daniel was there also. He was seated in a chair next to Emily, and they must have been enjoying a pleasant conversation, for her whole aspect was bright and cheerful. It was a big change from the way she'd been sulking this morning over the family's change of plans.

Daniel rose. "Good afternoon," he said with a bow.

"Mr. Hibbitt has graciously joined us for tea today," Lady Cardington said, as two servants followed Lucinda into the room with heavily laden trays.

"How nice to see you again," Lucinda said to Daniel. She wished her heart would leap for joy when she saw him, as it did whenever she was around James. Even thinking such a thing only increased her guilt and distress.

By contrast, Lady Cardington's happiness was increasing in exact proportion to the number of times Daniel kept returning. Today she was positively preening with satisfaction. Once the servants had retreated, she rose and said, "Mr. Hibbitt, will you excuse me? I've just thought of an important matter that needs handling right away."

"Shall I go with you, Mama?" Emily said quickly.

"That would be wonderful. Thank you, dear."

This unnatural interchange between her mother and sister, followed by their swift exit, aroused every one of Lucinda's suspicions. She was not ready for this. Not today. With a quick apology to Daniel she raced out into the hall and caught up to them, speaking to her mother in a furious whisper. "Mama, don't you think this can wait? You know I'm leaving for Lincolnshire in a few days. Papa promised I could go. It's all arranged—"

"Yes, yes, you can go," her mother said. "But that is the very reason why Mr. Hibbitt is here today. He knows we are preparing to leave London, and so he came and had a private chat with your father this morning."

"He knows? How could he know? Didn't you just decide this morning?"

"Never mind all that," her mother said, attempting to shoo her back toward the parlor. "Just talk to the man, and be aware that your father has given his blessing."

"His blessing! Shouldn't he have spoken to me first? I'm not ready. I need more time——"

"Don't waste time arguing!" Lady Cardington commanded. "You have an actual suitor in there!"

"And a very nice one, too," Emily chimed in. "Mr. Hibbitt is perfectly charming, and you are a fool if you throw away this chance to be the wife of a baronet! He does go on about the opera, but he's such a sensible man, too. A perfect match for you, I am sure. Besides, think of me! Think of James!"

Unfortunately, it *was* James she was thinking of. But James was promised to Emily—a fact Lucinda must strive to remember above all else. She wanted desperately to do the right thing. *Trust in the Lord, and do good…* That was an admonition she ought to heed. If Daniel was going out of his way to be with her, she ought to at least talk to him. She owed him that much. "Fine," she said with resignation. "I will hear what he has to say. But that doesn't mean——"

Emily gave a little squeal and hugged her. "Oh, Lucinda! You will be so happy! I just know it!"

Lucinda disentangled herself and turned away. If this had to be done, it would be better just to get it over with. She returned to the parlor to find Daniel standing by the window, looking not entirely at ease. That made two of them. She took a seat on the sofa. "May I pour you some tea?" she asked, although she knew it was only an attempt to delay the inevitable.

"Perhaps in a bit."

To her dismay, Daniel did not return to his chair, but took a seat next to her on the sofa. He smelled strongly of soap, as though he'd taken extra care with his morning ablutions. Lucinda's heart skipped, but not from excitement. He took hold of her hand. His touch was not unpleasant, but neither did it set her pulse racing. It was nothing like the heightened sense of pleasure that coursed through her whenever James was near. In short, everything about this moment felt distant and unreal, like she was acting in a play.

"Miss Cardington." He cleared his throat. "Lucinda. I believe you may have some idea what I am about to say."

"Mr. Hibbitt, I wonder if we might be a bit premature—"

"Hear me out, please," he urged. "I know this isn't easy for either of us, but I hope you will allow me to say my piece."

Lucinda took a deep breath, prayed for wisdom, and nodded for him to continue.

"There comes a time in every man's life when he must do the responsible thing and get married. For me, that time is now. As you know, my mother is not well. The truth is, she may not be long on this earth, and her greatest wish is to know that I am settled and the Hibbitt family line will continue."

"I see," Lucinda murmured. "I'm sorry to hear your mother is ill."

He frowned. "I won't pretend my relationship with her has been an easy one, but I know she has always had my best interests at heart. She remembers you, by the way, and sends her regards."

"She does?" Lucinda was startled by this unexpected tangent.

"She says you met at some soiree or other four or five years ago."

"Yes, it was at the Duke of Cherville's ball. It's kind of her to remember, although I hope it's due to some conversation we had and not because I tripped over his grace's feet and fell into a potted plant." She probably shouldn't be mentioning such things, but if Daniel was serious about marrying her, he'd better know full well what he was getting into.

This drew only a mildly curious look, however. "She made no mention of a plant. She said only how charming you were and how pleased she was that I was considering marrying you."

Lucinda pulled her hand away. "You told her that? When we hardly know each other?"

"Don't be offended. You can't deny this was the whole reason James introduced us. Our situations are similar; we both have parents who are pressuring us to marry."

"This is true," Lucinda admitted.

"Therefore, I suggest we meet their demands. Once you and I are married, they will be appeased and you and I will have the freedom to conduct our lives as we see fit."

Freedom. It was an odd word to use in conjunction with *marriage*. True, she would escape her parents' dominion over her, but would she really be *free*? She said cautiously, "And just how, exactly, do you envision us conducting our lives?"

He shrugged. "As I said, it will be as we like it. Your

sister told me you don't enjoy going out in society. Neither do I, as I'm sure you are aware. Most of what passes for conversation at dinner parties bores me to no end, and I personally cannot abide dancing."

"Can't you?" A few weeks ago, Lucinda would have said the same thing. But then she'd enjoyed one enchanting waltz in a sunlit parlor. Now she had periodic daydreams of floating across a ballroom, swept up by the music and a man's embrace. Sharply she told herself not to assume that one dance with James guaranteed she was no longer a failure on the dance floor. If she and Daniel were to attempt to dance, it could well be a disaster.

"I wish to listen to music, not exercise to it," Daniel said firmly. "I will attend anything with real merit, such as the opera, but I draw the line at going out afterward."

"It sounds as though you envision a life of quiet domesticity," Lucinda said. It was not an appealing vision. There were so many places she wanted to visit, and dreams she had yet to accomplish.

"Don't misunderstand me. I do not expect us to be always at home, tripping over one another. I spend many evenings at my club. I'd expect you as the lady of the house to watch over the servants and meals and so on, but you are a sensible and capable woman so you shouldn't find those tasks too onerous. Beyond that, you are free to do as you like."

There it was again, that word *free*. She supposed his vision of marriage ought to be appealing to her. Why wasn't it, then?

"Your sister also mentioned how you both prefer living in London," Daniel continued.

"Did she?" It would appear Emily had managed

to tell Daniel plenty of things about her, most of it not entirely accurate—or at least, not any longer. Lucinda was changing, but her sister would never take any notice. "I don't know that I *prefer* London to the country, but I do take pleasure in the work I do at Caring House while I'm here."

Daniel took this halting agreement as hearty confirmation. "Precisely! Therefore you'll be happy to know we shall live primarily in town. The family estate at Highgate is full enough with my parents and sister living there."

"It won't bother you to have a wife who is so directly involved in the lives of women who were...that is, who are trying to recover themselves?"

"Not at all. I think it's commendable."

"Do you really? I'm glad to hear you say it." Lucinda's heart lifted a little. Here was a topic they'd not yet broached during the brief time they'd known each other. One that was vitally important to her. "I believe we have a moral and religious duty to help our fellow man. Don't you?"

"Yes, well..." Daniel tugged at his collar. "I'm not a religious man, not in the sense of someone who goes to church every Sunday. There are too many hypocrites under those steeples, and I will not be found among them."

"So you believe actions speak louder than words," Lucinda prompted, trying to discern the actual depth of his religious feeling.

"*Some* actions speak louder than words," Daniel corrected. "As I said, I have no intention of sleeping off my Sunday mornings in a pew, so I'll tell you right now not to expect it."

"And yet you do believe in God, don't you?" Lucinda persisted. She could never marry someone who was an unbeliever. It would be unthinkable. No other "advantages" offered by a marriage could ever compensate for that lack.

"Well, naturally I believe in God," Daniel replied. "He has set everything in order—'all things great and small,' as the poem says. Those of us who have been blessed with abundance ought to render help to those less fortunate. For example, I'm very interested in this project that Henry Petersen is organizing over at the Lord Mayor's office. The city needs a proper sanitation system, and they are working to design one that could be the envy of all nations—if the politicians will let us build it."

"Yes, I have read about that," Lucinda said. "It is an admirable goal."

He nodded. "I'll wager, too, that in your charity work you have seen streets where refuse heaps and sewage can be cheek-by-jowl with wells. Medical science has now proven conclusively that cholera is spread by tainted drinking water. So you see, having a proper sanitation system would not only be more pleasant, but it would save many lives as well." He was speaking eagerly now, almost as animated as he'd been when they were discussing the opera. "I believe that falls under the heading of doing one's moral duty, don't you?"

Was this good enough for her? She had often told the girls at her school that God could be found both within a church building or outside it. She supposed it was better for a man to prefer good deeds to false words. But were good works confirmation of an inner spiritual life, or merely a replacement for it? She could not tell.

When she did not reply, Daniel leaned back and

smiled contentedly. He clearly believed he had proved his point. "So there you have it. You will live your life, and I will live mine. I think it can work out admirably, and we won't have to trouble each other too much."

This statement was probably a logical conclusion to everything he'd said so far, yet it still managed to surprise her. "So if I understand you correctly," she said with slow deliberation, "you think we are a good match because we both wish to be left alone?"

"Precisely! I do like a woman who can get straight to the point." He eyed her. "So, what do you say? Shall we become engaged, then?"

For a proposal, it was hardly the stuff of dreams. But then, Lucinda had always tried to approach life rationally and not allow herself to be carried away by foolish whims as her sister had been. Unfortunately, the taste of romance James had given her had turned her life topsy-turvy and ruined everything she thought she knew about herself. He'd shown her what genuine attraction between a man and woman ought to be...

Her hands flew to her cheeks. In all this rationality, Daniel had not touched on one very important problem with the arrangement he had just described. Was this to be a marriage of convenience only? Would they have separate rooms, with him never approaching her bed? If he was to seek his pleasure elsewhere, she couldn't bear it. It would be too humiliating.

She squared her shoulders and looked Daniel straight in the eye, ignoring the heat now burning her cheeks. "Daniel, if we never...ah...disturb each other, how are we..." She coughed. "That is, if we are to carry on this illustrious family lineage of yours..." She pushed down her embarrassment and blurted out, "I expect you to visit no woman's bed but mine!"

Daniel laughed. It was, in fact, the first time Lucinda had ever heard him laugh out loud.

Disconcerted, she said, "It's no laughing matter. I assure you I am quite serious."

"I believe you." Daniel placed an arm on the back of the sofa, drawing closer to her. Again she could smell soap, plus the faint scent of his hair tonic. "I have no intention of going elsewhere. Not so long as you and I can glean satisfaction from our marital duty." He touched a hand to her cheek. "In that, as in everything else, we each have an important role. I will play my part. Will you play yours?"

His hand strayed, lightly tracing the edge of her jaw line. She shivered, confused, not knowing what to make of this sensation. He had not been this forward with her before. He gently grasped the back of her neck, pulling her toward him. She allowed him to do it, curiosity driving her. Could she really give herself wholly to this man? What would his kiss be like? After the fiery branding of James's lips on hers, she had to know. Perhaps, she told herself wildly, all kisses were like that. If so, then Daniel would be able to draw out that same desire from her, and fill her with that same craving for more. She desperately hoped this was so, if only for the sake of her bewildered and battered heart.

Daniel's kiss was firm, his lips cool against hers. She found herself instinctively wishing to pull back, but she forced herself to lean into him instead. He tried to coax her mouth open, to deepen the kiss. She complied, but she had the sense he was pushing his ardor forward, forcing something that wasn't there. She was doing the same, disillusioned that the kiss was not setting off a string of heady sensations. In fact, she felt...

Nothing.

She drew away, more horrified at this complete lack of sensation than she would have been if the man had repulsed her.

He looked as disappointed as she felt. Surely this was a sign things were not right, that they should not even be considering marriage. But he merely patted her hand and said, "It was a first kiss. In time you will learn. We will each of us have to learn what pleases the other."

He said this with a confident, almost patronizing air, but Lucinda could not believe him. She was too aware of the way James's kiss instantly enthralled her without any hesitation or coaching. She stared at him, unable to speak and utterly perplexed.

"So I suppose I may take your answer as a yes?" Daniel pressed.

"Well, I... That is..." Lucinda stammered. What was wrong with her?

His cool gray eyes watched her intently, which only made her more uncomfortable. She rose hastily from the sofa and crossed the room, tripping as her skirt caught a table. Catching herself, she leaned a steadying arm against the mantel, trying to think clearly. If she accepted Daniel's offer, she could meet her father's demands and ensure that her sister and James had the money they very much needed, and she would still have a reasonable degree of autonomy. But she would be committing her life to a man she hardly knew. She just didn't have enough confidence in him to do it.

All the expectations of both their families were like

a giant weight pressing down on her, pushing her to go where she was not ready. The very walls of this room seemed to be closing in around her. Quietly she began a desperate prayer. *Lord what should I do?*

Wait.

The word came to her, simply and easily, bringing with it a sudden peace. It made perfect sense. She did not have to answer him today, and in just a few days she would be seeing Margaret and Tom. Surely they could give her sound advice—something she could not get from anyone in her family.

Slowly she turned to face Daniel. "I am truly honored by your offer, but this is such an important decision and I need time to think it over. May I give you my answer in a few weeks?"

Clearly this was not the reply he wanted. She saw his hands grip his knees tightly, and a furrow creased his brow. He must be impatient to conclude this business. "All right," he said at last, his frown straightening to a more neutral expression. "Your parents have invited me to the house party at your estate next month. Can I expect your answer then?"

"Yes," she said in relief. It was a reprieve, not a solution, but she would take it.

Chapter 19

"That's got it, I think." James pulled the glass plate from the water bath and held it over a burner to dry, slowly moving it back and forth over the flame. He was pleased at how well the photograph had turned out.

Kate and Peter's wedding at the small church had been short and simple, attended only by James and Lucinda and the women from the school. The wedding breakfast having been concluded, they were now gathered in the tiny courtyard behind the school. Everyone crowded around, eager to see the photograph James had taken of the happy couple.

"It's like magic!" Mary exclaimed. She was one of the younger students, and she'd been watching James with undisguised awe.

"Much of science is perceived that way," James told her. "But it's really just the result of trial and error—not to mention a vast array of chemicals."

Kate peered at the plate with a puzzled expression. "It looks odd."

"This is the negative. That means the lights and darks are reversed. It will look spectacular once I make the prints. Then you and Peter will each have one, and you'll always be able to gaze upon the face of your beloved, no matter how far apart you are." He couldn't resist glancing over at Lucinda as he said this, for he fully intended to take a photograph of her today. He hoped it wouldn't be too hard to convince her to do it.

She was standing a short way off, smiling at the proceedings, but in a distracted sort of way. All morning she'd maintained a distant air. She'd even begged off helping with the picture-taking process, claiming she didn't want to risk staining her gown. But James had an idea there was another reason for it.

"Speaking of being apart," said Tessa, "isn't it time the bride and groom left us? I do believe you should go and inspect your new lodgings—if you take my meaning." She gave the pair a grin and a knowing wink, which brought hoots of laughter from the ladies.

"Yes, indeed!" Peter said heartily. He took hold of his new wife's hand and kissed it. Kate beamed. She was dressed in a modest, Sunday-best gown, but she was positively radiant. James marveled, as he had done many times, at how a wedding always had this effect on the bride, no matter how humble the circumstance.

Peter turned to Lucinda. "With your permission, Miss Cardington?"

Lucinda looked distressed and more than a little embarrassed, for everyone here knew exactly how Peter and Kate were about to spend their afternoon. She cleared her throat. "Yes, of course you may go. Just remember I shall need you back here by five in order to take me home."

"I could escort you home," James offered. "Then Peter and Kate can have another hour or more together."

Lucinda looked doubtful. "It won't go unnoticed at the house if I return without my footman."

"Why don't you just say you sent him on an errand? Important business for the school, or something?"

Peter and Kate looked at Lucinda hopefully as she pondered this idea. *Poor souls,* James thought. *I know exactly how they feel.* Becoming engaged to Emily had imposed a life of celibacy on him. It hadn't been easy, for he'd been obliged to give up many other things in order to remove himself from the distractions of women. Nor had it freed him from guilt, for now his fiancée's sister had proved a far bigger distraction. He could understand how desperate Peter and Kate would be to lose themselves in each other's arms, and they would want every minute they could get.

"I suppose that will be acceptable," Lucinda said at last. "But you must be home by seven, or Mr. Jennings will have my head as well as yours."

"Yes, miss!" Peter said happily. "Thank you!"

"Off with you, then!" Fannie said with a grin. Just like a mother hen, she rounded up the other ladies, and they all clustered around the newlyweds, laughing and teasing as they bustled them out the front gate to where a hackney coach was waiting.

James and Lucinda remained behind in the little courtyard, but they could hear the comments tossed to the happy couple as they drove away, including Tessa's, "Go easy on him, Kate!" This brought on a fresh round of raucous laughter.

Not surprisingly, Lucinda's face was flushed pink. "Well, that's that," she said with a resigned sigh. "I am happy for them."

"So am I," James said. "I admire what you've done. You've made such a change in all those women's lives."

She gave a humble shrug. "I only wish I could do more."

He cocked his head at her. "Tell me, why do you always try to deflect compliments?"

The question only made her look uncomfortable. "Perhaps I am not always so deserving of them." That was pure nonsense, but before James could say so, she pointed to the plate in his hands. "Is it dry now?"

"It is." He looked down at his handiwork. "I think it might be one of my best compositions yet. What do you think?" He held it out for her to inspect. When she stepped nearer to do so, he took a moment to breathe in a soft hint of lilac. He'd never been enamored of that scent before he'd met her. "Would you like to come to my house—to Lady Thornborough's, I mean—and I will teach you to make prints?"

He knew this was straining the bounds of respectability, but he had to ask. He wanted to find a place where they could talk privately, where he could find out what was on her mind.

Lucinda took a step back. "Thank you, but I think we should remain here for the afternoon." She pointed toward the school. "There is work to do—"

James took hold of her arm to prevent her from going inside. "I have a better idea. Let me take a photograph of you."

"Me?" She looked genuinely surprised taken aback. She motioned toward the rough table they'd set up, which was now littered with trays and bottles of chemicals. "My picture is not worth all that time and effort."

"I beg to differ." With a gentle hand he lifted her chin,

studying the attractive line of her jaw, and her expressive, ever-changing eyes. It was all indescribably appealing. "In fact, if I may steal a line from Shakespeare, 'Lady, you are the cruelest she alive if you will lead these graces to the grave and leave no copy.' "

"He can't have been speaking of photography," she said primly, although her breathing was slightly ragged. "In fact, I believe he was speaking of marriage and—" Her eyes got wider and she took a step back, flustered. "In any case, you needn't use Shakespeare just to flatter me."

He smiled, for he truly loved setting her off-balance like this. He'd enjoyed it ever since that night on the Trefethens' balcony. It was a big step toward lowering her walls. "Despite my reputation, I do speak truth sometimes. You ought very well to be photographed, for you are looking incredibly lovely just at the moment."

She took in a startled breath. "Thank you," she said quietly. "But really, there's no need."

What would it take to convince her? An idea quickly came to him. "Let me tell you the real reason. I already have a photograph of Emily—that one we took in Hyde Park, remember? I want to take one of you as well, and present both to your parents as a gift. It will be a lovely memento of their daughters." He held out his hand in appeal. "Please. Wouldn't you like to do this for them?"

"Well . . . it is kind of you to think of that," she said hesitantly.

"Wonderful!" James lost no time pulling out another plate and the collodion mixture before she could think of another objection.

As he prepared the plate, he realized the other women had not returned to the courtyard. He had an idea, based on several things Tessa had said and done throughout the morning, that she was as interested in seeing James and Lucinda paired as she was in getting Peter and Kate off to their marriage bed. If she was the one ensuring they were undisturbed, he would have to thank her for it later. Noise from the city and the occasional shouts of children drifted over the high brick wall, and yet it felt like they were in their own private sanctuary.

Once the plate was ready, James led Lucinda to a rough wooden bench near the little garden's lone rose bush. "If you will sit here, the sun is reaching this corner now. That will shorten the exposure time."

She obeyed, although she still looked uncomfortable at being the subject of a photograph.

James carefully set the position of the tripod and adjusted the angle of the camera. He ducked his head under the cloth to check the picture. There she was, beautifully projected onto the ground-glass focusing screen, the image upside-down—just like so many things in his life. If this was what he had to do for the opportunity to stare at Lucinda without her shying away, then he would find a way to take dozens of photographs. He took his time, trying to decipher what she was thinking. All day she'd been cheerful and even a bit misty-eyed, just as the other ladies had been. But James also saw evidence of strain around her eyes. Something was troubling her, and James wished very much to know what it was.

"Is everything all right?" she finally called out. "You've been under there an awfully long time."

James pulled his head out from the cloth. "The angle isn't quite right—your head was turned a little to the side. I think it would be better to look straight at the camera."

It was an excuse, and nothing more, but she seemed to believe him. She did as he asked, and he dove under the cloth again, studying her features once more. "Perfect!" he exclaimed. "Stay exactly as you are."

He quickly made the camera ready. "Now, take a deep breath, and then don't move. The exposure is going to take about thirty seconds. Give me a signal when you are ready." She breathed in. When she dropped her chin in the tiniest of nods, James reached for the lens cap.

He tried hard to concentrate as he counted the seconds. It was difficult to do, because at the moment he started the exposure, her face took on the most lovely, wistful expression he'd ever seen. Her lips were parted just a fraction, and tiny wisps of hair framed her face perfectly. "And... thirty!" Swiftly he set the lens cap back in place.

She breathed out and visibly relaxed. "Will it do?" she asked.

"Oh, yes," James said, his heart playing an intense game of rackets against his chest. "It will do."

He would happily have stood there, gazing at her. Only the need to treat the plate before it dried finally propelled him to the dark tent. He could not lose this moment that had been captured for all time. The dark tent's small red window gave James just enough light to see Lucinda's image slowly begin to emerge on the plate. This was always the most exciting step for him, because it was the exact moment when he knew whether his choice of lens and exposure time had paid off. But never had he been more thrilled than he was right now. The picture, and its subject, were perfect.

He set it in the wash tray and brought it outside the tent. "Here it is," he announced. "It's going to be wonderful."

He set the tray on the makeshift table. "Lucinda, what were you thinking about while I was taking the exposure?"

There was that strain around her eyes again. "Do you really want to know?"

"If you are embarrassed by the question, then yes, I most definitely want to know."

His teasing response brought out a ghost of a smile. "It's a silly thing, really. To tell you the truth, I was thinking about weddings."

"That's not surprising, given today's events."

She sighed. "Not just this wedding, but others I've attended as well. I was thinking about Geoffrey and Lizzie's wedding, so different from this one. It was on a cold morning in early December."

"I remember it well," James said. "There was a biting wind and a fresh layer of snow. But the church was warm with happiness and a multitude of good wishes, and of course Lizzie's smile could melt even the hardest ice."

"It was lovely," Lucinda agreed. "So was Margaret and Tom's wedding, which took place the following autumn."

"I remember that wedding even better," James said. "You and I stood up together with the bride and groom, and you were wearing that lovely dress—which I believe I've mentioned to you before."

She gave him a modest smile. "Now, here we are again, both of us attending yet another wedding—this time in summer."

"Three weddings, all at different seasons of the year. And here I thought weddings always took place in the spring."

"Well, yours will be a spring wedding, at any rate."

"Yes." The word came out without even a hint of

enthusiasm. With more energy he added, "It's terribly dull of me to be so conventional. But since all the other seasons have been tried, I suppose it will have to do."

"Conventional?" She shook her head. "It will be the highlight of the season. The *London* season, I mean." She tried to smile as if in jest, but it took on more of a melancholy air. "You will find a way to make it extraordinary, for you are extraordinary."

James felt something twist inside at the way she was looking at him just now. "And will you be at my wedding, too?"

"Yes." Her lower lip trembled a little. "I will."

I will. Those two little words suddenly painted a powerful image in James's mind. He saw Lucinda, no longer a bridesmaid but now a bride, resplendent in a white silk gown, her hair decorated with orange blossoms, her sweet lips uttering a promise of a joyous lifetime together. "I wish more than the world to be at your wedding," he said.

He spoke impulsively, but even as the words came out he realized it was a mistake. She stiffened. "Did Emily tell you, then?"

"I haven't seen Emily for two days," James replied, worried at this sudden shift in her demeanor. "What did you think she would have told me?"

Lucinda sent a quick glance toward the school as if to ensure no one else was nearby. Quietly she said, "Daniel Hibbitt has proposed marriage to me."

There it was—the news he'd been dreading. James turned back to the table and set about moving the plate to the second bath, primarily to hide his grimace of pain. "And...did you accept?" He waited, every nerve on edge. Behind him, there was a long pause.

"I—I told him I needed time to consider it, and that I will give him my answer at the house party next month."

James exhaled. "I see." If Lucinda was not ready to accept Daniel's offer, she was undoubtedly torn over it. That would explain the worry he'd seen in her eyes—worry that was still there when he turned to look at her again.

Now he saw anguish and uncertainty as well. "You can imagine how well that was received by my family. Daniel was polite about it, but as soon as he was gone from the house my mother and sister immediately attacked me, telling me I was ungrateful, insensitive, and wickedly selfish."

"They have no right to say those things!" James said angrily. "I may not be allowed to reprimand your mother, but you can be sure I will tell Emily in no uncertain terms to never again treat you that way. You are the kindest, most thoughtful person in the world, and I won't allow her to insult you." He stopped short, realizing that Lucinda's eyes were tearing up at his tirade.

"It's nice to have someone in my camp," she said softly.

"Do you not want to marry Daniel, then?"

"I don't know!" She twisted her hands together in frustration. "It seems like the right thing to do, and yet I cannot reconcile myself to it. I prayed fervently to God, asking what I should do, and the only answer I got was *'Wait.'* But I can't put off the decision forever." She gave him a searching look. "Do you think I should marry him, James?"

The way she was looking at him, pleading for help, nearly tore his heart out. How could he possibly be the one to give her the right advice? He lifted the plate from the second bath and began the process of drying it over the flame, grateful to have something to do as he took time to compose his answer.

He ought to say yes, of course. So many things about his future were dependent on Lucinda making that choice. And yet he was jealous of anyone who might have the chance to marry her. It occurred to him that he had equally selfish reasons for answering either way.

No, he told himself. It was not selfish to urge her to marry. He agreed with her father's opinion that Lucinda would not truly be happy alone. She ought to be able to enjoy the pleasures and comforts of married life, and he certainly could not offer her that. But he could not—would not—be the one to make that decision. She had to make it for herself. He stared down at the plate, only to see Lucinda's image looking back at him. "Well, I would never have introduced you if I didn't think it was a good idea."

She walked around the table until she stood opposite him, forcing him to look at her. "And now?" she pressed. "You told me at the opera that I shouldn't marry a man I don't love."

"I did," he acknowledged. Those, too, were words that he had uttered spontaneously and that were now coming back to bite him. "Perhaps that's why God told you to wait. Perhaps your love for Daniel will grow with time."

James was not happy with that answer on a number of different levels, but for now it was the best he could do.

Lucinda did not appear pleased either. "That's a very convenient interpretation, isn't it?" she accused.

She turned away, her shoulders slumped, heavy with disappointment. No doubt he'd confirmed her belief that he would say anything to gain his own ends. Only he would know how much it had cost him to appear so self-serving.

Chapter 20

Lucinda and Margaret leaned against the low wall of a little stone bridge, relaxing in the morning sun. The day was fine, the sky dotted with soft, white clouds. Lucinda had been in Lincolnshire for three days now. After the emotional turmoil that had preceded this trip, every day here had felt like heaven. Margaret and Tom were so happy, their love for each other evident in everything they did. What a delight it was to spend time with a husband and wife who loved each other so tenderly and so deeply. It gave Lucinda hope, an example to strive for.

Adding to her pleasure was the joy of being free from her overbearing family. It was a small taste of the independence she craved. Marriage would offer her that independence; it lured her to keep considering Daniel's proposal. Should she marry him? She'd had yet to broach the subject with Margaret, but perhaps now it was time. "Margaret, there's something I've been wanting to ask you about."

Margaret looked up from where she'd been dreamily watching the ripples in the tiny brook below. "Yes?"

"I am glad to see how happy you are with Tom, especially since you had some reservations about marrying him."

"It's true that at the time I was not entirely sure I was doing the right thing." She smiled. "But I have no doubts now. Marrying Tom is the best thing I've ever done."

Margaret had changed so much, Lucinda thought. So many weights seemed to have dropped away, leaving only this peaceful, contented woman. *If this is the result of a good marriage,* she thought, *I would welcome it wholeheartedly.* "So would you say that even if two people are not in love at the time they marry, it can still grow into love?"

"Well, perhaps that isn't *always* the case. In our society there are plenty of people who marry for reasons other than love. They want social status or financial security. Unfortunately, true love never quite blossoms."

"Do you think there's any way to know ahead of time what will happen?" Lucinda asked anxiously. "Can a person be sure, before taking that irrevocable step, they are not making a huge mistake?"

Margaret leaned an arm on the bridge and studied her thoughtfully. "Tell me, why are you suddenly so interested in discussing marriage? Has some gentleman proposed to you?"

"Well, yes."

"How wonderful!" She clapped her hands in delight. "Who is he? I've been praying for you, that you would find a good husband and be blessed just as I have been."

"Wait!" Lucinda protested. "We are not engaged just

yet. I still have many concerns, which is why I knew I had to talk to you."

"Dearest Lucinda, you know I'll be happy to help you in any way I can." She wrapped her arm in Lucinda's. "Shall we take a walk? Then you can tell me all about it."

As they strolled along a sunny path that followed the stream, Lucinda told Margaret everything, describing the events from the night in Cremorne Gardens right up to Daniel's offer of marriage. Everything, that is, except the day when James kissed her. She could not bring herself to speak about that just yet. Even so, it felt good to share the rest of it, and she felt her burden lift a little.

Margaret listened intently, nodding and asking occasional questions. "I had no idea of the financial conditions your father was putting onto James and Emily's marriage," she remarked, sounding every bit as indignant as Lucinda had been. "You poor thing! You must feel like a chess piece or something."

"I do, rather," Lucinda agreed.

"Yet you say that you and this Mr. Hibbitt have found each other agreeable, and that he seems to be showing a genuine interest in you."

"Yes, and that's what's confusing me."

"I think it sounds fairly simple. If you love him, you should pursue the marriage. Don't turn him down just to spite your parents."

"That's the problem," Lucinda said miserably. "I cannot truly say that I love him. But you didn't love Tom at first either, right? So I keep thinking that perhaps in time, with me and Daniel it *could* grow into love, just like what happened to you."

Margaret shook her head. "I think I gave you the

wrong idea. Before my wedding I may have said I didn't love Tom; I most assuredly told myself the same thing. But the truth is, somewhere, deep down, I *did* love him, right from the start. In time I came to realize that."

"You did love him?" Lucinda pulled up short. "And yet you didn't realize it at first? I'm so confused! How do you know? How can I know if it's the same for me?"

Margaret pondered this. "I think if you harbor any spark that could grow to love, you can sense it."

"A ... spark? What does that mean?"

"It's a quiet feeling, deep down, that you *want* to trust him, or at the very least, you want to walk with him to the next bend in the road and see what lies beyond. The first time Tom took my hand, there was something very like a physical spark. A thrill ran through me that I will never forget. It was intense and undeniable."

"Undeniable," Lucinda repeated softly. She had felt a touch like that. But it was not from Daniel's hand.

"There was something that drew me irresistibly to Tom. Every time he was nearby, even if it was a huge ballroom with hundreds of people, I always knew it. I could sense it." She gave Lucinda an apologetic glance. "I'm probably not describing it very coherently."

"As a matter of fact, I understand you completely." Lucinda knew that feeling very well. It was a perfect description of what happened whenever she was near James.

"So you have felt it?" Margaret said hopefully. "The first time Tom kissed me, it was so glorious I never wanted it to stop. Has Mr. Hibbitt kissed you?"

Lucinda let out a long sigh. "Once."

"And ... ?"

"There was no spark." A feeling of helplessness welled up inside her. What was she to do if the only man she'd had a genuine attraction to was the one she could most definitely *not* marry?

"I'm only describing what happened to me," Margaret qualified, watching her with worry. "Perhaps for you it will be different. If you were to try again..."

Lucinda shook her head. "You are trying to talk me into getting married, and yet you just gave me a good reason not to."

Margaret gently hugged her. "Lucinda, you are my dearest friend. Even better, next spring when your sister marries James, you will be my cousin, too. I want nothing more than to see you happy." She gently nudged Lucinda's chin upward. "Don't give up hope. Maybe you should give Mr. Hibbitt another chance. I have heard of instances where two people did not realize at first that they were right for each other. They were acquaintances, perhaps even friends. But then one day, they suddenly realized how much they meant to each other."

"Yes, I've heard that, too." At what point had she become so drawn to James? She'd known him for years, and they'd had some pleasant conversations, but nothing more. Then something had changed. It began the night he'd caught her with the borrowed book on Lord Trefethen's terrace. She hadn't understood it then. Nor had she allowed herself to admit it after all that had happened between them in her quiet, sunlit parlor. Only now, as Margaret's words began to clear the fog from her brain, could she admit the truth in the depths of her heart.

Lucinda sank down onto the grass. "I am in love," she moaned. "With James Simpson."

"What? Oh, my dear." Margaret sat down beside her. "How do you know?"

Lucinda felt the sting of tears, but she was laughing too—probably from hysteria. "He kissed me, and it was everything you described! The spark, the fire—it was all there!" She grabbed hold of Margaret's sleeve. "I love James Simpson!"

Margaret looked thunderstruck. "He kissed you? When did this happen?"

"There was a day when he and I were alone. He was teaching me to dance, and—oh, what does it matter? The point is, we kissed, and it was wonderful, and I never wanted it to stop. Then I was so racked with guilt because he's engaged to Emily, but even so I have not been able to get him out of my mind. Or my heart. What am I to do?"

There was a pause after this long and ragged speech. Lucinda looked beseechingly at her friend, desperately hoping for comfort or guidance, but there was only dismay written across her features.

"Lucinda, listen to me," Margaret said sternly. "You know how James is with women. He might simply have been flirting with you. Besides, he's engaged to Emily."

"That's why I feel so guilty! But I told you how they got engaged—she trapped him into it."

"Has James ever said he loves you?" Margaret's question was pointed, as though she knew the answer already.

"No," Lucinda admitted. "Not in so many words." Her mind returned, as it had done many times, to the last time she saw him, when he had told her she ought to marry Daniel. She had foolishly been hoping for more from him that day, some sign he was in love with her.

"So you think it was nothing more than a mere flirtation? You're telling me I should forget him?"

"I'm urging you to guard your heart. You know what kind of reputation he has. He's broken plenty of hearts over the years. For your sake—and your sister's—think very carefully about what you do."

It was a hard truth, but Lucinda could not deny the wisdom of it. "You're right. I can't believe I was so foolish as to let myself fall in love with him." She wiped away a tear, trying to regulate her breathing as cold resignation settled over her. "Thank goodness I came here to talk to you."

Chapter 21

"They're here!" Emily cried, racing into Lucinda's room. She ran to the window and threw back the curtains. "Why are you brooding here in the darkness, when our guests are arriving today?"

Lucinda remained where she lay, fully clothed, on top of the bed. "I'm not brooding. The afternoon sun was making my room too warm, and I have a headache." To make her point, she indicated the cold compress on her forehead.

Emily, however, was not paying her any attention. She peered out the window, bouncing from foot to foot with excitement. "Do come and see the carriage. It's magnificent—and drawn by four beautiful bays."

With a sigh, Lucinda slowly sat up, wincing as her aching head complained. The moment she'd been dreading had finally arrived. A trying week lay in store for her, as she would have to wrestle with her own desires while meeting the expectations of everyone else. Although she was resolved on her course of action, she found she still had no stomach for it.

While she was at Tom and Margaret's home, it had seemed a simple thing to shore up her heart and do what was best. But since she'd returned to Hampshire it had been considerably more difficult. The entire household had been in a frenzy of excitement getting the house prepared for nearly two dozen guests. Her mother had relied on her heavily to oversee many of the arrangements. Lucinda had dutifully done everything asked of her, but beyond that she'd kept to herself as much as possible. The knowledge that she owed Daniel an answer weighed heavily on her.

One thing she'd determined after careful reflection was that even if James had been merely flirting with her, she had seen and responded to something deeper. She was not suffering from the same schoolgirl infatuation that every other woman seemed to have for this vibrant man who was the life of every party. She was in love with the man beneath that frivolous façade he wore so well. The man who had gone out of his way to visit her school, mend her reputation, and treat her students with respect rather than scorn. The man who had kissed her so fervently, who'd insisted she was beautiful, a creature worthy of admiration and love. The man whose touch made her feel wondrously, gloriously alive. Margaret had pointed out that he'd never actually declared his love. But Lucinda had decided the reason for that could well be his inescapable bond to the girl who was now gesturing wildly for her to come to the window.

"Lucinda! Hurry! You must see this carriage!"

This was it, then. Lucinda had decided she had no choice but to set aside her feelings for James, and now was as good a time as any to begin. She rose from the bed and joined her sister by the window, fully expecting to see James and Lady Thornborough. But the crest on the side of the carriage was one she did not recognize. A footman opened the door and Daniel Hibbitt alighted. "Why, that's Daniel," she said with surprise. "I'd have thought you were looking for James."

"Oh, James has been here these two hours already," Emily said dismissively.

"He has?" This news gave her a jolt. She must have been lost in a truly deep fog not to have heard his arrival. "Then why are you here with me, and not with him?"

"To be honest, I'm quite put out with James," Emily declared. "Do you know how many times he has written me during these past three weeks?"

The throbbing in Lucinda's head picked up afresh. "I couldn't hazard a guess."

"Twice." Emily uttered the word with disdain. "Twice! I wrote to him every day, and he sent back only two short letters. What keeps a man so busy that he hasn't got time to write to his fiancée? I've decided he can just wait before seeing me. It serves him right."

Her sister's pettiness really was astounding sometimes. Lucinda rubbed her temples, trying vainly for any kind of relief, as she watched the scene below. Daniel was helping his mother out of the carriage. Everyone had been surprised that Lady Hibbitt had accepted the invitation to come, since she was reputed to be in poor health. Evidently she had decided she was well enough to travel. Her presence only increased Lucinda's worry, for the woman would surely expect an engagement announcement by the end of the week.

"Let's go down and greet them," Emily urged. "Mr. Hibbitt will want to see you." She looked at Lucinda critically. "Your hair is mussed, but I can fix it." She reached a hand toward Lucinda's hair, but Lucinda put out a hand to stop her. "I'm not going to go tearing down there. Where's your sense of decorum?"

"Fine," Emily retorted. "I will go and greet them myself."

Emily was out the bedroom door and halfway down the hall before Lucinda reconsidered. Daniel and his mother would be tired after the long journey. They would want to settle in their rooms and refresh themselves, not be subjected to Emily's energetic and wearisome company.

She did pause long enough to repin a few loose strands of hair and splash some water on her face. She still felt miserable, but it was time to forge ahead anyway, and she wanted to make a good impression. When she reached the top of the stairs leading down to the main hall, she saw that the Hibbitts were already in conversation with Emily. She allowed her gaze to rest on Daniel for a moment, hoping for any kind of warm reaction to seeing him again. There was nothing, but perhaps it was simply because at the moment she was too vexed with her sister to allow for any other emotions.

"I remember you well, Miss Cardington," Lady Hibbitt was saying to Emily. "I was thrilled when Daniel told me he'd made your acquaintance." She took one of Emily's hands in hers. "I look forward to getting to know you better, my dear!"

Lucinda began rapidly descending the staircase. Daniel cleared his throat and said, "Mother, I believe I should clarify. This is Miss Emily Cardington—the one who is engaged to Mr. Simpson." As Lucinda reached them, he said, "May I present Miss Lucinda Cardington."

Lady Hibbitt was a small woman with snowy white hair. She was leaning heavily on a cane, but her demeanor projected a will of iron. Her expression changed noticeably when her eyes alighted on Lucinda. She was probably recalling Lucinda's disastrous run-in with that potted plant. If Lady Hibbitt was disappointed to discover her error, it was just one more obstacle Lucinda would have to overcome.

"Lady Hibbitt, I'm so pleased to see you again," Lucinda said. "Welcome to our home. I was not aware you and my sister were acquainted."

"We are indeed." Her gaze traveled back to Emily. "We met at—where was it?"

"Lord Brower's home," Emily said. "I was visiting his daughter."

"Yes, that was it! You two girls snuck down to get a look at the party, for you weren't quite old enough to attend. We had a most lively discussion in the library about—"

"Literature!" Emily cut in. "But please don't mention that to my mother. I'm an adult now, but even so, she wouldn't like to hear that I was somewhere I shouldn't have been."

Lucinda was astonished by this exchange. It was hard enough to hear Emily use the word "adult" in reference to herself, but the word "literature" was even more jarring. Emily never read anything but lurid novels.

"It will be our little secret," Lady Hibbitt assured her with a wink, but her voice was loud enough to be heard by everyone in the grand foyer—including the butler and a half dozen servants.

The older woman's obvious preference for Emily was making Lucinda uncomfortable. Daniel, too, seemed perturbed at the way the conversation was going. He gave Lucinda an apologetic smile, and she tried to keep up a brave face.

"Shall we go upstairs, Mother?" Daniel suggested. "I'm sure you want to rest up before dinner."

"Yes, that's a good idea." Turning to Lucinda, she added, "That journey has nearly done me in. My heart is not good, you know."

"Yes," Daniel said, with the air of one whose patience has grown thin. "We know."

"I shall be only too glad to show you to your room," Lucinda offered.

It was not the way she had hoped her first encounter with a prospective mother-in-law would turn out, but she tamped down her disappointment as she accompanied the Hibbitts up the stairs. It was only when they'd reached the first landing and Lady Hibbitt paused for breath that Lucinda looked back and saw James crossing the great hall. Emily must have forgotten her previous anger toward him, for she was now hugging him enthusiastically. He looked up over Emily's shoulder. His eyes met Lucinda's, and in that moment she felt all the warmth and joy she'd hoped to get from the sight of Daniel. It could not be; she would not allow it. She turned away and vigorously renewed her attention to the Hibbitts, determined to not permit her traitorous heart to govern her actions this week—or the rest of her life.

*

"Where is Mr. Hibbitt?" Emily asked anxiously. "Everyone else is here, and Mama will be quite put out if she has to delay dinner."

It had been a busy afternoon at the Cardington mansion as carriage after carriage rolled up the front drive. Now, as they were all assembled in the drawing room, James saw the guest list was evenly split between young and old. In the older camp were several of Lord Cardington's political cronies from the House of Lords and a high-ranking Member of Parliament. They had all brought their wives, of course. Then there were Mr. and Mrs. Paddington, no doubt here at the invitation of Lady Cardington, and another lady named Mrs. Wiggins, whom James guessed to be about a hundred years old.

At the moment he and Emily were chatting with the friends she had been allowed to invite in order to mollify her for having to quit the London season early. There were Bob Chapman and his fiancée, Miss Lucy Hallowell, and the newly married Myron and Jane Stonewell, fresh from their honeymoon in Scotland. There was Miss Georgiana Evers, who was Miss Hallowell's dearest friend—this month, anyway. She was a talkative creature, and had been vigorously relaying to Jane and Emily all the gossip they'd missed since being gone from London. Rounding out their little group was Hopkins, who made a good addition to any house party because he invariably did something that was good for a laugh.

"You know how Hibbitt hates crowds," Chapman pointed out.

"More likely he's avoiding his mother," James observed, knowing how Daniel and Lady Hibbitt did not get along. "But Lucinda has been fearless enough to face her, at least."

It was true; Lucinda was now seated deep in conversation with both his aunt and Lady Hibbitt. James had not missed the awkward interchange between Lucinda and Lady Hibbitt in the entry hall today. Perhaps Lucinda was attempting to smooth things over. Knowing Lucinda, she might well have chosen to sit with the pair anyway, for she never had been comfortable around Emily's friends. Daniel wasn't making things any better by reverting to his hermit-like ways.

"I think I saw Hibbitt skulking about in the library," Chapman said. "Shall I go fetch him?"

"I'll go," James offered. "Your fiancée looks very lovely draped on your arm, and I should hate to separate you."

"Quite right," Miss Hallowell said, clinging to Chapman in a proprietary way. "I shan't let him out of my sight."

"So you will leave your own fiancée?" Emily asked James with a hint of peevishness.

"You are to act as hostess," James pointed out. "I won't be gone long."

In fact, James did not have to go, for Daniel was just coming through the door. As he joined them he said morosely, "Looks like all of London is here."

"Oh, we won't have to bother about them," Emily replied, giving a dismissive wave in the general direction of some of the most influential men in government. "They will do whatever it is old people do, and we shall have fun!"

"Daniel, shouldn't we go rescue Lucinda from your mother and my great-aunt?" James suggested.

"I don't see why you should have to," Emily put in. "She seems content to me."

"Come along," James said, giving Emily and Daniel a firm nudge. "We will all go."

Lucinda stood up as they approached, although the

two older ladies stayed seated as everyone exchanged greetings.

"You are looking exceptionally well this evening, Lady Hibbitt," James said. "I see you have recovered from the long drive."

"I am tolerably well, thank you," she replied. "How kind of *you* to ask." She threw a chiding look at her non-dutiful son. Daniel didn't even flinch.

"No word on how exceptionally well I look, I suppose?" Lady Thornborough said.

James grinned. "Hello, Auntie. How are you?"

"Unfortunately my rheumatism is acting up. It's a sign we'll have rain tomorrow."

"Oh, surely not!" Lucinda exclaimed. "There's not a cloud in the sky."

"My aunt's bones are never wrong," James assured her.

"That would be a shame. I was planning to go into the village tomorrow. The wife of one of our tenant farmers gave birth last week. It's her third child, but this time she has had trouble recovering. I wanted to take her a food basket and see if there was anything else I could do for her."

"How very thoughtful of you," Lady Thornborough said. "I always try to do the same with our tenants at Rosewood."

"Emily, why don't you go too?" James suggested.

"Me?" Emily looked horrified. "Why should I go?"

"It will be good training for your future duties. It's all part of being a conscientious landowner."

"Oh, I don't expect Emily to go," Lucinda interjected, looking uncomfortable at the growing dissention. "She really doesn't do well around sickbeds."

She probably intended this as a way to excuse her sister, but for James it was just one more thing to fuel his growing frustration with his wife-to-be. He'd given up so much for this woman, but she had not the slightest concept of it and was giving him precious little in return. "You know, Emily, it wouldn't hurt you to start learning a few things about compassion from your sister."

Emily glared at him. "We are in the middle of a house party, in case you didn't notice. I shall stay right here and do my duties as hostess." She said this last part with a touch of triumph, throwing James's words back at him.

"I don't see why you don't just send the basket with one of the servants," Daniel said.

"No," said his mother. "You wouldn't."

*

"Rain, and more rain! Can you believe it?"

This came from Miss Hallowell, who was seated with Emily and several other ladies near the window.

It was, in fact, the third day of rain. The storms had begun the day after the guests arrived, just as Lady Thornborough had predicted, and showed little sign of letting up.

"It's so vexing," Emily agreed. "I wanted to show you all the lovely walks we have. There's simply nothing to do inside."

Lucinda set down the book she'd been trying unsuccessfully to read, thanks to the chatter of Emily and her cohorts. Here was a whole room full of books, and they were complaining about nothing to do.

"At least the gentlemen are able to amuse themselves in the billiard room," Miss Evers observed.

"Every gentleman except one," Emily pointed out. "We know you're behind that newspaper, Mr. Hibbitt!" she called out in a teasing tone to Daniel, who was seated in the far corner.

Daniel peered at her from over the top of his newspaper. "Don't mind me, ladies. Carry on." And he went back to reading.

Emily laughed. "Are we entertaining you?" She snapped her fingers and rose from the window seat with excitement. "That's it! I have the most excellent idea. We shall gather up everyone and split into two groups, and then each group will present some kind of little play or *tableau vivante*. We can take tomorrow to plan and rehearse, and present them tomorrow night."

"Oh, that's a brilliant idea!" Miss Hallowell said. "Let's go tell the men!"

Emily went over and rapped on Daniel's newspaper with a flick of her finger. "Don't think you shall be excluded, Mr. Hibbitt! You and Lucinda must both join in!" Then the whole cluster of women sailed from the room, laughing and tossing out story ideas as they went.

Daniel set aside his newspaper, his gaze following the women. "Aren't you going with them?" he asked Lucinda.

She shook her head. "I have no desire to join in those antics."

"Nor I. But at least it will keep them occupied for a while, and I think I shall enjoy seeing what they come up with." He crossed the room and took a chair close to Lucinda. "I'm also glad it gives us a moment or two alone."

Lucinda tensed. Over the past few days she had dutifully spent time with Daniel, looking for some indication their acquaintance could grow into love. But she had not been successful. It wasn't that she didn't like him. He was intelligent and well read. Although he could be brusque when pressed to interact with a crowd of people, in his actions toward Lucinda he'd been attentive and considerate. Was it asking too much to want more? This was the question that tormented her. She gave him a nervous smile. "I'm sorry you've had to spend a week cooped up with these magpies."

"I don't mind. I've actually enjoyed myself this week." His gaze strayed once more toward the door before turning back to Lucinda. "I think my mother has been happy, too." He took hold of her hand. "She's really warmed up to you, especially after that lovely piano recital you gave us last night."

Lucinda fought to remain calm, to think of something to say. "I—I am glad she shares your love of music."

He gave her hand a little squeeze. "She has also been growing anxious for news, as I'm sure you might imagine. Lucinda, the week is drawing to a close. May I expect your answer soon?"

Lucinda felt her throat constrict. She could see Daniel's frustration mounting at not getting an answer. It seemed wrong to put it off any longer, and yet still she hesitated. "Yes. That is, yes, I will give you my answer very soon."

"By tomorrow, then?" he pressed.

"By tomorrow."

"Excellent." He leaned in and gave her a brief kiss, his lips cool against hers. "I shall look forward to it."

*

James sat in a tall wicker chair surrounded by an abundance of leafy plants. Drizzling rain spattered against the glass roof and walls, adding a sense of privacy. This little conservatory was far from the main rooms where the guests spent most of their time, and over the past few days it had become a refuge for him. Here was a place where he could sit, undisturbed, and think. He didn't used to be the sort who sought solitude, but recent events had made it both desirable and necessary.

He'd been here for at least an hour, with his feet propped up on another chair, staring down at the photograph he'd taken of Lucinda at her school. He traced a finger lightly over her image—her slender figure, her fine chin, and her nose with its enchanting tiny left turn at the tip. Everything he loved about her.

This little portrait was as good as careful work with the best equipment could make it. Yet there was something it could never truly capture: Lucinda's inner beauty. That was what James had come to adore most about her, and this week he'd seen it more clearly than ever. He'd never had any qualms about dropping down to the servants' hall, and today he'd gone there to strike up a conversation with Peter, her footman. Peter spoke admiringly of how, despite the rain, Lucinda had spent the last three mornings at a woman's sickbed in the village, praying for her and giving encouragement and practical advice to her family. She'd taught the two little children how to cook and clean, and even helped them do it. But mostly, Peter was convinced it was Lucinda's prayers that had set the woman on the road to recovery. For James, the whole affair was a perfect example of Lucinda's compassion and kindness. It illustrated just one of many reasons why James was in love with her.

It still seemed too momentous to grasp. Love had

come from out of nowhere, blindsiding him. Back in that little courtyard when she'd asked him what he thought about her marrying Daniel, he ought to have spoken the truth. He should have told her then and there that he loved her. But at that point he'd still been bound by irrational definitions of right and wrong. Now he understood with painful clarity that he'd had it backward: loving Lucinda was right, and pretending anything else was wrong.

"So here you are," said a familiar voice behind him.

Caught off guard, James hastily tucked the photograph behind a chair cushion. He dropped his feet to the floor and rose out of his chair, turning to see Lady Thornborough standing not ten feet away. "Auntie! You surprised me."

She gave a little smirk of satisfaction. "May I join you?"

"Certainly." He motioned toward a chair. "Although I warn you this conservatory is rather chilly."

"I think my bones can bear it for a few minutes." Her cane tapped on the tile floor as she walked, and James wondered how he'd not heard her initial approach. Once she'd settled herself, James resumed his own seat.

His aunt studied him, her lips pursed and her forehead wrinkled in thought. "It's not like you to sulk in a corner, James."

James shifted uncomfortably. "I'm not sulking. I'm . . . ruminating."

"Over that?" She pointed toward the photograph, a corner of which was sticking out from behind the cushion.

James gave her a sheepish grin. "I never could fool you, Auntie."

The old woman held out a hand expectantly. With a sigh, James handed her the picture, wondering what she would think when she saw its subject. After studying it for several long seconds, she lifted her gray eyes to his. Her expression held no surprise at all. She said quietly, "I thought as much."

James's burden lifted a tiny fraction, just knowing she understood. "Lucinda does things to me, Auntie. Things I can't explain."

She handed him back the photograph. "How about giving it a try?"

He raked a hand through his hair, wondering how to put his feelings into words. "Well, for example, I was talking with her footman today. He was filled with her praises. Told me he didn't used to be a religious man—until he went to work for Lucinda." James leaned back in his chair, looking down once more at the face of the woman who had quietly stolen his heart. "But then, she has that effect on people."

"And you?" Lady Thornborough prodded. "What effect has she had on you?"

James hesitated. A heart-to-heart talk was not something he normally indulged in with his great-aunt. But who else was there to confide in? "Lucinda and I got to talking one day and, well...somehow I found myself telling her about my parents. I got to remembering my mother's account of how she prayed for my father after the battle at Quatre-Bras. I hadn't thought about that for a very long time." He closed his eyes, remembering how oddly freeing it had been to share those long-suppressed details about his parents.

Lady Thornborough said gently, "I suppose you realize

that if your father had died, you would never have been born."

"Yes." He eyed her. "Some might have thought that a better outcome."

"Never!" the old woman replied staunchly. She punctuated the word with a sharp tap of her cane on the hard floor. "When God answers a prayer, it is always for good. I think He has some purpose for you."

James let out a sigh. "You'll pardon me if I don't agree with you on that score, Auntie."

She cocked her head to one side, still studying him. "What about all those times you dined with the Reverend Lord Somerville, back before he got married? Did nothing he shared with you about the Almighty soak into that hard head of yours?"

"Not much," James admitted. "At the time I wasn't very interested. But now..."

"Yes?" she said, looking at him expectantly.

James stood up, blowing out a breath in exasperation. "I don't know." He walked over to the glass wall and stared out at the steadily falling rain. Behind him, his great-aunt said nothing, waiting patiently. She was like this when James was younger, too, whenever she used to confront him about anything. He knew she wouldn't rest until they'd gotten to the truth. Slowly he turned to face her, feeling, for the first time in his life, intensely humbled. "All I know is that I've grown tired of the shallow life I've been leading. Something about Lucinda makes me want to be a better person. To do... *more*, somehow."

"Have you told her this?"

"What good would it do? Our futures are set. She's bound to announce her engagement to Daniel any day now."

Lady Thornborough wagged a finger at him. "Ah, but she hasn't yet, has she? Did it ever occur to you that she's hesitating because she's waiting for you to declare yourself?"

"Waiting? For me? Nonsense. She—" He cut himself off in mid breath as the word *wait* pricked something in his memory. "Now that I think on it, Lucinda told me that when Daniel proposed, she prayed to God for help with her decision. The answer she got was, 'Wait.'"

His great-aunt nodded her head knowingly—a gesture that in the past had always irritated him. Now, however, he was thrilled to think she might have given him an answer that would save him. He strode back to her. "Do you really think that's what I should do—declare myself?"

She lifted a gray eyebrow. "I can't believe I have to urge you, of all people, to go after a woman."

"But it's not that simple! What about Emily? How can I withdraw from our engagement without hurting her or ruining her prospects?"

"Our help cometh from the Lord," said his aunt calmly. "Who—*by the way*—made heaven and earth," she added, finishing the quote with her own unique interpolation thrown in. "I'd say He has the ability to take care of Emily as well."

James knelt down before his aunt so that his eyes were level with hers. "Do you really believe this, Aunt Thornborough? Because if you think it's the right thing to do, I'll do it!"

Her mouth quirked into a smile. "Yes, I'm sure you will."

A huge sense of relief washed over him. This week of

being in the same house with Emily had been enough to show him he couldn't possibly endure a lifetime with her. If Lucinda loved him, as he was sure she did, she'd have to agree that it was wrong for either of them to marry someone they did not love. With her penchant for honestly, how could she say otherwise? Perhaps, with this divine help his great-aunt spoke of, there was a way out after all.

James placed a kiss squarely on her wrinkled cheek, then rose, shaking the dust off his trousers. "If you'll excuse me, Auntie, I believe I have some business to attend to."

She said approvingly, "It's about time."

He whistled under his breath as he strolled down the hallway leading back to the main wing of the house. He knew what he must do. First off, he would tell Lucinda he loved her. He had no idea what the next step would be, but he was going to take his aunt's word for it that everything would work out. It *had* to. James couldn't bear to think otherwise.

At this hour, the ladies would be resting or changing for dinner. Lucinda was always one of the first to arrive at the salon where they all gathered before going into the dining room. If James was quick about changing into his evening clothes, he might be able to meet her there for a private chat before anyone else showed up.

He had just picked up his pace when he was arrested by the sound of a woman calling his name. He turned to see a servant standing there, looking distressed. "If you please, sir, I was asked to come and fetch you right away. Will you come with me?"

"Of course," James responded instantly, trying to

think where he'd seen her before. She was one of the ladies' maids, but whose? "Did...er...Miss Cardington send you?"

"Yes sir, and it's quite urgent! There's no time to be lost!" She turned and hurried down the hall. Still confused, James followed. What choice did he have?

The maid rounded a corner, taking them down a hallway he didn't recognize. She tapped twice on a door, then opened it, swiftly ushering him through before he had a chance to think.

He stopped cold when he saw Emily. She was standing in the middle of the room, almost entirely undressed. A light silk wrap did little to conceal her undergarments. With a sinking heart, he realized he was in her bedchamber. Behind him, the door closed with a firm click.

He'd known Emily might attempt something untoward this week. He'd been equally determined to prevent it, which is why he'd locked his bedchamber door every night before going to bed. But he hadn't expected the little minx to trick him into her room.

He turned to go, but she swiftly cut him off, leaning against the door. "What's your hurry?" she purred.

"Let me out, Emily," James said through clenched teeth. "You know this isn't proper."

She reached out a hand and tugged at his cravat, drawing him closer. "I suppose you think it's proper to ignore your fiancée? Where have you been all afternoon? I couldn't find you anywhere. I had to send my maid to scour the house for you." She leaned into him suggestively. "Now that you're here, who's to stop us from doing what we like? We're betrothed, after all."

James took hold of her shoulders and firmly pushed

her away. "I'm not going to seduce you in your father's house."

She gave him an ill-natured glare. "You're no fun anymore. Ever since we've become engaged, you've turned into a real bore. Where's the charming James I used to know?" She pressed into him again. "Just one kiss, please..."

Panic rose in his chest. He had to get out of here before anyone found them. Especially now that he'd made up his mind about Lucinda. He needed to have a serious conversation with Emily, too, but this was certainly not the time or place. He drew her toward him, as though to kiss her, but the moment she relaxed he gave her a chaste peck on the cheek and whirled her around so that he had access to the door. "I have to go," he said, turning the handle. "I'll meet you downstairs."

"Don't be late!" she said petulantly, following him into the hallway. "Or I shall just go into dinner with someone else!"

"Emily, get back inside," James commanded. "What if someone sees you?" He sent a quick glance in both directions and choked on his words. Lucinda had just stepped into the hallway from a nearby room.

"James!" she said in surprise. "What are you—" Then her eye fell on her scantily clad sister. In two seconds, she had sized up the situation and drawn her own conclusions. He could see it in the shock that crossed her face just before revulsion settled there. "On second thought, I don't even need to ask."

James wanted to protest, to explain that it was all innocent. But he could see he'd fallen low enough in her eyes already, without trying to put blame on her sister.

"This is what lovers do, Lucinda," Emily said defiantly. "If you would stop pushing men away and get engaged yourself, maybe you'd understand that."

Lucinda made a kind of strangled noise, which she covered with a cough. Straightening to her full height, she said, "Oh, I understand it fully." She turned to focus her angry disgust on James. "You'll be relieved to know I accepted Mr. Hibbitt's offer of marriage today. I hope you enjoy your money, as well as"—she pointed a finger at her sister's obvious state of undress—"everything else."

And with that, she turned and walked away.

"Lucinda, wait!" James cried, but before he could follow her, Emily had taken a painful grip on his arm.

"Don't you go after her," she hissed. "If you do, I'll start screaming, and you'll have much more to contend with than my prudish sister."

Chapter 22

The drawing room was stifling hot, crowded with chattering guests, its windows tightly shut against the pelting rain. Lucinda longed to escape, but with the Hibbitts standing at her elbow, she had no choice but to remain.

She was committed to marrying Daniel now. In truth, the decision had been made for her the instant she'd realized that James and Emily had already breached the bounds of decency. It had forced upon her two equally terrible facts: James was every inch the rogue he was reputed to be, and Lucinda must do whatever was necessary to get her sister married to him. Now that Emily had been truly compromised, no other man would ever marry her.

With a few quick words to Daniel, the engagement had been made. At dinner he had announced the news, much to the delight—and evident relief—of her parents. Lady Hibbitt seemed satisfied, and the other guests offered hearty congratulations. Lucinda couldn't say how James had reacted; she had refused even to look at him. The entire dinner had passed in a haze. She felt, just as she had when Daniel had proposed, that she was acting a part that belonged to someone else.

"Now, my dear, we must begin planning the wedding immediately," Lady Hibbitt said. "There are just four weeks remaining before Advent Sunday, so there's no time to be lost."

Lucinda fanned herself, trying to clear her mind. "I don't understand. Why should that matter?"

She was, in fact, looking forward to Advent Sunday, which this year fell on the last Sunday of November. It was the official start of the Christmas season. Her family always celebrated Christmas quietly at their estate in Hampshire, and Lucinda was desperate for time alone to prepare her heart for the new life she would be facing in the spring.

Lady Hibbitt looked at her as if she was daft. "You must be aware that weddings are not allowed between Advent Sunday and the new year. Happily, there is just enough time for the reading of the banns and the wedding before the season begins."

"But..." Lucinda threw a confused glance at Daniel. "I thought we were going to wait until May."

Lady Hibbitt's declaration seemed to have taken Daniel by surprise, too. He stared at his mother, nonplussed.

Suddenly, the old woman's face pinched in a grimace, and she clutched at her chest. "Help me to a chair, won't you? My health... it's not good..."

Lucinda and Daniel immediately complied.

"That's better," Lady Hibbitt wheezed, once she was seated. "Would you two be so good as to find me a glass of water?"

As soon as they had moved away from his mother, Daniel said quietly, "Wouldn't you like to be a Yuletide bride, Lucinda? You know how happy it would make my mother."

He made no mention of his own feelings, but Lucinda hardly expected that. They were both well aware of their reasons for getting married. While Lucinda tried to think of a response, her gaze landed unexpectedly on James and Emily, who were walking in her direction. Neither looked especially happy, although Lucinda thought they ought to be ecstatic that they were finally getting what they wanted. Perhaps they were angry at having been discovered after their indecent tryst. At the very thought of it, Lucinda was seized with a terrible fear. What if Emily were to get pregnant? What if she already was? They couldn't wait until May, or the obvious shame would ruin them.

There was nothing for it. Lucinda had to get married right away, so that Emily and James could do likewise.

And then she wished above all else never to see either one of them again.

Pulling her eyes away from the two people who had been the cause of all her torment, she said, "Yes, Daniel, I think it's a wonderful idea." Even as she spoke the words, she was overcome with nausea. The heat...the pressure...she couldn't take any more just now. Nor could she bear the idea of speaking to James and Emily tonight. "Let's talk more about it in the morning, shall we? If you'll excuse me, I—"

No longer able to hide her distress, Lucinda gave up the effort and dashed from the room. She had to find somewhere to be alone. The best way to keep from being followed was to head for the servants' hall. She slipped down the stairs, through the kitchen, past the startled exclamations of the scullery maid, and out the door into the rain.

Her goal was a little gazebo that overlooked the lake. She raced across the lawn, heedless of the rain soaking her dress or the way her shoes kept slipping in the mud. When she reached the gazebo, she stepped inside and sank down on a bench to catch her breath.

She sat for a long time, listening to the tapping of the rain on the roof, watching the patterns formed by the raindrops as they danced on the lake's surface. Tomorrow she would think more rationally about how to move ahead with her new life. Tonight she would just allow the reality of it to sink in, and pray to be at peace with her decision. Had this really been why the Lord had said to "wait"? Did He know things would reach a point where there was no other recourse than to marry Daniel? Was this the only way for her to understand that it was the right thing to? It seemed an absurd notion, but she could think of no other way to reconcile these events.

Truly, there were worse fates than marrying Daniel. He would treat her well, and they would live comfortably. Better to marry a man who made no pretense about who he was and what he wanted from life. Unlike James, whose actions toward her had been nothing but a charade. She'd known from the beginning that he was a master at it. The events of today had only given her the final, irrefutable evidence.

Slowly, a sense of peace—or at least, of resignation—began to settle over her. She closed her eyes, hugging herself to ward off the chill, listening as the patter on the roof began to subside. The storm was passing. There would be new storms ahead, but somehow she would face them.

"Lucinda."

Reluctantly she opened her eyes. James was standing there. His clothes were limp from the rain, and his hair, normally slicked down, now showed its natural curliness. The sight of him sent heat and desire and pain through her all at once. She stood up and turned her back to him. "Leave me alone. You've done enough for one day."

*

James ignored this command, of course. Not that he could have moved anyway. He was rooted to the spot, staring at the woman who meant more to him than anyone in the world. "I had to find you. I had to tell you that I love you."

"What?" This brought her round to face him. She was soaked through, and shivering a little. Her fine silk gown seemed pasted to every part of her, the bodice clinging to her breasts with shocking clarity. A few rivulets of water seeped out of her halfway tumbled-down hair. She stared at him, incredulity mixed with pain and anger. "How can you dare say such a thing, after what happened today?"

"It's not what you think."

"But I saw—"

"I know what you saw," he interrupted fiercely. "It was a trap. Her maid shoved me into Emily's room before I even knew what was happening. I swear to you, *nothing* happened." He spoke with urgent honesty, willing her to believe him. She merely kept looking at him, unmoving and unconvinced. "Lucinda, you know how your sister is. You know what she did at Cremorne. Why is it so hard to believe me when I tell you I never touched her?" He began to close the distance between them. "Tell me you believe me," he urged.

She tensed as he approached, but did not back away. He could see a flicker of comprehension, an indication that she *wanted* to believe him, and that was enough. "You can't marry Daniel," he said fervently. "He doesn't understand what a treasure you are."

Her eyes briefly squeezed shut in a spasm of pain. "I have made a vow and I will not defer to obey it. I suggest you do the same."

"But what about love? Surely that has to enter into it?"

"Love?" She spat out the word. "You want to talk to me about *love*?"

"Yes! Before it's too late." He placed his hands on her arms, feeling the heat the two of them began to draw from each other, generate in each other. "You will never love Daniel as much as you love me now. And I will never love any woman as much as I love you."

There. He had said it. He might go to his grave now and be happy. Perhaps he ought to, since living without her would be hell on earth.

"You seem very sure of yourself," she said coldly.

"I believe you have never been moved by Daniel's kisses," James persisted. "Can you look me in the eye and deny it?"

Her jaw was set, her expression unyielding. "What passes between me and Daniel is none of your affair."

"I think it *is* my affair. Tell me his kisses are better than the one we shared."

He could see her struggling for an answer, not wanting to lie, but not wanting to give in. "I suppose one's first kiss is always exhilarating and memorable. But all memories fade with time."

"No," James contradicted. "Not always. I have kissed many women, and"—she started to pull away at this, but he held her tight—"not one of them ever made me feel so alive, so full of this amazing quality that is like searing fire and unbounded joy at the same time."

"It was one kiss," she said stubbornly. "How can you be certain it was not some trick of the moment, some wild fancy caused by the unusual circumstances?"

James pulled her closer. "All right then, let's test your theory. Prove to me that what happened between us once cannot be repeated." It was a reckless challenge, but James had to know he was right, that despite her unwillingness to admit it, she loved him.

At some point the rain had ended, leaving only a gentle calm and the mist rising from the grass. Lucinda looked at him with intense, unblinking eyes, but he sensed she was thinking over what he had said. The moments passed. At last, the hard denial in her expression softened, replaced by a look of uncertainty and then—his own pulse began to race as he saw it—with need. She raised her hands and placed them on his chest. He could feel his heart hammering against her palms. Her breathing was shallow, her breasts rose and fell rapidly, the damp silk clinging tantalizingly to every curve.

James ached to crush her against him, but he forced himself to remain still. He savored her nearness, the scent of her, and the now-unveiled desire in her eyes. When at last she began to tilt her mouth ever so slowly toward his, it was all the invitation he needed. He met her halfway. Their lips touched, instantly igniting a flame of recognition.

He grasped her waist, pulling her toward him as he kept kissing her, claiming her for his own. Her arms came up around his neck, returning his kiss with equal passion, and James knew this was the woman he was destined to kiss for the rest of his life, and no other. Surely now she would allow herself to admit she felt the same way?

After a long while—though not nearly long enough for him—she pulled back. Her lips were gently swollen. It was a look which decidedly suited her. "Such a kiss will never be forgotten," he murmured, trailing more kisses along her neck. "Not until it is lost among the thousands of kisses we will share in the future."

Lucinda exhaled a deep, shuddering breath. Slowly and, it seemed unwillingly, she released her grasp on him and took a step back. "No," she said. The word came out ragged, as though it had caught in her throat. "There can be no more kisses."

"What!?" James protested. "You can't mean that."

She hugged herself, as though she too felt the chill of the damp air now that they were separated from one another's warmth. "What do you think will happen if we go in there and blithely announce that you are abandoning my sister? Do you know how that will crush her? Emily may drive me to my wit's end sometimes, but I do love her. How could I hurt her like that?" She leveled an accusatory glare at him. "You said you were going to be a good husband to her. And yet here you are, already unfaithful to her."

James knew it would not help his cause to point out that Lucinda was just a culpable, for she had returned his kiss, and willingly, too. "Emily is not my wife yet," he insisted. "There is still time to set this situation right."

"But she loves you! She—"

"No." James cut her off sharply. "Emily will soon realize her feelings for me are not love, merely infatuation. After I refused her advances today, she's barely given me a civil word. I daresay it wouldn't be long before she thanked her lucky stars she never married me."

"You can't possibly know that for certain. Emily is always cross if she does not immediately get her way. What *is* certain is that breaking off these engagements would bring scandal and disgrace upon my family. How could I do that to them? Family loyalty has to count for something!"

"So you are saying you would throw away your future happiness—and mine—merely for fear of scandal?"

"Merely," she repeated with a bitter laugh. "That's an easy word for you. Such things as honor and sacrifice may not mean much to you, but they are vitally important to me."

He shook his head, unwilling to accept this charge against him. In times past he might have deserved it, but no longer. "Ever since that night at Cremorne, I have been attempting to do the right thing, the noble thing. But now I see there is a very big difference between being noble and making sacrifices that benefit no one. Surely God, if He is as loving to us as you say He is, does not want this for us?"

Her eyes grew round, her body stiffening in anger. "You are hardly qualified to lecture me about God. You, who can toy with two women's hearts at once."

She might just as well have physically slapped him. She spoke out of disappointment and regret, he knew; yet it also showed how much she still distrusted him. Everything he'd done to show himself worthy of her had been to no avail.

"Very well," he said curtly. "I see now what you really think of me. Perhaps you will allow me to explain with the same brute honesty exactly how I perceive *you*."

He saw her lower lip tremble, but she stood firm and unmoving, as though bracing herself for a blow. "All right."

"You are so wrapped up in your notions of sacrifice and suffering that you will not even give a tiny place to the idea that God might want you—yes, you, *Lucinda Cardington*—to be happy. You think nobleness and happiness must be mutually exclusive. You wish to live like the stoics of old, those who believed life was a joyless struggle from start to finish. You do not think yourself worthy of happiness."

She bristled like a threatened cat. "Now see here—"

"I happen to feel differently. If God doesn't want us to be happy, why does the Bible say He gives us all things richly to enjoy?"

This question stopped her cold. She rallied, however, angrily pushing back her damp and tangled hair as she spoke. "I'm not surprised to hear a libertine like yourself quote that verse. But the truth is, people make mistakes. The Lord cannot control that."

"But He can forgive, can't He?"

"The Lord may forgive, but there are still consequences. Those cannot always be undone. And in any case, I cannot imagine the Lord forgiving us for the dishonorable things we have said and done here tonight." Her fists clenched. "I have a reputation to uphold. I will *not* disgrace my family, and I will *not* ruin my sister."

"Lucinda—"

"Don't say any more," she cut in ferociously. "True faith does not lead people to grasp at straws. We must forget any of this ever happened." She turned away, her hands gripping the low railing that edged the gazebo. "For the last time, *go away!*"

It was clear James would get no further with her tonight. If neither his words nor his caresses could win her, he had nothing left. She'd pushed him to the brink, forced him to feel more deeply than he had in years. He'd bared his soul to her, tried to show her there could be a power in her faith that not even she knew existed. What more could he do? He was hopelessly in love with a woman who could extend boundless compassion to everyone except herself. Or him.

He combed his fingers through his sodden hair and straightened his damp cravat. "I see your mind is made up. Well, so is mine."

She straightened, reacting with a start to his uncompromising words, but said nothing.

He left the gazebo and crossed the lawn in slow, measured strides, not looking back. It was with no small sense of irony that he found himself thinking the oft-used phrase, *It's in the Lord's hands now.* The trouble was, he believed it. If marrying Emily really was the right thing to do, then he would do it. And yet, despite all that had happened, he was not ready to give up the outlandish belief that somehow there would be a better way.

Chapter 23

James slipped into the library through the French doors, then paused to allow his eyes to adjust to the gloom. The room was dark and quiet, as he had hoped. The door to the hallway was open, and he could hear the sounds of guests in the distant salon—the clink of glasses, a melody from a piano, the voices which were only a dim murmur from this distance. They were plenty occupied with their gossip and cards. No one would miss him.

He sank down on one of the chairs in the dim room. Sagging back against the overstuffed cushions, he contemplated what to do next. What was left? He fought a surge of helplessness. How could he get Lucinda to let go of her misguided beliefs about what was right and wrong? If she didn't, everyone would be worse off because of it. There would be no way out.

No *honorable* way out, at any rate. The old James might genuinely have contemplated making a run for it, leaving now in the middle of the night, and getting as far away from this place as he could. He could go to the Continent, the Far East, or even Australia if he had to. Anything to escape his own marriage and the daily torture of seeing the woman he loved on someone else's arm. He was reasonably certain no one would be at all surprised if he did this. They'd expect it from someone who was a useless as his father had been. It would prove that adage about apples not falling far from the tree.

But he knew he wouldn't do it. Lucinda's urging and example made him want to be a better man, a man of principle. A man truly worthy of her. But what if in order to do that, he really did have to give up all hope of her? He was discovering why he'd always thought being a man of principle didn't suit him in the least.

Suddenly, a clink of glass much closer to hand alerted James that someone else was in the room. "Is someone there?" he said to the darkness.

"Have a good swim?" It was Daniel's voice. James heard a soft tread as Daniel crossed the room and appeared in the gloom. He lifted his glass in salute, then took a chair next to James.

James eyed him as he took a long drink from his glass. "What are you doing in here, Daniel?"

"Needed a quiet drink. The babblers were driving me mad. This seemed a good place to escape the noise."

"Yes, some of them can go on. Emily especially."

"Oh, Emily's not the problem. In fact, she's already retired for the evening. Poor thing has a headache."

"I'm sorry to hear it," James said, but his heart wasn't in it. He was too distracted with thoughts of Lucinda.

"In fact, that's why I decided to come in here. The party isn't interesting without her. She really does light up the place."

James lifted an eyebrow. "That's high praise from someone who once said he was glad he wasn't the one marrying her."

Daniel gave a sanguine shrug. "I may have judged her too hastily at first. By the same token, I think you are the one judging her too harshly now."

"Me?"

Daniel nodded. "I heard the way you were chastising her the other day, telling her she ought to have more common sense like her sister. But Emily will never be like that. She has an entirely different sensibility. She brings energy and excitement to everything, and a simple, unbridled passion. She takes the world as it is and enjoys it."

James recognized something very familiar in Daniel's tone. He was trying to sell James on the idea of marrying Emily—just as James had initially worked to interest Daniel in Lucinda. How much easier it was to see the good points in a woman one wasn't attached to. "You seem awfully enamored of the girl," James said, repeating the words Daniel had spoken on the first night they had discussed Lucinda. "I wonder why you don't marry the girl yourself."

Daniel grunted. "Don't think it hasn't crossed my mind."

James sat straight up in his chair, leaning so far forward that he was within inches of Daniel's face. "What did you say?"

Misunderstanding this instant change in James's attitude, Daniel held up a defensive hand. "Sorry, Simpson. That was out of line." He held up his nearly empty glass. "Put it down to too much brandy."

"I call it *in vino veritas*." James took hold of Daniel's lapels and pulled him to a standing position. Daniel jerked awkwardly, dropping the glass to the small side table as he rose, but James's grip held firm. "You love Emily, don't you?" James demanded.

Daniel's eyes were wide with surprise. "Simpson, what has gotten into you?"

"Don't you?" James said again, punctuating his words by giving Daniel a little shake. The thought that he might be on the verge of freedom electrified him.

"Are you daft?" Daniel protested, grabbing James's wrists in an effort to get him to loosen his grip. "I didn't mean anything by it. I never would have pegged you for a jealous sort of fellow."

"Just admit it," James persisted, not caring how he sounded, too excited to know how to even explain himself properly. He was half giddy with a sudden surge of hope, and he didn't care whether Daniel thought it was anger or insanity. He wanted only the truth. The truth—as the Bible saying went—just might set him free. "Tell me you love Emily and not Lucinda."

"I never claimed to love Lucinda," Daniel hedged. "I merely said I was content to marry her—"

"But you are fond of Emily, aren't you?" James's grip tightened again, but Daniel only stared obstinately back at him. He was not a man to be cowered. Finally it dawned on James that he would get further with his friend if he was not so aggressive. He forced himself to release Daniel's lapels and took a step back. "Please, Daniel," he said with forced calmness. "This is important. I'm begging for your honesty as a friend."

There was no mistaking the confusion and wariness in Daniel's expression. Using deliberate care, he smoothed down his lapels and straightened his jacket. "Well, naturally I've grown fond of her," he said cautiously. "Who wouldn't? She's a lovely girl, spritely and fun, and clever in her own way."

"Are you happy about being engaged to Lucinda?"

He gave a shrug of resignation. "My mother is happy. Lucinda and I will make it work somehow. It's just that..." His voice trailed off.

"What were you going to say? Tell me!" James urged.

Again the maddening shrug. "I thought I was getting rather a bargain in Lucinda. Someone who would not trouble me. We'd go our separate ways, insomuch as two people can when they are married. But now I see it won't be like that at all. I think she may turn into a bit of a nag. She's always questioning me about how am I using science to better the lives of my fellow man, or badgering me about my lack of religious feeling. I'll tell you, that can wear a man down exceedingly fast."

James was tempted to laugh. Those were exactly the ways in which Lucinda had been prodding at him, too, pushing and challenging him to rise up to her high expectations. The lovely irony, as James saw it, was that he had come to love Lucinda for that exact reason. A wild sort of hope was sprung up full-fledged now, if only he could be sure he was right.

"You'll have much more freedom with Emily, I'll wager," Daniel was saying. "She'll be happy to go shopping for new clothes, or to call on her friends or plan parties. I'll bet she won't even care if you spend an afternoon playing rackets or relaxing at the club. And she'll let you watch *La Traviata* in peace, without giving you a lecture over it."

"Are you saying you would marry Emily if you had the chance?"

Daniel scrutinized him before answering. James did his best to look as nonthreatening and disinterested as possible. "Only asking for your honest opinion," he said with an encouraging nod. "I'm not daft, nor angry, nor jealous. I simply want to know."

Another long pause, during which James was almost dizzy with anticipation.

"Yes," Daniel said finally.

"Hallelujah!" James whooped. He grabbed Daniel's right hand and shook it vigorously. "God bless you, sir," he said with feeling. "God bless you."

These actions understandably bewildered the man. "Do you mind telling me what this is about? Are you saying you don't want to marry Emily?" His eyes narrowed suspiciously. "Is there something wrong with her?"

"Not at all," James hastened to assure him. "She is exactly as she seems. Mindless and sweet and silly and utterly charming. And Lucinda is exactly the woman you have found her to be."

"Exacting, stiff, demanding, and dull?"

"Precisely!" James said happily. He didn't care how the rest of the world saw her. He knew what lay hidden under that starchy exterior. "Don't you see? We're engaged to the wrong women!"

Daniel threw a quick glance toward the brandy glass he'd been holding earlier. No doubt he was wondering if this was some kind of alcohol-induced hallucination. "Are you saying you want to marry Lucinda?"

"Yes!" James exclaimed. "Don't you see? Our problem is solved!"

At last he saw the same glimmer of hope that he knew had been lighting his own eyes. But Daniel's natural pragmatism—and pessimism—kept him from jumping in elation too quickly. "There are still issues," he said flatly. "We don't know whether the ladies would even agree to this. And their parents..." He shook his head. "It would raise such a scandal they'd likely toss us both out on our ears, and then where would we be? My mother would die of a stroke—or worse, she'll live forty more years and never stop hounding me about it."

"Let's handle this one step at a time," James suggested. "First of all, I can tell you for a certainty that Lucinda loves me."

"What?" Daniel looked incredulous.

"No, truly. I'm afraid that over the past weeks we've...well, fallen for each other." He gave Daniel a sheepish grin. "Sorry to break the news to you, old chap. I apologize for stealing her from under your nose, but these things can't be helped."

"You really are a heartless rogue, aren't you?" Daniel chided. His voice held no rancor, however. Only warmth and something that sounded to James like relief.

"As for Emily," James said, "I believe you have been quietly stealing her heart as well."

"Me?" Daniel looked more incredulous than ever.

"I've seen the way she hangs about you whenever the four of us are together. The way she playfully baits you, which is just her way of trying to attract attention. And tonight when I was gone from the house, she came to you, didn't she? You said she'd gone upstairs with a headache, so I assume you knew this because she told you?"

"Well..." Daniel rubbed his chin, thinking it over. "She has been bending my ear rather a lot this week, mostly about how unkind you've been to her lately, and how you seem to have lost your charming ways. I confess I was beginning to think she enjoyed being around me better than you." He paused, pondering the idea further. "Now that I think on it, tonight I'm sure she held on to my arm longer than was strictly necessary as she was bidding me good night. And for a moment I could have sworn she wanted me to—" He cut himself off with a little cough.

"Why Daniel, you heartless rogue," James said, throwing back the man's accusation with a smirk. "You stole the woman right out from under my nose."

Daniel beamed—actually beamed—at the prospect. It was a look James had never known the man could possess. "Do you really think so?" A sliver of uncertainty crossed his features. "I mean, do you really think so?"

James slapped him on the back. "There's no doubt in my mind. Whether she knows it or not, Emily is head over ears in love with you, my friend. All you have to do is make her fully aware of it. Here's how I suggest we do it—and it will solve the problem of the parents as well..."

And just like that, James was back in his element. As James outlined his idea to Daniel, he realized he hadn't felt this good nor been this sure of himself since the night Emily had followed him to Cremorne. But this was more than simply a case of his matchmaking *savoir faire* returning to him; this time it was an utter, unshakeable confidence that he was doing the right thing. For despite Lucinda's dogged attempts at martyrdom (which James now solemnly swore he would soon wipe out forever), her example had shown him many important things about the spiritual side of life, and what was truly important.

She once quoted a verse in Romans about how all things work together for good to them that love God, but James was convinced that not even she understood the fullness of that truth the way he had seen it tonight. Surely no one but God could turn such a ridiculously wrong situation into an unqualified triumph.

Chapter 24

"A h, there you are. We've been looking all over for you."

It was with no small sense of dread that Lucinda looked up from her book when she heard James's voice. She'd been hiding herself away in the library all morning, figuring it was the best way to avoid seeing James. The pain was tearing her heart in two. How she was going to survive the next few days until this house party was over, she had no idea.

She had expected James to be equally torn up over last night's events, but she was very quickly shown otherwise. He was grinning at her with the sunniest, most carefree-looking expression she had ever seen. It was a look he hadn't worn in quite a while, and it stunned her. After his fervent declarations of love last night, had he really just shrugged and returned to Emily without a backward glance?

Emily, too, was beaming brightly, clinging to James's arm with such radiant joy that Lucinda's own heart felt scorched by it. How was she ever going to find the strength to withstand such happiness, on today of all days?

"Yes, what is it?" she said tersely, making a great show of irritation as she closed her book with a snap.

"Don't you remember? We agreed that we would meet this morning to work on our tableau."

Lucinda closed her eyes and tried to repress a sigh. With everything else that had been going on, she'd given no thought at all to the tableau for tonight's entertainment. Perhaps James and Emily were happy to indulge in such foolishness, but she had no heart for it. "You can easily come up with one by yourselves. I will not be participating."

"Oh, but you must!" Emily insisted. "We've worked out the most excellent idea, and we can't do it without you." She said this in her most insistent, whining tone—no doubt it was meant to be cajoling, but it only shredded Lucinda's nerves. At least Lucinda could take comfort in the fact that by marrying Daniel she would no longer have to live with her sister.

James held up a piece of paper. "Here's what we've worked up. I think it will be splendid. But we must practice."

"What is there to practice?" Lucinda said with frustration. "It's a *tableau*. All we do is arrange ourselves and stand there."

"Actually, we've decided on something a bit different." He thrust the paper into her hands.

Lucinda looked down and read it. "*A Midsummer Night's Dream*?" She nearly choked on the words, for she saw that just below the title he had written a famous quote from the play: *"The course of true love never did run smooth."* She thrust the paper back at him. "As I said, I won't be participating."

James looked entirely unruffled. She even had a bizarre feeling he was pleased by her vicious tone. "Oh, but as Emily said, you must. You see there are four parts there—two men, and two women. You will play Helena."

Surely James was trying to goad her. Lucinda was familiar with the play, and with Helena's role in it. She crossed her arms. "You want me to play Helena, the plain one whom nobody loves?"

"I don't think she's ever called 'plain' in the play," James protested mildly. "I think she merely views herself so." Before Lucinda could launch another objection he said swiftly, "Don't you see, it's perfect! Helena does obtain Demetrius's love in the end, right? So you see, Emily and I will play Hermia and Lysander, the two lovers—" Here he stopped to send a ludicrously loving gaze toward Emily, and Emily batted her eyelashes back at him with such fervor that Lucinda worried she might hurt herself. Emily was the world's worst actress, and today James wasn't doing any better.

"And then you shall be Helena, who's in love with Demetrius, although poor Demetrius is in love with Hermia…"

"And I suppose you want Daniel to play Demetrius? You know he won't do it. And in any case, I haven't seen him." She had in fact expected him to seek her out first thing, pressuring her to begin making plans for their future together. Although she had been relieved to be alone all morning, now she was beginning to worry that he was having second thoughts. Perhaps he was deliberately avoiding her.

"Precisely!" James said joyously.

"Oh look!" Emily squealed. "Here he is now."

Sure enough, Daniel was just entering the library. As his eye caught hers, Lucinda hurriedly tried to think of something to say. The few possibilities that popped into her head left just as quickly when Daniel kissed her on the cheek and said, "Hello, darling. Am I late for rehearsal?"

"You...are you...going to..." Lucinda stammered. Try as she might, she was too overtaken with shock to finish a coherent sentence. Everyone in the room was acting far too strangely. It was as if she'd dropped into some upside-down version of the world.

"Well, of course, I'm going to be in the play!" Daniel said cheerfully. "I wouldn't dream of missing out on all the fun."

Something in the way he said *fun* sounded just a little off. It hinted at the irascible Daniel that Lucinda had come to know over these past few weeks. There was no time to dwell on it, however, for James was ushering them all to the corner of the library which had the least amount of furniture in it. "We can practice here, I think. Then we must go and prepare our costumes. We must all wear togas, since the play takes place in ancient Greece. Those should be easy enough to fashion from some bedsheets."

"Mama will be livid if you ruin any of her fine linens," Lucinda warned.

"Never fear, we shall do them no harm," James assured her. "We shall only drape them carefully around ourselves. Here, I brought one down to show you." He opened the satchel he was carrying and pulled out a sheet. He unfolded it and placed one corner on Emily's shoulder. With a gentle push he set her into a twirling motion.

Giggling, she turned herself around so that she was soon very neatly wrapped in the sheet. Lucinda watched, sickened, as James's hands traveled all over Emily's body, helping her adjust the toga.

Daniel never took his eyes off the two of them, watching the demonstration with such intense interest that one would have thought he'd never before seen either a woman or a toga. "Careful, there," he cautioned. "You two are sliding dangerously close to impropriety. Remember that Emily is not your—" He coughed as though a word had stuck in his throat. "Not your *wife* ... er, *yet*."

"Right you are, Daniel," James said with a saucy grin. "Appallingly rude of me." He turned back to Emily and placed her hands on her shoulders, showing her how to hold the draping in place. Then he took a step back to observe the effect. "There we are. You get the general idea. When it comes time to dress for the performance, you ladies can help each other pin these in place."

"Well I hope this isn't *all* we are going to wear," Emily said with a twitter.

"Certainly not!" Lucinda exclaimed.

"Oh, I'm sure you'll come up with something very proper to wear underneath," James said. "I only ask you to find something that won't spoil the overall effect." This time he allowed his gaze to travel over Lucinda. "What a shame togas are no longer the fashion. I think you would look breathtaking in one. I can imagine long, shapely legs, bare except for a bit of delicate draping and some sandals—"

"Careful," Daniel warned him again. "That's my fiancée." But it seemed to Lucinda that his heart wasn't in the reproof.

This was all growing painfully ridiculous. "Let's just get this over with, shall we? Since you seem to be the director, James, suppose you tell us what we are to do."

"It's simple, really. You are Helena, so you will stand here." James took hold of her arm and pulled her gently. She could not help but remember the way he'd held her last night, sending heat coursing through her. But James gave no indication that he was thinking of anything other than this cursed play. "Stand here," he directed. "You will be looking with longing at Demetrius..." He took Daniel and placed him about two feet from Lucinda, pointing him so that his back was to her. "Now Demetrius is in love with Hermia, so Daniel, you will be looking at Emily..." He placed Emily in the same relative position to Daniel, with her back to him, so that the three of them formed a line and all were facing James. "And since I am the irresistible Lysander and Hermia is in love with me, she will be looking at me." He took Emily's hands. "Now, look at me as though you were in love with me." Emily giggled. Lucinda could not see her facial expression, but she had no doubt Emily was acting like a ridiculous flirt. That certainly would not be a stretch for her.

James raised his hands in triumph. "See? So easy, and positively brilliant."

"Are we done now?" Lucinda demanded.

"Well, we've added a bit of dialogue, but I believe you can practice that on your own." Once more he gave her the paper she had refused earlier.

Emily allowed the folds of the sheet to fall around her feet. "Oh, this will be so much fun! I can hardly wait!"

Scooping up the sheet, James grabbed Emily's hand and the two fairly skipped out of the room. Daniel made as though to follow, without even giving Lucinda a backward glance.

"Wait!" she said, taking hold of Daniel's arm. "I think we need to talk, don't you? Shouldn't we start thinking about our future plans?"

"Don't worry, there'll be plenty of time for all that." His attention still seemed focused on the door that James and Emily had just exited. "Now, if you will excuse me, I need to go ask James something. I need his help with the costume."

*

"All right, everyone! Are we ready?" James clapped his hands to draw attention to the makeshift curtain that had been hung across the large doorway connecting the salon with the library. Chairs for the audience had been set up in two neat rows facing it, with plenty of space between the chairs and the curtain for their little play to take place.

Already seated were Lord and Lady Cardington, who were giving James their undivided attention. Even old Mrs. Wiggins, who normally slept so soundly through the evening activities that James worried she would topple off her chair, was bright-eyed and alert. So was Lady Hibbitt. She had been watching all the events of the week very closely—too closely for James's comfort. Once or twice she'd given him a censorious glance when he'd approached Lucinda, as though she thought he was poaching on Daniel's game. But that was all past now; in just a few minutes everything would be set to rights and Lucinda would be his.

There were still a few empty seats, however. There was no sign of his aunt, and James was not going to start the show without her. Her absence worried him, because it was not like her to be late for anything. James sincerely hoped that she had not taken ill. There were times when cold rain made her rheumatism nearly unbearable. But he reminded himself that he had just seen her two hours ago chatting with Lady Cardington, and she seemed all right then. No doubt she was on her way. In the meantime, James decided to make sure everyone backstage was in their places and ready to go. He stepped behind the curtain and into the library.

Immediately he was met by Chapman and Hopkins. James had persuaded Chapman to dress as Queen Titania, and except for his prodigiously full mustaches, he'd done a credible job of looking like a fairy queen. Flowers were strewn in his hair; a few were even stuck into his full side whiskers. His toga was bedecked with jewels. In fact he looked truly ridiculous, but he was not the least bit abashed about it. This was a quality James admired very much. "What do you think?" Chapman said proudly.

"Perfection," James answered with a grin.

Hopkins was going to play Bottom, the simple peasant whom Oberon, the fairy king, gave the head of an ass just at the time Titania unwittingly takes a potion that causes her to fall in love with him. This was definitely going to add even more fun to what already promised to be an exceptional evening. Hopkins wore the thick corduroy trousers and rough shirt of a peasant. There was even a faint whiff of barn emanating from his clothes. Hopkins must have borrowed those trousers from some nearby farmer. His ass's head was huge and roughly made, but what it portrayed was unmistakable. The mask covered most of the upper part of his head, leaving a small round opening at the eyes and mouth to allow him to see and speak.

"This is incredible!" James said with approval. "Have you been hiding some latent artistic ability from us all these years?"

Hopkins snorted. "Not likely. Truth is, I went looking for an ass to model it on. I never did find one, but I did meet a very pleasant farmer in the next valley. He also has a lovely daughter. Turns out she has *many* talents."

James lifted an eyebrow. "Are you saying she did more for you than simply fashion this mask?"

"Nothing improper, I assure you," Hopkins replied, although his lascivious grin seemed to contradict his words. "For some reason, her father never let her out of his sight. She's a fetching lass, though. Tomorrow I shall go back and thank her for sure."

"You and Chapman are going to make a fine spectacle," James said. "I only hope you do not steal the show before we get to the important part."

"Yes, about that . . ." Hopkins's look sobered. "Are you sure you know what you're doing?"

"I've never been more sure of anything in my life," James replied. "You need only worry about yourself. I daresay you've got plenty to think about, wearing that." He cocked a critical eye as he surveyed his friend. "I have to say it suits you."

Hopkins snorted again, and this time it was nearly a very good imitation of a donkey's bray. "You'll be the one wearing this permanently, James, if things do not go as you plan."

"Then we must make sure that Queen Titania spreads extra good magic spells on the audience," James said.

"Like this?" Chapman made several elaborate gestures that looked either as if he were trying to sprinkle holy water or chase away flies.

"Perfect," James said, laughing. "Now, we must get this enterprise under way. Most everyone is in place, but I saw some empty chairs on the way in. Hopkins, will you go out to the hallway and urge in any of the stragglers? I can't start the show until everyone has arrived."

"Go out like this?" He pointed to his mask. "Won't that spoil the effect?"

"Good point." James considered him for a moment. "You're dressed reasonably enough except for the head. Take that off and leave it here. And make sure my aunt—Lady Thornborough—is in that front-row seat I reserved for her next to Lady Hibbitt."

"All right." Hopkins removed his mask and slipped out to the other side of the curtain.

"If you'll excuse me for a moment," Chapman said, "I need to go make some...adjustments." He tugged at a portion of his toga that kept slipping from his waist. "I don't want to shock the ladies, so I'll just step over here..." He disappeared behind a very thick and tall potted plant.

James turned his attention to the others in the library. Daniel and Emily were standing together, chatting quietly. James was dismayed to see that Daniel was not even attempting to give his attention to Lucinda. At least he and Emily were standing a respectable two feet or so from each other and looked as though their conversation was casual and innocuous.

Lucinda showed no signs that she resented being left alone. In fact, from her expression and the way she was looking at nothing in particular, James had the impression her mind was a long way away from this room. She was standing quietly in a corner, so still that James fancied she was trying to once more blend in to the wall. And yet who could miss her? The toga was wrapped around her tall and slender frame in artfully draped folds that gave her an exotic elegance. Her rich brown hair, lightly threaded with flowers and a gold chain, flowed softly around her shoulders. Even the simple gown she wore beneath the toga for propriety's sake could not detract from the effect. As he drew closer to her he saw that the only thing marring her appearance was a telltale redness around her eyes. She'd been crying, and James's heart ached to think of it.

"You look lovely," he said. In fact, she looked like a Greek goddess come to life, but James had to bite back that lavish compliment. He could not afford to give himself away before his plan was fully realized.

"Thank you." Her eyes, which had once looked into his with such fire, now returned his gaze with only a flat, bleak stare.

"I mean it," James insisted. "You will be the best Helena ever portrayed on stage."

"I'm sure I will not carry off my part as well as you. You are an expert in dissembling."

Her answer stung him. He was tempted to stop the entire charade at once and fall down at her feet and beg forgiveness. But he reminded himself that she was not the only person who had to be won over today.

For the moment, James had to pretend she meant no more to him than she had in times past. He must act as though he'd already forgotten everything that had happened between them since that night at the Trefethens' ball. It pained him to the depths of his soul, and he could only hope and pray she would forgive him when the time came. But he was certain this was the only way to win her and gain the blessing of her parents. They all had to be put on the spot and unable to refuse. An expert at dissembling? Indeed he was. He'd been doing it all his life. Tonight, however, it would surely be his redemption.

Hopkins came into the library through the other door. "Everyone's in place!" he announced.

James was glad for the excuse to turn away from Lucinda, to escape her look of contempt. He must be the clown for a few minutes longer. He strolled over to take Emily's arm. "Are you ready for your grand debut, my love?"

Emily giggled. "I can't believe you got Mr. Hopkins and Mr. Chapman to be Bottom and Queen Titania. It's too funny! Even Mr. Hibbitt thinks so." She turned her joyful gaze on Daniel. "Don't you, Mr. Hibbitt?"

Daniel gave a curt nod that was intended to convey grudging acquiescence, but there was a little sardonic smile playing around his lips.

"It's just what we need," James proclaimed. "Everyone has grown quite cross thanks to the rain, but after tonight I think they'll agree this was the most entertaining week they have ever spent in the country."

Chapter 25

"Ladies and gentlemen, thank you for coming all the way out to our modest little theater on such a cold and dreary evening."

This drew laughs from most people. "Don't see as how we had much choice," Lord Cardington said, whereupon his wife poked him in the ribs.

"Now I know you came out to see an ordinary little *tableau vivante*. And yet, as we have a long night ahead of us, we are going to incorporate a few speeches into our show as well. We shall, however, retain the custom of allowing you to guess what we are portraying. And now, we begin!"

The audience clapped. Lucinda knew this was her cue to come forward from behind the curtain. She had done all she could to prepare, but now that the moment was upon her she froze.

"Go on!" Emily said, and gave her a push.

Lucinda half-walked, half-stumbled into the salon. She stopped to regain her balance, not daring to look at anyone in the audience. Her eye paint and lip color had been applied by Emily with a heavy hand, making Lucinda feel like some kind of doll or scandalous woman. Many of the older guests were bound to think her costume too scanty, although she was adequately covered. The applause died away into what she could only imagine was stunned silence.

Slowly, deliberately, she lifted her eyes, expecting to see only shocked expressions. There were a few of those—particularly among the wives of her father's friends. Mostly, though, people were staring at her with something like pleased incredulity.

"My heavens," her father said, breaking the silence. "She's lovely."

Then the applause began again. "Bravo!" This came from Lady Thornborough, of all people. She was smiling at Lucinda with admiration.

"It's *Antony and Cleopatra*!" Jane Stonewell shouted gleefully. "I can tell because of the toga!"

Despite the crowd's approving reaction, Lucinda's legs felt weak and she began to tremble.

Beside her, James whispered, "Don't forget what you're supposed to do."

Lucinda took a deep breath. She could do this. She had no choice. "Oh, how I pine for another!" she rasped, extending her arms toward the curtain.

This was Daniel's cue, and he stepped out boldly. He struck a pose and smirked a little, drinking in the fresh round of applause. Once things had quieted down he proclaimed in a booming voice, "I, however, pine for another!"

He pointed toward the curtain as Lucinda had done, and out stepped Emily.

"Who's she supposed to be?" Miss Evers asked.

"This cannot be *Antony and Cleopatra*," Mr. Stone-well said. "There were no other women."

"My father says I must marry him!" Emily said, between bouts of giggles. "And yet I pine for another!" She extended her hand with a dramatic flourish and placed it on James's arm.

"And that man returns your love deeply," James said, so ardently that Lucinda thought her heart might break all over again. "But how shall we escape the tyranny of your father?"

"I have got it!" Miss Hallowell squealed. "It's *Romeo and Juliet*!"

"Don't be daft," Miss Evers said deprecatingly. "There were no togas in that play."

When Chapman came forward, dressed so outrageously as the fairy queen, the audience dissolved into helpless laughter. "Oh, how I pine for another!" he said, his voice a tremulous falsetto. "What angel wakes me from my flowery bed?"

With a loud bray, Hopkins burst into the room. "Who, me?"

Instantly a dozen voices shouted out over the laughter, "It's *A Midsummer Night's Dream*!"

Miss Hallowell was laughing so hard at the sight of her fiancé as Queen Titania that she was crying. She fanned herself, but her face was flushed with joy.

Everyone was partaking in the merriment except for Lucinda. She wanted only to melt in the background, never to be seen again. For several long moments she considered it seriously, as Hopkins and Chapman were making such fools of themselves that all attention was focused on them.

She took a cautious step toward the curtain, but James

intervened. "Not so fast," he whispered. "We're not done yet." He turned toward the audience and announced, "As we all know, because this is one of Shakespeare's comedies, everyone is going to live happily ever after. The Fairy Queen will return to the Fairy King, Bottom's spell will be broken, and he will return to his rustic little village." He shot Hopkins a wink at this. "And finally, let us not forget that even poor Helena will find true love."

Daniel took hold of her hand. Following James and Emily's had, they bowed to the audience. There was more applause, and shouts of "Bravo!"

Now we are done, Lucinda thought, her relief mingled with pain. She wished only for this evening to be over. Seeing James and Emily looking so ecstatic only added to her sorrow and confusion. How could James appear so utterly content, after what he had told her last night?

Suddenly, however, James's smile faded. "Something is amiss," he announced to the audience. "I know you all think we did a smashing job, and no doubt we did." He turned to survey Lucinda and the others. "And yet now as I look at our little troupe, I realize the casting is all wrong."

"I'll say," Mr. Stonewell called out cheerily. "I'm surprised you weren't the one with the ass's head!"

"That's enough out of you," James chided. "No, that's not the mistake I'm talking about. I believe Hibbitt should be playing Lysander and I should be playing Demetrius." He dropped Emily's hands, and instantly Daniel dropped Lucinda's as well.

"What's going on?" she whispered to Daniel.

"You heard what he said," Daniel whispered back. And with a broad, easy smile that Lucinda had never seen on him before, he turned and took Emily into his arms.

Emily squealed in delight, and then—oh, heavens! Daniel tightened his hold and kissed her! Lucinda thought her heart must have stopped as she watched Emily return the embrace with total abandon.

"Emily!" Lady Cardington shrieked in outrage. "Mr. Hibbitt! What is the meaning of this?"

"Now see here!" Lord Cardington joined his blustery objections to that of his wife. "This is most improper! I demand you stop immediately!"

James gently pried Daniel and Emily apart. "That will do, I believe," he said in a happy stage whisper.

Lucinda was still frozen in shock. "What are you doing?" she hissed to James. "Are you trying to humiliate me further by proving that my own fiancé doesn't want me?"

"Bear up a moment longer," James said. He turned and addressed the audience. "Ladies and gentlemen, perhaps this gentle lady's stunned expression reminds you of the scene in the play where poor Helena thinks the men are playing a joke on her. But I assure you, this is no joke. Since I have now switched to playing Demetrius, I shall borrow his words from the end of the play." He took hold of Lucinda's hands. She yielded them freely, as she was too dazed to object.

His clear blue eyes were staring into hers, without any hint of teasing. "The object and the pleasure of mine eye, is only Helena," he said tenderly. "Once, as in a sickness, did I loathe this food; but now as in health come to my natural taste, I do wish it…" He brought her left hand up to his lips, and his soft kiss sent tingles down Lucinda's spine. "I do love it…" James continued, now kissing her right hand. "I long for it…" He placed both of her hands on his heart. "...and will for evermore be true to it."

He seemed to be in complete earnest, but Lucinda's brain still could not take it all in. It wasn't supposed to be like this. She was going to be strong, and they were going to move on. But now he was gently kissing her palms and the inside of her wrists, a gesture that felt impossibly intimate. The lump in her throat grew so large she could barely breathe.

Somewhere, dimly, she heard a gasp. She was fairly certain it belonged to her mother, but she was not brave enough to look over at her and find out. This was a spectacle, to be sure—in every sense of the word. James stopped kissing her hands, and once more his gaze locked on hers. "What say you, Helena?" His smile was both teasing and tender in that irresistible way he had, his lips tempting her to draw closer...

"What are you waiting for, James? Kiss her!" This command came—could it be possible?—from Lady Thornborough!

Lucinda pulled in a breath, but before she could even think of what to say or do, James was sweeping her into his arms and kissing her. It was passionate, fierce, shocking, and wonderful. It had to be wrong...yet it felt so utterly right and perfect...Every conceivable emotion broke and swirled inside her, crashing against her fears and objections like waves on a rocky shore. "James," she whispered at last, pulling her lips away just enough to speak. "Is this really true? Daniel...and Emily...and you want..." Her voice trailed off, for she still could not find enough air to speak coherently.

"This is what the Lord wants for you," James murmured

against her ear. "God help you. It will be an altogether different sort of martyrdom."

"I believe...I shall be able to bear up under it," she replied, still trying to collect her breath. "Any man who believes as relentlessly as you do for God's deliverance will surely make the very best sort of husband."

"Careful, my love, or you shall give me a big head."

"Impossible for it to get any larger."

"Wench," he said with a grin, and putting his hand behind her head brought her to him swiftly for another kiss. This time Lucinda gave in to the sheer joy of it, oblivious of anyone or anything else.

The room erupted with cheers and applause. It was astounding, really, how a relatively small group of people could produce enough joyous fervor to shake the mansion.

"Ah, 'tis almost time for our curtain call," James whispered.

"Almost?"

Slowly he tore himself away from her and held up a hand to calm the audience. It was only at that moment that Lucinda dared to look at her parents. They had not been among those cheering. They were, in fact, staring at her, completely dumbstruck. It was quite a feat, Lucinda thought, to have rendered even her mother speechless. Lucinda brought a hand up to her cheek, which felt like fire, and the magnitude of what they had done began to hit her very hard. What on earth had James been thinking, to instigate something he knew would bring only scandal and her father's wrath upon them?

Worse, Daniel and Emily had been in on it, too. But neither of them looked the least bit worried. Lady Hibbitt appeared to have fainted dead away. She was leaning against Lady Thornborough, and that venerable lady kept Lady Hibbitt upright and fanned her gently, all the while smiling at James and Lucinda with obvious approval.

James cleared his throat. "Ladies and gentlemen, if I may borrow a few lines from the great Bard himself—" Holding his hand to his mouth as if speaking an aside, he added, "—with a few *minor* alterations." He opened his arms wide and bowed to Lord and Lady Cardington, showing that he was specifically addressing them. "If we shadows have offended—think but this, and all is mended: This is not a trifling dream—your daughters are exactly as they seem. She loves him…" He lifted up Daniel's and Emily's clasped hands. "And—heaven help her—she loves me!" He planted a fresh kiss on Lucinda's cheek, which brought a round of whistles and laughter. "Each now has a husband to cherish and love; you cannot object as your purpose has been won." He gave Lucinda's shoulders a quick squeeze, and then walked over to Lord Cardington. "And as I am an honest swain, I have put this all to rights again. So give me your hand if we be friends; and Hibbitt and I shall restore amends."

Lord Cardington gave him one last, hard look, before his face slowly cracked into a smile. He stood and extended his hand to James. "She's too good for either one of you," he declared. "But upon my soul, I have never denied her anything."

This was a patent lie, but Lucinda had no intention of calling him out on it. She was too ecstatically happy to care.

Lady Cardington rose imperiously from her chair. "I should like to say something," she announced.

She looked excessively stern and serious. Lucinda held her breath, and beside her she felt James stiffen.

"I shall now reveal something to you all." With a broad sweep of her arm, she included everyone in the room. "I always knew Mr. Simpson was the best match for my Lucinda!" Turning to Lord Cardington, she added, "Didn't I say that very thing to you just last night?"

He looked at her, temporarily confused. But then Lucinda saw a look pass between the two of them that she was certain she'd never seen before. It was filled with amusement, tenderness, and joy—a sign they understood each other on some inexpressibly deep level. Could it be that her parents really did love each other after all? Lucinda's heart overflowed with happiness at the thought.

Lord Cardington took hold of his wife's hand and kissed it soundly. Then, sending a wink toward Lucinda, he replied, "So you did, my love. So you did."

"And I shall be married to a baronet!" Emily exclaimed, mimicking James's earlier gesture as she happily tossed out this non sequitur.

"Hurrah!" someone shouted, whereupon Daniel drew Emily toward him again.

"You know, Lucinda, I've been thinking," James said, returning to her side. "There are still four weeks until Advent Sunday. Would you like to—"

"Yes!" Lucinda cried, and cut him off with a kiss. James's arms encircled her and she gave herself once more to the wanton joy of kissing her beloved in a shockingly public way.

And somehow, over the shouts and clapping and the bubbling of her own joyous soul, she heard Lady Thornborough exclaim, "Oh, what fools these mortals be!"

Epilogue

Christmas Eve, 1854
Somerville Estate, Kent

"Don't you think we should be getting back?" Lucinda murmured. They're bound to wonder what happened to us."

James nuzzled his wife's neck, unwilling to let her go just yet. He'd gone the whole afternoon without kissing her, and he was beginning to feel like a starving man. He was happy to have cornered her behind a potted tree in the hallway which—for now, at least—was free of servants. He transferred a kiss to her cheek. "I expect they'll know very well what happened to us, and I doubt anyone minds a bit."

"But—"

"I'll stop your mouth with a kiss," James answered, and did so. This time, she did not protest.

In all his years as a bachelor, James had never once truly considered the possibility that kissing one's own wife might be the most scintillating pleasure known to man. He knew it now, however, and he was doing all he could to make up for lost time.

They might have stayed there until dinnertime, had not the sound of Margaret's voice coming from the parlor arrested them. "There he is!" she cried happily. "He's just coming up the drive now."

Also from the parlor came Geoffrey's response: "I told you he'd make it. On that fine horse of his, how could he fail?"

Lucinda pulled away gently. Her cheeks were that lovely pink that James wanted to spend the rest of his life teasing out of her. She caressed his face and smiled, but the firm look in her eyes said it all.

James sighed. "I'll admit defeat. For now." Stealing one last kiss, he took her by the arm and led her into the parlor.

Marriage must truly be turning him into a sentimental man, James thought, for he found the sight of his family gathered in this room truly heartwarming. Margaret was seated by the window, where she'd been eagerly watching for Tom's arrival. Geoffrey stood by the mantel, and next to him Lady Thornborough was doing some needlework in a chair by the fire. She gave a sly, knowing smile to James as he and Lucinda entered the room. James simply grinned in return.

Lizzie, who sat on the sofa nestling her sleeping son, said, "I'm so glad we shall all be together for Christmas."

"Is there any sign of a carriage?" Lucinda asked Margaret.

"I'm afraid not." Seeing the look of concern on Lucinda's face she added, "I'm sure Tom will have news of their whereabouts."

Tom lost no time shedding his hat and coat and coming

up the stairs. He strode in swiftly, his damp hair still curling around his ears. "Hello, everyone." This may have been addressed to the room at large, but it was clear he had eyes only for his wife. Margaret ran to him and he folded her into his arms. "Best be careful, my love," he warned. "I'm cold and damp yet." But she made no move to pull away.

"At that rate, I don't think you'll be cold long," James observed with a smile.

"Do you have news of Emily and Daniel?" Lucinda asked anxiously.

"I do," Tom said. "I found them about five miles from here. Their carriage broke down near Amberly, and they've decided to stay at the inn. No one will be able to repair the wheel until after Boxing Day. I took the liberty of offering one of your carriages, Geoffrey, but Daniel said he wouldn't hear of putting us out in such a way—nor the driver, who ought to be able to spend Christmas day at home with his family."

"Really?" James said. "I've never known Daniel to concern himself about the servants."

Tom shrugged. "It's a charming inn, they've got a comfortable set of rooms, and the proprietors are overjoyed to have the business. I'd say they are resigned."

"I wonder they even attempted the journey, when they might have stayed more comfortably in town," Lady Thornborough put in.

Lucinda gave an embarrassed grimace. "That was Emily's doing. When she gets her mind set on something, it's hard to refuse her."

"I'm going to wager Daniel is more than resigned," James said. "He's probably happy for the excuse to stay away. As I recall, he and Master Edward did not get along so well when last they met. Claims Eddie bit him or some such nonsense."

"Impossible," Geoffrey declared, sending a tender glance toward his dozing son. "Eddie is too well-mannered for that. Although I grant you, he may be rambunctious at times, just like his namesake."

"He certainly looks a little angel now," Tom observed. "I'm surprised he's not already tucked into bed."

"He insisted that he wanted to stay up until you came home," Lizzie said. "You are his favorite uncle, after all. And since it's Christmas Eve, I indulged him."

"Looks like he didn't quite make it." Tom bent down to lightly ruffle Eddie's hair. The little boy moved, muttered something incoherent, and snuggled deeper into his mother's arms.

"I prefer him when he's awake and tearing through the house," Geoffrey said. "It's those times that I really see Edward in him." He sat down on the sofa, and Lizzie gently transferred the sleeping boy to his father's arms.

"I'm glad to see our progeny are taking after their namesakes," James said. He reached over and placed an arm around Lucinda's waist. "If our first child is a girl, I have every intention of naming her Ria."

"Your first child…" Lady Thornborough's needlework slipped from her hands. "Do you mean—are you trying to imply—?" Her face lit up with joy and she couldn't finish her words.

"No!" Lucinda hastened to say.

She was blushing again, and James knew why. She was not pregnant yet, though it was not for lack of trying. He smiled to himself, remembering how much fun it had been. She had begun as a hesitant lover, but it had not taken long to gently break down every last one of her shy barriers. Even now, with this newfound confidence in herself, James was pretty sure those bright blushes weren't going away anytime soon. He was glad for it, for he had discovered something no one else had even remotely suspected. Lucinda's vivid blushes were a mirror of the fiery woman she was on the inside. But as long as she kept showing that part of herself to *him*, James didn't mind in the least if no one else saw it.

"Who will be next, then?" Geoffrey asked. "Little Eddie is pining for cousins to play with."

*

Tom cleared his throat. "Well, as a matter of fact..." His gaze dropped to the woman in his arms. The most beautiful woman in the whole world. It had been a hard, cold ride today through deep drifts, but Tom would have faced much worse to get home to her. She was smiling serenely. Practically glowing. Tom wondered that no one else had yet caught on. "You haven't told them, my love?"

Lizzie was the first to grasp the meaning of his words. "Oh, my dearest Margaret!" She rose from the sofa, nearly tripping over the blocks Eddie had strewn on the rug, and threw her arms around Margaret's neck. Margaret laughed, but was unable to speak.

"Easy now," Tom advised. "Don't crush the baby."

*

All the ladies were crying now—sobbing and yet smiling and making happy exclamations all at the same time. Tom and James wore more bemused expressions—and Geoffrey was sure the look on his own face was similar.

So much happiness. How far they'd all come, he reflected, in just a few short years. The tragedies of the past could never be forgotten, but they could, perhaps, be laid to rest, remaining only as bittersweet memories that could not dampen the joys of today.

In all that had happened since those terrible days, Geoffrey had seen the hand of God at work in things great and small, to bring them all together. To heal the brokenhearted. To bind up the wounds. The Lord's declaration in the Scriptures was poignantly real to him: *To everything there is a season, and a time for every purpose under heaven.*

*

Later, when Eddie had been put to bed and they'd enjoyed an excellent dinner, they all gathered once more in the parlor.

"I have a surprise for you all," Lizzie announced. She took a seat at the piano. "I have been learning to play."

Her words did indeed bring gasps of surprise from everyone—all except Geoffrey. "Turns out she has a gift for it," he told them. "Just like her sister Ria did."

This news made James very happy indeed. Across the room, Lady Thornborough was misty-eyed and smiling. James knew she missed Ria more than anyone. Even so, she had never let it dampen her love for Lizzie, who held a different but equally special place in her heart.

Here was one more wonderful thing to celebrate. He rose, took his wife into his arms, and said to Lizzie, "Any chance you know a waltz?"

After five years of exile, Lizzie Poole returns
home, taking on a new identity. But when she
falls in love with a handsome clergyman,
will her secret cost her true love?

An *Heiress* at Heart

Please see the next page for an excerpt.

London, June 1851

"If you've killed her, Geoffrey, we will never hear the end of it from Lady Thornborough."

Geoffrey Somerville threw a sharp glance at his companion. The man's flippancy annoyed him, but he knew James Simpson was never one to take any problem too seriously. Not even the problem of what to do with the young woman they had just accidentally struck down with his carriage.

The girl had been weaving her way across the street, seemingly unaware of their rapid approach until it was too late. The driver had barely succeeded in steering the horses sharply to one side to keep from trampling her under their massive hooves. However, there had not been enough time or space for him to avoid the girl completely, and the front wheel had tossed her onto the walkway as easily as a mislaid wicker basket.

Geoffrey knelt down and raised the woman's head

gently, smoothing the hair from her forehead. Blood flowed freely from a wound at her left temple, marring her fair features and leaving ugly red streaks in her pale yellow hair.

Her eyes were closed, but Geoffrey saw with relief that she was still breathing. Her chest rose and fell in ragged but unmistakable movements. "She's not dead," he said. "But she is badly hurt. We must get help immediately."

James bounded up the steps and rapped at the door with his cane. "First we have to get her inside. People are beginning to gather, and you know how much my aunt hates a scandal."

Geoffrey noted that a few people had indeed stopped to stare, although no one offered to help. One richly dressed young lady turned her head and hurried her escort down the street, as though fearful the poor woman bleeding on the pavement had brought the plague to this fashionable Mayfair neighborhood. At one time Geoffrey might have wondered at the lack of Good Samaritans here. But during the six months he'd been in London, he'd seen similar reactions to human suffering every day. Although it was no longer surprising, it still saddened and sickened him.

Only the coachman seemed to show real concern. He stood holding the horses and watching Geoffrey, his face wrinkled with worry. Or perhaps, Geoffrey realized, it was merely guilt. "I never even seen her, my lord," he said. "She come from out of nowhere."

"It's not your fault," Geoffrey assured him. He pulled out a handkerchief and began to dab the blood that was seeping from the woman's wound. "Go as quickly as you can to Harley Street and fetch Dr. Layton."

"Yes, my lord." The coachman's relief was evident. He scrambled up to the driver's seat and grabbed the reins. "I'm halfway there already."

Geoffrey continued to cautiously check the woman for other injuries. He slowly ran his hands along her delicate neck and shoulders and down her slender arms. He tested only as much as he dared of her torso and legs, torn between concern for her well-being and the need for propriety. Thankfully, nothing appeared to be broken.

James rapped once more on the imposing black door. It finally opened, and the gaunt face of Lady Thornborough's butler peered out.

"Clear the way, Harding," James said. "There has been an accident."

Harding's eyes widened at the sight of a woman bleeding on his mistress's immaculate steps. He quickly sized up the situation and opened the door wide.

Geoffrey lifted the unconscious girl into his arms. She was far too thin, and he was not surprised to find she was light as a feather. Her golden hair contrasted vividly with his black coat. Where was her hat? Geoffrey scanned the area and noted with chagrin the remains of a straw bonnet lying crushed in the street. Something tugged at his heart as her head fell against his chest. Compassion, he supposed it was. But it was curiously profound.

"She is bleeding profusely," James pointed out. "Have one of the servants carry her in, or you will ruin your coat."

"It's no matter," Geoffrey replied. He felt oddly protective of the woman in his arms, although he had no idea who she was. His carriage had struck her, after all, even if her own carelessness had brought about the calamity. He was not about to relinquish her, not for any consideration.

He stepped grimly over the red smears her blood had left on the white marble steps and carried her into the front hall, where James was again addressing the butler. "Is Lady Thornborough at home, Harding?"

"No, sir. But we expect her anytime."

Geoffrey knew from long acquaintance with the Thornborough family that Harding was a practical man who remained calm even in wildly unusual circumstances. The childhood escapades of Lady Thornborough's granddaughter, Victoria, had developed this ability in him; James's exploits as an adult had honed it to a fine art.

Sure enough, Harding motioned toward the stairs with cool equanimity, as though it were an everyday occurrence for an injured and unknown woman to be brought into the house. "Might I suggest the sofa in the Rose Parlor, sir?"

"Excellent," said James.

As they ascended the stairs, Harding called down to a young parlor maid who was still standing in the front hall. "Mary, fetch us some water and a towel. And tell Jane to clean the front steps immediately." Mary nodded and scurried away.

Another maid met them at the top of the stairs. At Harding's instructions, she quickly found a blanket to spread out on the sofa to shield the expensive fabric.

Geoffrey set his fragile burden down with care. He seated himself on a low stool next to the woman and once again pressed his handkerchief to the gash below her hairline. The flesh around the wound was beginning to turn purple—she had been struck very hard. Alarm assailed him. "What the devil possessed her to step in front of a moving carriage?"

He was not aware that he had spoken aloud until James answered him. "Language, Geoffrey," he said with mock prudishness. "There is a lady present."

Geoffrey looked down at the unconscious woman. "I don't think she can hear me just now." He studied her with interest. Her plain black dress fit her too loosely, and the cuffs appeared to have been turned back more than once. Her sturdy leather shoes were of good quality, but showed signs of heavy wear. Was she a servant, wearing her mistress's cast-off clothing? Or was she a lady in mourning? Was she already sorrowing for the loss of a loved one, only to have this accident add to her woes? "If she is a lady, she has fallen on hard times," Geoffrey said, feeling once again that curious pull at his heart. He knew only too well the wretchedness of having one's life waylaid by one tragedy after another.

A parlor maid entered the room, carrying the items Harding had requested. She set the basin on a nearby table. After dipping the cloth in the water, she timidly approached and gave Geoffrey a small curtsy. "With your permission, my lord."

Something in the way the maid spoke these words chafed at him. He had been entitled to the address of "my lord" for several months, but he could not accustom himself to it. There were plenty who would congratulate him on his recent elevation to the peerage, but for Geoffrey it was a constant reminder of what he had lost. Surely nothing in this world was worth the loss of two brothers. Nor did any position, no matter how lofty, absolve a man from helping another if he could. He held out his hand for the cloth. "Give it to me. I will do it."

The maid hesitated.

"Do you think that is wise?" James asked. "Surely this is a task for one of the servants."

"I do have experience in this. I often attended to the ill in my parish."

"But you were only a clergyman then. Now you are a baron."

Geoffrey hated the position he had been placed in by the loss of his two elder brothers. But he would use it to his advantage if he had to. And he had every intention of tending to this woman. "Since I am a baron," he said curtly, motioning again for the cloth, "you must all do as I command."

James laughed and gave him a small bow. "Touché, *my lord.*"

The maid put the towel into Geoffrey's hand and gave him another small curtsy. She retreated a few steps, but kept her eyes fastened on him. Geoffrey suspected that her diligence stemmed more from his new social position than from the present circumstances. It had not escaped him that he'd become the recipient of all kinds of extra attention—from parlor maids to duchesses—since he'd become a baron. The years he'd spent as a clergyman in a poor village, extending all his efforts to help others who struggled every day just to eke out a meager living, had apparently not been worth anyone's notice.

Geoffrey laid a hand to the woman's forehead. It was too warm against his cool palm. "I'm afraid she may have a fever in addition to her head injury."

James made a show of pulling out his handkerchief and half covering his nose and mouth. "Oh dear, I do hope she has not brought anything catching into the house. That would be terribly inconvenient."

Harding entered the room, carrying a dust-covered carpetbag. He held it in front of him, careful not to let it touch any part of his pristine coat. "We found this near the steps outside. I believe it belongs to"—he threw a disparaging look toward the prostrate figure on the sofa—"the lady."

"Thank you, Harding," James said. He glanced at the worn object with equal distaste, then motioned to the far side of the room. "Set it there for now."

That bag might be all the woman had in the world, Geoffrey thought, and yet James was so casually dismissive of it. The man had a long way to go when it came to finding compassion for those less fortunate.

He turned back to the woman. She stirred and moaned softly. "Easy," Geoffrey murmured, unable to resist the urge to comfort her, although he doubted she could hear him. "You're safe now."

James watched from the other side of the sofa as Geoffrey cleaned the blood from her hair and face. "What a specimen she is," he remarked as her features came into view. He leaned in to scrutinize her. "Look at those high cheekbones. And the delicate arch of her brow. And those full lips—"

"This is a woman, James," Geoffrey remonstrated. "Not some creature in a zoo."

"Well, it's clear she's a woman," James returned lightly, unruffled by Geoffrey's tone. "I'm glad you noticed. Sometimes I wonder if you are aware of these things."

Geoffrey was aware. At the moment, he was *too* aware. He could not deny that, like James, he had been taken by her beauty. Except her lips were too pale, chapped from dryness. He had a wild urge to reach out and gently brush over them with cool water ...

"Good heavens," James said, abruptly bringing Geoffrey back to his senses. He dropped his handkerchief from his face. "This is Ria."

Geoffrey froze. "What did you say?"

"I said, the young lady bleeding all over Auntie's sofa is Victoria Thornborough."

No. Surely that was impossible. There were occasions, Geoffrey thought, when James seemed determined to try him to the absolute limit. "James, this is not the time for one of your childish pranks."

James shook his head. "I am absolutely in earnest."

"But that's preposterous."

"I think I should know my own cousin. Even if it has been ten years." He bent closer as the woman mumbled something incoherent. "You see? She heard me. She recognizes her name."

The room suddenly became quite still. Even the servants who had been hovering nearby stopped their tasks. All eyes turned toward the sofa.

Was this really Ria? Geoffrey had to take James's word on it for now; he had never met her. He had been in Europe during her brief, clandestine courtship with his brother. This woman, to whom he had been so curiously drawn—for some reason he could easily believe her to be a lady, despite her dirty clothes and bruises. He had no trouble believing Edward could have fallen in love with her—had he not been taken with her himself? *No,* he told himself again. It had been mere compassion he'd been feeling. And it was utterly incomprehensible that his sister-in-law should appear like this out of nowhere.

"If this is Ria," Geoffrey said, "then surely Edward would be with her?"

"So one would expect," James replied. "I agree that the situation is most unusual."

"Unusual," Geoffrey repeated drily. The word might describe everything about what had happened between Ria and his brother. Their elopement had taken everyone by surprise, causing a scandal that was bad enough without the embarrassing fact that Ria had been engaged to his other brother, William, at the time.

"At least we can surmise that they were not aboard the ill-fated *Sea Venture*," James said. "Where *did* they go, I wonder?"

"That is only one of the many things I'd like to know," Geoffrey said. He'd exhausted himself with searches and inquiries after Edward and Ria had disappeared without a trace. The best they could discover was that the couple may have booked passage on a ship that had sunk on its way to America. And yet all was conjecture; there had never been answers.

Geoffrey took hold of the woman's left hand and began to remove a worn glove that was upon it. He heard the maid behind him gasp, but he was beyond worrying about the possible impropriety of his actions. If this was Ria, he wanted evidence that Edward had made an honest woman of her. He did not think his brother would deliberately trifle with a woman's affections, but he also knew Edward was prone to rash whims and irresponsible actions. Anything might have kept him from carrying out his plans.

With one last gentle tug from Geoffrey, the glove came off, revealing a hand that was rough and calloused. It was a hand that had done plenty of manual labor.

Though she was not wearing a wedding band, she was wearing a gold and onyx ring that Geoffrey recognized as having once belonged to Edward. The sight of it nearly devastated him. He could think of only one reason she would be wearing it instead of his brother.

"Why?" Geoffrey asked roughly, as his concern melted into consternation. "If they were in dire straits, why did they stay away? Why did they not ask us for help?"

"If you were in their shoes," James answered, "would you have wanted to face William's wrath? Or Lady Thornborough's?" He looked at the woman thoughtfully. "Perhaps they were not always so destitute. Look at her, Geoffrey. Look at what she is wearing."

Geoffrey allowed his gaze to travel once more over the slender figure in the plain black dress that seemed to declare her in mourning. "No!" Geoffrey said sharply. How could she have survived, but not Edward?

Geoffrey rose and gave the towel and the glove to the maid. He walked to the window and peered through the lace curtains to the street below. It was filled with carriages moving swiftly in both directions, but he could see no sign of either his coach or the doctor's. He knew it was too soon to expect their return, but he could not quell the anxiety rising in him.

Which was worse: the continual pain of not knowing what had become of his brother, or the final blow of discovering he really was dead? If anyone had asked him that question before this moment, he might have given an entirely different response.

He had to get Ria well again. And he had to get answers.

Society beauty Maggie Vaughn is horrified
to find herself engaged to a gold prospector from
humble beginnings. But what begins as a marriage
of convenience may blossom into
a true affair of the heart...

A *Lady* Most Lovely

Please see the next page for an excerpt.

"Aren't you the man who rode a horse twenty miles to shore after a shipwreck?"

Tom Poole grimaced in irritation. This had to be the twentieth time tonight that he'd been forced to answer some inane question. He turned to see who had addressed him.

The man looked about the same age as Tom, but he was much shorter and a good deal more rotund. His weak, watery eyes were focused on Tom with complete fascination. Apparently everyone in London had heard his story—or some wild, exaggerated version of it. Tom had been answering questions like this all evening, trying to set the record straight for dozens of questioners who had been buzzing around him like mosquitoes. "It was only seven miles," Tom told him pointedly. "And I didn't *ride* the horse."

With a vain hope that this would satisfy his inquisitor,

Tom turned away. He no longer cared if his answers were too brusque. He'd done more than his share of socializing tonight, and in any case his real attention was elsewhere—held captive by the most beautiful woman he'd ever seen.

She was breathtaking—tall and stately, with every feature that Tom had always found desirous in a woman: gleaming dark brown hair, high cheekbones, and a full, sensuous mouth. A generous portion of her smooth, ivory skin was displayed to great advantage by the low-cut neckline of her emerald-green gown. Tom had spotted her the moment he'd come in. Although he'd been introduced to just about every other person in this overcrowded ballroom, somehow she had remained far away—unreachable, like a star or a distant planet.

Since no introductions had been forthcoming, Tom had decided to ask James Simpson who she was. James, who was the cousin of Tom's half sister Lizzie, was an affable roué who seemed to know everyone in London. Tom had been just about to ask him about the woman when they'd been interrupted.

James now looked askance at the man. "Carter, hasn't anyone told you to obtain an introduction before butting into a conversation?"

"Oh, I beg your pardon," Carter returned in an exaggerated tone, not looking the least bit contrite. He gave Tom a showy bow. "Bartholomew Carter, at your service."

Tom replied with a brief nod. Carter's lack of protocol revealed he was just like so many men Tom had met at this party: self-indulgent, self-important gentlemen who would not have given him the time of day before

he'd left England. Now that good fortune in the Austra-
lian gold fields had elevated Tom from a poor farmhand
to a wealthy man, he was suddenly on everyone's list of
people worth knowing.

His sister Lizzie's social status had also risen dramat-
ically. Last year she'd married a baron, and now she was
Lady Somerville, a member of London's elite social circle. For her sake Tom had done his best to endure the lessons on deportment and all these irritating interactions
that passed for conversation with the upper classes. He
knew it was an unavoidable duty, given his new station
in life, but his patience was growing short. Especially
tonight. Tonight he wanted only to meet the woman who
had kept him spellbound.

Once more Tom's gaze strayed in her direction. She'd
spent much of the past hour speaking with a very slender, rather shy-looking young lady—one who might
have been pretty, but whose features seemed to fade
into her pale, peach-colored gown. On the surface these
two women could not have appeared more different, yet
they were chatting with the air of close friends. For some
reason Tom found this intriguing. He'd seen plenty of
so-called friendships that were nothing but two people
pretending to like each other in order to gain some
social advantage. Tom wondered if perhaps this one was
genuine.

"You mean, you didn't ride to shore on a wild
stallion?"

Wild stallion? With great effort, Tom turned back
to Carter. "It's a *Thoroughbred*. A champion racehorse.
Took first place three times at Homebush."

"That's not the way I heard it," Carter persisted. "I

heard he could barely be contained in his stall during the voyage to England."

Tom frowned. "The horse is, understandably, leery of ships."

That wasn't the half of it, of course. It was a wonder the creature had survived the voyage at all, given its constant restlessness that verged on panic whenever the seas were rough. But now that the stallion was on dry land, it was easily controlled by any competent rider. But this information would be lost on Carter. No doubt the only time he got near a horse was when he placed his generous rump into a finely appointed carriage.

Irresistibly, Tom glanced at the woman again. She looked so poised, so cool and collected, as though she didn't realize that the horde of people in the room had sucked all the air out of it.

It was hot, and Tom's collar chafed. Every part of his attire, from his elaborately knotted cravat to his trim-fitting coat and trousers, was too confining. He was still adjusting to the sheer volume of clothing that custom dictated for gentlemen. In his humbler days he'd rarely needed more than a simple shirt and trousers. He tugged at his cravat in an attempt to loosen it, even though he could imagine the look of disapproval this would bring from his new valet. Stephens was not just a servant but a mentor. He was teaching Tom how to dress and how to allow others to do dozens of things for him that any man should be able to do for himself. Being waited on hand and foot chafed Tom even more than the cravat. He would never forget that hard work alone brought his success. He would never become like the buffoon who was still questioning him.

"What was it like to be captured by savages?" Carter prompted.

"The Aborigines didn't *capture* me," Tom said sharply. "They *found* me washed up on the beach, half dead. They took me to their camp and helped me recover."

This drew a look of disbelief from Carter. He evidently preferred to visualize Tom pinned down by the point of a spear. That alone illustrated the vast difference between them. Tom had lived for weeks among the Aborigines, but it was only now he'd returned to England that he found himself among a truly different race. He had been excited about returning to London—he'd always loved the energy of its noisy, foggy, bustling streets. But he was seeing a new side of the city now. He'd been dirt-poor when he'd left for Australia seven years ago. He had lived in parts of London that nobody in this room was aware even existed. Or at least, they did not acknowledge it if they did. He'd only seen these grand homes from the outside, only observed their inhabitants from a distance. Now he was one of them. Well, not exactly *one of them*. Perhaps *among them* would be a better way to describe it.

Despite his joy at being reunited with his sister, Tom had begun to question whether coming back had been a good idea. Only now, as he watched the statuesque brunette gracing the room with her sweeping gaze, did he think all his pains had been worth it. It had been a very long time since a woman had taken such complete hold of his attention. Longer than he could remember. He *had* to get James to introduce him. "James," he said, "who is that woman?"

James looked toward the place where Tom was indicating, but Carter cut him off before he could answer.

"Tell me, Poole, is it true the Aborigine women walk around all day without a stitch of clothing?" His mouth widened into an ugly leer. "I should like to see that."

This remark swept away the last shred of Tom's patience. He took hold of Carter's coat, bringing the smug idiot close enough to sense his anger. "Do you think they are no better than animals? There are far worse savages in England, I assure you."

Carter's mouth actually fell open in shock. But then he collected himself and shook free of Tom's grasp, sputtering, "How dare you handle me like that, sir!" His right arm came up, as though he was foolishly considering taking Tom on—something that Tom, God help him, would have relished. His fists clenched, and he might actually have taken a swing if James had not stepped in and smoothly steered the man several steps away.

"Carter, you've plied Tom with quite enough questions," he admonished. "Why don't you go find the billiard room or something."

Carter straightened his coat. After throwing an icy glare at Tom, he turned and stalked off.

"Thank you for rescuing me from that fool," Tom said.

"I had the impression I was rescuing Carter from *you*," James countered with a smirk. "I could see you were ready to throttle him. Not that I would have blamed you. He is an insufferable bore."

Tom waved away James's well-meaning words. "No. It was my fault. I should not have allowed him to anger me. I should not have used force against him." He shook his head ruefully. "I keep forgetting all those things Lizzie has been trying to teach me. Not to mention—" He cut himself short.

James lifted an eyebrow. "Not to mention what?"

Again, Tom waved him off. "Never mind." There was no point trying to explain; James probably would not understand. Despite the multitude of resolutions Tom had made over the past year, there were still far too many times when he lost his temper. Why was it so hard for him to act with the patience he was supposed to have if he was truly a Christian?

"Forget about Carter," James said. "As far as I'm concerned, you acted admirably. I'm sure everyone else thinks so, too."

Startled, Tom looked around and realized what James was referring to. The gentlemen and ladies who had been standing nearby had apparently noticed his little run-in with Carter. Many were still staring at Tom, their expressions ranging from alarm to undisguised amusement. He had made a spectacle of himself.

Had *she* seen it? What would she think of him?

Tom looked quickly over to her. She may have been watching him, but it was impossible to tell. Her attention seemed to be focused on an old man with enormous whiskers who was kissing her hand. "James," he said, though his eyes never left the woman, "who is she?"

"I see you are determined to meet her," James said with an exaggerated sigh of resignation. "Well, come on then." He dove into the crowd, and Tom quickly fell in step with him. All around them, people moved aside and pretended to go back to their own conversations, although Tom still sensed that they were watching him.

"I'm surprised you should be interested in her," James remarked as they went.

"Really? Why shouldn't I?"

"Well, don't misunderstand me...Miss Cardington is a very respectable young lady to be sure, but she's a bit...bland. Sad to say, she's probably on a direct route to spinsterhood."

"Are you daft?" Tom exclaimed. "She's the most beautiful woman in the room!"

James paused, looked at Tom, and then followed his gaze back to the two women. "Oh, I beg your pardon. Were you referring to the lady in green?"

"Of course!" Tom replied, amazed that someone as astute as James could have misunderstood.

"Ah," said James. "Of course." He shook his head and gave an odd little smile, as though amused by some private joke. He started forward once more. "I told you about her before we arrived," James said as they skirted a small group of boisterous men who were on their way to the card room. "Miss Margaret Vaughn is the reason we're at this gathering. Well, half the reason. She's engaged to Paul Denault. Our host, the Duke of Edgerton, is Denault's uncle. He's throwing this party in their honor."

"Engaged?" Tom repeated.

The word came out as a gasp, and James gave him a curious glance. "She's quite beautiful, as you have noticed. She's also the wealthiest heiress in London. Inherited mountains of money when her father died two years ago. Denault is one happy man."

"Who is this Denault?" Tom demanded. "Surely not that old man!" he added in dismay, pointing to the old man with the prodigious whiskers who was still speaking with her.

"Oh, dear Lord, no," James said with a laugh. "Although

he wishes he *was* her fiancé, I'm sure. That's Mr. Plimpton—a pillar of London society, and he'll be the first to tell you so."

"Where is Denault, then?" Tom said impatiently. During the past hour, he'd seen Miss Vaughn chat with scores of people, including those he pegged as would-be suitors. But he could have sworn she had not bestowed particular attention on any one man.

"Let me see..." James scanned the room. "He's usually in the smoking rooms chatting up the barons of industry, unless he's entertaining the—ah! There he is." He pointed to a tall, sandy-haired man, impeccably dressed, who had a cohort of young ladies clustered around him.

"He has many admirers," Tom said drily.

"Oh, yes," James agreed. "Both Denault and the ladies agree that he is a very handsome man indeed."

But why wasn't he with Miss Vaughn? How could he possibly find other ladies more appealing? Remembering James's remark that she was an heiress he said, "Denault's marrying her for her money, then."

James shrugged. "I doubt it. He has plenty of his own."

"Inherited?" Tom figured that as the nephew of a duke, Denault was in that privileged class whose money was handed to them at birth. Tom was beginning to loathe that sort of man, for the simple fact that they all now loathed him.

"Not at all," James said, surprising him. "Denault's branch of the family is well connected, but not as wealthy as it once was. He made his fortune on investments in America. He is, as the Americans would say, 'a self-made man.' I suppose that's something you two have in common."

At that moment, Denault finally deigned to send a glance in Miss Vaughn's direction. As their eyes met, Denault gave her a smile and a look that seemed to say, *All the world knows that I am yours—and you are mine.* When Miss Vaughn serenely returned her fiancé's smile, an irrational jealousy wrapped itself around Tom's heart. He and Denault shared something much greater than business sense, that was certain.

"Do you still wish to meet her?" James asked.

"Yes," Tom said resolutely. Even knowing she was engaged could not curb his desire to speak to her.

She had taken note of their approach. Tom was sure of it. He could tell by a subtle shift in her posture, an extra alertness in his direction, even as she kept her eyes fixed on Plimpton. He felt a surge of excitement at this realization. Suddenly he was far too conscious of his tight collar, his heavily starched shirt, and his overpolished boots. In fact, everything he had on was foreign to him. He told himself this must be the reason why he felt as though he were moving through heavy sand.

They were stopped by Denault, who broke away from his little group of admirers and strode over to intercept them. "Simpson!" he said warmly, holding out his hand.

While James returned the greeting, Tom watched as Miss Vaughn excused herself from Miss Cardington and Mr. Plimpton and came to join her fiancé. Now that she was so close, Tom found he could hardly breathe. He marveled at her flawless features. Her eyes were deep green—nearly the same shade as her gown—and rimmed in the center with yellow gold. They studied him with cool interest.

"I'd like to introduce you to my cousin," James said. "This is Mr. Thomas Poole."

"Tom," he corrected. "Just Tom."

One of Miss Vaughn's delicate eyebrows lifted a fraction, but she said nothing.

"Tom Poole?" Denault repeated. "The man who made a fortune in the gold mines?"

News traveled fast among London's elite. Faster than the wildfires in Victoria. "You've heard of me?"

"Heard?" Denault echoed. "You might buy and sell the Crown now; that's what I've heard. You're a lucky man."

There was admiration in his eyes—and avarice as well. Tom had seen it in plenty of people, from the poor ex-convict gold miners in Australia to the highborn folk in England. That look always put Tom on his guard. He'd seen how dangerous men could be when driven by greed. He also knew what hypocrisy it bred. The upper classes might abuse him behind his back for his lowly origins, but to his face they could only compliment him for having so much money. "It was a lot of work," Tom pointed out. "The gold don't mine itself."

"Of course," Denault said, waving off Tom's remarks. He turned to his fiancée. "Miss Margaret Vaughn, may I present—"

She cut him off as she extended her hand and said, "How do you do, *just* Tom?"

Tom didn't miss the hint of derision in her words. Most everyone he'd met tonight had approached him either with awe or as some kind of phenomenon to be marveled at. Yet the woman he'd been admiring all evening was actually speaking to him with condescension! It was a challenge he could not ignore. Calling him as she did by his Christian name, even in jest, she might have been speaking to an errand boy or a servant. This thought, ironically, cued something his sister had taught him to say during introductions. He grasped her hand and said with gentlemanly dignity, "Your servant, madam."

Her hand was cool but it sent a curious warmth through him. Her stunning eyes widened, as though she, too, were startled at the sensation. Tom's lessons in etiquette completely left him and he forgot what he was supposed to do with her hand. So he continued to hold it, savoring the opportunity it gave him to be close to this woman. He was fascinated by the strength and fire in her gaze.

"Will you be in London long, Just Tom?" She sounded a bit breathless.

"I..." he faltered like an idiot. Suddenly he felt as unsteady as if he were back on the stormy seas. *Keep your wits about you, man,* he told himself, and released her hand. "I will be in England for the indefinite future."

"How wonderful." Her gaze held his. "We shall be glad to get to know you better."

"Indeed we shall," Denault broke in briskly. "Mr. Poole, perhaps you would like to be my guest for lunch tomorrow at my club? I've a business proposition for you."

Denault's offer jerked Tom back to his senses. He should have expected this, even from a man as rich as Denault. Everyone, it seemed, wanted to discuss business ventures with him. So far, he'd deflected or turned down all such proposals. He could have found some reason to avoid Denault, too, but he found himself agreeing to the appointment instead. He had an unreasonable urge to find out what kind of man Miss Vaughn had agreed to marry. "Will Miss Vaughn be joining us as well?" he asked.

Denault threw a condescending look at his bride-to-be. "Heavens, no," he said with a laugh. "Women aren't allowed at the club. And in any case, she has no head for business, poor thing."

Something like annoyance or anger flashed across Miss Vaughn's face. It was brief, and she quickly suppressed it, but it did not escape Tom. As an heiress in her own right, surely she was capable of handling business affairs. Why didn't she correct him? Tom was aware of the adage that when a man and woman were married they became *"one person, and that person is the husband."* Even so, he could not imagine Miss Vaughn in the role of a meek wife.

"I could not possibly join you in any case," she said lightly. "I am far too busy. The wedding is days away, and there are a thousand details to arrange."

At the mention of their wedding, Miss Vaughn and Denault exchanged a look so amorous that Tom wondered if he'd been mistaken about her apparent irritation. She must love Denault. Once more Tom felt himself awash in jealousy, even though he had not the slightest right to be. Miss Vaughn was betrothed to another man, and it was evidently a propitious match. Certainly there was nothing he could do about it.

She turned her attention back to Tom. "Will you also marry soon, Mr. Poole?"

Steeped as he was in thoughts of Miss Vaughn, this

question took Tom utterly by surprise. He could only look at her blankly.

"I thought perhaps you were searching for a wife," she said. "I saw how intently you were studying each lady in the room."

So she *had* been watching him, just as he had been watching her. Tom found this knowledge incredibly intoxicating. He would gladly have explored this mutual attraction, if not for the unwelcome fact that she was already taken.

No, he was not considering marriage to any of the other ladies he'd met tonight. They seemed too vacant, too pliable. Tom wanted a woman who was spirited and strong. He wanted what the Bible called a *helpmeet*—a true companion, not a mere accessory. He'd thought Miss Vaughn might possess those qualities, but now that he'd seen her with Denault he wasn't so sure. He shook his head in answer to her question. "I might have to return to Australia for that. The ladies there have more backbone."

Her eyes narrowed. "Do they?" She rose up a little taller, and her gaze swept over him from head to foot. He gladly withstood her scrutiny, pleased to have drawn a spark from her again. "Everyone in Australia seems quite...resourceful," she said. "Including you. I should like to hear more about your famous shipwreck. It seems a fantastical tale."

For the first time this evening, the mention of the ship-wreck did not annoy Tom. He did not try to analyze why. "I'd be more than happy to tell you about it. At times I have trouble believing it myself."

"Paul, dear," Miss Vaughn said without even looking

at her fiancé, "I am dying of thirst." She thrust her empty champagne glass in Denault's direction.

Denault looked at it in surprise, clearly taken off guard.

"That's an excellent idea," James interposed. "Don't worry, Denault. We'll entertain Miss Vaughn while you're gone."

Denault looked mistrustfully from his fiancée to Tom. Could he possibly feel threatened by him? The thought was more than a little appealing.

"I have a better idea," Denault said. "I am sure you are famished, Margaret. Why don't we both go to the supper room?" He took hold of her elbow, as if to lead her away. With a nod to Tom and James he added, "If you gentlemen will excuse us."

Miss Vaughn gently extricated herself from his grip. "I only asked for something to drink," she said, her voice edged with irritation.

"Yes, my darling, but you've eaten nothing this evening. We cannot have you fainting away from lack of food." His annoyed tone left no doubt this was an order rather than an expression of concern. She answered him with a frosty look.

Yes, there was trouble beneath those apparently smooth waters. Miss Vaughn and Denault were not as madly in love as they wished to portray. Of course, being *in love* was no requirement for marriage, certainly not among the upper classes. Even a commoner like Tom knew that. Why, then, should they pretend?

He could see her wavering, undecided. If he were a betting man, Tom would have wagered half his gold that Miss Vaughn did not have it in her nature to be docile.

He'd just as gladly give away the other half just to find out what was going on in that head of hers. He was hoping for a good display of fireworks.

To his disappointment, Miss Vaughn relented. She gave Denault a crisp nod of assent before turning back to Tom. "I do hope we shall meet again, Just Tom."

Something flickered in her eyes that gave Tom the wild hope that her words were more than mere formality. Tom kept his gaze fastened on hers. "I should like that very, very much."

Her lips parted in surprise, and he knew his meaning had reached her. She swallowed and looked away. Denault took her elbow again, and this time she did not demur.

As Tom watched her retreating form, he was captivated by a stray curl that had made its way down the back of her long, elegant neck.

And he knew with dangerous certainty that he must see her again.

Fall in Love with Forever Roman...

LAST CHANCE FAMILY
by Hope Ramsay

Mike Taggart may be a high roller in Las Vegas, but is he ready to take a gamble on love in Last Chance? Fans of Debbie Macomber, Robyn Carr, and Sherryl Woods will love this sassy and heartwarming story from *USA Today* bestselling author Hope Ramsay.

SUGAR'S TWICE AS SWEET
by Marina Adair

Fans of Jill Shalvis, Rachel Gibson, and Carly Phillips will enjoy this sexy and sweet romance about a woman who's renovating her beloved grandmother's house—even though she doesn't know a nut from a bolt—and the bad boy who can't resist helping her... even as she steals his heart!

Fall in Love with Forever Romance

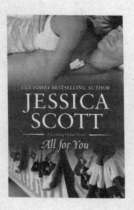

ALL FOR YOU
by Jessica Scott

Fans of JoAnn Ross and Brenda Novak will love this poignant and emotional military romance about a battle-scarred warrior who fears combat is the only escape from the demons that haunt him, and the woman determined to show him that the power of love can overcome anything.

DELIGHTFUL
by Adrianne Lee

Pie shop manager Andrea Lovette always picks the bad boys, and no one is badder than TV producer Ice Erickksen. Andrea knows she needs to find a good family man, so why does this bad boy still seem like such a good idea? Fans of Robyn Carr and Sherryl Woods will eat this one up!

Fall in Love with Forever Romance

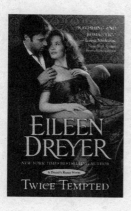

TWICE TEMPTED
by Eileen Dreyer

As two sisters each discover love, *New York Times* bestselling author Eileen Dreyer delivers twice the fun in her newest of the Drake's Rakes Regency series, which will appeal to fans of Mary Balogh and Eloisa James.

A BRIDE FOR
THE SEASON
by Jennifer Delamere

Can a wallflower and a rake find happily ever after in each other's arms? Jennifer Delamere's Love's Grace trilogy comes to a stunning conclusion.